ISLAND MAGIC

ISLAND MAGIC

ROCHELLE ALERS
SHIRLEY HAILSTOCK
MARCIA KING-GAMBLE
FELICIA MASON

St. Martin's Paperbacks

ISLAND MAGIC

ISBN: 0-312-97300-4

Printed in the United States of America

St. Martin's Paperbacks edition/February 2000

St. Martin's Paperbacks are published by St. Martin's Press, 175 Fifth Avenue, New York, N.Y. 10010.

10 9 8 7 6 5 4 3

CONTENTS

ISLAND MAGIC

ENCHANTED

FELICIA MASON

ONE

Regine Bryant liked what she saw—a lot. He stood about six-foot-two, had a smooth-as-honey complexion, a trim mustache and goatee, and a slight wave in his hair. He reminded her of the sexy actor Shemar Moore. As she handed her platinum credit card to the hotel desk clerk, Regine decided that the man checking in a few feet away would be the one.

As much as she loved her friends, she didn't want to spend this vacation exclusively with them, particularly when they were all happily married. She'd tried, in vain, to get out of this vacation, but Shayla, Camille and Alicia wouldn't hear it. They didn't know—couldn't know—how difficult it was for her to keep up the happy front. To them, this excursion would be about sun and fun. For Regine, the original Miss Unlucky in Love, it could be a chance to possibly find someone special.

She'd come to Martinique for a vacation with her three best girlfriends, the annual outing they'd dubbed the Sisterfriends' Fiesta. But Regine's goal for the week had nothing to do with getting a little sun and a lot to do with getting a little bit of what was standing near her at the hotel check-in counter.

At first she resigned herself to listening to them chatter about their men the entire week. Then, on the plane, she'd decided to stop worrying about finding Mr. Right and to settle for a little of Mr. Right Now. The "settling for" part didn't sit with her very well, though. Regine had never settled for anything. But a second look at the brother standing nearby eased the concern.

"What is taking Shayla so long? I swear, the woman brought enough luggage to last a month. Did anybody tell that diva this is a seven-day trip, not a seven-month journey?"

"Calm down, Camille," Regine told her friend. Camille was the intense one in the group. Everything she did she accomplished at warp speed and gave one hundred fifty percent. Coupled with a fine attention to detail, Camille made the perfect magazine editor.

"You hopped out of the cab like demons were chasing you," Regine said. "As a matter of fact, you've been in a mood since we got on the plane. What's up with that?"

Camille rustled in a straw handbag and pulled out a pack of Virginia Slims menthol. "I'm overdue for a vacation. I'm ready to relax if we could ever get this show on the road."

"First you're going to have to learn how to relax."

"Madame, this is a nonsmoking facility," the desk clerk said in French-accented English.

Camille stuck the cigarette in her mouth. "I know. I know. Every place I go is nonsmoking. I'm just getting a taste." The statuesque beauty paced the small area where they stood. A moment later she stopped and looked around. "This would be a nice place for a photo shoot." From her bag, she pulled out an electronic planner and scribbled a few notes as she resumed pacing.

"No, you didn't bring that thing with you," Alicia complained. "And be still. You're making me nervous with all that fidgeting."

"Yeah, okay," Camille said, her usual response when she was caught up in an idea and not paying a bit of mind to the people around her.

Alicia shook her head. Camille tucked the stylus and planner back in her bag and fingered the cigarette.

"And let me tell you right now, you will not be smelling up my room or my clothes with your cancer sticks," Alicia said. "It took two trips to the dry cleaner's for me to get that stench out of my raw silk jumpsuit."

The mention of that doomed trip made all three women wince.

"You always forget that I bought you another suit," Camille reminded Alicia.

"That's not the point."

Regine ignored the dispute between her friends, the argument a three-year-old one. It all started on that nightmare vacation to Belize. Regine, Shayla, Alicia, and Camille had been taking week-long trips together every year for the last seven years. The fiesta had been everything but a holiday when they chose the Central American country. From delayed and rerouted flights to lost luggage, major diarrhea, a stolen purse, and a hotel undergoing major renovations, the friendship had been sorely tested that year.

But now, Regine knew Camille wouldn't light up in their suite or anywhere near the three nonsmokers. Camille had been trying to quit for about six months. The fact that she even had cigarettes with her meant something was stressing her. Regine knew she'd have time to talk to Camille while they vacationed on Martinique.

As the hotel clerk processed their arrival, what she didn't have time to lose was the opportunity to make a connection with Mr. Too Fine.

Careful not to mess up her slick pageboy 'do, Regine perched her sunglasses on the top of her head and glanced over at him.

"Here you are, monsieur. Your usual room is prepared."

"*Merci,* Marcelle."

Regine catalogued that bit of information. If he had a usual room in this upscale resort, she figured he was a businessman who did work on the island on a regular basis. The information she'd read in advance indicated that could be the case with people who frequented Martinique.

He turned and Regine found herself caught staring. She did what any woman would do under the circumstances.

"Bonjour," she said with just enough smile to convey that the simple hello was more than a simple hello.

His answering smile let Regine know the message had been received and was welcome.

"Français ou anglais?" he asked.

"English, please," Regine answered as she took the two steps that put her in front of him. "My French is very rusty."

"Beauty speaks all languages, mademoiselle."

"Thank you," she said, sporting what she hoped was a pretty blush. While she dated at home, Regine didn't have a lot of confidence in or patience with her small-talk abilities. "My name is Regine."

"I am Emil. You are visiting Martinique for the first time, no?"

"*Sí.* I mean, *oui.* My friends and I. This is our first time."

Regine could've kicked herself. She'd enrolled in a French class and didn't have time to take more than the first night's lesson. And now, of all times, her high school Spanish was coming out of the woodwork of her memory. An English-to-French dictionary remained tucked in one of her bags. But she couldn't whip it out in midflirt. Shayla spoke fluent French and the three of them had relied on her expertise up until this point.

"Would you look at girl friend over there?" Alicia stage-whispered.

"Regine! The hotel clerk is trying to give you your credit card," Camille said loud enough so Regine couldn't feign lack of hearing.

Regine glanced back at her friends for a moment, then turned her full attention to Emil.

With a nod toward her waiting friends, "I'd better get going," she told him. "Nice to have met you."

"Le plaisir est partage," he said, lifting her hand and kissing it.

She could hear Alicia's impatient sigh and the click of

Camille's Prada heels on the marble floor. Regine ignored both of them.

"I have no clue what you just said, but it sounded wonderful," she told Emil.

His chuckle intrigued her. "I said, the pleasure of meeting you was all mine, Mademoiselle Regine." He kissed her hand again, then picked up the garment bag at his feet and went in the direction the desk clerk indicated.

"Regine Bryant, you ought to be ashamed of yourself."

Accepting her credit card from the front desk clerk, Regine tucked it into a slot in her wallet. "Just because you have a band of gold on your finger isn't going to stop me from having some fun."

Before Camille could respond, a large commotion at the entrance drew everyone's attention. Shayla had finally made it inside. A trio of men stumbling over themselves to assist her followed in her wake, lugging suitcases and bags.

"Why does she drag so much stuff with her all the time?" Alicia complained.

"Because you always leave whatever it is at home and Shayla always has it," Regine pointed out.

"Leave the woman alone," Camille said. "She's still a newlywed and is already missing her honey-do."

"Sure doesn't look like it," Alicia muttered as the men all came to a halt when Shayla did.

Regine glanced at Alicia, who seemed to be complaining about things even more than usual. Regine made a mental note to talk with Alicia as well.

"This place is gorgeous," Shayla declared as she dropped a small case on the floor. "Thank you, darling," she said to the official bellman who'd assisted her. "And thank you all, too," she told the other two as she slipped them generous tips.

"I'll be just a moment."

"*Oui, madame,*" the bellman said.

"Did you all see the flowers outside? My gracious,"

Shayla enthused to her girlfriends. "I'll have to see if Scott can make those grow at home. I doubt it, though, with all the cold weather and snow. Regine, are we checked in yet? Camille, honey, put that cigarette away, and Alicia, good heavens, stop looking like we're here for a funeral."

Shayla raised her hands and did a pirouette. "Let the fiesta begin."

Regine could only shake her head. How the four of them, opposites in every way, ever found themselves in a lasting friendship, she didn't know.

Shayla, a former model, owned a public relations firm that specialized in celebrity endorsements. Alicia tended to be dour, while Camille, the workaholic perfectionist, ran herself into the ground with work. Regine believed herself to be the most balanced of the quartet. She loved her job as a stock analyst but also recognized the need for outside interests, hobbies, and some well-deserved R&R. All she had to do now was find a man with a similar disposition and outlook.

So far, though, her attempts to do just that hadn't amounted to much. Regine wanted a forever love. All she'd been able to find at home were men who were interested in what *she* could do for them, not what they could do for each other as a couple. Shayla, in particular, seemed to have found her soul mate without even trying. She and Scott, the newlyweds, had set Regine up with one of the groomsmen who had been in their wedding. But after two dates and twenty requests to "hook up my boys with some inside stock tips," Regine had called it quits with that joker.

No matter their differences, these women were her best friends in the world. They met and instantly clicked in college at Howard University. After graduation and a few years of work under their belts, they upgraded their Spring Break flings to real vacations. Independent women with disposable income had it like that. Until the husbands started arriving, Regine thought.

With Mexico, Hawaii, Jamaica, Brazil, St. Lucia, Barbados, and the disaster that had been Belize behind them, they'd come to the French West Indies for sun, fun, and a girls-only holiday. With money to burn and nothing but time on their hands, the week promised Caribbean delights.

And if all the men looked like Emil and the ones bowing and scraping after Shayla, Regine knew she'd be in for a good time.

With bellmen in tow, the women made their way to the suite they'd call home for the next seven days.

"Nothing but the best," Shayla had demanded.

"As if you'd settle for anything else," Regine dryly commented.

Used to luxury from the crib, it had never even dawned on Shayla that the four might not be on equal financial standing. Shayla had money and had married even more of it. Money wasn't a problem for Regine; she had more than she knew what to do with. But that wasn't the case with Alicia, who Regine knew was struggling to keep up appearances. The two kept a secret from Camille and Shayla: Regine had loaned Alicia the money for last year's Hawaiian fiesta. Even though Regine told her not to worry about it, Alicia was still in the process of paying Regine back for that trip.

As they stopped in front of a pair of French doors, Regine vowed that the one thing she would do this week is have a talk with Alicia about her financial situation. Alicia made decent money in her civil service job; she was a GS-14, in the uppermost tier of government salaries. With the right kind of assistance and some solid investments, it wouldn't take much to get her back on solid ground.

The bellmen stepped forward and the group swept into the luxury suite. Fresh-cut tropical flowers in a riot of reds, yellows, and purples scented the foyer and accented the rooms.

Shayla dropped her purse and dashed across the room to the windows. "Oh, my. This is perfect. Would you look at that water! Oh, my God. There's a waterfall over there!"

Alicia glanced around, spotted the bar, and made her way to it.

Hanging back, Camille and Regine glanced at each other.

"I'm worried about her drinking," Camille said.

"I am, too."

"Is everything okay with her and Howard?"

Wondering the same thing, Regine could only shrug. With an eye on Alicia, they took in the rest of the main room. The rattan accent pieces gave the place a tropical feel. The rich mahogany furniture and a smattering of antiques lent it an elegant ambience.

Shayla twirled around and plopped into an overstuffed chair. "I'm in heaven. I just wish Scott could be here."

"Don't start that again, please," Alicia said as she stirred her drink.

"I just didn't want our honeymoon to end," Shayla said on a dreamy sigh. "I almost couldn't bear to be away from him so soon after the wedding. Maybe I'll call him and tell him we arrived."

Alicia rolled her eyes. "The wedding was four months ago."

"Hey, guys, let's not start fighting," Regine the peacemaker said. "We just got here. Why don't we unpack, get settled, and then we can figure out what to do next?"

"I know what I'm going to do next," Camille said. "If I don't get a nap, I'm not gonna be any good the rest of the day."

The bellmen showed them the bedrooms and then departed. The four had already agreed that Alicia and Regine would share a room, and Camille and Shayla would share the other one. Each of the bedrooms had two queen-size beds, an abundance of closet space, a bath area to die for, and spectacular views of the gardens that ringed the resort.

While Shayla called her husband and Camille headed for a nap, Regine quickly freshened up, unpacked her luggage, and grabbed a small shoulder bag for a tour of the hotel. She liked to get her bearings early so she knew where everything was.

"I'm just going to walk around a bit," she told Alicia.

From the terrace where she'd curled up on a chaise with a drink, Alicia waved Regine on. "See ya."

Regine eyed the tall tumbler. "Alicia, don't you think it's a little early—"

"Chill out, Regine. It's juice." To prove her words, Alicia reached for and held high a pitcher of something tropical-looking.

Giving her friend the benefit of the doubt, Regine didn't sniff the contents. Instead she reached for Alicia's shoulder and gave it a gentle squeeze. "I worry about you, you know that. Alcohol can't drown problems."

"I'm fine, Regine. Really. And it's not liquor. Taste," Alicia said as she put the pitcher down and held up her glass.

This time, Regine did take a sip. All fruit juice.

"Satisfied?"

Instead of answering, Regine handed the glass back to Alicia. "What's going on with you and Howard?"

Alicia's heavy sigh told a part of the story. "We're having some problems," she admitted. "But it's nothing we can't work out, I'm sure. As a matter of fact, he encouraged me to take this trip this year. The week away will give us some time to breathe."

"Howard—your husband Howard—encouraged you to come with us?"

Alicia chuckled. "Yeah, amazing, isn't it? He even paid for it."

Regine's eyes widened. The scumbag had to be up to something. He'd objected to every vacation the four girlfriends took together and made no secret about it. It didn't matter that the college pals had been traveling together long before he ever showed up in the picture. That he objected to the friendship the four shared didn't exactly endear him to Shayla, Regine, and Camille. But Alicia seemed to love him, and since her friends loved her, they tried to overlook his pushy ways and support Alicia. Just what Alicia saw in him was something they'd been trying to figure out for a while.

Regine reached for the second chaise and pulled it closer to Alicia's.

"No," Alicia said halting Regine. "I know you're headed out. Don't worry about me. I'm just soaking in the sun."

Pausing for a moment, Regine considered Alicia's words as she leaned back on her chaise and repositioned her sunglasses.

"Go ahead. I'm fine."

"You sure?" Regine asked.

"Go. I know you're itching to explore every little nook and cranny in this place. Come back and give us the report."

Regine hesitated a moment longer. Then, "We'll talk later, okay?"

Alicia nodded.

With another glance at her longtime friend, Regine headed toward the door. Howard and Alicia had been married for almost six years. From phone conversations with Alicia, Regine knew that his business had been in trouble. Now it seemed that those problems had extended to their marriage as well.

Regine left the suite and walked toward the lobby. Her mind on Alicia, she didn't see Emil until she trampled over his feet.

"Ah, Mademoiselle Regine. It is with pleasure I see you again."

Regine beamed. "Hello, Emil. I'm sorry. My mind was

occupied. I should have been paying attention to where I was going."

"As you Americans say, no problem."

He smiled. Regine decided on the spot that if he was willing, she'd have a wild fling with this man. Not only was he good-looking, he was, well . . . good-looking. Regine harbored no expectations or delusions that a Caribbean fling would or even could lead to what she really wanted—a long-term relationship that would ultimately see her to the altar. But in the meantime, there was not a single reason she should miss out on the opportunity to make a few vacation memories with Emil. His nails were clean, his clothes pressed. He spoke English, was breathing, and had flirted with her. What more could a woman ask for?

Hot on the heels of that came the thought, *How pathetic—a grown woman deciding to have a fling with somebody based on such a superficial thing like physical appearance.* Regine, however, knew people who'd entered relationships on much less.

"I was just going to look around and see what the hotel offers," she told him. "Do you know where the pool is?"

Emil took the question as an invitation to join her. They strolled around the grounds, stopping briefly at the indoor pool, the outdoor pool, the tennis courts, and a garden that looked like it was designed specifically for moonlight trysts.

"Everything is beautiful here," she told him.

"*Oui.* Like heaven."

They eventually made their way back to the lobby area and sat on a rattan love seat. Surrounded by large tropical plants, it was easy to believe they'd been transported to Eden. Emil ordered fruit juice cocktails for them, sipped from his, then leaned toward Regine.

"There are many places you must see while you visit Martinique."

Regine's smile was coy. It seemed he *was* willing. She

knew exactly where to take that opening. "What places did you have in mind?"

"Well, there is my—"

"Regine, there you are! I've been looking all over for you."

Regine wanted to grit her teeth, but she kept a perfect smile on her face as Shayla made yet another dramatic entrance, this one a total interruption.

Shayla had changed into a flowing lounge outfit in dazzling gold. "Hi, there. I'm Shayla," she introduced herself.

Emil rose and completed the introductions.

"Would you care to join us?" he politely asked.

Regine tried to motion for Shayla to disappear, but her friend either ignored the signal or decided that whatever she wanted was far more important. Emil glanced between the two women; then, with a distinguished kiss on Regine's hand and an elegant bow to Shayla, he finished off his drink.

"I see the two of you have much to discuss." Then, claiming a prior appointment, Emil excused himself and slipped away.

"Now look at what you've done," Regime whined.

"What? That gigolo? Regine, honey. I really need to talk to you. It's about Alicia. I think something's wrong."

That got Regine's attention. "I do, too," she said. Then, "What makes you think he's a gigolo?"

Shayla nodded toward a lounge where he seemed to be headed. A stunning brunette leaned toward him. They clasped arms and strolled away.

Regine sighed. "So he has a date. That doesn't mean he's a gigolo."

"Um-hmm," Shayla said as she inspected a claw-shaped flower on a plant next to the love seat. "And what about the woman I saw him with at the airport?"

"What woman? What are you talking about?"

Shayla gave a little shrug. "While the three of you were gawking at everything else in the airport, I saw him putting the moves on a woman at least twice his age."

Regine smiled. "Now you're just telling tales. You didn't really see him at the airport."

"Believe what you want, sisterfriend," Shayla said.

Reflective, Regine took a sip from her drink. "Do you really think he's a . . . you know?"

"Of course, honey. He's one of those types who hang out in hotel lobbies and pick up American tourists—just the women, though." Shayla affected a Caribbean accent, "You know, you American women are all *tres* rich. If you are married, your husband does not satisfy you the way I can. If you are single, you must need some *really* bad."

Regine rolled her eyes. "That's just those Jamaican men, namely Andre and his posse of buddies who thought they were God's gift."

Shayla settled on the love seat, reached for Regine's drink, and took a sip from it. "Mmm. That's good. I think I'll have one, too. Believe what you want, sisterfriend. I'm just telling you what I know to be true. And it's not just Andre. A lot of Caribbean men think like that."

"Now you're really stereotyping," Regine said. "And that's not fair."

Shayla shrugged, then leaned forward to catch the eye of one of the roaming wait staff. Regine took her drink back, but before Shayla could protest, a crisply clad waiter appeared at her side and placed an identical juice cocktail on the table for her.

"*Merci,*" Shayla said automatically. "As I was saying, forget him. He's just a pretty boy. What do you think is up with Alicia?"

Regine crossed her legs. "I don't know," she hedged. The one thing she was sure of was that Alicia didn't want her marital and financial woes discussed all over the place. Until she had a chance to talk with her, Regine figured she'd best keep quiet.

"Camille's taking a nap," Shayla reported. "I think she's pregnant."

Regine sat up. "What makes you think that? Surely she would have said something."

Shayla waved a manicured hand. "You know Camille. She's not going to say anything. She probably hasn't even told Roger."

"What are you, a psychic or something these days?"

Shayla stood. Drinking down the last of her refreshment, she reached a hand down toward Regine. "No, honey. I'm just observant. Come on, let's go see what this paradise has to offer."

"What about Alicia?"

"She went to the spa for a massage or something. Come on."

The one thing the friends had decided early on when they started vacationing together was that they didn't have to do things in a group. While they enjoyed each other's company and did many things together, they didn't have to all agree to do any particular activity at the same time. Shayla and Regine shared a passion for shopping, so the two asked for directions, then hopped in a taxi headed toward downtown Fort-de-France.

Hours later, they returned to the suite laden down with packages.

"Good grief, did you save any stuff for us to buy?" Camille said.

"I told you they went shopping," Alicia piped up. "We're sitting up here wondering what happened to you two."

Regine dropped her bags on the sofa next to Camille. "Stop being such crybabies. We just scoped out a few stores. Besides, the two of you hate to shop."

"I don't hate it," Alicia said in her defense. "I just shop with a purpose, not for the so-called pleasure of wandering around."

"You'll enjoy it here," Shayla said as she pulled a bouquet of multicolored flowers from a mesh bag. "These are for you," she said, presenting them to Alicia.

Charmed out of her surly mood, Alicia laughed. "No harm, no foul. Now can we go eat?"

"Yeah," Camille added. "I'm starving."

With a knowing look toward Regine, Shayla deposited the rest of her packages in a chair. "We found a lovely restaurant where the chef makes all the food from the island's fruits and vegetables."

"Fruit and vegetables," Camille whined. "Girl, I want a steak and double mashed potatoes, with gravy."

Camille and Alicia grabbed their handbags and headed for the door. Trailing behind them, Shayla caught Regine's eye.

I told you, Shayla mouthed.

TWO

The next morning, Regine slipped from the suite early. She wanted to get a run in before her Sleeping Beauty pals stirred. They'd discovered a karaoke bar and proceeded to make fools of themselves acting as Diana Ross and the Supremes half the night.

With the words to "Stop in the Name of Love" running through her head—and messing up her rhythm—Regine ran what she estimated was two miles, then jogged back to the resort.

Emil appeared from nowhere. She caught his quick frown before he transformed it into a welcoming grin. Shayla's assessment of the man came back to her. So did the image of him with that other woman. Before completely throwing him back, Regine decided to test the water for herself. She was a grown-up and could come to her own conclusions about people.

"*Bonjour*, Mademoiselle Regine."

"*Bonjour* to you, too," she said. "Sorry about yesterday. It was our first day and my friends were kind of anxious to get started on seeing the sights."

"No, problem," he said with a quick glance to his left toward the elevator.

"Waiting for someone?" she asked.

His gaze—was that guilt?—met hers again. "*Non*. My time is for you."

Regine knew a way to test that assertion. "I was just about to have some breakfast. Would you like to join me?" she invited.

"I have a better idea," he said in accented English.

I'll just bet you do, Regine thought. *How much is it going to cost me?* She'd halfway decided that Shayla, who knew about such things, probably had him pegged. But

Regine was a woman who came to her own conclusions, based on fact, not assumptions or cultural stereotypes.

"What's that?" she asked.

"Let's have supper. Tonight. *Oui?* I shall pick you up at eight? I shall take you to Fort-de-France's finest restaurant."

Flattered despite herself and wondering if she'd live to regret it, Regine agreed. If *he* was taking *her* to a restaurant, that meant he was paying. Gigolos mooched off women; they didn't pick up tabs. In the next few moments, Regine agreed to meet him in one of the hotel's lobby lounges.

With another look toward the elevator, Emil leaned forward, kissed her on the cheek, then excused himself. As Regine headed back to her suite, she smiled, pleased with herself. Her plan seemed to be unfolding just right. If Emil wasn't one of those, she'd be well on her way toward accomplishing her vacation goal. She knew exactly the dress she'd wear for her dinner date with Emil. And she wouldn't mention anything to Shayla until she had the evidence to prove her wrong.

"Who knows?" she said out loud. "Dessert might lead to breakfast."

Later in the day, ready to haggle for tourist trinkets and bargains, Shayla and Camille decided to check out the Place de la Savane. The craft market was a haven for bargain hunters in search of things like beach towels and T-shirts. Regine and Alicia, who both preferred museums and cultural sites, decided to see the house where France's Empress Joséphine was born.

From there, they hailed a taxi and asked the driver to take them to a place off the beaten path where they could see how regular people lived on the island.

"This is even better than one of those organized tours," Alicia commented as they drove around, with the taxi driver commenting along the way.

By lunchtime, the two had seen quite a bit. Alicia, claiming too much sun and not enough water, decided to head back to the hotel.

"You'll be okay by yourself?" she asked Regine.

Regine nodded. "Look at this place. It's as safe as my backyard. Besides, it's broad daylight."

"Well, people do get mugged in broad daylight," Alicia pointed out.

"You, friend, need to spend more time away from Detroit."

"Um-hmm. You just be careful out here."

"I will, Mom," Regine said as she shut the door on the taxi that would take Alicia to the resort.

On her own a few minutes later, Regine wandered the avenues, peering in shop windows. At a jeweler's, a necklace caught her eye and she entered the establishment.

"Bonjour," she gaily greeted the clerk.

A torrent of French followed her simple hello. Regine reached in her bag for her English-French dictionary and came up empty-handed.

"Oh, dear. Uh, *parlez-vous anglais?*" she said, hoping she was asking if the clerk spoke English.

"Je parle un peu anglais, madamoiselle."

Regine glanced around. "Uh . . . let's see." She pointed to her neck and then toward the window.

"Un collier?" the clerk answered.

Well, that sounded sort of like *collar,* she figured. "*Oui, un collier* . . . in the window." Regine walked back toward the display and pointed to the necklace she'd admired.

The clerk's face lit up. "*Tres, belle. Un moment. Un moment, s'il vous plait.*"

Regine nodded and smiled. *"Merci."*

She'd actually made a connection and recognized a word or two. Either Alicia left with her small dictionary or she'd accidentally put it down somewhere. Regine did remember Shayla's number one rule about traveling in French-speaking countries: Always say "please" and "thank you." Those two words, along with "Where is the bathroom?" and "Take me to the American embassy," were the few she actually remembered.

Regine watched as the clerk retrieved the gold-and-gemstone necklace, then took a seat where he indicated. Emeralds, amethysts, and diamonds sparkled in the intricate design of the piece.

"It's beautiful," Regine said.

Another customer entered the store and the clerk said something in melodic French. A middle-aged woman appeared from an office Regine had not noticed and went to assist the customer.

The clerk indicated her neck and Regine nodded. "I'd love to try it on."

She leaned forward and bowed her head so he could place it against her skin. Then, straightening to face the clerk again, Regine picked up an oval hand mirror to admire the necklace. The gemstones were interesting, but not quite as beguiling as the man she saw reflected in the glass.

Regine shifted the hand mirror to get a better view.

He seemed about medium height. The salt in his hair lent just enough age to tell her he was in his late forties or very early fifties. Regine had always liked older men. They knew how to treat women. They also had a certain sensual appeal that Regine had never questioned. A man in his prime, he appeared very distinguished in a confident yet self-composed way. Very sexy.

As a matter of fact, she decided, all the men on this island must be descended from the same bronze god. That great diviner of genes had obviously lingered over Martinique and run out of the good stuff by the time he got to the States, particularly Minnesota, the place she called home.

When he smiled and nodded his head just so, Regine had to smile. *Caught! But who cares?*

In a flurry of French, the sales clerk asked her a question, or what at least sounded like a question. Regine placed the mirror on the glass counter and touched the necklace.

"It's very beautiful," she said. "Very expensive, too, I bet."

The clerk's hopeful look encouraged her. Maybe he'd understood something after all.

"*Oui,* beautiful, mademoiselle."

From seemingly out of thin air, he produced what suspiciously looked like a sales slip. Regine got worried. She didn't speak French, but diamonds and gemstones cost a lot in any language.

"Uh, no," she said with a worried glance at that sales slip. "English, *s'il vous plait?*"

The clerk nodded and smiled and pointed toward a pair of colorful stickers. Regine had no trouble recognizing the MasterCard and Visa logos. That language was universal.

Shaking her head as she reached to undo the necklace's clasp, she felt a presence behind her. A glance confirmed the presence as the man from the mirror. A moment later, he and the enthusiastic clerk exchanged French that Regine had no hope of understanding. Instead, she focused on the stranger's melodic voice. She didn't understand the words, but she knew she'd like to hear him whisper a sweet nothing or two in her ear. French was such a beautiful language. Coupled with the dulcet tenor, Regine knew she could listen to him talk for hours.

A moment later and with a deferential "*Oui, monsieur,*" the clerk slipped away.

Regine turned toward her rescuer. Her breath caught. Close up, he was even more handsome than he'd appeared in the mirror. Tiny laugh lines at his eyes added character to a face that at once was both relaxed and primed for battle. He stood about three inches taller than she did and wore a casually elegant cream-colored ensemble. He put her in mind of a model she'd seen in a men's fashion magazine.

Without a word specifically to her, he put Regine at

ease. She recalled scenes from movies when Hollywood capitalized on its dashing leading men, men like Sidney Poitier and Sean Connery, who were suave and sexy and chivalrous.

"Did you just tell him I'm not buying this?" she asked.

He smiled. "Something like that. I told him we wanted a few more moments to decide."

"Thank you."

She placed a steadying hand on the countertop. Hearing him speak directly to her did strange things to Regine—strange delicious things. For one, her breathing deepened and she felt that unmistakable lurch of excitement and awareness. It had been quite a while since she'd experienced that particular rush. She couldn't recall the last time she'd had such an overwhelming response to a man. Emil from the hotel elicited lusty but unspecific wouldn't-it-be-nice thoughts. This man made her weak in the knees.

She hadn't experienced *that* in . . . in ever, she realized with a surprise. In her thirty-one years, Regine had dated—mostly players and jokers, though. She had been seriously involved a time or two, but she'd never, ever experienced the instant knowing or the secret fire that romance writers rhapsodized about in their novels. Not until, that is, this very moment.

Wow!

"Sometimes, merchants attempt to take advantage of Americans. You are all perceived to be rich, particularly when you come in and choose a piece like that," he said, indicating the necklace still at Regine's throat.

"It's that expensive?"

He shrugged. "In U.S. dollars, about twelve thousand."

"Oh, my God." Regine made fast work of undoing the necklace. She carefully placed the piece back on its velvet display box.

"A little out of my price range for an island memento," she said.

"It is very beautiful," the man said.

His finger traced a cluster of the emeralds and amethysts, but his eyes remained locked with hers. Regine's heart beat triple-time. She wasn't at all sure he was still talking about the jewelry.

The clerk appeared and asked the man a question.

"*Non,*" he replied, then added something Regine didn't comprehend.

The clerk looked disappointed as he returned the necklace to its display area.

"Is there something else you'd like to try?" the man asked her.

"I think I'd better quit while I'm ahead."

"As you wish," he said.

With parting words to the clerk, the man led Regine out of the jeweler's shop.

"Thank you," she told him. "I can buy pretty jewelry anytime. I came to Martinique to enjoy the local culture and to take home souvenirs I wouldn't be able to get anywhere but on the island."

With a slight but nonetheless courtly bow, the man introduced himself.

"I am Demetrius Fielding and it was an honor and privilege to assist you, mademoiselle."

Regine stuck her hand out. "Regine Bryant. American tourist."

They started walking down the sunny street.

"That part I gathered," he said with a smile. "You should carry a small English-French dictionary with you, particularly when you tread off the beaten paths here. Some merchants speak English, but many of them do not. That fellow doesn't speak English, but his wife does. He would have confirmed the sale with her before it was finalized."

Regine nodded. "That's good to know. By the way, was that a reputable shop?"

"Oh, most definitely," Demetrius said. "As you saw,

the English he understands is made of little squares of plastic."

Regine laughed. "Good credit is a universal language."

"That it is," he replied.

Regine noticed and realized that the smile in his voice and on his face reached his eyes. She liked that. A lot.

Demetrius pointed out sites and landmarks as they walked. At one point, they stopped for a cool drink and sat on a bench in front of a garden.

"The flowers are all so beautiful here," Regine said as she sipped the fresh fruit concoction. "It's like Eden must have been."

"The first explorers to Martinique believed the same thing," he said. "The early settlers, Carib Indians, called it Mandinina, which means 'Island of Flowers.' "

As they sat, watching people go by, Demetrius gave her a short history of the island, from its slavery days through Napoleon's reign and the eruption of Montagne Pelée.

With a worried glance around their peaceful surroundings, Regine asked, "Is the volcano still active?"

"*Oui.* It erupted almost one hundred years ago. That makes it active to geologists. But do not worry, Regine, Pelée is on the northern coast of the island. You are safe here."

His teasing grin charmed her. But more than that, Regine thrilled at the way her name sounded when *he* said it. All her life, Regine wished that her fanciful parents had named her *Regina* like normal girls. It had taken years for her to fully appreciate the French spelling of the name, and now to hear it roll from this man's tongue . . . ooh la la.

Regine smiled and Demetrius smiled back. He finished off his refreshment, then rose and held his hand out to her.

"If you like, I will show you the most beautiful spot on the island."

Game, Regine stood. "Okay."

He placed their cups on the bench and took both of her hands in his. "Close your eyes, Mademoiselle Regine."

She did as he requested.

"Take a deep breath." When she complied, he continued. "Now slowly exhale and open your eyes."

When she did, he stood before her, closer than before. He was close enough to kiss and Regine found her thoughts roaming down that very path.

"The most beautiful place on the island is standing before me," he said. "You are enchanting and I am glad we've had this opportunity to share a part of the day."

Regine's breath caught. She leaned forward just a bit, enough to let him know she wanted his kiss, anticipated his caress. Her eyes drifted closed again. But nothing happened.

She opened her eyes to discover him standing farther away. Regine was all woman and recognized the look in his eyes. But before she could act on it or say anything, he shielded himself, shutting her out emotionally. Unbidden and unwanted, Shayla's assessment of Emil came to mind. *Gigolo.*

Surely Demetrius wasn't one of those types. He'd been nothing but her Sir Galahad from the moment they met.

"Regine, I have enjoyed your company today. I did not mean to monopolize your time. I am sure you had other plans."

She reached a hand toward his. "I didn't. And you didn't monopolize anything. I enjoyed the afternoon. Thank you."

A glance at her watch made Regine start. "Good heavens, I had no idea it was so late. We've spent practically the entire day together."

"I will see you to a taxi. We are some distance away from the downtown hotels."

Regine had always relied on her instincts to guide her. Everything in her told her that if she let Demetrius Fielding leave, she'd never see him again.

Throwing caution to the wind, she bolstered her courage and took a deep breath. "Would you have dinner with me, Demetrius?"

THREE

As soon as she uttered the words, Regine regretted them.

First of all, because she remembered she'd made a date with Emil. And even more important than that, with Demetrius she didn't want to come across like a floozy or worse. If Shayla's assessment was actually true, American women already had a hot-to-trot reputation in the Caribbean.

But there was something about Demetrius, something beyond the casual elegance of his outward appearance. While she found herself extremely conscious of his virile appeal, she sensed in him a depth and a need that equaled or rivaled her own.

Taking her hand, he lifted it to his mouth and pressed an oh-so-gentle kiss first on the back side and then, without his gaze ever leaving hers, he turned her hand in his and kissed her palm.

Her heart jolted and her pulse pounded. Surely he could hear it. Regine stopped breathing.

"Not tonight, *chère*. You are here to see Martinique with friends, *non*?"

Regine nodded, but was more than willing to forget about her friends for the time being.

"It would not be fair of me to keep you from them."

Regine searched his face, looking for . . . what? She didn't know.

He hailed a cab that scooted to their side in seconds. Demetrius opened the door for her.

"Will I see you again?" she asked.

"That depends on you, Regine."

"I want to."

She didn't at all like the neediness she heard in her own voice. She did, however, know that everything in her being responded to him. The insistent voice of her subconscious told her something special, very special, could happen if she trusted her instincts. Could he possibly know how very much she wanted him? Right now. In the midst of these beautiful flowers, with the sun setting around them.

He leaned forward to assist her into the cab.

She had one last shot before it was forever too late. She settled into the backseat and he shut the door.

"Demetrius," she said. "I'm staying at Chateau Fleur de Lisse."

His eyebrow rose, but he didn't say anything as the taxi took off.

Halfway back to the hotel, and with her mind still on the very intriguing Demetrius Fielding, Regine regretted making the date with Emil. The afternoon with Demetrius left her wanting to know more about him. His knowledge about the island's history and people impressed her. So did his air of sophisticated but unpretentious confidence.

Regine would honor her commitment with Emil, but she had to find out one thing. "What is the brother's last name?"

"*Qu'est-ce que vous avez dit, madame?*" the taxi driver asked.

"Huh?"

"What did you say, madame?" the driver repeated in heavily accented English. "*Non à l'hotel?*

"*Sí,*" Regine said. "I mean, *oui.* Take me to the hotel, uh, what you said, *l'hotel.*"

"*Oui, madame,*" the driver said as he settled back in his seat.

Regine expelled a frustrated sigh. Next time, they were either going to a place where English was the primary language or she'd just have to take a week or so of vacation and enroll in a crash course.

Back at the resort, she made fast work of changing into an alluring peach-colored sheath. The color, she knew, accented and complemented her skin tone. High-heeled strappy sandals on her feet, diamond studs in her ears, and a spritz of a sultry perfume at her wrists, behind her knees, and behind her ears completed the ensemble. Regine stepped away from the mirror to get a better look at herself.

"You go, Miss Thing," she told her reflection. Then, with a naughty grin, she reached for the perfume bottle again and applied strokes to the inside of her cleavage.

She picked up a tiny clutch purse and deposited her ID, the room key, cash, her platinum charge card, and three condoms, not because she planned to use them, but because as a savvy woman in this day and age, it was best to be prepared.

She went to the resort lounge where they'd agreed to meet. The soothing flow of water from a fountain relaxed her as she crossed her legs at the bar. When the bartender approached, she ordered a glass of Chablis while she waited.

"This is the life," she said.

A little while later, when the bartender asked if she'd like a second glass, Regine said yes and looked around. People-watching was a sport she didn't have time for back home. Here, it seemed all the more interesting, particularly as she recalled the afternoon and how she'd watched Demetrius in the mirror at the jeweler's shop.

She smiled to herself, not at all realizing how approachable she looked.

"Hello, *chérie*. Buy you a drink?"

After listening to Demetrius's melodic French-accented English all day, Regine knew a fake accent when she heard one. She gave the guy a once-over. Plaid pants. Striped shirt. Thick-lensed glasses with heavy plastic rims on the nose. Sunglasses perched on the head. He looked as if he'd just stepped out of central casting for geeks.

"No, thank you. I'm waiting for someone."

"Your loss, babe," the guy said, sauntering away.

"I doubt it," she murmured. The bartender replaced her wineglass with a full one. "Thank you. Excuse me, what time is it?"

The bartender pointed toward a small digital clock behind him. Regine's eyes widened. No, it wasn't that late.

Regine couldn't remember the last time she'd been stood up.

So lost in her thoughts about Demetrius and wrapped in the easy atmosphere of the resort, she hadn't realized Emil had yet to make an appearance until the nerdy American guy tried to pick her up. She sipped from her third glass of Chablis and muttered a few choice phrases about Emil Too Trifling.

She paid and tipped the bartender, slipped off the high stool, and walked straight into a solid wall of man. Her tiny clutch purse fell to the floor at the impact. The man bent down to retrieve it.

Taking a deep breath, she launched into Emil. "How dare you show up almost two hours late?"

"Did we have an appointment?" he said.

Regine snatched her handbag back and two seconds later realized it was Demetrius who stood before her and not that gigolo Emil.

"Oh! Hello. I'm sorry. I thought—"

"You had a dinner appointment and he has let you down," Demetrius surmised. "I apologize for my countryman, Regine."

"How'd you know?"

Demetrius smiled and casually shrugged. Regine's knees grew weak . . . Again.

She wondered how and why this gorgeous older man had such a physical effect on her. All he had to do was say her name and she was putty waiting to be sculpted.

"You have the look of a woman who was anticipating an enjoyable evening," he said.

Regine held her breath as his gaze wandered from the bodice of her clingy sheath to her slim waist. She thanked

God she'd put in all those hours at the gym.

"I know the hour is late, but would you object if I substituted for your tardy dinner guest?"

She didn't need to think about her answer. "I'd love to have dinner with you, Demetrius."

Tucking her arm through his, Regine let Demetrius lead her out of the lounge.

"I know a lovely little place not far from here that I believe you would enjoy," he said.

And enjoy she did. From the wonderful French wines that accompanied every course to the delicacies she couldn't pronounce but knew she'd love forever, Regine found herself in the unique position of being seduced by a smile and a superb chef.

"What?" she asked when a small smile tilted the corners of his mouth.

He finished the last of his wine. A waiter hovering not too far away was quick to refill both Demetrius's and Regine's glasses. Only after he stepped away did Demetrius answer her question.

"You are like a goddess who has suddenly discovered her powers," he said.

Regine's smile could have been interpreted several ways. But the finger that she stroked along his gave the meaning. "And what powers do I have?" she asked.

She could have blamed the sultry tone of her voice on the wine and the food, but Regine was a big girl. She knew what she wanted. And it wasn't the lobby-hopper Emil.

"I think you know," he quietly said.

Regine didn't say anything. Her finger ceased its light caress. For a long, tension-filled moment they simply stared at each other. Regine had never been more aware of herself as a woman, a woman who wanted a man—this man.

She licked suddenly dry lips and felt her body quicken as he tracked the movement.

How, she vaguely wondered, did she ever find herself

attracted to that gigolo Emil? An older man like Demetrius would know how to treat a woman. If his actions during the day had been any indication whatsoever, Demetrius had more than a touch of Old World charm mixed in with the attributes of a Renaissance man.

She smiled at the whimsy of her thoughts.

"What?"

His question eased the tension between them. Regine sat back in her chair. He still leaned forward in his.

"I was just thinking," she said. "It's funny how the best-laid plans tend to go awry."

"What were your plans?"

This time her smile was shy, almost embarrassed. She drank from her glass, then ran a finger along the rim of the delicate crystal, all the while observing him through lowered lashes.

Watching the play of emotions on her face reminded him of a summer storm. Demetrius didn't know if he was intrigued more with her subtle flirtation or with the fact that it didn't seem to occur to her that he was practically old enough to be her father. Regine stirred up too many longings, desires that needed to remain dormant. It wasn't about sex.

Well, yes, it was sex or at least the potential for it, he thought as he watched her. But Regine stirred something in him that went deeper than a physical urge that was easy enough to appease. A willing and beautiful woman to share a few hours with wasn't what he wanted. Those encounters had always left him feeling let down and empty. Regine, however, filled the emptiness without them having even shared as much as a kiss.

He reached for her free hand and held it in his. "Tell me what you are thinking."

Regine smiled. "I'm thinking that my original plan for coming to Martinique has had a few holes shot in it."

"And this shooting . . . who did it?"

She laughed, the sound a sweet melody to him.

"That's just an expression," she said. Then, "Oh, you mean what happened?"

"*Oui*. Tell me."

Now, truly embarrassed to admit to this man her slutty little plan for her Caribbean holiday, Regine plucked up her white linen napkin. "I . . . well, it's not important."

She felt him watching her.

"All right, then," he said. "We shall talk of something else. What would you like me to tell you of the island?" . . .

"I'm not in a relationship and so on the way here I decided I'd find someone to have a hot, meaningless fling with." The words tumbled from her mouth like a confession to a priest.

A cloud crossed his face. Demetrius sat back. "I see."

He sounded so disappointed in her that Regine wanted to take the bold words back.

"And this man who did not take you to dinner, he was the one of your choice?"

"Well, at first I thought . . ." she started. "But then I met you. I mean, that's not what I meant. You are very . . ." She stumbled over the words, trying to extract the big foot she'd managed to shove into her mouth. Regine twisted the napkin. Had it been paper, it would have shredded under the assault.

"I am very what, mademoiselle?"

Regine grabbed her wineglass and drained the contents.

"Are you trying to get intoxicated so you can have your way with me?"

Her mouth dropped open and she stared at him.

A moment later, her shoulders shook as she tried to stifle the laugh that threatened. When the waiter returned to refill their glasses, the two sat laughing together. The first awkward moments of their mutual attraction had been handled in a most unconventional way.

"You're a nice man, Demetrius Fielding. I'm glad I met you."

He bowed his head in a small acknowledgment of the compliment.

After that, the rest of their meal was easy. The conversation flowed. Demetrius told her more about Martinique and its people. Reginc shared with him details about life in Minneapolis and her work analyzing stocks for a large investment firm.

When they left the restaurant, they strolled back to the hotel. Demetrius saw her to her suite.

"Thank you," she said.

"Thank you, Regine. The pleasure was mine."

He leaned forward. Everything in Regine cried for, begged for, wanted his kiss. Her eyes closed in preparation. Everything about the night led to this moment, Regine waited.

Then, Demetrius kissed her on the cheek and whispered "*Bon jour,* Regine."

Surprised, and oddly pleased, she opened her eyes. With one last smile for her, he turned away. From the open door, Regine watched his retreat.

"Now, that's a sexy man."

Camille had turned in early. Alicia, claiming a headache, did the same. Shayla raised an eyebrow when Regine came in, but was too engrossed in one of her longwinded kissy-cooey calls to her husband to do much more.

Regine, too keyed up to sleep yet too mellow to do anything else, opted for a luxurious soak in the suite's spa.

The candles lit around the elegant bath gave the room a sensual ambience As she lounged in the fragrant water, her wandering thoughts kept winding back to Demetrius. No matter what she tried to focus on—a meditative thought, her bank balance, or the varied and beautiful tropical flowers she'd seen during the day—her mind remained on the man she'd spent most of the day with.

She'd been attracted to him from the moment she spied him in the mirror at the jeweler's shop. She wondered what it might be like to share a bath like this with him. Lifting a handful of warm water, she let it trickle across her breasts. Sighing a not-quite-contented sigh, she contemplated what it might feel like if Demetrius's hands did the very same thing. Closing her eyes, she let herself run with that delicious thought.

After a while, Regine rose from the tub. She dried and lotioned her body, then crawled into bed. Her last waking thought was of walking with Demetrius through one of the enchanting Edens on the island. . . .

Slowly he trailed the soft petal of the hibiscus along her breasts. A moment later, his mouth followed the same sensuous path. She arched into the sweet embrace, panting . . . aching for him to relieve the pressure that built inside her lithe body. Higher and higher he drove her. Tighter and tighter she answered the call. She wanted it to end. She never wanted him to stop.

His mouth closed over her breast. She moaned his name as he suckled her.

When he inched a long finger into her to test her readiness for him, a thousand stars exploded around her. She yelled his name. But he quickly muffled the sound as his lips found hers. A moment later, they locked together in a dance as old as Eden, as wild as distant thunder, as hot as the ancient lava that flowed from Montagne Pelée.

Regine woke up in a sweat.

"Huh? Whassamatter?"

Regine guiltily glanced at Alicia sleeping in the next bed. "Nothing. Go back to sleep."

Mumbling, Alicia rolled over. Regine's gaze roamed the dark room. While luxurious, it was just a room. It wasn't a garden filled with flowers. Demetrius Fielding wasn't there waiting to tease her needy body. But her body was definitely ready for him. From her hardened nipples to the dampness she felt between her legs, Regine knew that her body cried out for a real-life completion of the erotic dream.

FOUR

The next day, the four friends explored more of the island. They took a tour that had them visiting the northern coast of Martinique. Regine and Shayla managed to get some shopping in. Camille sampled every food she could get her hands on. Alicia sulked.

"What in the world is wrong with friend girl?" Camille asked Shayla.

"I don't know. But I plan to find out right this minute," the diminutive Shayla decreed. She hustled to catch up with Alicia's long strides as they walked through the butterfly garden at the botanical museum.

"Alicia, honey. We're worried about you. What's going on?"

"Nothing. I just have some things on my mind," Alicia said. "Are we going to spend all day in here or are we ever going to get over to that volcano Reggie wants to see?"

Regine and Camille looked at each other. With both hands on her hips, Shayla frowned at Alicia's retreating back as she made her way to the exit.

With Alicia in a mood and Camille stopping to eat at every bakery they passed, the rest of the day was spoiled for Regine and Shayla.

"This is not how I planned to spend this week," Shayla pouted as she waited with Regine outside a restroom.

"Tell me about it," Regine concurred. "I didn't even want to come."

Shayla nudged her friend. "Well, Miss Stay Out Half the Night. You sure made up for it fast. Who were you with last night?"

Regine smiled. "A gentleman I met."

Shayla frowned. "Not that gigolo from the lobby."

"No. Not Emil. I met Demetrius. . . ."

"Ooh. He sounds sexy already," Shayla said.

This time Regine's knowing smile spoke of secrets and a confirmation of Shayla's guess. "He is. I met him after Alicia left yesterday."

"She came back to the room and ordered a fifth of—"

Camille's and Alicia's appearance from the rest room cut off the rest of Shayla's and Regine's conversation.

Later, Shayla mouthed. Regine nodded.

The later came when the two of them went to the hotel's live music lounge. Shayla and Regine had always been close. The two had more in common than they did with either Camille or Alicia.

"Do you think she's an alcoholic?" Shayla asked.

"I think she's super stressed and not working it out in the right way."

"What should we do?"

"I don't know," Regine said. "I'm going to talk to her."

After listening to a couple sets of music, they went for a walk around the resort. When they returned, they came through an entrance they had not yet used. Shayla, confident that she knew exactly where she was going, marched off down a corridor—a corridor that took them straight to a dead end.

"One of these days I'm going to stop listening to you," Regine groused.

Shayla turned around, trying to get her bearings. "Well, honey, I thought this was the way."

"Let's go back," Regine said. "If we head down that other hall we passed, we'll probably run into an elevator or something."

This time, with Regine leading the way, they retraced their steps. The soft chime of an elevator landing let them know they'd made their way through the maze of corridors. Regine turned the hallway corner and came up short. Shayla bumped into her.

"What's wrong?"

"Shhh." Regine pushed Shayla back, then retreated herself.

"What's going on?" Shayla said.

"Shhh. They might hear us."

"They who?"

With a finger at her lips, Regine urged Shayla to peek around the corner. Leaning over, Shayla did.

"Busted! I told you so!" Shayla stage-whispered.

Regine yanked her girlfriend back. With their backs against the wall, they stared at each other. "Now what?"

"What do you mean, now what? Let's go back to the suite."

"We can't do that. They're standing right there in front of the elevator."

"Well, I'm not going to stand around here in the hallway all night, Regine. My feet hurt."

Regine glanced down at the fabulously cute but totally impractical sandals that Shayla wore. With Shayla's inappropriate footwear, the brisk walk Regine had hoped to take after dinner turned to a pace slower than a stroll.

Right now, though, Regine had more on her mind than Shayla's feet. She peeked around the corner again. They were still there. Regine watched as Emil leaned forward and whispered something in the woman's ear. The woman twittered a girlish giggle and swatted his hand away. Emil put his arms around her thick waist. The woman had to be at least sixty.

"She's as old as my grandma," Regine mumbled.

"What was that, honey?" Shayla asked.

Regine waved for Shayla to be quiet. A moment later, it dawned on her. The woman probably was *his* grandmother. "That would explain it."

"Regine, I don't plan to loiter in this hallway with you all night. It's almost time for Scott to call."

"Okay. Okay. Just a minute," Regine whispered as she leaned farther around the corner.

"I told you that boy is a gigolo," Shayla said. Then, a

beat later and in a speculative tone, "I wonder how much he gets paid an hour. Do you think the rates are higher or cheaper than in the States?"

"Will you please be quiet?" Regine hissed.

Shayla harrumped and reached for a nail file in her shoulder bag.

So wrapped up in their conversation, the people near the elevator didn't hear Shayla's loud comments.

A moment later, Regine's eyes widened. Emil and the woman were locked in an embrace that no grandma and grandson should ever be in.

Shayla yanked Regine away from the view.

"What?" Regine complained.

"Now aren't you glad you didn't hook up with him? I can spot 'em a mile away. Come on, honey. Let's go plan our shopping for tomorrow."

Regine didn't feel in the mood for that. She instead questioned her judgment as she and Shayla backed down the hall, then found the parallel elevator. It took them just moments to reach their suite. Shayla pulled out the key. Regine glanced at her, about to voice her concerns to her girlfriend. A moment later, though, she changed her mind.

Demetrius couldn't be like Emil. Could he?

What do you really *know about him?* her pesky conscience asked.

"Enough."

"Enough what, honey?" Shayla asked as she opened the door.

Distracted, Regine walked in. "Nothing. Nothing important."

Shayla shook her head. The motion sent the curls that cascaded down her back into swing. "Don't stress about that playboy. Sure, he was good-looking, but good-looking men come a dime a dozen, particularly in the Caribbean. Substance is what matters, Regine. Substance."

"Uh-huh," Regine said knowingly. "And that's why

Scott is all substance and has the looks of a hound dog, right?"

Shayla grinned and reached for her purse. "Hey, I lucked out. Tall, gorgeous, and intelligent."

"And richer than Midas."

"We all have our burdens to carry." The two women chuckled together. "I like 'em like that," Shayla added.

"Like what?" Alicia asked as she joined Shayla and Regine. The red eyes, deep circles under her eyes, and blotchy makeup let them know something was amiss.

"Good Lord, Leesha. What's wrong, honey?"

"What happened?" Regine asked on top of Shayla.

"Nothing," Alicia mumbled. She gathered her terry-cloth robe around her body and paced the lounge area. "What could possibly be wrong?"

Shayla marched over, grabbed Alicia's arm, and walked her to the sofa. Regine headed to the wet bar to get some ice water for Alicia.

"Don't give us that cock and bull," Shayla said. "You come out here looking like a shell-shocked refugee and expect us to believe nothing's wrong? You've been crying, for goodness' sakes. What happened?"

Regine pressed the cool glass into Alicia's hands, then sat next to her on the sofa. "Is it Howard? Did something happen to him?"

Alicia harrumped. Then her bravado collapsed. "Yeah, I guess you could say that."

"What happened, Alicia? Whatever it is, you know we're here for you." Regine left unsaid the fact that neither she nor Shayla had ever liked Howard and couldn't figure out how and why Alicia ever hooked up with him.

"You all were right," Alicia said. She took a sip of water, then placed the glass on the coffee table. "Hindsight is twenty-twenty, though."

Regine and Shayla exchanged a glance but remained quiet. A moment later, Alicia bit her lip, cussed a blue streak, then started crying. Before Shayla or Regine could ask what was wrong again, Alicia sniffled, sat up, and took a fortifying drink of water.

"This arrived about half an hour ago," she said, pulling a crumpled piece of paper from her robe pocket.

Regine took the paper, smoothed it out, and read it. "Oh, God. I can't believe he did this."

"What? What is it?" Shayla said, trying to snatch the paper from Regine.

Alicia stared straight ahead. "I can't believe it. I just can't believe it."

Shayla put her arms around Alicia. "Whatever it is, we'll work it out with you, okay, honey?"

Alicia shook her head. "How could he do this to me?" She turned toward Shayla, then looked at Regine. "Howard declared bankruptcy yesterday. And . . . and . . ." Alicia broke down again.

Shayla rocked and held her friend while Regine ran a comforting hand along Alicia's back as she sobbed. Catching Regine's eye, Shayla silently mouthed, *What?*

Regine held up the single page fax so Shayla could read it. A moment later she blurted out, "Who the heck is Miriam?"

Alicia's tears fell in a steady stream, faster than she could wipe them away with the sleeve of her robe. "Miriam is the bookkeeper! Howard sunk all of our money into that stupid business of his and now he's run off with Miriam."

"Well, I say good rid—"

The always-blunt Shayla was cut off by loud knocking at the suite door.

"What in the world is going on out here?" Camille asked as she padded into the living room. "Is somebody sick? I'm starving. Are there any more olives left in the fridge?"

Alicia moaned. Shayla held her close. Regine got up to answer the door.

"What's wrong?" Regine heard Camille ask as she went to the door.

"Shayla, do something," Regine said with a wave toward Alicia. With one eye on the drama unfolding in their suite, Regine yanked open the door. "Yes?"

Demetrius turned around. "Hello, Regine."

FIVE

Regine's mouth dropped open. "Hello. Hi. Uh, what are you doing here?"

"I gave him nine of the best years of my life!" Alicia wailed.

Regine glanced over her shoulder; so did Demetrius.

"Now is not a good time," he surmised.

Regine winced. "Not exactly. We're in the middle of—"

"How could he do this to me?" came from inside the suite.

"Uh, can I call you a little later?" Regine asked Demetrius.

He nodded as he reached into his inside jacket pocket and retrieved a card and a pen. The very elegant and very expensive fountain pen didn't go unnoticed by Regine. He wrote something on the back of the card.

"Here is my number on the island," he said. "Is there something I can do for you or for your friends? Is a physician needed?"

Before Regine could answer, another outburst came from within. "I'm going to kill him! I swear on my grandmama's grave I'm gonna kill the man."

Demetrius took a step backward. "On second thought," he said, "maybe you need *le gendarme*."

Regine butchered the word trying to repeat it. "What is that?"

"Police. *L'agent de police*. There is a station nearby," he offered.

"No, what we need," Regine said with another glance back into the room, "is a good divorce attorney." It was more than apparent that Alicia had quickly shifted from distraught victim to woman scorned. It promised to be a long night. Shayla frantically paced alongside Alicia. From where she stood, Regine couldn't see Camille.

Closing the door a bit, Regine stepped into the hall area with Demetrius. He took the small white card from her hand and wrote something else on its backside. "Here," he said, handing it back to her. "I have a cousin in the States, in Chicago. He is one of the best divorce attorneys in the world. Call him. He will help your friend."

Regine took a look at the name and number. "I can't impose like that. I don't know the man—although if he's your cousin I'm sure he's just wonderful. Besides, I think Alicia needs some time to sit down and think things through before hiring a lawyer."

Demetrius smiled. "You know, this seems like a scene from that movie the American women of color loved so much a few years ago.

Regine's answering smile held a slightly flirtatious bent. "Well, no one's setting fire to any cars around here tonight."

"That is good to hear."

"Breakfast?" she asked.

"I beg your pardon?"

Belatedly realizing what he thought she was saying, Regine blushed.

The smile at Demetrius's face accentuated the laugh lines at his eyes. Regine felt that familiar tingle she'd come to associate with being near Demetrius. Maybe it was just the tropical weather that kept making her overheated.

Yeah, right, her conscience smirked.

"Maybe we can have breakfast together tomorrow, or rather later today," she said, clarifying the invitation.

"I, mademoiselle, will be counting the minutes."

He leaned forward. Regine did, too. She let her hands softly rest on his shoulders. For a long, comfortable moment, they stared into each other's eyes. It was an awakening moment, one that Regine felt more than a call to answer. Not only right, this moment had been destined.

Her eyes closed. Less than a heartbeat later, his mouth covered hers.

The kiss bypassed the exploratory politeness of first kisses. Demetrius staked a claim that Regine willingly granted. His lips had been sculpted for hers. Hungrily they explored each other in a dance that sent sparks shooting through Regine.

Perfect.

Right.

Meant to be.

In all her years, a kiss had never been like this one. He deepened the embrace and her knees grew weak. The moan came from him. Or was it her? Regine didn't know or care. Yes, she'd been kissed before. She'd been French-kissed before. But this . . . this feeling of rightness, of passion, of perfect knowing seemed out of her realm of experience. And yet, she'd known all along it would be like that with this man.

Time ceased to be while Demetrius showed her what a man kissing a woman was truly supposed to be about.

Glass shattered.

Regine and Demetrius jerked apart.

"What?" a dazed Regine managed to mutter.

Demetrius stroked a gentle fingertip along her temple. "I think your referee skills are needed inside."

For a moment, she stared at him, clearly confused.

"Alicia, don't!" Shayla's voice beyond the door jolted Regine back to reality.

"I forgot," she mumbled. "Alicia's husband—"

"Shhh." Demetrius quieted her with a finger at her lips. "Your friend needs you now," he said. "My need—our need—" he added as he stroked her back, "can wait."

She wasn't at all convinced of that. Her gaze meandered south toward a certain region of his anatomy. His need appeared just as pressing as her own felt.

Demetrius smiled as he took her hands in his. "Until breakfast, chère."

Regine hoped for a quick but passionate kiss on her already swollen lips. Demetrius fooled her, though, as he leaned forward. He lifted her hands into his. While never letting his gaze leave hers, he kissed her hands. Then he was gone.

Regine stared after him as though the man were an apparition come to haunt her.

A moment later, the door flung open.

"Regine, what are you doing out here? Girl, get in here and help Alicia calm down before she tears this place apart. I've never seen her so pissed off."

Regine heard Camille. But even as she followed her girlfriend into the suite to deal with the crisis, her mind stayed on the personal crisis she experienced. Was it truly possible to fall in love at first sight?

Yes, she realized at breakfast.

Demetrius cut a piece of tropical fruit for her. Regine leaned foward, accepting the morsel from him.

"Is your friend better today?"

Regine nodded as she chewed. She then chased the fruit down with a sip of orange-mango juice. "Their marriage has been falling apart since about an hour after their wedding reception. She got a fax from him yesterday that really upset her."

"Is there something I can do for you or for her? I am not an attorney-at-law, but I can telephone my cousin and inform him of her plight."

Shaking her head, Regine declined the assistance on Alicia's behalf.

"She was on the phone with her own lawyer, her brother, shortly after you left."

"I hope, then, for her that things work out on her behalf."

"They will," Regine said, thinking about the rest of the mostly sleepless night.

After someone scrounged up a sleeping pill for Alicia,

she fell into a fitful sleep. Shayla, Camille, and Regine then spent half the night coming up with a financial plan that would ease their friend through the rough months ahead. Getting Alicia to accept the assistance would be another battle . . . one they figured they could worry about later.

"She's flying home this afternoon," Regine told Demetrius.

"So you cut your holiday short for your friend. That is very charitable."

Regine's look of chagrin stopped Demetrius. "No?" he asked.

Regine shook her head. "She insisted we stay."

Demetrius took that in stride. "Well, that is bad for your friend, but good for me," he said with a sudden and arresting smile.

Her body responded to the invitation in his eyes. Then Regine remembered why she had to remain cautious. For whatever reason, Shayla's assessment of Emil stayed with her. Wary now, she wasn't sure if she could trust her own instincts about Demetrius. Never mind that those instincts had helped make her one of the best stock analysts in Minneapolis and probably in the country. That was her professional life. Her personal life, particularly when it came to choosing men, left quite a bit to be desired.

She'd managed to get herself involved with some true characters as she navigated the dating arena. There had been Ramon, the Latin lover who neglected to tell her about his wife and three children. She'd fallen hard for Victor, a stockbroker. Thank goodness she'd wised up early. It didn't surprise her one bit when she picked up the newspaper one day and saw that he'd been busted on an insider trading charge. Then there was Charles. He was all talk and no cash. The third time he "forgot" his wallet, Regine paid for her half of the meal and left him sitting in the expensive restaurant.

If her track record with men was any indication, it

would be just like her to travel all the way to the islands just to have a fling with a, a . . .

"Are you a gigolo?"

Her face flamed.

Demetrius choked on a piece of croissant. *"Excusez-moi?"*

"I'm sorry. I didn't mean to blurt that out like that. It's just that . . ." Regine waved a hand as her words faded away. *Great, just great.*

He looked stunned. "You believe me to be a man who takes money from women?"

Regine wanted to crawl under a rock. "No. No, that's not it at all."

Demetrius's eyes narrowed as he sat back and folded his arms. "Explain."

She sighed. Where to begin?

Taking a moment to gather her thoughts, Regine realized she had absolutely nothing to lose. He was already offended, she thought. She should go ahead and tell the rest; it couldn't get any worse. He already looked as if he'd been mortally and morally assaulted.

"I'll start at the beginning," she told him.

"That would be an appropriate place."

Regine winced at his biting sarcasm. "I'm the only one of my girlfriends who isn't married yet," she began. "As a matter of fact, I've been so busy building my career—"

"Where do you work?" he interrupted.

"I told you. I'm a stock analyst for an investment firm. And you?" she had the presence of mind to ask.

"I manage my family's estate and assets. Vineyards. Hotels. We own property here."

Regine nodded. A sinking feeling crept through her. She'd managed to mess things up with a good one. Well, she thought, at least he worked. Managing those kinds of assets didn't exactly sound like a gigolo's work.

"I'm sorry about what I said," she apologized.

He nodded. "You have not yet told me how you came to believe I was a kept man."

She sighed as she broke off a bit of croissant. Instead of eating it, though, she rolled the pastry between her thumb and index finger.

"As I was saying, I'm the single one in the group. And it's been a while since I was in a significant relationship. Without telling my girlfriends, I decided to have a hot fling while here this week."

He frowned. Regine's spirits sank. Now he probably thought she had no morals at all. Her little plan had seemed so rational at the time. Now, it just seemed pathetic, particularly when viewed from his perspective.

"So it wasn't one of my better ideas," she confessed. "I just thought the sun, the flowers, the anonymity . . . I thought it might be fun."

His deeper scowl made Regine want to slither under the table.

"I have been careful all my life of not pandering to stereotypes," Demetrius said. "You, however, are confirming many of the not-pleasant things that are said about Americans, particularly female American tourists."

"Don't," Regine said. "You can't judge my thoughts and actions against others. I'm thirty-one years old—"

"Very young," he said.

"It depends on who is judging," she replied. "By many American standards, particularly the ones my parents and grandparents adhere to, I'm an old maid." A rich old maid, as her brother always made a point of noting, but nonetheless without a husband and gold ring on her finger. She didn't have the two things that mattered.

"And now who is stereotyping?"

Regine smiled. "Touché."

A waiter refilled their juice glasses and topped off Demetrius's coffee.

"I still do not understand how—"

Regine cut Demetrius off. "I was just getting to that

part. When we checked in, there was a man at the counter also checking in. He caught my eye. I decided he'd be the one to . . . well, you know. We chatted. We made a date. He didn't show up. And then, last night, Shayla and I saw him with an older woman. A much older woman. They were doing more than, uh . . ."

"I get the picture," Demetrius said blandly. "And based on that you thought I wander around hotels and the streets doing the same thing?"

She winced again. "I'm sorry. My friend spotted him for what he was the moment she laid eyes on him. I questioned my own judgment about you since I didn't recognize him for what he was."

Demetrius gazed at her. Regine kept her eyes on the piece of crossaint that now resembled little bits of dough on the tablecloth. He reached for her hand.

"Look at me, Regine."

Reluctantly, her gaze met his.

"I am not a gigolo. I am in Martinique for a meeting with my staff. After that, I head to another island to do the same thing. When I saw you in that jewelry shop, I was struck by the optimism, and the panic," he added with a smile, "in your eyes. I entered looking for a gift for my youngest daughter."

"Buying that necklace wasn't exactly in my plans for this holiday," she said.

"Well, I am glad I came along when I did."

"You're not angry with me, are you?" she asked.

"*Non.* I am just wondering if maybe your experience with this man is the universe trying to tell you it was not a wise course of action."

"Boy, what a nice way to say 'stupid,' "

Amusement brightened his face. "I would never call you any such thing, and I would not think it, either."

"Thank you," Regine said. "How old is your daughter?"

"She will be sixteen in six weeks. She lives with her

mother. Unfortunately, I do not get to see her very often."

"That's too bad," Regine said. She wanted to ask more about the mother and whether he had any other children, but she'd already pressed her luck with him once today. That was enough.

A glance at her watch told her she needed to get back to the suite so they could get Alicia to the airport in time for her flight.

"Thank you for having breakfast with me, particularly given the circumstances with your friend," Demetrius said.

Regine glanced at her watch. "We're going to see her off and then do some more exploring."

Demetrius spent the next minutes suggesting places for them to go. When they parted company, it was without any future plans, a fact that didn't escape Regine's notice. He'd shut her out and off without making a scene.

"When you blow it, you blow it big time, my friend," she said as she closed the door to the suite.

The friends said a tearful farewell to Alicia. Sober, angry, and ready for battle, Alicia boarded the plane that would eventually see her back to Detroit. Shayla, Regine, and Camille spent the rest of the day lounging at the pool, no one really in the mood to do much else.

Regine counted Demetrius a loss due to her own stupidity. She tried to make the most of the next few days, but the sparkle that had been on the garden of flowers seemed to diminish, given Alicia's problems and the way she'd insulted Demetrius's character. Regine couldn't even do anything with her friends. Camille was sick in the mornings. And given Alicia's marital woes, Shayla found herself missing her new husband even more. The luster of the island faded in Regine's eyes. Her thoughts kept straying to Demetrius and their breakfast together.

She'd managed to alienate the one man who was legitimate.

Friday morning, their last full day on the island paradise, Regine woke to knocking on the suite's entry doors.

A resort employee delivered an arrangement of tropical flowers that included several beautiful ones Regine couldn't identify.

She searched for a card and found it near a lovely hibiscus bloom.

My work has kept me in meetings, but I think of you each day.
Would you honor me by having dinner this evening? Eight o'clock.

The note was signed with a bold *D* and included a telephone number. Regine smiled. Then she grinned. Then she placed the call, confirmed the dinner date with Demetrius, and spent the rest of the day smiling.

Maybe Martinique wasn't a wash after all.

SIX

"I thought you were angry with me," she told Demetrius as they settled at a cozy table in a small but lovely restaurant.

"Why would I be angry with you, Regine?"

"Because of what I said the other day."

He shook his head. The sommelier approached. In the French she loved to hear him speak, Demetrius ordered wine. Regine didn't even mind that he didn't ask her what she preferred.

Moments later, Demetrius returned to their conversation. "Regine, given the circumstances, I understand. I think," he added. "As long as you realize I am not one of those men, then—how do you say it?—no harm, no foul."

Enchanted, Regine laughed. She stuck her hand out. When he did the same, they shook on it. But Demetrius carried the frivolity a step further. He ended the embrace by holding her hand a moment longer than necessary. Then he kissed it.

Regine sighed, even as her body trembled with awareness and wanting.

Demetrius wined her, dined her, and seduced her. For the first time in her life, Regine appreciated and understood the small talk. Their dinner conversation was a form of foreplay, the idle talk of two people who knew exactly where and how the evening would end. Maybe. She hoped. She prayed.

After dinner they strolled along the avenue that led back to the resort.

"We leave tomorrow afternoon," she said.

"Have you enjoyed Martinique?"

"Very much so. It's beautiful here. Peaceful, too."

"Then you must return someday," he said.

Regine stopped walking. She turned to him. "I hope to."

For a long time they simply stared at each other. Regine's entire being seemed filled with waiting. The sweetly intoxicating scent of tropical flowers filled the air, but Regine didn't notice. The night spoke of unfulfilled longings, desire that had been held in check for too long. Regine stared into the eyes of the man she wanted. But Demetrius didn't smile. This moment would begin or end all of their future moments.

His silence let her know it would be her call, her choice.

Of its own voilition, Regine's hand reached up to caress his face. His eyes darkened, his stare bold and assessing. He waited. The moment was Regine's to determine.

She cupped his head and brought it to hers, the kiss a vow sealed.

"Do you trust me, Regine?"

"Yes."

"Then come," he said.

Demetrius raised his hand, and moments later a car appeared. He helped her into the backseat. "Home," he told the driver.

"*Oui,* Monsieur Fielding."

Demetrius closed the window between them. Then he turned to Regine. She came into his arms, willingly and passionately.

The next morning, Demetrius drank a cup of rich, dark coffee and stared at the tableau from his balcony. He didn't see the courtyard fountain or even the verdant hills of the land stretched before him. His mind was on Regine Bryant.

He hadn't planned on last night. Making love to Regine complicated things, for him if not for her. She was a tourist, leaving today. He'd never see her again. But he knew he'd always remember the way she responded to him. The plan he'd been determined to carry out was to grant her the island magic she'd come to Martinique to explore. He'd planned to make love to her, then walk away without a regret, without the expectation of anything more. The way a gigolo would.

Demetrius sighed.

He'd make a poor kept man. He got too emotionally involved. And that's exactly what he was with Regine—emotionally involved, despite the odds, despite everything, including his plans.

The plan had been to show her exactly how unsuited they were. He was almost twenty years her senior. Yet, Regine came to him. She wanted him.

"She wanted anyone," he reminded himself. The thought that she would even consider a casual affair with a stranger angered him.

A moment later, Demetrius realized he was more angry with himself than with Regine. He'd played with fire and gotten singed to the core of his being. In a few short days, the beautiful Regine had crawled up under his skin and made him forget the vow he'd made to himself. He placed the coffee cup on the balcony railing.

In all his years, no woman had ever made him feel the way Regine did—as though he were king of the world.

"And your track record stinks, monsieur," he reminded himself.

Regine didn't know much about him. He'd told her about his youngest daughter. He'd even given her a vague description of his so-called job. Could a man who had the blood of kings running through his veins claim to have a mere job?

"Yes," he told the balcony. Long ago his impoverished family sold away their claim to royalty. At seventeen, Demetrius had been thrust out of luxury's lap and into poverty. By the time he turned twenty-seven, his rich relatives were coming to him for money. Demetrius Fielding had made a name for himself in the Caribbean and in France.

From the ground up, he'd restored his side of the family's name and fortunes.

Demetrius had shared none of his background with Regine. That, he knew, was for the best. He knew because he'd had lots of experience with women . . . and more specifically with would-be brides.

From her own mouth, Regine told him she wanted a wedding ring, a band of gold just like all of her girlfriends. But that, he knew, was impossible.

Four times now he'd said "I do." And with the exception of his first wife, who was buried near the Mediterranean in her native Provence, he'd sat at an attorney's table dissolving the memories and the revenue earned during each disastrous union.

The only good thing that had come of his marriages were his children. Four of them. And Arianne, despite her mother's games, was his pride and joy.

The very last thing Demetrius needed was a woman with starlight, moonbeams, and forever after in her eyes.

He conveniently ignored the fact that in the few short days he'd known Regine, he'd found himself more enchanted than he'd ever been, and that included the short months he'd had with his beloved Larette.

"And she didn't want marriage," he reminded himself of his first bride. He had been the one who insisted upon it.

American tourist Regine Bryant had come to Martinique to explore the tropical and sensuous side of the French Caribbean. Demetrius simply gave her what she came for.

For once, he vowed, he would not be the chivalrous knight who spoiled the maiden, then asked for her hand.

Regine sat up in bed. With Alicia gone, she'd had the big room all to herself most of the week. Suddenly Regine wished that Alicia lay snoring in the other bed. She needed something, anything to keep her mind off the one thing her brain seemed one hundred percent focused on: Demetrius Fielding.

Regine's sigh was everything but dreamy as she clasped her arms around her knees and hugged herself. Her plan had backfired.

"Big time."

The idea had seemed so simple, so flawless. All she had to do was have a hot, torrid, no-strings-attached affair while on vacation.

"No strings and no regrets," she reminded the empty room.

But here she was, the morning after the most fabulous night in her life, having big-time regrets—not regrets that she'd made love to Demetrius, but that her time remaining on Martinique and therefore in his arms had all but ended. He'd given absolutely no indication that he wanted to see her again.

Even if she abandoned Shayla and Camille, found her way to Demetrius's house in the hills, and spent the next few hours ravishing him, Regine didn't think that would be near enough time to get him out of her system.

"Or to prove that he isn't even in my system," she said.

Regine flopped back on the bed. "This is a fine time in your life to turn into a nympho," she groaned.

She'd been without sex for months at a time. There'd even been a stretch of two years one time a while back. After a wildly passionate night with Demetrius whispering in her ear, touching her here, loving her there, Regine didn't think she could ever get her fill of him.

Flipping onto her stomach, she pouted. It wasn't just the sex, which had been the best she'd ever—

A rat-a-tat-tat on her bedroom door interrupted Regine's thoughts. Before she could turn over or say *Come in,* Shayla and Camille burst into the room.

"I told you she was by herself," Shayla said triumphantly. "I'm a very light sleeper, you know. I would have known if she'd had company." Shayla stretched the word *company* out into a long, knowing tease.

Camille peeled a banana. "Uh-huh. And who was the one who completely slept through a panty raid that had six police squad cars and a fire truck at the dormitory?"

Shayla waved a hand as she plopped onto Regine's bed. "Ancient history. That was then. I'm a light sleeper now."

Camille settled on Alicia's vacated bed.

"So, tell us about him," Shayla prompted.

"Him who?"

"Don't even try it, sisterfriend. You have that glow," Shayla said, waving a manicured hand around Regine's face and body.

"What glow?" Regine asked.

Camille chuckled. "The same one that got me in my present state."

Shayla whipped around and pounced on that juicy morsel. "So you admit it!"

"Admit what?" Camille asked as she took a bite of banana.

"You're pregnant."

Camille smiled and placed an open palm on her flat stomach. "I must be. I've had some of the oddest cravings. How'd you know? I haven't even said anything to Roger."

"It's that glow," Regine said dryly.

Shayla grinned. "So, when are you due?"

Camille shrugged. "I don't know. I'm going to make an appointment when we get back."

"Did you do one of those pregnancy tests?" Shayla asked.

"No. It wasn't until the other day that I had morning sickness."

"Ooh. I'm so excited," Shayla said, hitting Regine's leg. "We're going to be aunties."

Regine smiled, and admitted to herself a bit of wistfulness. Demetrius had been well protected. The fruit of their passion would be the kind you remembered, not the kind that showed up in nine months.

"Don't forget Howard's kid," she reminded them. "We're already step-aunties."

"That little monster. I don't know how Alicia puts up with the beast," Shayla said. "At least he just shows up once a month when Howard has visitation rights."

"Did either of you talk to Alicia yet?" Regine asked.

"She said she'd probably be too P.O.'d to call," Camille reported. "I'll ring her place when we get to the airport."

"You think they're gonna be okay?"

"Who?" Shayla asked. "Howard, his beastly child, or that hoochie-mama bookkeeper he ran off with?"

"I meant Alicia and her mother," Regine clarified. "Alicia's mom depends on her for a lot of things."

"Well, I, personally, think she's better off without that loser," Camille added. "All he ever did was beat all of her self-esteem out of her."

"He hit her?" Shayla shrieked.

"No, not physically," Camille said. "But the mental damage was probably the same. Nothing she did was ever right as far as Howard was concerned. Frankly, Alicia has too much going for her to let somebody like that bring her down."

"I wish I lived closer to her," Camille added. "We only talk through E-mail."

"Well, with the plan we've come up with for her, she'll be okay. At least financially," Regine said.

"Maybe I should encourage her to move to Colorado. It's beautiful," Shayla said. "Scott and I love it."

"You all know that child is not going to leave Detroit," Camille said as she finished off her banana and stretched out on Alicia's bed.

They all knew that to be true. The three women were quiet for a little while, each lost in her own thoughts about Alicia.

Shayla broke the silence.

"Okay, honey," she said, patting Regine's leg under the top sheet. "You've had enough time to get your little thoughts together. Tell us about this man."

Regine slipped from bed on the opposite side and grabbed a light robe that she wrapped around her body. "He's a gigolo. You know that."

Camille choked and sat up. "You paid some guy . . ."

"No," Regine said.

"Not *that* guy," Shayla said at the same time.

"What are you two talking about?" Camille asked.

"Sisterfriend here met somebody," Shayla said with a sly grin. "That's who she spent the night with."

Regine bit her lip. "Hey, guys, I really don't want to talk about it right now, okay?"

Camille and Shayla glanced at each other.

"Okay, honey," Shayla said as she rose from the bed.

For once, Regine appreciated the perceptiveness that Shayla occasionally displayed.

"I need to finish packing," Camille announced.

Regine absently nodded as she walked into the bathroom. She left her girlfriends staring after her wondering about the man who seemed to have Regine's complete thoughts.

SEVEN

Three months later

Winter still gripped Minneapolis, and all Regine had to keep her warm were the memories of the vacation that seemed like a lifetime ago. She sat at her desk twirling a pencil. The screen-saver photo of one of Martinique's picturesque beaches popped up. All it did was remind her of what she'd lost. Even after all this time. Regine still found herself unwilling to talk with her friends about the man she'd met and given her heart, body, and soul to on Martinique. Regine didn't truly understand the concept of loneliness until she'd spent these long weeks since Martinique alone and lonely.

Camille was enjoying her pregnancy. Alicia was in the middle of divorce proceedings. Shayla and her husband had returned to Martinique for an early second honeymoon. And Regine was alone and missing Demetrius.

Since returning from the island, she'd heard from him once. A week after arriving back home, a package postmarked Fort-de-France, Martinique, arrived at her office. Curious, Regine peeled the paper away and opened the box.

Stunned, she stared at the gold-and-gemstone necklace—the very one she'd admired in the jewelry store the day she'd met Demetrius.

Without a second thought, Regine returned the expensive piece to the jeweler.

Months later, she didn't regret the action. But she wondered about Demetrius and where he might be.

Her interoffice line buzzed. Regine hit the button on her telephone that activated the headset she generally wore while conducting business.

"This is Regine."

"Bonjour, mademoiselle."

Her heart suddenly pounded furiously. Regine stood up so fast she knocked over a paper cup of coffee. The voice was unmistakable.

"Demetrius?"

"Oui."

Regine stared at her telephone console. The line that rang was one inside the building that housed her investment firm's offices. "Where are you?"

"At your assistant's desk," he replied. "I have missed you, Regine Bryant."

Her mouth dropped open. Regine stared from the telephone console to her office door. A moment later, the door opened.

Demetrius stood there with a telephone receiver at his ear. Beyond him, her assistant grinned and waved. He looked the same. Tall, distinguished, and Old World sexy. A little more gray peppered the hair at his temples. The blue wool suit he wore would have seemed pompous on their tropical island. Here in the city, he looked like one of the stockbrokers or lawyers who did business in the building.

Other than that, he remained the same sun-bronzed man she'd fallen in love with on Martinique.

Regine tugged the headset free and watched as Demetrius handed the receiver over to Melody.

Melody mouthed, *Good luck,* to Regine as she closed the door.

"What are you doing here?"

"I came to see you," he said. "I had business nearby and thought I'd stop in."

"Oh," Regine said. So this was simply a courtesy call. She could handle that, she figured. She'd just fall apart after he left.

He took a step toward her. "You returned the necklace."

Regine took a step backward. "You shouldn't have sent it."

"I know. And I apologize for that."

Part of Regine's heart broke at his words. In the end he'd given her exactly what she said she'd wanted from her island vacation: a hot affair with no strings attached.

Demetrius took the steps that put them face-to-face. Regine leaned against the edge of her desk—for support, she had to privately acknowledge.

"I . . ." she licked her lips. "How have you been?"

"I've missed you, Regine Bryant. I've missed you every day we've been apart."

"But . . ."

Demetrius silenced her with a finger at her lips. Regine thrilled at the contact. She fervently hoped he couldn't see or hear her heart pounding a mile a minute. She'd never thought she'd see him again.

"Why did you come here today?" she managed. Feeling his finger as she said the words made Regine weak in the knees—a phenomenon that hadn't happened since she'd first met and loved Demetrius so many months ago.

"To give you this," he said as he pulled something from his suit jacket.

Gemstones sparkled in his hands.

Regine's eyes widened when she recognized the necklace. "But—"

"Let me finish," he said. "I should not have sent this to you."

"That's right," she said. "It's far too expen—"

He silenced her with a finger to her lips again. Of its own volition, Regine's tongue licked the bit of flesh.

Demetrius jerked his hand back and turned away from her. A moment later, when he faced her again, a fire burned in his eyes. Vaguely withdrawn, Regine wondered if the volcano Pelée on Martinique had given warning before it exploded. The fire that burned in Demetrius's eyes was, she was sure, a warning. But of what? He seemed angry, even tense, but surely *she* hadn't angered him.

"I should not have sent you the necklace, Regine," he said again in that wonderfully accented English. "I should have hand-delivered it."

Regine gasped.

"You are surprised? I was as well when I realized my feelings for you."

"You have feelings for me?"

Regine's outside line buzzed. She ignored it, knowing her assistant would get it.

"Yes, I do," he said. "I have strong feelings for you, Regine Bryant. But I do not think you want to be involved with a man like me. I carry with me lots of what you women call emotional baggage. I've been married before."

"I don't care," Regine said.

He smiled. "I have children who are just a bit younger than you are."

She licked dry lips. "I'd love to meet them."

Demetrius's hungry gaze tracked the action. "You test my strength, Regine."

"Turnabout is fair play."

His chuckle warmed her even more than his presence did.

"The short time we spent together on Martinique was magical. It was . . ." He shook his head, unable to come up with a word that matched his feelings.

"I know," Regine said. "I feel the same way."

"Then why did you send this back?" he said, holding the necklace before her.

"I thought you were paying me back for what I said about you."

For a moment, Demetrius looked confused. Then it dawned on him what she was talking about.

"Regine, I sent you this gift as a token of my love. Not as a payoff."

"Love? Did you say a token of love?"

Demetrius smiled. "Yes, *chère.* I have missed you tremendously."

"And so you just stopped by here while in town on business?"

Regine didn't want to jump to any conclusions. Wherever this was leading, she wanted to make sure they were talking and operating from the same page. She'd almost lost him the last time when she jumped to incorrect assumptions.

"*Non,*" he said. "I stopped by after leasing a space in a downtown building. I believe it is time for my family to do business in Minneapolis. That means my real reason for being here," he said, pointing to her desk, "is to determine if there can be more for us than a few days of island romance."

"Do you mean it?" she said.

"*Chère,* you ask too many questions. Let me show you."

He lifted the necklace and placed it around her neck. Regine bent her head so he could close the clasp. A second later, she moaned. He'd closed the clasp and then kissed the back of her neck.

"Demetrius."

"Yes, Regine?"

She turned in his arms. The fast beat of her heart slowed to a more normal rate. She slipped her hands around his shoulders.

"I want to know exactly what we're talking about. I don't want any misunderstandings or confusion between us. So, what are you talking about?"

He smiled as his arms circled her waist. "*Amour,* Regine. That means love."

"I knew that."

"And did you know this?"

"What?"

"That I love you, Regine Bryant."

"I love you, too," she said.

"Show me."

"That, monsieur, is something that can be arranged."

AN ESTATE OF MARRIAGE

SHIRLEY HAILSTOCK

PROLOGUE

URL: http://www.TrueVacations

Bored with the usual? Need a change? Want some magic in your life? Willing to take a risk? Let the magicians at **TrueVacations** plan the perfect getaway for you. Packages from one week to the end of time. Put yourself in our hands. SATISFACTION GUARANTEED. E-mail Adrian and expect perfection. Adrian@TrueVacations.com

ONE

Stephen Weller would have kissed Adrian if she were here. No travel agent had ever followed his rules as close to the letter as she had. He was sure he'd have complete privacy behind the stone wall he'd been passing for the last half mile. He turned the rented Lexus convertible into the driveway and stopped. Outside a massive, ornately forged wrought-iron gate he punched in the security code the online travel agent had included with his packet of travel documents. The gate slid sideways and he proceeded up the divided driveway. The center was a garden ringed with low hedges, a single row of dwarf palm trees running up the middle. Brightly colored flowers had been planted at the base of the hedges to give a colorful and welcome entrance.

Stephen didn't often notice things like flowers, but coming to the island meant being draped in the floral scents of hibiscus. At every glance there were people holding or wearing flowers, in their hair, around their necks, or as bracelets. It was impossible not to notice them.

He stretched as he got out of the car and looked at the impressive house in front of him. It was two stories, with an upper balcony that ran the length of the front supported by strong white pillars that gleamed in the morning sun. He wondered if the pattern continued along the back. He could smell the ocean, hear it roaring in the background. Palm trees waved gently in the tropical breeze and bird-of-paradise grew profusely along the front of the house. Hardy roses, which must need constant care in this salty environment, spread out about the grounds. He could only wonder what the back looked like.

Stephen smiled. The estate was perfect. Oahu, Hawaii, was worth the last eleven hours he'd spent on airplanes to get here. He could relax, enjoy himself, and be completely isolated from anyone who might interrupt his ability to finish the musical score he'd put off for far too long.

Gathering his suitcases, he went inside. Going through the living and dining rooms, with their panoramic views of the ocean, Stephen approved of everything he saw. The music room could have been set up by a major record company. From a grand piano to a CD cutter, equipment gleamed at him as if it were telegraphing him silent messages. Stephen turned everything on. Like a kid during Christmas, he darted from machine to machine, forgetting the luggage he'd abandoned at the entrance. He wanted to play with all his toys at the same time.

Adrian had promised this would be the perfect vacation. He had to agree with her. If he couldn't finish the score here, it wasn't meant to be finished.

Naomi Davenport had reached that point in the jogging trail where her mind was free of constraint. No thoughts crowded her. Nothing filtered in to disturb her endorphin-induced euphoria. Just the natural communion with herself and the elements around her. She ran along the beach behind the estate as she'd done each morning of the week she'd been here. It was quiet, undisturbed, beautiful. The sea accompanied her, joining her rhythm and singing a song that she understood as she continued her exercise program. Her body, usually a light brown, had deepened to a golden, healthy color. Even the lighter-colored skin around her third finger had deepened to hide any trace of the engagement ring she'd removed when she arrived on the island. She also hadn't thought of Burt in days, either.

The place was ideal for her needs. She'd explained them to Adrian precisely and the wonderful travel agent must have been her twin in another life, for Naomi couldn't have chosen a better place herself.

Returning to the estate, she slowed her run to a walk and covered the last fifty yards, which brought her to the back gate. Pushing the wrought-iron portal open, she entered the estate and headed directly for the pool. A swim would finish her workout. Again Naomi thought how perfect the estate was as she stepped onto the diving board and looked out on the calm waters of the Olympic-size swimming pool that was totally hers. Her jogging clothes, shorts, and top doubled as a swimsuit, but she could have easily swum nude in the seclusion of this privileged area.

She dove cleanly into the water, cut through the liquid with strong even strokes. It was refreshing, smooth, and cool against her heated skin. Naomi came to the surface and started her routine of swimming laps. She'd done seventy-five yesterday and she wanted to add another twenty-five today. Her count started when she got to the shallow end. She turned and, using the wall as a push-off point, began her swim back the other way. She was at number thirty-seven when she reached to touch the tile at the shallow end and a set of bare feet stopped her.

Naomi stood up, pushing the water out of her eyes and slicking her hair back from her face. The feet she'd seen were connected to bare legs, strong, dark brown, athletic, and long. He wore bright red swimming shorts and had a towel slung over his left shoulder. He smiled at her with a wide grin. His shoulders were broad and she remembered her thought about swimming nude. Thank God she hadn't.

Climbing out of the pool, she wondered how he'd gotten in here. She knew the front gate was locked. Her towel was at the other end of the pool and she had no choice except to approach him with water sluicing down her legs and dripping from her shoulder-length hair.

"Do you come with the house?" he asked. The smile on his face may have been playful, but her body turned indignantly hot. The implication was clear and she frowned.

"Who are you? And what are you doing here?"

"According to my lease, I live here. Now, why are you in my pool?"

Naomi had seen many men wearing various amounts of skimpy clothing. In her line of work as a film consultant she'd seen more than her share of men wearing nothing on their muscular frames, but this man's body made hers stand at attention. Even through her anger she was aware of the sex appeal he exuded. What was he doing here? She didn't like how he made her feel. She didn't like that he could make her feel things she had no right to feel or time to research. She didn't even know if she wanted to research them. His washboard stomach and Tarzan-size shoulders made her aware of everything about him, including the small bit of fabric separating him from indecency. His eyes, dark and interested, made her aware of her own lack of dress.

He took a step toward her. Naomi stepped back before she could stop herself. She hadn't meant to let him know he intimidated her, but she'd lived in New York too long not to remember caution. It was instinctive. She didn't know this man; no matter how much he looked like someone she'd want to know, he could be a serial killer.

"I have no weapons on me." He obviously read her reaction correctly. He lifted his arms for her inspection. With the trunks as his only garment, she could tell he was unarmed, but the sexuality that radiated from him was enough to overpower any female under the age of dead.

"What do you mean, you have a lease? I've leased this estate through the end of the month."

She could see the change in him. Her words seemed to have awakened an anger in him. He stepped toward her again.

"You must be wrong," he said. "My lease begins today and runs for the next sixty days."

Her peace on the beach had been instantly destroyed. She didn't like his attitude: Of course, she had to be the one in the wrong. Well, if he thought he could just walk in here and run over her, he'd met the wrong woman.

"Then it's invalid," she stated in the best lawyer voice she could muster. "I'd like to see this alleged lease of yours."

"And I'd like to see yours."

Naomi took a deep breath. Her heart was beating fast and her ears were burning. So much for the peace and quiet she'd had on the beach. Now she had a man to deal with.

"Meet me in the kitchen in fifteen minutes."

By way of assent, he brought his heels together and extended one arm in an exaggerated gesture of a gentleman. Obviously, she was to precede him into the house. The display angered her even more. Naomi wanted to push him into the pool, but she lifted her chin and walked past him, glad the water had dried on her skin or he'd be able to see the steam evaporating.

In her bedroom she quickly showered and dressed in a yellow sundress. There was little she could do with her hair other than pull it into a wet ponytail. She added lip gloss to her mouth and returned to the kitchen. Her adversary was already there. He turned from the pot where she'd made coffee and held her cup in his hand. When he lifted it to his mouth, another stab of anger replaced the calm she'd achieved in her bedroom. He hadn't changed clothes and Naomi had the distinct feeling he was using his body to throw her off her guard.

It was working.

On the table was a legal-looking document. Naomi went to it.

"Read it and weep," he said.

Naomi threw him a withering glance and tossed the lease in her hand at him. He caught it with his free hand. Agile, too, she thought, as not a drop of the coffee spilled. She read through the pages of his lease, looking for something that would give hers superiority over what was in his.

"Obviously, there's been some mistake," she said.

"I'd say so."

"You'd needn't act so superior. I have possession and I'm sure that will hold up in any court."

"When would you like to go to court?" he challenged.

"I'll kill Adrian. She obviously isn't as good an agent as I thought she was."

"Adrian Bledsoe?"

Naomi looked up at him. "Yes, why?"

"She's my agent."

A thought niggled in the back of her mind, but Naomi rejected it. Adrian didn't know her. The two of them had never met face-to-face, although Naomi had seen a digitized photo of the travel agent on her personal web site. All arrangements for this vacation had been made on the Internet. Yet some of the travel agent's messages had been laced with personal questions. Mostly about men. Was she seeing anyone? Was she interested in meeting men on her trip? Should she book Naomi on some trips were there were single men? Naomi hadn't told her much about her life, only enough to let her know she required absolute privacy. Which meant *no men*. But for a split second she wondered if the agent hadn't taken her seriously.

"Why don't we sit down and discuss this like two intelligent adults?" he suggested.

Naomi thought of it as one of those questions like, *Do you still beat your wife?* There was no way you could answer without looking bad. She took a seat and waited. She looked directly at him for a moment. He came forward and pulled a chair back, turning it around to straddle it. She noticed the darkness of his skin and the muscles flexed in his arms. She also thanked God she couldn't see his legs.

"Have any ideas?" he asked.

"One of us has to leave, and since I've—"

"I'm not leaving." His interruption had finality to it.

"Why not? You've only just arrived. You can't have any affinity for the place."

"That music room alone is enough for me to never want to leave."

"Oh, no, not a musician." She got up and walked to the sink. Looking out on the grounds, she took a calming breath. Except for the gentle wind, which she knew from her week here was constant, everything outside was exactly as it had been since she'd arrived five days ago. Yet things weren't the same. He had changed them. She turned back. He stared at her. His eyes had interest in them. Interest of a man for a woman. It was only there for a moment, then gone as if a set of blinds had closed.

"What did that mean?"

"What?" She was confused. She'd lost her train of thought. They were talking about the lease.

" 'Oh, no, not a musician,' " he mimicked.

"It meant nothing."

"It must have meant something."

"It means musicians are usually loud, but we're not here to discuss music. So can we stick to the subject?"

She was the one not sticking to the subject. She was the one whose mind was full of hormones, but he was the one practically undressed. How was she supposed to act?

"What do you do?"

"Why is that important?" she asked.

"You seem really stressed out. If you've been here a week, I'd expect you'd be more relaxed."

Naomi had been relaxed. That was before Adonis arrived. "I am not stressed out," she said slowly. "I'm just surprised and a little annoyed." She paused. "I have some things to work out, and this place was ideal before . . ."

"Before I showed up." He finished the sentence she'd left hanging.

She nodded. "I'm sorry. I apologize."

"You want to tell me what the problem is?"

"You're a musician, not a shrink."

"What do we do about living arrangements? It's a big

house. I'm sure we can share it and never run into each other."

Naomi weighed this. Share a house with this . . . man. She wasn't sure. She'd never done anything like this before. She'd never considered it. Burt had never asked her to live with him. And here was a total stranger wanting to share her house and thinking nothing of it.

"From what I've seen, we could ramble around here for weeks and never see each other."

Naomi wouldn't have to see him. She could feel his presence.

"No, that is a bad idea." She shook her head. "I couldn't possibly consider it."

"You're already considering it."

She looked at him. In a flash, an erotic fantasy popped into her head. She could see them sharing not only the house, but every room in it, especially the bedroom. Her own naked body covered by his, sprawled over the satin coverlet of her bed, heated her skin. Naomi had to blink to get rid of it. Nothing like that had ever happened to her. Not with Burt, at least.

Suddenly she could see her life. Safe. Contained. Unexciting. She didn't like the reference. She'd lived at home with her brothers, but never with another man. What would it be like?

"We'd need to do some scheduling," he was saying when her mind came back to the present. "There is only one kitchen."

Naomi nodded. They would need to think about that. There were many things they needed to think of, but right now she was having a devil of a time concentrating.

"What do you think?" he asked.

She frowned, confused.

"About the kitchen?"

The kitchen, she thought, looking around as if she'd never seen it before. "I like to cook," she said. Then realized he was smiling. "But I am not going to be responsible for your meals."

"Then we can try this?"

"We can try it," she finally said, already sure this was a bad idea. But he did have a lease and she really wasn't sure of the legal implications. And the thought of having him around was more exciting than anything she could remember.

He gave her a winning smile. It irritated her that he'd won so easily. Naomi put her hand out toward him, palm up. "Not so fast. We have to set some rules."

"You go first," he conceded.

"The kitchen—"

"I can cook my own meals," he interrupted. "The most I'll probably do here is coffee and donuts. If you want it, the kitchen is all yours."

She might have known it, junk food, but seeing him in the skimpy trunks, she knew the effects of fat had nothing on him.

"I've taken the front bedroom in the East Wing. You'll occupy the West Wing."

He nodded. "My stuff is already there."

"And there is to be no forgetting the directions."

"I wouldn't dream of it, honey."

The way he said it made her feel small, as if he found her unattractive. She shrugged, rolling her shoulders as if she could virtually drop his words to the floor, but they hung on.

"Anything else?" he raised his eyebrows.

"That's all."

"Now it's my turn." He pushed himself up from the chair. Naomi had to look up as he stood. "First, I told you I'm here to write music. I do like to play it loud, but I will probably do more composing than playback. I work late into the night. I do not wish to be wakened early in the morning. So if you're a morning person, keep quiet when you get up."

"I'm sure I can manage that," Naomi said.

"Second, I came here to be alone. I don't want my time encroached upon for any of the little things like getting a lizard out of your room or reaching something on the top shelf or—"

"I get the picture. You don't need to worry about those things. I'm very self-reliant. I'm sure I can manage to reach whatever needs reaching. Your time is certainly your own, and this house doesn't have lizards."

With that, she snatched her lease from the table and headed for the door.

"One more thing," he said when she was about to go through the arch leading to the back stairs. She stopped, but did not turn to face him. "My name's Stephen Weller. I see from the lease yours is Naomi Davenport. It was nice to meet you, Naomi."

Naomi said nothing. She left the kitchen. In her room she grabbed the phone and dialed the number of the travel agent. Too angry to think straight, she forgot there was a time difference between Oahu and New York. She got Adrian's personal message saying she was not at her desk, but her call was important so please leave a message. She left one that could curl the naturally straight hair of the travel agent.

Stephen should be as angry as Naomi. He had invaded her space, even though he had a perfectly legal claim to the property. He wasn't angry. In fact, he felt good about having her here. She was certainly beautiful, clear brown skin the golden color of autumn leaves, dark brown eyes he'd like to find staring at him from a pillow some morning. And a body that couldn't have been built any better if it had been sculpted by Michelangelo himself.

TWO

Naomi sat straight up in bed as if she'd been propelled by an angry puppeteer. "What is that?" she said out loud. Her heart beat wildly from the sudden jerk out of a deep sleep. She grabbed her head as the jarring music pounded. *It's dark,* she thought, unable to immediately determine what was happening. Then her thoughts focused. *Stephen Weller!*

She had the east side of the house. Not even a finger of light filtered in through the curtains. And Stephen had his music blaring loud enough to wake Pele. Naomi pulled the pillows over her head, but the action only muffled the words and left the thumping bass to reverberate throughout the room. It bounced off the walls and sent vibrations through her body.

This was not going to work, she told herself as she threw the pillows on the floor and shoved back the covers. Her head had been pounding since she'd found him standing over her in the pool. And now he was disturbing her sleep. She got out of bed and, grabbing her robe, went toward the ungodly sound that filled every room of the huge estate.

She marched across the spacious living room that separated the east side from the west and into the room that held all manner of musical equipment. Going straight to the offending machine that spewed the awful sound, she snapped it off, uncaring if she broke the darn thing. The room became gloriously silent.

"What the . . ." Stephen stopped as soon as he saw her.

"Do you know what time it is?" she attacked. Her teeth clenched as she spoke. "It's three o'clock in the morning and you're playing your music as if it were high noon." Her arms gestured wildly.

"I told you I liked it loud."

"I thought loud meant during daylight hours. Have you no consideration for people who live normal hours, sleep normal hours—at night?"

"Have you no respect for a man's domain? You could have knocked."

"What would be the purpose? You couldn't have heard me if I'd shot a cannonball at the door."

She glared at him, wondering if this was just a ploy to get her to leave. "If you think this little episode will get me to leave, you can think again." He started to speak, but she cut him off. "And if you start this music up again, I'll call the police."

"Just what do you think the police will do? This is private property. It is well off the road. There are no other houses around. What I do in the privacy of my own home is my business."

Naomi smiled and lowered her voice to a menacing quiet. "This is not your home, and the law is on my side. I had the first lease, which takes precedence over yours. She'd checked that this afternoon, phoning her own lawyer back on the mainland. If you'd care to test the validity of that, just turn this thing back on and you'll be spending the night someplace other than that comfortable bed in West Wing, preferably jail."

Naomi left, waiting until she had closed the door behind her before bringing her hands to her pounding head. Her vision was nearly blurred by the effects of the headache. She hated confrontations, but she refused to be run over roughshod by some brute from the city who had no consideration for his fellow human beings. If he wanted her to show him how stubborn she could be, she was up to the task.

Returning to her room, she went directly to the medicine cabinet and swallowed two aspirins, then tumbled back into bed, knowing this arrangement would not work. In the morning she would tell him he had to go. Half an hour later, the pain in her head had eased and she closed her eyes. What she saw on the inside of her lids was the picture of Stephen Weller standing in front of her as she dressed him down. He wore no shirt. The warm night air blew through the windows of the room, billowing out the gauzy curtains and bringing the outdoors inside. No shoes, no shirt, no socks, only a brief pair of shorts covered him, leaving the rest of his body for her to feast on.

Naomi groaned and she turned on her stomach. She pulled the pillow over her head. He was more than good-looking, she told herself. He was gorgeous. She'd thought of him as Adonis before, and now she could see each feature of his corded arms and well-defined chest in her mind. His skin was a dark, rich brown as if some medieval courtesan had fashion him from clay just to torment her.

Sleep evaded her for the rest of the night. By five A.M. Naomi had tossed and turned all she planned. She got out of bed and pulled on white shorts and a jogging top. She usually jogged at seven, but it would be light in an hour. She'd begin a little earlier this morning. Going to the kitchen, she filled the well of the coffeepot with water and prepared the machine for her return. After her normal swim, she'd hit the button and make breakfast. Then her day would begin.

On the back veranda she pulled her hair into a ponytail using a rubber band and did some rudimentary stretches. The air was cooler, caressing her skin with a soft kiss. She liked this time of the morning, before the sun rose, before the heat woke to warm the air. Everything remained asleep and still. Night anticipated the day, and life waited on the fringe of beginning. She could hear the grass grow and see the flowers open. After she stretched, she ran in place for a minute, then struck out toward the back of the property and the gate leading to the beach.

Naomi glanced to her side. The far western sky was at its darkest. She thought of Stephen, probably sleeping soundly, then quickly she moved her thoughts away from him. When she turned back to look where she was going, a giant stood in front of her. She couldn't brake. He was too close. She ran smack into the naked chest of the object of her thoughts. Did this man ever wear clothes? Together they went down. He broke her fall but rolled over, pinning her to the ground. The rubber band on her hair snapped and her hair fell over her face.

"Just where do you think you're going?"

"None of your business." She struggled to get out from under him, but it was a waste of effort.

"Do you know what time it is?"

She thought he was trying to give her a dose of her own medicine. "Of course I know what time it is."

"Do you also realize how dark it is on the beach?"

"Your point, Mr. Weller?"

"My point . . ." He lifted himself up to look her square in the face. "My point is that it is not safe for you to be alone on the beach before sunrise."

"Don't be absurd. I run here every morning."

He stood up, dragging her with him, as if she weighed no more than a rag doll. "Not any longer."

Naomi snatched her arm free of him and turned.

"Take one step and I'll tackle you."

Slowly she turned back as if he'd said the one thing that got her hackles up. "You don't have the balls." She challenged his command.

"Balls are the last thing you ought to be concerned with."

The menace in his voice matched her own, but she had the upper hand and she knew it. He'd arrived yesterday from New York. He hadn't slept much, been up all night; she had no idea what, if anything, he'd had to eat, and he looked like he could use a good eight hours. In a moment Naomi decided to accept the gauntlet. She smiled slowly, then swung around and took off. In seconds she was over the gate, not taking the time to open it.

He followed her, but she outdistanced him easily. She

was used to running in sand. She'd done it here for the past week. Her job took her to Los Angeles several times a year and she always stayed at the beach and jogged every day. In New Jersey she had a house at the shore. She was intimately acquainted with sand. Stephen, on the other hand, had his size and weight against him, plus the abuse to that beautiful body, but he was gaining on her. Naomi stretched her legs and made the terrain harder. She angled into the trees, running along the outside of the estate. They paralleled the beach. She knew the area. There was no path, but Naomi had made her own as she'd traversed this area in the daylight. In the darkness, if you didn't know where you were going, it was murder.

She ventured a glance over her shoulder. Stephen was closer than she'd expected. He was only a few feet behind her. She had to get away. If he leaped, she'd be in his grasp, and she knew she didn't want to be there. He only needed a foot or so and he'd be on her. She had to do something quick.

Along the woods ran the wall to the estate. It was over six feet of melded stone that had been placed there decades ago, long enough for the cementing to adhere to the stone and make them one unit. She struck out more, reaching inside herself for all the strength that remained in order for her to get farther ahead. He must have anticipated her move. She felt more than saw him go for the tackle. Luck was with her and she zigged right as he zagged left, only milliseconds before his hands would have touched her. She veered farther right and headed for the wall as Stephen's airborne body propelled itself through nothing that could support him, then fell like a stone to the soft dirt of the ground. Naomi took no time to determine if he'd been injured. She scaled the wall as surefooted as a billy goat and headed back toward the house, never breaking her stride.

Then she heard him. Before she could look around, strong hands closed over her shoulders and the rushing weight of him broke her rhythm and pushed her to the ground. She skidded under him across the soft grass. Her lungs whooshed air out as they came to a halt. She lay spent beneath him, unable to speak or move. For long moments she lay still dragging air into her lungs and exhaling, panting like a dog to return her body temperature and heartbeat to its normal rate.

She couldn't help but think of the man lying on top of her. She was already sweaty and hot, yet she felt the heat from his body seeping into hers. There was nothing she could do to control the elevating temperature.

"Could you please get off of me?" she asked, feeling more out of breath now than when she'd run two miles trying to evade him.

"Yes," he said, then turned her over, but keeping her under him. His legs straddled hers.

"Haven't we already done this?" She struggled.

"Not quite," he said. Then, before she knew what he intended, his hands anchored her head and his mouth covered hers. Naomi was too surprised to react. His mouth was hard and insistent. She pushed at his shoulders, but it was like trying to move a bulldozer with a toothpick. His tongue slipped between her lips. She kept her teeth clenched. Then his mouth changed, as if he'd decided on another course of action, as if the bad cop had finished and the good cop was now playing the role. Naomi understood this. Her brain still functioned and she was determined to resist him, but then her body relaxed. And his fell on top of her. The groan in her throat sounded in his mouth. Her legs opened to give him room and desire shot through her like a drug. His hands released her head and gathered under her shoulders, pulling her into his arms. She held her breath as long as she could, then on an intake of air Stephen's tongue filled her mouth and she gave up resistance. The hands that had pushed at his shoulders encircled them. The teeth that were tightly closed released. Her body molded to him and her mouth melded with his.

Feelings she hadn't known in years pumped through her as his mouth did magical things to her mind and body. He gathered her closer, keeping her under him, making her aware of every inch of his long, hard frame.

Naomi didn't know what was happening to her. She understood that Stephen was asking more of her than anyone had ever asked. And she was giving all he asked for. She wanted to. Stephen lifted his head and looked at her. She could see the desire in his eyes and feel the want inside herself. She felt good in his arms and she wanted to stay there. His mouth was different when it returned to hers. It was tender and soft. He kissed her cheeks and her eyes, then returned to her mouth. Cradling her against him, he deepened the kiss, holding her close. Naomi could feel his erection grow hard against her. She couldn't keep her legs from moving against him, couldn't stop the rapturous sensation that streaked through her with each movement, couldn't dampen the need that wanted him.

When they finally separated, Naomi's breath was ragged. She lay against Stephen, hearing his labored breathing as he tried to take air into his own lungs. Her head remained against him for a few minutes. Then she leaned back to look at him.

He stood up, this time leaving her alone on the ground. "You were saying something about balls."

What was wrong with him? Hadn't his engagement ended only a week ago? What would the fair Tara Patterson say if she knew that only seven days after their broken engagement he already had another woman in his arms and he had wanted to make love to her? This was not him, not his character. He was a rational man, a man who understood women, knew what they wanted and what they wanted from him. He understood himself, his needs and desires, yet this morning Naomi Davenport had called his bluff. In fact, she'd called his bluff from the moment he'd arrived.

He wasn't used to women challenging him. He wasn't used to anyone doing it. He'd guided the careers of some of the best-known people in the music business. When he presented plans, people listened to what he had to say. When he spoke, no one questioned him. He had a flawless record for being a good judge of character. Yet she'd stared him in the eye and challenged him to put his money where his mouth was and she'd almost won—no, she had won. She might not know it from the parting comment he'd thrown at her as he left, but she had the upper hand. Naomi was good, *real* good. If it hadn't been for those white shorts and her bra-looking sports top that seemed to glow in the dark, he would have lost her the moment she went over the fence.

He had to admit she'd gotten to him when she'd outrun him. She was barely heavy enough to maintain her own in a light wind, yet she'd evaded him with apparent ease. He only began to enjoy it when he knew he could reach her, but when she went down under him, everything changed. He enjoyed the feel of her under him, the resistance she put up, and the surrender. He enjoyed it too much.

This wasn't the reason he had come here. He had work to do. He'd put off this score for years. Something more pressing always took precedence over finishing this music. First it was his business, building a clientele, getting into the right places, getting noticed by the right people, and putting his clients in the best places. Then Tara came along and took up the little amount of free time he had. They'd gotten engaged. He'd known it was a mistake from the beginning, but his chances of finding the right woman in his circle was a small probability. She knew the score, too. Neither of them was in love with the other. When their engagement broke up, getting away seemed ideal. He'd had all kinds of plans and Adrian seemed to know exactly what he was looking for. He had to admit, as he looked about the room, she knew him inside out. This place was as perfect as they came. But he couldn't stay here. He couldn't stay with *her*. He'd survived one relationship gone sour. He wasn't about to begin another.

One of them had to go.

Naomi virtually dragged herself to the pool. She'd didn't think she'd have the energy to swim after that kiss had weakened her. Changed her from a full-grown woman into a mass of melting Jell-O; she knew the water, with its slight mist rising due to the temperature difference, would disband her molecules into millions of separate entities and she would dissolve into nothing. She started to swim her laps, beginning in the deep water and going toward the shallow end. If she ran out of energy before she got there, she wouldn't drown. That was how she'd felt in Stephen's arms, as if she were coming apart. And she liked it. She'd never felt like that when Burt kissed her.

Burt! Naomi stopped and tried to stand. She was in deep water and immediately got a mouthful as she began to sink to the bottom. Choking, she recovered, surfaced, and, spouting water, kicked out toward the shallow end of the pool. Burt was the reason she was here. And she hadn't given him a thought since Stephen Weller had arrived.

She didn't want Stephen Weller upsetting her. She had other things to think about. She had work to do and she didn't need the complication of another man.

She looked up as she reached the end of the pool. Stephen was coming toward her. Naomi completed her lap and turned for another. He no longer wore shorts as his only covering, but had on light beige slacks and an open-neck shirt. It didn't matter what he wore, she thought. The man would look gorgeous in golf clothes.

It would be easy to have him around. He must be six feet tall. He had a strong face, square jaw, cheekbones that softened his face when he smiled, eyes that would be piercing when he was angry, and, oh, so loving when aroused. His hard body she was fully aware of, his eyes crinkled when he laughed, and she liked the way he made her feel.

Maybe she was being rash in her judgment. Maybe they could stay here together. It was a big house. If she didn't get in his way, they could exist together. She could gaze on him whenever he wasn't looking. Maybe once in a while they could have a congenial jog along the beach.

"Naomi," he called.

She came to a halt at the shallow end of the pool. One day earlier she'd met him at this same spot. Her mouth went dry and she felt as if she were the generator heating the pool. She couldn't do this.

"Stephen, you have got to go."

THREE

Burt Mitchum looked like a medieval knight. Naomi had first seen him on the set of *The Merry Adventures of Robin Hood,* a children's version of the famous myth that they were shooting at Western Studios. Burt wrote the music, and even though he wore jeans and a sweater, not the traditional tights and tunic of the period, Naomi could see it in his face, ruggedly handsome, although unsmiling.

Naomi got out of the car at Sunset Beach and perched on a flat rock. Surfers in the distance danced on their surfboards as they searched for the perfect wave to ride to shore. The beach was famous for the high waves, and surfers came from all over the world to challenge them at this particular beach. Naomi had tried her hand at surfing. She wasn't very good. She spent more time in the water than on the board. This beach was out of her league. The water, however, was calming, and this was far enough from the estate at Makaha to put some distance between her and Stephen.

She needed to think about Burt. He was her fiancée, the man she was engaged to marry. She looked at her left hand, where Burt's engagement ring had been. She'd taken it off when she arrived. There was no sign of it ever having been there now, but Burt was expecting her to set a date when she returned to New York. Two more weeks and she would be on a plane, leaving this paradise and returning to the life she split between New Jersey and Los Angeles, and Burt.

Why couldn't she make up her mind? It wasn't this hard with Kenneth. They'd set a date and immediately began making plans, but look how that had turned out. She was naturally cautious the second time. She wasn't the twenty-one-year-old she had been when she impulsively decided to marry her college sweetheart. She was thirty-one now, a wiser woman, she hoped. This decision was for always, since she had no intention of becoming another divorce statistic. She'd told Burt this, told him she needed time to think about being married. Her first marriage had ended sadly when Kenneth died in a traffic accident, but it had been finished long before that. Naomi wanted to be sure this time, and this small vacation was where she was supposed to decide.

Her first week here, she'd done nothing but drink in the wonder of living in the Garden of Eden and doing a little work on the proposal for the next movie she planned to consult on. When she went back, Burt would meet her at the airport in Los Angeles. She knew he'd want her answer the moment she came through the jetway at LAX. What was it going to be?

Would she marry him? Was this the man she wanted to spend the rest of her life with? Wake up next to every day for fifty, sixty, seventy years?

The sun glazed over the water. She squinted even behind the huge sunglasses that protected her eyes from the brightness of the day. The surfers looked as if they were racing, all standing in a row, perfectly balanced on the slender boards. Naomi smiled, remembering the spray on her face, the taste of the salt water, the feel of the splash against her skin.

Why couldn't she stay here for the rest of her life? Forget Burt and forget Stephen . . . Stephen? Where did he come from? She didn't have to forget Stephen. He was as good as forgotten. She told him to call Adrian and have her or some other agent get him a place to live. No way would she share the estate with him. Even with its size, it was too small for the two of them. They had nothing in common. Their lifestyles were too different. She was a morning person. He was a creature of the dark. He liked his music at two hundred decibels, high enough to kill a normal human being. She liked hers soft and smooth. And she couldn't keep her eyes off that body he appeared to like to parade in front of her.

She'd done the right thing. It wasn't her fault the agency had screwed up the leases. She had possession. She was right. They had to fix things for him. Her needs were important, too, and she didn't need or want some man interrupting her plans. She shook her head as if confirming her decision.

Naomi sat on the rock long after it had become hard on her backside. Her stomach growled. She refused to listen to it until it was speaking louder than that niggling voice at the back of her mind. She stopped along the drive back to the estate and picked up some Japanese food. Eating in the Jeep, she stayed away as long as she could.

Turning into the driveway, she stopped in front of the door. Suddenly her heart was beating fast. Had he left? Would she go inside and find him standing in the kitchen pouring coffee, or was he in the music room leaning over the piano, studiously working on his music?

Naomi went inside and instantly knew the house was completely empty. There was a hollowness about the place. Her footsteps echoed off the wood flooring. She shouldn't be able to tell that he wasn't there—the West Wing was too far away for her to hear anything—but she knew.

She turned toward his wing, knowing what she would find when she got there. Yet when she opened the drawers and closets, finding them empty of anything except drawer-lining paper, it didn't make her feel good about her actions. She felt like a landlord evicting a tenant and making him homeless.

Where was he? Did Adrian find him another place to stay? Was he comfortable there? Would he be able to finish his score there?

Naomi sank down on the bed. She didn't care, she told herself. He was not her responsibility and he was not a child. He was full-grown man. What a man. Heat sliced through her like a flash fire. She crossed her arms over her stomach, pushing thoughts of them on the grass out of her mind.

She was right, she repeated over and over in her mind. Why shouldn't she think of her needs? She had rights, too. All she'd done was exercise them. What would he have done if Burt had been here with her? Would he have tired of staying? She'd done nothing wrong.

So why did she feel as if she had?

For the second night in a row, Naomi slept badly. She was up at first light with no will to jog or swim or even perform the aerobic workout she often did in her New Jersey bedroom. She made coffee and sat on the lanai looking over the grounds at the pool. Everything reminded her of Stephen: his smile that first morning as he asked if she came with the house, the place on the ground where he'd turned her over and kissed her—her ears burned with the memory of that consuming kiss—the gate leading to the beach where she'd started the chase.

Two days, she thought. She'd only known him for two short days and they had covered so much territory and covered it without hours of conversation. She knew so little about him and she liked most of what she knew. She sipped her coffee. Of course they argued, but he stimulated her. He made her think about herself, her life, what she wanted to do. He made her think of things, experiences she didn't have, and wonder why she'd never thought of them before.

She wanted to talk to him again. She wondered what he was doing now. What woman's kitchen was he in this morning? And did she come with the house?

"Excuse me. Do you come with the house?" Naomi jumped when she heard the familiar voice behind her. The smile on her face was unmistakable. Her coffee cup dropped to the floor of the lanai. It bounced, spilled, but didn't break. "Good," he said. "You missed me."

Recovering, she said, "I didn't miss you. What are you doing here?"

He took a step toward her and was rewarded when she moved back. "I thought I could get a cup of coffee."

She hesitated, then said, "The coffee . . . is in the kitchen." She gestured to the door behind him. He noticed the crack in her voice.

He glanced over his shoulder, then turned as if to walk to the door. Before going into the darkened kitchen, he turned back. "Would you like to go to breakfast with me?"

"I . . ." She closed her mouth, at an obvious loss what to say.

"Don't worry about the coffee. We can clean it up when we get back." He grabbed her hand and pulled her through the door, into the kitchen. He kept going toward the front door and the car parked behind hers in the driveway. He'd left it there last night when he came in. She'd been asleep, or at least in her room.

He'd done as she commanded and called Adrian from the local Holiday Inn. Adrian had apologized profusely for the mix-up, but during his conversation somehow she had convinced him that he and Naomi could work things out. It was her suggestion that he return to the estate and discuss things with Naomi over breakfast.

Stephen had been reluctant to return, but the smile on Naomi's face before she closed the mask she hid behind had been worth the trip.

He drove her to a local restaurant. The place was small, with bare, worn floors and only half a wall to keep out the sun or rain. The roof was made of long straw that had once been wheat-colored but now hung in a drab gray over the top of the building. It grew locally and would take over the island if people didn't keep it cut back.

Naomi looked around when he led her to a table. "The food's good," he told her.

The place was too small to boast a waiter. Stephen went

to the bar in the center and ordered for them. He came back and set a plate of fruit and a pitcher of pineapple juice in front of Naomi. He'd discovered that no matter where you ate or drank on the island, the local fruits and pineapple juice were served like grits and iced tea in the South or pretzels with mustard in Philly.

Knowing there would be nothing like a bagel and cream cheese, he ordered eggs over easy with bacon, toast, and coffee for two. Naomi ate heartily. He expected her to balk at the fat content, since he'd discovered her exercising the two mornings he'd been at the estate, but she said nothing.

"Naomi, what are you here for?" he asked when he pushed his plate aside and poured a second cup of coffee.

She slipped a slice of cantaloupe in her mouth and sucked the sweetness from the fruit before swallowing the pulp. "I came to rest, get a little work done, and make a d—" she stopped. "Make up my mind about several pending projects."

He didn't think that was what she'd intended to say, but he didn't press her. "What kind of projects?"

"I work for several film production companies in Los Angeles."

"I thought the lease had a New Jersey address on it."

She raised her eyebrows.

"Good memory," he explained.

"My time is split between the two coasts. I work for film companies in LA and New York. I consult on Broadway plays and occasionally travel to Florida and Nashville on business."

"This sound interesting. What do you do?"

"I'm a specialist in medieval history and I consult on the authenticity of costumes, props, settings, castles. I work with the dialogue to make sure it's both understandable for today's audience and that it remains virtually true to the period."

"This all sounds very academic."

"It is," she agreed. "So tell me, what it is you do?"

"In my normal life I direct the public careers of some of the most temperamental people in the world." He smiled. "I'm a publicist for several musicians." He didn't bother to name them. For some reason he decided she would be unimpressed with the list that would have another woman giving her eyeteeth. It had impressed Tara.

"In your other life . . . ?" she smiled. He liked seeing her smile.

"A long time ago I began a score for a musical. I want to finish it. This is where I chose to do that."

She nodded. "That's why there is so much equipment in that room. Was it brought here especially for you?"

"I didn't request it, but Adrian asked for specifics about what I wanted to do and what would make me happy."

"Did you ask for a woman to go with the house?"

His chin came up and he stared at her. The smile in her eyes told him she was kidding. He shook his head. "I didn't think of it." *But I'm glad it was you,* he added silently.

She dropped her chin. He wondered if she was trying to hide an expression.

"What about it? I know we got off to a pretty bad start. But we've both had time to cool off. Do you think we could share that place? It's got everything I need. And if you've been here a week, it must have what you need, too."

"I'd like to apologize for yesterday. I didn't mean—"

"Neither did I," he stopped her. "So do we have a deal?"

"All rules still apply?"

He nodded. "I'll also try to be more considerate of you."

"And I, you."

They toasted each other with coffee cups.

* * *

They left the restaurant, if that was what it could be called. It was little more than an open-air hut. There were hundreds like it all over the island. Most of them sold trinkets tourists bought to take back to the mainland and show they had been to the islands. Naomi had spent a day walking along Waikiki Beach and watching the many people lining the streets hawking their wares as if it were any midtown street in New York.

Everything from expensive, pearl and coral jewelry to T-shirts and shell-covered boxes that wouldn't survive the trip to the airport, let alone the mainland, had been offered to her. She didn't buy anything. The only person she had to get something for was Burt, and she could find nothing he didn't already have. She couldn't imagine a man who had several Rolex watches, custom-made clothes, and monogrammed shirts wearing a necklace of shells.

"Where did you sleep last night?" Naomi asked, shifting her mind away from the subject she should be pursuing. She and Stephen, by some mutual agreement, had passed the car and were walking toward the water. It was hard to find places that weren't in direct view of the ocean unless you went inland. The estate was just off the beach and this restaurant sat in the sand at the base of Makaha Valley Road near Lahilahi Point. They headed toward the point even though they had no apparent destination in mind.

"I checked into the Holiday Inn, but left after a few hours. I returned to the estate in the early morning and slept there."

Naomi smiled. She hadn't known he was in the house, but somehow it was comforting to find he had been there, even now. Naomi felt like taking his hand. It seemed so natural for her do so, but she didn't. Stephen was almost a stranger; granted, a stranger she had kissed with as much abandon as a low-born handmaid.

"Why did you come back?" She paused, then rushed on. "I was pretty mean to you. I know that."

Stephen turned and stared at the sea. The sun was high in the sky as it rose quickly this close to the equator. He raised his hand shielding his eyes and searched the horizon. Blue sky meeting blue water.

Naomi followed his gaze. "It is gorgeous here, isn't it? Each morning I'm thrilled at the sheer wonder of the place."

Stephen agreed with her. He hadn't answered her question. He couldn't say why he'd returned, at least not out loud. Lying in the hotel room, all he could do was stare at the ceiling and think of her. He thought of their wild chase along the beach and into the trees. His tackling her and turning her over, his mouth on hers, and how good she felt in his arms. He remembered the way her body felt stretched out along his and how he'd wanted more than her kisses. He couldn't stay in the hotel room any longer. He thought of the smell of her, the way her hair slid over his fingers as he cradled her in his arms. Trying to sleep, all he could see when he closed his eyes was the dark gold flesh of Naomi and what it was like to run his hands over her. Finally he left. If he was to be tormented, he could at least have her close by.

"Tell me about the music you write."

"It's a musical score," he answered, latching on to this safer topic than the one his thoughts had been following.

"Did you write the play, too?" They stopped and sat on the beach facing each other. The lapping of the waves was gentle and they spoke softly.

He nodded. "I wrote the play about ten years ago. Three years ago in my spare time, usually on airplanes traveling to meet a client or in a hotel room, I updated it. Working on it made me feel good and I wanted to finish it. I realized if I was ever going to finish the score, I'd better get to it."

"Well, then." Naomi stood up. "We'd better get back so you can go to work." She reached for his hand without thinking and helped him to his feet. "You'd be surprised how fast your time will go by, and you don't want to waste a moment of it."

Stephen noticed she dropped his hand immediately. He would have liked to hold on to her for a while. He wanted to get his music finished, but he also wanted to spend time with her. She was already walking toward the car. Stephen caught up with her and took her arm. He turned her to face him, but dropped his hands so they wouldn't caress her skin.

"How about we both work until three o'clock, then we go swimming? I don't want to spend the entire time working."

Naomi cocked her head to the side. "Well, I didn't exercise this morning."

"I'm not talking about exercise."

She looked confused.

"Have you ever been surfing?" he asked.

Naomi stopped and looked directly at him. Her eyes opened as wide as saucers. Her mouth formed a huge smile. "I've tried it once, but I was awful. I'd like to try it again, but everyone looks so comfortable and I've never been able to stay on a board." Then her expression turned serious. "Do you know how to surf?"

Stephen laughed at her. She looked as hungry-eyed as a child staring through a window at diners feasting. He took her arm and turned her toward the car. "Of course," he said. "Every New Yorker knows how to surf. It's the course directly after Graffiti Painting 101 and Principles of Jumping Subway Turnstiles."

Their laughter mingled as they returned to the car. Stephen felt better than he had in months. He might go so far as to say years. Naomi was refreshing, nothing like Tara. She seemed to bring out the kid in him. He knew there was a time for work and a time for play. In his career, he'd seen so many people confuse those two things, but Naomi helped him separate them. He couldn't see Tara donning a bathing suit for anything other than to take a photo or laze by the pool. The thought of going onto the sand was like stepping into a sewer for her, while Naomi was willing to try anything.

Stephen thought he'd like to try many things with her, and in the next two weeks he planned to get significantly down the list.

FOUR

Stephen hadn't worked this well in years. The way he felt, he could have stayed at the piano forever. Since they'd returned from breakfast and their walk on the beach, he'd spent the day right where he was. Music poured through his body. Song sheets spread across the piano and onto the floor. The room looked as if a paper explosion had taken place, but the song that had eluded him for the better part of the last year was in his head as if it had always been there, ready for him to recall. His hands worked with both the grand piano and the computer keyboards he'd set up directly next to the instrument. He had no doubt that his inspiration was in another part of the house. Momentarily he wondered what Naomi was doing. Quickly he dragged his attention back to the song. If he thought about her, he'd lose all concentration. But it might be worth it. He smiled and went back to the keyboard.

Finally he finished it. He sat up straight and reached for the ivory keys. His hands skimmed the melody as part of the introduction. Then he launched into the first verse and played straight through to the end. He wished there was someone who could sing the words, but he knew them in his head and his heart:

Feel the Warm

From birth our spirits linked
Though five years separate us
You share my memories
Our shoulders hold each other's tears
Our hands each other's hearts

Many nights we talked till dawn
Others we never spoke

Through our veins flow identical blood
Our minds identical thoughts

Years have passed since we shared a house
Between us miles are endless
But if I spread my hands to the fire
I know you feel the warm.

When the final note died he sat back, knowing this was no longer the rough draft. This was the final product. The female lead would sing this song for her dying brother. He visualized her standing at a window, a fire glowing warmly. She'd end with her hands stretched toward the flames.

Stephen stood and pushed an audiotape into the machine on his right. He sat down and played the song again. He could send the tape to one of the many producers he knew and have them record it exactly as it stood. But this was not what he would do. His name was on several copyrights and they provided him with a steady income, but this song was part of a score. He knew it was the cornerstone of the show. And he'd written it, almost from the beginning, in one day.

He stretched, removing the kinks in his shoulders and back. He'd been in the same position for a long time. His shoulders were tired. His back hurt from sitting, but he felt invigorated. He stood again, stretching and wondering where Naomi was and what she was doing. He hoped her day had been as productive as his. Leaving the music room, he went to look for her. It was past three o'clock and he wanted to find her and tell her everything that had happened.

She wasn't in the kitchen, on the lanai, or in any part of the house where he looked. Then he rushed up the stairs and went toward the East Wing. At the end of the hall was a balcony. Stephen saw her sitting there. He started forward, careful not to disturb her. He took a moment to look at her, unobserved and without care for his expression. She intrigued him more than anyone had in a long time. Suddenly he wanted to know everything about her: where she went to school, what she was like at twelve, what was her favorite ice cream, who had taught her to swim. He wanted her to begin at the beginning and tell him her life story. But when he got close enough to see her face, instead of the happy or contended expression he expected, she looked sad, sadder than he'd ever seen anyone.

Impulsively he started to rush toward her, then stopped. If she wanted to share her pain with him, she would do it. He had no right to take the decision from her, and from their previous encounters he knew she would strike out against him. He backed up to the stairs.

"Naomi," he called from that distance, giving her time to compose herself before he reached her. "I'm ready for the beach."

The Naomi who faced him had a smile on her mouth, although her eyes were overly bright. If he hadn't seen her already, he wouldn't have noticed the doubt that appeared in her brown eyes.

"I'll be ready in a moment," she said. "Why don't I meet you at the pool in a few minutes?"

Stephen didn't ask her anything about her thoughts. "Fine," he said. "I had a wonderful day." Then he gave in to the impulse that said she needed him more than she might know. He went to her and pulled her into his arms. Her hair smelled clean, with an intangible scent that reminded him of sunshine. For a moment he let her lay against him. He buried his face in her hair and kissed her temple. She clung to him. His body grew pleasantly warm. "I'll meet you downstairs," he said, and pushed himself back.

She nodded and he left her. What was it? he wondered. Why was she sitting there looking as if she had no friends in the entire world? Why would a person sit in paradise and look as if she'd been responsible for its destruction?

He didn't know, but he vowed he'd make sure she never had to sit alone and be sad again.

The estate sat in Makaha, a spot due west of Honolulu, almost to Ka'ena Point, the westernmost place on the island. From the balcony where Naomi perched, she could see the ocean. The water rushed to the sand. While it had been calm near the restaurant, the waves at the back of the estate were more robust. Naomi eyed them with reservation. She'd been enthusiastic earlier, but she wasn't so sure anymore. She'd never done much more than swim in the ocean and she was careful to stay close to shore and away from anyplace where there might be an undertow. She much preferred the pool.

She wanted to go surfing, however. Naomi was daring, often doing things that she'd never done before, like that challenge to Stephen. She liked him. That was her problem. She was engaged to another man and she was falling in love with the one living on the other side of this house.

Naomi went to her room and changed into her suit. Instead of the normal exercise bra and shorts she ran and then swam in, she put on a yellow one-piece suit with straps that crisscrossed her back. The suit didn't cover the same amount of skin as her usual outfit did. Her tan lines outlining the bra shape were clearly visible. Naomi tried to ignore this, but heat flowed into her face when she thought of nude bathing. On the wake of that thought came a mental image of Stephen equally naked and looking every bit as beautiful as a black god.

She tied a beach wrap around her waist and clamped a hat on her head. Then she sat down in front of the dressing table to apply sunscreen to her face and shoulders. Setting the tube down, her hand bumped into the small velvet box containing her ring. She opened it and fingered the stone. Six carats, pear-shaped, flawless. Burt wouldn't stand for any less. She snapped the box closed and looked at her reflection.

While Stephen had worked, she'd tried to make a decision. Why was it so hard? Why couldn't she just make up her mind to marry Burt? She had his ring, had agreed to wear it and to marry him at some time in the future. Why now, when he'd issued an ultimatum, was she hesitating? Burt could offer her a secure future. He was handsome, fun to be with, had a rewarding career that he loved, and he wanted to marry her. Why couldn't she say yes outright?

Naomi's vision blurred and she saw Stephen's features in the glass in front of her. He was tall, tan, and strong. She knew very little about him. He had a career like Burt, one that demanded one hundred percent of his time and energy, yet he'd come to this island to fulfill a promise he'd made to himself. She liked that. She liked knowing that a man could follow a dream, shed the life that was comfortable, where he had power and status, where he was comfortable with the rules and rituals, to pursue a wish that could evaporate as fast as water on a hot day. It wasn't the succeeding that mattered. It was the desire to do it, the drive that sent him on a mission that only mattered to him, and success wasn't the ultimate goal. The goal was to prove to himself that he could complete something he had begun.

She couldn't say that of Burt.

Naomi didn't realize there were surfboards on the estate, but when she found Stephen on the lanai, he stood between two of them. Her breath caught. She'd been thinking of Burt. Seeing Stephen, she'd forgotten the effect he had on her senses whenever she got near him. He wore dark trunks and a smile, no socks, no shoes, exactly as he'd looked the previous day when they'd strolled down the beach like two playful children. The sun shone on his dark skin. Naomi was used to seeing good-looking men,

Hercules look-alikes, basketball players, men in kilts or tights. Often she walked past them as if they were props. There was no walking past Stephen. The others paled in his shadow. He should come with a surgeon general's warning—*Wear protective lenses when coming upon this man*. Naomi pushed her sunglasses higher on her nose.

Stephen smiled a bright, even grin and Naomi's spirits lifted. She could forget her decision for the moment. She would only think of the fun of being with Stephen. The fact that in his presence all other thought processes were blocked out was beside the point.

"Where did you get those?" she asked.

He indicated the white one was hers. "There is a shed over there"—he nodded to his left—"with beach equipment. Everything from surfboards to Jet Skis."

She took a deep breath and accepted the board.

"Do you mean you've been here a week and all you've done is jog and swim in the pool?"

"Not quite," she said. But he was closer to the mark than she was willing to let him know. She hadn't spent all her time on the estate, but other than the one trip to Waikiki, and going to a couple of beaches, she'd been no farther than the back of the estate.

They set out now for the gate that led to the beach. All the beaches in Hawaii were public, but Naomi had seen very few people on this stretch of the white sand. She wondered now about that, but knew no explanation. She was glad it was deserted when her feet sank into the soft sand. Overhead gulls cawed as they swooped through the air in their poetic dance above the sea.

Stephen held a blanket and his board. She'd only noticed the blanket when he dug his board into the sand and began spreading it out. The water looked sinister and unforgiving. Her heart beat fast. Even though she wanted to experience the ride, she was afraid. She remembered the surfers at Sunset Beach. They were the professionals. She was glad none of them were here to see her fall on her face, as she was sure she would do the first time out.

"Scared?"

She looked at Stephen. How had he known? She thought of tossing her head and giving him her usual answer, but something told her she would always have to be absolutely honest with this man. "A little," she replied.

"I bet the only surfboard you've seen was on television."

"I tried it once before, but I never got up on the board. Each time I went to push myself on it, the wave would hit and I'd go spinning toward shore like a beached whale."

His laugh was strong, from the belly. Naomi liked hearing it. "You could never be a whale." He gave her an up-and-down look that warmed her. "Don't worry," he began. "You're not going alone your first time out. And you start out face down *on* the board."

So he did know how to surf. His answer earlier had told her nothing. She felt slightly safer knowing it wasn't his first time.

The ride out was without incident except for the fires consuming her as she lay facedown on the board practically beneath him, paddling with her arms. Thankfully the coolness of the water dampened the threatening flames periodically and kept her sanity in tact. She concentrated on her task to keep her mind off of him. Waves came at them. Stephen steadied her as they rode over it. The ocean between the swells was rocking, and Naomi's blood pumped. They kept going, farther and farther. Ahead of her was nothing but water and horizon. They were out a long way, farther than she had ever ventured. Somehow she didn't feel afraid. Stephen's hands held the board right at her waist and she felt he would keep her safe.

The shore looked miles away when Stephen finally turned. He let wave after wave pass them, high ones, low ones, as if he were waiting for a specific one. Finally it came and he signaled they would take it. Both of them crouched on their knees. She took her instruction from his greater experience. Fear and excitement battled for dominance within her, but Stephen's presence made her feel confident on the borrowed fiberglass board.

In one fluid movement, simultaneously with the cresting wave, they stood up. The water pushed them forward. Naomi couldn't find a balance. There was no ground below her, only the constantly shifting and shapeless water. Stephen's hands spanned her waist and kept her in place, and she bent her knees as he had demonstrated. It took some getting used to and it was easier when she decided that falling wouldn't be the end of the world. With that decision, the ride was exhilarating. She felt the wind on her face, blowing her hair behind her. She could feel every movement Stephen made shifting his body weight to keep them balanced as they rode the waterfall shoreward. Naomi hadn't known what it felt like to stand alone against the forces of nature, with only the swift shifting of weight harnessing the tremendous force behind them, but she was learning.

Stephen had complete control of the surf and she moved with him instinctively, following his guidance. The rushing wind caught in her throat and took her breath, but this did nothing to decrease her excitement.

When finally they waded onto the sand, she turned, almost colliding with his figure. "That was wonderful!" She smiled excitedly. "Can we do it again?"

In all they rode five more waves together. Then he told her it was time for her to try it solo. Naomi wanted to do it, but she distrusted her ability. With Stephen behind her, she had someone to control the board. He was heavier, giving more stability to the light fiberglass. Could she do it alone?

She took her board and started rowing as she'd practiced, in the facedown position. As far out as Stephen went, she followed. Her mouth went dry in the midst of billions of gallons of water. The symptoms of fear were evident, but she refused to let Stephen think she was anything but the confident student.

When they stopped, she tried to read the water, gauge it as she had seen Stephen do, but it didn't cooperate for her. It moved in the standard manner of a liquid; unstable, without form, and changing from second to second. She didn't know which wave to choose and she looked to him for a clue.

"The next one," he said without noticing any discomfort on her part.

Naomi got to her knees. The wall of water rose up like a mighty hand. The crash behind the board was a roar in her ears. She stood in front of the powerful force, her knees bent, her back foot controlling the rudder on the bottom of the board. She wavered but compensated, keeping herself balanced, keeping her eyes on the shoreline and her body in complete complement with the forces behind, below, and around her.

She was afraid to breathe for fear she'd lose some part of her confidence and pitch into the surf, her board lost and crashing to shore without her. Naomi went onward toward the beach, propelled toward her goal fifty feet ahead, the white sand beach that ended at the gate to the estate.

She made it. Almost. The wave lost its power not gradually, but like a balloon deflating in a snap. With Stephen on the board behind her, he would have controlled it. Alone, she lost her footing, shifting too hard toward the rear. The board pitched out from under her. She fell backward, and it shot into the air like a jockey thrown from a horse. Water closed around her, filling her mouth and gushing into her throat. Naomi came up coughing in the shallow pool that was only a few feet from the shoreline.

When Naomi stood up, Stephen was sitting on his surfboard. His powerful legs dangled in the water on either side of the bright red board. His head was thrown back and he laughed that belly laugh which Naomi loved to hear. Her ears grew warm, but soon she saw the absurdity of the situation and the higher notes of her voice mingled with his, the salt, the sun, and the romance of the moment.

"Did you have fun?" Stephen asked as they restored the cleaned surfboards to the shed several minutes later.

It was dark inside the small building. When she turned, the light silhouetted him. "I can't remember the last time I had such a good time."

"I'm glad," he said. He remembered her earlier, sitting on the balcony and looking sadder than anyone he'd ever seen.

"Can we do it again?" She took a step toward him, smiling.

"If you like."

"I like." Naomi stepped closer. The light from the open doorway was behind him, throwing his face into shadow. In the darkness she put her hands on his shoulders and, standing on tiptoe, kissed him on the cheek.

Stephen's hands grasp her waist. She told herself it was for balance, but she wanted him to touch her.

"What was that for?" he asked.

"Teaching me to surf."

For a moment Stephen only looked at her. His face was close to hers. Even in the darkened space, she could see desire in his eyes. The air around them seemed charged with heat. Naomi could feel the fire building inside her. Stephen lowered his head.

"Here," he whispered. His voice was low, intoxicating, sexy. "This is for future lessons." He pulled her body in contact with his and settled his mouth over hers. This time there was no fighting, no shifting her head from side to side. Her mouth opened to him and he settled in as if he were a long-lost lover, or a husband returning from a long trip. He crushed her to him, his mouth brushing, exploring, seeking. And she gave.

Naomi knew she shouldn't do this. It was wrong. She should pull away, not let Stephen kiss her like this, not feel as if the entire world had disappeared and they were the only people left on earth. She shouldn't feel as if his body had been carved into an exactly matching shape for her to fit into. She shouldn't feel as if tiny men were inside her veins rapidly carrying her blood to the far reaches of her system. She shouldn't feel this burning desire to climb up his frame and close her legs around him.

But she did.

She was engaged to be married to another man, but Stephen's hands threaded into her hair and pulled her to him. He smelled wonderfully like the sea, the sand, and the salt. Naomi's arms charted him as if she were a mapmaker. They moved over a strong back and up to bone-hard shoulders. She went up on her toes, stepping even closer to him. His hands skimmed up and down her back. They brushed over her waist and settled over her buttocks. Sensation rocketed through her and she heard the groan in her own throat as pleasure so sweet it reached the point of pain threatened to burst out of her.

Stephen's erection pressed into her. She could barely breath through the fire around them. The heat was so intense, she wondered why the small building didn't explode from projected flames. She wanted to climb onto him, take him inside her, and go for a ride even wilder than the one in the ocean, the ride his body promised would be like none she'd ever experienced. Fantasies rushed though her mind of things she would like to do to Stephen and have him do to her.

Then his mouth slid from her and he held her closer. She didn't dare move. Her body had turned to warm Jell-O, without form or substance. Without support, she would melt to the floor. Her breath was ragged as she sucked air into her lungs in hard gasps. She could hear Stephen's labored breathing in her ears and feel his arms squeezing her to him. Together they stood this way until it seemed time ended.

Naomi moved back and stared into Stephen's passion-drenched eyes. His mouth was wet from her kisses and he looked at her as if she were beautiful, delicate, precious, all the things she wanted a man to see when he looked at her.

And she knew in that instant, in the infinitesimal space of time moving forward in her universe, what her decision had to be.

There was no way she could marry Burt after this.

FIVE

Naomi stretched like a languid cat in the bed. Stephen's music filtered into the bedroom. Not the jarring noise of a few nights ago, but a soft, tender rendition of some type of ballad. She liked it. She liked him. She felt so much freer this morning, like a huge iron weight had been lifted from her shoulders. Today was a whole new day, a whole new life. It was a beginning. She hadn't realized until now how much the decision weighed on her. Now that she knew what she wanted, life was so much clearer.

Quickly, she showered and dressed in shorts and a T-shirt. The doorbell rang as she reached the bottom step on her way to the kitchen. She didn't need coffee this morning. She was wide awake. Humming Stephen's tune, she went to the door. A man in a blue uniform sporting the orange and white Federal Express logo waited. She signed for the package and, taking it to the kitchen, found Stephen had already made coffee. She smiled at the morning ritual that had become habit between them. Pouring a full cup, she drank deeply, letting the reviving liquid course through her. Putting the cup down, she immediately opened the small box. The script for *The Lost Prince* was inside. She lifted it out, whirling about when she saw what it was. She'd wanted to work on this film, and according to the note from her office, the deal had finally gone through. Filming would begin in two months.

That would give her just enough time, she thought, taking a seat at the table and sipping her coffee. When she left here, she'd stop in LA to confer with the producers and costumers and take a look at some of the props. The average person didn't realize how much work went into a production before an actor ever walked onto the set. Ideas started running through her brain. Adrenaline pumped through her along with the coffee. She couldn't wait to tell Stephen.

"What's happening? You look like you've discovered the secret to life."

Naomi swung around. Stephen stood there in shorts and a shirt unbuttoned all the way down. Naomi's smile must have been as wide as the Pacific when she saw him. She hadn't noticed the music stop. She had her own symphony going on in her head. Stephen picked up her cup and drank the rest of her coffee. Today she didn't mind.

"I've been assigned a new script. It's one I wanted." She told him how she'd worked to get assigned to the film; that she often worked on the historical reality of both language and props.

He took the script as Naomi turned it around so he could see the title. He flipped through a few pages. "The story of Prince Michael in the 1500s in Scotland."

"You know the story?" she asked with surprise. Michael wasn't a real character from history. He was a myth of the Scottish Highlands.

"My mother gave me book about him when I was in grade school. During a trip to Scotland she became fascinated by the story. She brought the book home as a gift for leaving me behind. How are they planning to film it?"

"I've worked with the director and producer before on other projects and they tend to stay very close to the original. I'm sure they'll do the same to this, too."

He smiled. "I'll be glad to see it when it's done. I can tell all my friends I knew you when. . . ."

He didn't sound happy. Naomi wondered why, but she didn't ask. From someplace inside her she knew he wouldn't tell her and that he didn't want her to ask. Or was it she who didn't want the answer?

"Come," he said, offering her a hand. "We'll go celebrate."

* * *

The streets of Honolulu boasted crowds at most times of the day and night. People flocked to the earthly paradise for the vastness of the blue ocean or the stretch of sand that went on for as far as one could be seen. Palm trees swaying over Waikiki Beach witnessed vacationing couples, outdoor weddings, spectacular sunrises and sunsets, and the constant throng of people.

The sun rose quickly in the tropics. Honolulu was only twenty-one longitudinal degrees above the equator. By the time Stephen and Naomi reached the bustle of activity, the sun was directly overhead. People meandered about the shops in the International Marketplace. Mainlanders, wearing colorful muumuus they'd never be able to use once they arrived back in Kansas or Illinois or Washington or even Florida, bought hand-woven baskets, coral rings, velvet pictures of the island during sunset, flowers, and more colorful clothes. Naomi had on a bright blue-and-white-flowered dress that the sales clerk said could be tied in at least thirty ways to provide different looks. The dress came with a card showing all thirty styles.

Naomi managed only one of these. She'd wrapped it about her from back to front, twisted the ends around several times to form a rope that climbed up to her collarbone, where she tied the ends behind her neck. The dress fell almost to her ankles with a soft pull upward in the front that allowed a peek of her legs when she walked. She noticed the darker tone to her skin, a result of spending so much time outdoors since her arrival.

"See anything you like?" Stephen whispered in her ear as she ran her hand over a bolt of fabric.

Naomi felt his breath. An inward shudder passed through her and she clamped her teeth together to prevent the sexual sigh that wanted to escape. She shook her head. She had no one to buy for anymore. Her parents were both dead and she wasn't really close to her brothers. Her only other relative was an uncle in Wisconsin whom she hadn't seen in fifteen years. Since she'd decided not to marry Burt, she didn't even have him to buy a souvenir for.

"How about this?" Stephen took her arm and led her to a stall full of basket products. He reached up and grabbed a hat made of ti leaves and clamped it down on her head. It was shaped like an upside down wastebasket.

Naomi turned and looked in the mirror on the counter. She laughed at her reflection. "It looks awful."

"It looks wonderful."

She reached to take it off. Stephen's hands came up at the same time, forestalling hers. Their hands touched and he held hers. Naomi met his eyes. What gripped her she couldn't explain, didn't understand. It was the chemistry between them, the attraction she no longer tried to push aside, the attention of having someone treat her as if she were the most important person in the world, the need for companionship and love. Whatever it was, she couldn't tear her gaze away. She didn't know what she was seeing. There were depths in his eyes she hadn't seen before, dark, rich, phantoms that pulled her closer to him. She felt as if she were falling, falling up into those dark, beautiful, mesmerizing eyes.

Abruptly he turned toward the clerk, who appeared as if by magic, and whispered, "We'll take it."

Naomi couldn't stop him. She'd lost the capacity to speak by some hysterical paralysis of her vocal cords. She was completely out of breath, her heart pounding, her knees struggling to keep her upright. Her mouth had as much moisture as the Mohave Desert. And all Stephen had done was hold her face in his hands. She was lost. And in love.

They left the International Market hand in hand. Naomi couldn't say how they'd linked hands. It wasn't that it was so crowded they needed contact so they wouldn't lose each other. It was that lost moment. The one when Stephen should have kissed her, but by some form of control he realized they were in a bazaar while she could think of nothing but him. He'd linked his fingers with hers as surely as her soul had become linked to his, and they'd begun walking together, no longer like two people who'd arrived at the same time, but like lovers, two people who were intimately acquainted with each other's body. People who knew the secret and power of adding two hearts together and arriving at the correct answer of one.

Naomi looked at the wares of the stalls differently. She no longer saw the shell necklaces as junk, but as mementos, something with which to remember this time, this moment; something that would transport her back to this place for an instant, that would bring this man to her memory for the rest of her life. She shuddered. This was way too fast for her. She knew little of Stephen Weller. Then she knew a universe about him. She was falling in love.

Naomi would never be able to remember what they did the rest of the day. The cocoon that wrapped around her was warm and fuzzy. She had vague memories of laughing a lot and telling stories about her childhood. They had gone to the zoo and up Diamond Head to view the city. What they did, didn't matter. What mattered was they were together in paradise.

With the sunset that evening they were on the beach outside the estate on a blanket. Next to them sat a plate of cheese and fruit and a bottle of wine in a silver cooler on the sand. Stephen reached for her and pulled her against him. Her back settled against his chest and like this they watched the sun drop below the waterline at the horizon.

It was the most beautiful day of her life. Naomi didn't want it to end. She wanted to stay here, trapped in this moment with her back against Stephen's chest for all time. She took his hand, bringing it to her mouth and kissing it.

"I had a wonderful time today," she said.

Stephen's arms tightened around her. "It was perfect," he said. They lapsed into silence. A moment later she felt him laugh against her. Naomi turned around. "What's so funny?"

"I was thinking about that Kodak moment today."

Naomi joined him. A few of the silly things that lovers did came back to her. She'd gone to one of the picture sites and posed. Stephen took an imaginary camera, pointed it at her, and snapped. Then he'd joined her and they posed for an imaginary photographer. Many tourists looked at them as if they were several sandwiches short of a picnic. It was childish, silly, and freeing. Naomi couldn't remember having so much fun or laughing more. She knew it was because of the man in whose arms she was lying. She wished they really had taken a camera. She would like to have a captured moment in time to keep with her.

"How much longer will you be here?" Stephen's question took her by surprise. She stiffened despite herself. She knew he felt the change in her.

"I'll need to leave by the end of the week," she whispered. "I've done what I came here to do."

"What was that?"

Naomi moved away from him. She didn't look at him, but stared out at the quietly lapping water. Across that sea was a man she'd promised to marry. "I had a decision to make and I've made it."

"Now you can go back to your life?"

"Yes," she nodded.

"What was the decision?"

Naomi turned back. She stared him directly in the face. "I'm engaged," she said, speaking the words almost as if she were challenging him. "I've been engaged for almost three years. I came here to decide if I really wanted to marry or not."

She could hear the silence in the spacc between them. She felt as if they were enclosed in a huge invisible shell. It was deafening inside it. Did he care? Did it make a difference to him that the reason she had come here involved another man?

"What . . . what did you decide?"

She threw her hair back over her shoulder. What had she heard in his voice? Did it crack? What did he want her to say? Would either decision matter to him? It was important to her. She'd discovered that today. "I decided not to marry Burt."

"Burt, is that his name?"

"Burton T. Mitchum."

"The lyricist?"

"One and the same," she said, dropping her shoulders and staring at the lovers' moon. It was huge, golden, perfect for this garden, for lovers, for the first people to visit this place, sit on this shore, and watch the sun drop away and the moon magically rise. "I knew you would know him."

"That's why you never mentioned his name or your plans to marry him."

"I didn't exactly conceal it, but it was my decision and I came here to make it without anyone's influence." She knew that hadn't happened. Even if Stephen knew nothing of her purpose, he certainly influenced her. There was no way she could feel what she felt in his arms or even just thinking about him and marry another man.

She'd fallen in love with Stephen.

The two of them sat apart as they hadn't done since this morning in the kitchen. Naomi knew they were coming back to reality now. The day had been wonderful. She couldn't have asked for a better celebration of her good fortune, but it was over now.

"Why did you get engaged in the first place?" Stephen's voice was low and filled with some indefinable note when he spoke. Naomi couldn't read it.

Naomi sighed. "We met on a film. I was consulting and he was working with the music director. He came to the set one day when the director was having a particularly difficult time with the star of the show. Burt stepped in and charmed her until they got the performance the director wanted.

"You were impressed?"

Naomi nodded. She caught her knees and pulled them to her chest. Resting her chin on top of them, she looked out at the water and smiled. Burt had been very charming then. Where had the charmer gone? The question startled her. That was why she could never bring herself to set a date. Burt wasn't the same man, at least not to her. The change had been subtle, so gradual she hadn't noticed it until now. Had it something to do with the accident?

"What happened then?" Stephen prompted.

She tried to smile but wasn't sure if she succeeded. "Outside of being charming, Burt had a wonderful sense of humor and was fun to be with. We saw each other a few times over the next year. We didn't start dating until four years ago. A year after that he asked me to marry him."

"And you became engaged." It was a statement and fully the truth.

"He gave me a big ring." Stephen looked at her bare fingers. "Its back at the house. I took it off so I could think about things rationally."

"From what I hear, *rationality* and *love* are mutually exclusive terms. And you have yet to mention that four-letter word."

"I thought I was in love with Burt," she said. Right up until she came to the island she thought she loved him and that they could make a life together. But the morning Stephen arrived and sprawled his body over hers and showed her what passion was like, what falling off a cliff and loving it was like, she knew their relationship was doomed. "He appeared to be everything I wanted in a husband. He was successful, confident, knew what he wanted in life, and treated me like a princess."

"A princess." He laughed. "I suppose I was a totally different animal."

"Animal is right. You treated me like a scullery maid," she said. *And I loved it,* she finished silently.

"Why have you decided against marrying him?"

Naomi knew he'd ask that. She couldn't tell him the truth, at least not the whole truth.

"I discovered I'm not enough in love with him to agree to spend the rest of my life with him. And he deserves that."

"You were engaged for three years?"

She nodded.

"Do you like long engagements?"

"I never really thought about it." Suddenly she saw herself in a white gown with flowers in her hair standing at the back of a long center aisle in church. Ahead of her was a man. He smiled and reached for her to come toward him. She smiled back. The groom wasn't Burt. In this fantasy Stephen waited for her at the head of the church. "Burt was in California working on a movie score," she continued. "I was on location in Canada consulting on a Scottish film. Setting a date wasn't a priority at the time."

"If you were my woman"—his voice, only loud enough to be heard above the ocean, was unmistakably carnal—"it would have been the uppermost priority."

Stephen stared at Naomi. He wanted to see her reaction to his words. He meant them, more than he'd ever meant anything he'd said to any woman in his past. He felt differently about her more so than he'd ever felt before. He'd been engaged, too. His experience was sterile, designed to achieve a goal. Neither he nor Tara had any illusion of love. Naomi did. She wanted to be in love with Burt. But she wasn't. He would have known that the first day when he kissed her, if he'd known that she had a fiancé.

The sun had fully set. The breeze off the water balmy, but he could feel the fire inside himself. His heart beat a drum in his chest. He thought of the song he'd written for his musical. "Feel the Warm." It was so appropriate to the moment. If violins had suddenly begun to play and an offstage singer voiced the words, he wouldn't be the least surprised.

Naomi sat as still as a statue. He could see the glow around them. They created it together, without thought or effort. Being together changed them, created friction, and fire. They were in the slow-burn stage, but eruption was imminent.

And both of them knew it.

He hadn't expected to find her when he E-mailed the travel agency, and even after he arrived and she upset him, he didn't expect to find how much she'd burrowed into his life. He reached for her, pulling her toward him, then pushing her down on the blanket. Stephen wouldn't let himself define the feelings that flowed through him when he looked at her. When he touched her, his mind could think of nothing except the softness of her skin and the sensual way her mouth looked, as if it were waiting for his kiss.

He framed her head with his hands, feeling her cotton-soft hair, caressing her tanned skin. "I remember you that first morning," he said. "When you'd run me through the thorns and bush and I finally caught you." He worked his fingers in her hair, looking at her features in the low light. Her hair was dark and he brushed it with his hands. "You were so soft under me. I thought, *I'm the luckiest guy in the world.*" His eyes played across her features, putting them together section by section, her forehead, her eyes, the space that separated them, her nose which tilted upward when she was angry, her chin, and that sensual mouth he couldn't resist. He found each feature unremarkable as a single entity, but put together, in this order, with the rises and falls of her character, her face was more than a song, it was an aria. "I'm glad you're not going to marry him."

Stephen's voice was gravelly. He lowered his mouth to hers, only touching her lips, brushing back and forth on her mouth. The sound of the ocean paled to the roar of his beating heart. Then he felt her arms encircling his neck. He gathered her closer, deepening the kiss. He'd been holding himself back, but as she opened to him he found it harder and harder not to crush her to him, not to let the dreams of her take root in reality.

He lifted his head and looked at her. Only moonlight illuminated her features, making them ethereal. "Naomi, we only have a few days." He tasted her neck, driving himself crazy with need. "Let's spend them together." She went boneless in his arms.

"What about your music?" Her voice was rash with emotion.

"You *are* my music." He took her mouth again, passionately, hungrily. This time she was as hungry as he. They devoured each other, trying to get closer, so close they could merge into a single being. Her head moved rapidly sideways as she bestowed one mind-blowing kiss on him after another.

Stephen pulled himself up, and Naomi with him. "Come on," he said. She didn't ask where they were going. They headed toward the gate. Stephen pulled her along with him. He needed to get her to the house. The beach was romantic, but he didn't want to make love to her on the sand. He wanted her in his bed. The wine and cheese they left behind as they went toward the estate. He wanted to make love to her tonight, all night. He wanted her next to him when he woke up, her dark skin contrasting with his and the sheets. Tomorrow he wanted to gather her close and make love to her again.

Without a word, they went to his room. He pulled her into his arms the moment they stepped over the threshold. He didn't bother to turn on lights, but ran his arms up her back and into the length of her hair to the crown of her head. He angled her head and settled his mouth on hers. His tongue danced in her mouth and his body found all the right places against hers.

He was already fully aroused and the softness of her only made him harder. He wanted her; more than any woman he'd ever known before, he wanted Naomi Davenport. He'd told her she was his music, and he meant it. He could feel the music in himself and he could feel the music in her. Her body was a complete song as he peeled her clothes away, exposing her skin to the moonlit room. His breath seemed to come from the deepest reaches of his body when she stood naked before him. When her hands lifted the hem of his shirt and pushed it over his chest with agonizing slowness, he knew he would explode.

Naomi had her own methods of giving pleasure. Her wet mouth kissed his shoulders and trailed down his chest to his stomach, while he gripped her arms and felt the blood in his body pool to the center between his legs. By the time she began her trek upward, he was harder than stone and ready to take her standing up. His arms squeezed her to him. His hands traveled from her shoulders to her hips.

Stephen took her to the bed and laid her there. Taking off the rest of his clothes, he joined her. He'd imagined her here, had had frustrating dreams of her lying on these pillows. The substance was more satisfying than his dreams. She was dark against the starkness of the covers. He let his eyes study her, moving with deliberate slowness up and down her perfect frame. Then he kissed her and covered her with his body.

He sank into her wetness. Rapture he'd never known, didn't believe could exist, existed. She clung to him, her legs wrapping around his body and pulling him into her. Stephen thought he had some control left before that, but with her he lost it immediately. He sank time and time again into her folds as if this were the first and last time anything like this would ever happen to him. He knew it was the truth. Naomi was unlike any woman in his past and he didn't think there was an equal in his future. Stroke after stroke burst through him until he thought he would die. He reached under her, taking her buttocks in his hands and stroking deeper into her, so deep that he thought the two of them would break the barrier of humanity and morph into joined flames.

Suddenly Naomi's nails dug into his arms and she writhed beneath him. Her body went wild as her hips lifted off the bed and met him, slammed into him. Primitive sounds came from her, guttural, animalistic, as her hands washed over his body, scraping his skin and completing the rhythm the two of them produced, taking it faster and higher until they exploded and dropped back to the bed.

The aftermath left the room filled with only the sound of two racers at the end of a long haul. Stephen couldn't move. He lay heavily on her, but his muscles were too tired, too relaxed, and he was too emotionally drained to move. He forced air into his lungs. Aftershocks hit him like cyclone waves. He shouted out then, unable to hold back the release. He gathered Naomi to him and with an effort slid next to her on the bed.

He wanted to talk to her, tell her what she had done to him, but he couldn't. He had no words adequate enough to describe the feelings that took root in his body. Each time he looked at her he'd felt a quickening in his blood, but what had just happened between them was indefinable. He could only tell her by showing her.

He smoothed the hair back from her brow and kissed her forehead, then her eyes and her cheeks, before taking her mouth and pouring every thought, every word, every description that was part of him into telling her that she'd changed his life. From today forward, nothing would be the same, look the same, taste the same. She had made a difference.

And he didn't think he could ever let her go.

SIX

Naomi couldn't remember how many times she'd laughed this week or how many times she and Stephen had made love. They were always hugging and holding hands. They'd walk the beach or the streets in Honolulu. They would meander through the marketplace, listening to the sounds of hula music, stopping to watch the dancers putting on shows for the tourists, all the while never breaking contact with each other. It didn't matter where they were or who could see them. They wanted to be together, with each other, without care for the rest of the world.

Stephen sat at the piano, playing, alternately writing and changing what he'd written on the sheets of music in front of him. He played every day, often while she sat in a chair and listened or read. Many times she'd become a distraction, Stephen told her, or he would distract her. Then he'd come to her chair or she'd go to his and they would find themselves making love on the floor of the music room or in one of the other twenty-two rooms in the estate. Naomi sat watching him now. The sun streamed in, a breeze keeping the room comfortable. Stephen seemed such a different man from the one she'd met the first day. He was sensitive and caring, attentive, inventive, outgoing, and he made her feel like royalty.

Naomi sat still now. A book lay open on her lap, but she hadn't read a word of it. Sixteenth-century costumes, vividly detailed in gold and white, went unnoticed to either occupant in the room. She listened to Stephen's stops and starts on the piano. Every once in a while he'd play several bars, then stop, write something, and play it again. And again.

She watched the curtains billowing at the windows. The air was fragrant with the smell of hibiscus. The gardens, a few steps away, were beautifully tropical as they spread toward the sea like an emerald carpet. Naomi understood why they called this paradise. It was her paradise. She'd met the man of her dreams. She couldn't believe how fast she'd fallen in love. Less than a week and she knew this was the man she wanted to spend her life with. He'd found a room in her heart which fit his exact size and, like the house, he'd taken up residence.

Soon it would all be different, however. She'd be on a plane to Los Angeles, back to her life, the one she'd left on the other side of the world, and he'd be here, working on his music exactly as he was doing now. Her heart fell, contracted painfully in her chest, but she wouldn't let that stop her. They had different lives, different priorities, and meeting each other, falling in love, wasn't in their plans when coming to this estate. But who ever planned to fall in love? It just happened. Like it had to her.

"You look awfully thoughtful. I hope you're thinking about me." Stephen eased her over and sat in the chair with her.

"My thoughts are always about you," she said.

"Good answer." He kissed her on the cheek. Naomi nuzzled against him. He felt good. She took in his smell. It aroused her. Leaning back, she looked up into his eyes and was surprised by the depth of passion she saw. It took her voice; the humor she bantered with him was gone. Her mouth went dry and she could feel her body flowing. As surely as if she were Pelé and made of fire, she let herself be drawn to him until his face was a gentle blur and his mouth was only a breath from her own.

It seemed like a year passed before he eliminated the millimeter of space between them and his lips touched hers. He kissed her slowly, rubbing his mouth over hers with the slowness of palms floating on the breeze. Naomi felt the tingle throughout her body. Her book crashed unnoticed to the floor. She raised her arms around his neck. She stretched her body, aligning it with his. She pressed close to him, falling gingerly onto the soft carpeting, never relinquishing her hold. In seconds they were fighting their clothes, pulling at each other's in a fit to undress as fast as possible. He took her fast and hard and in minutes they were spent, breathing hard, their hearts racing simultaneously.

They lay like that for several moments, Stephen covering her with his body, the fragrant air caressing them. Naomi felt content. She stroked his hair, his shoulders, reveling in the silky feel of his warm skin. Was anyone allowed to feel this much happiness? Surely she was using someone else's ration.

"We better get up and get dressed," Stephen said.

"Get dressed? We just got undressed." She kissed him on the shoulder. Deep inside she heard him groan. She kissed him again, this time on the neck. She slid her mouth across his jaw and chin. When her mouth touched his, she felt the snap in them both.

Anything other than the need to give and take of each other was lost.

Today wasn't a day for humming. Naomi wanted to sing. Out loud. At the top of her tinny voice. She wanted to shout. Stand at the top of Diamond Head and croon to the four winds, to the sea gods, to Pele and her sister, to the ages, to time itself, that she was in love. For the first time in her life she was in love.

Naomi had opened her eyes to the sunrise. She'd only been in bed a few hours, but she was too excited to sleep. The night had been wonderful. She and Stephen. The music. Their lovemaking. She rolled over in the bed, tangling her legs in the satin sheets. Where was he? He was the night owl, she the morning person. She wanted him beside her when she woke.

Naomi smiled. Coffee, she thought. She smelled it. He was probably in the kitchen. *The most I'll probably do here is coffee and donuts.* She remembered his comment early in their relationship. This morning Naomi wanted more than coffee. She'd go for the full American breakfast. She showered and, coming back into the bedroom, looked at the rumpled bed. It was evident from the tangled sheets, the depression in the pillows, the haphazard array of clothing lying about the floor, that they'd spent the night in that bed. Naomi's cheeks burned with the memory of the heights they reached, the passion that overtook her each time, the way each coupling was different, better. Would they ever reach a point where the excitement was lost? She shook her head.

Dressing in minutes, Naomi ignored her suitcases sitting near the door, packed and ready. She rushed from the room. She wouldn't let the suitcases change her mood. Her plane didn't leave until midnight. They had the whole day.

In the kitchen she expected to see Stephen in his usual place, sitting at the table or looking out toward the ocean, her cup in his hands. She was prepared to rush into his arms and pick things up where they'd left off last night.

She came through the door humming the song he'd been working on for the better part of the week, a broad smile on her face, and stopped in her tracks.

"Burt!" She was startled. Quickly she looked about the room, out on the lanai, to the grounds she could see from the window over the sink. Stephen was nowhere to be seen. The only person sitting there was her fiancé, Burt Mitchum.

Guilt suddenly attacked her. She hadn't thought of Burt in what seemed like ages. Her mind had been on Stephen and the way he made her feel. Her decision regarding their future had been made so long ago that it felt like he should have known already, but how could he? She'd forgotten to tell him, forgotten all about him. And what was he doing here?

"Surprise," he said with a quick smile, one that seemed to spread his lips and quickly shut them.

"I *am* surprised." She found her feet then and moved

across the kitchen. She bent down and kissed him lightly on the mouth. There was nothing spectacular about it, she thought. Nothing stirred in her like it did when Stephen kissed her. He didn't put his arms up to touch her or to return the kiss. Their meeting didn't speak much for their engagement. "What are you doing here?"

"I knew your vacation was up and I thought I'd come and escort you home. I also needed to do some business on the Big Island."

Naomi made herself a cup of coffee and sat down at the table with him. Her appetite for a large breakfast had disappeared. He really hadn't come for her. She was just conveniently located on one leg of a business junket to the island of Hawaii.

"It was nice of you to come, but I can fly alone. I got all the way here by myself." She smiled tightly. "Hawaii is a beautiful place. You should have come to see the beach and the volcanoes, listen to the music and watch the Polynesian dancers."

A frown marred his forehead. "I don't think the places where Polynesians dance and volcanoes rise will accommodate my wheelchair."

"Burt, you may not be able to climb Diamond Head, but everything else is within your reach." She took a sip of the coffee.

"I know what's in my reach," he snapped. Then, in a voice more controlled, he said, "Don't think it means anything. I've been in it for years now. I'm used to it."

The accident had only been a year ago. She knew it must feel like years to him. Her heart softened even as he hardened his own.

"Tell me about Stephen Weller. When did you meet him?"

So he had met Stephen. Someone had to let him in. Where was Stephen now? She didn't hear any sound coming from the music room and she couldn't see him on the grounds.

"I met Stephen here. Apparently we have the same travel agent and she booked the place to both of us for overlapping times. Both of us refused to leave." Naomi had to hide the smile that rushed to her mind when she thought of that fight with Stephen, and its resolution.

"You should have called me."

"Why?" He wasn't about to tell her so he could fix things. "I handled the situation myself."

"I wasn't implying that you couldn't handle things. Its just that Weller is a very important man in the industry. It would do me well to know him."

Naomi almost groaned. He wasn't interested in the fact that she was living with a man, a stranger to her only a short time ago, but in his own career. Apparently he thought she should have called him, so he could ruin her vacation and advance his own purposes. How could she have thought she wanted to marry this man?

"Where is Stephen?"

"He mentioned he had to go to Federal Express to send a package."

His songs, she thought. They'd talked about them yesterday. He was sending them to a producer in New York. Naomi was sorry he wasn't here. She hadn't told Stephen much about Burt. She wished she'd been here to introduce them, at least to soften the surprise of his presence. She wondered what Stephen was thinking now.

"Are you packed, Naomi? Our plane leaves in a few hours. While I would like to stay a little longer, we should really be leaving soon."

"Burt, I'm not going back with you." She stood up. "I'm not going back today."

"What?"

Her decision was made in a flash, almost before she realized she was going to say it. She had to stay here. There was unfinished business between herself and Stephen. She couldn't sterilely walk onto an airplane, never to see him again. They needed to talk. She needed to tell him she loved him.

"There was no need for you to fly all this way," she told Burt. "There was no need for you to try and organize my life. There was just no need . . ." Naomi was too angry to finish the sentence. She paused a few seconds, then in a normal voice said, "Burt, I can't marry you."

For a moment he said nothing. Shock distorted his features. Naomi had rarely seen Burt showing any kind of emotion not involving charm, but his reaction showed surprise, anger, horror, incredulity, and rage.

"What are you talking about?"

"Burt, let's discuss this like adults. The reason I came to this island was to decide whether I wanted to get married."

"And after this brief consideration, you no longer want to be my wife?"

"Burt, look around." She spread her hands. "The air outside is fresh and clean. The breeze is fragrant. There is nothing here but beauty. It's like being in a time machine and looking at the world as it should be. I've thought a lot since I've been here about our lives together if we get married, and I can't see it."

"What can't you see?"

"I can't see the love, Burt. These islands are full of newlyweds, lovers, people who care about each other, people who can't tear themselves away from each other. We're not like that."

"You mean because I don't fawn all over you and kiss in public?"

"You're missing the point. That isn't it at all. People don't have to do that for their love to show." She had a sudden picture of herself and Stephen. He held on to her hand all the time and he'd kiss her anywhere and she didn't mind. She didn't mind if the world saw them. But she didn't need the demonstrations to know he loved her.

It was in the atmosphere, as fragrant as the orchids and the salt air.

"You're not in love with me?"

Naomi shook her head. "And you're not in love with me. If we get married we'd make each other miserable and eventually get divorced. I don't want to go into a marriage knowing it won't last."

She wanted to say more, but there was nothing she could think of that would be adequate.

"I guess my trip has been a waste, then."

He moved for the first time since Naomi had come into the kitchen. His chair was custom-made and had hand controls and a huge battery. He worked these controls and began moving toward the kitchen door.

"Where are you going, Burt?"

"Back to New York. There's nothing here to concern me."

Naomi stayed where she was. His lack of argument stunned her, but she'd known that was how Burt would act. Nothing bothered him that he couldn't handle. He offered her none of his charm, only the end of an affair.

"Burt," she said, to stop him. He spun the chair around to face her. "Why did you want to marry me? It isn't love." She was sure his heart wasn't part of his proposal.

"The usual reason. I love you."

Naomi's eyes widened at this. He'd never said he loved her.

"You find that hard to believe?"

She didn't answer and he continued. "Naomi, you're beautiful, talented, intelligent. You would complement me. You understand an artist and his moods. With you I could have everything: a home, a wife who's headed for an Academy Award one of these days, and . . ."

"And what?" she coaxed.

"And I said I love you."

"How, Burt? How do you love me? Like a wife or like a sister?" She waited, but he said nothing. "Our relationship has never had any of the fire that usually accompanies lovers. We barely touch each other. We spend more time apart than . . ."

It was clear to her then. As soon as she said it, she knew. He wanted a wife who wasn't around to encroach on his time, but was there when and if he wanted her. And especially if there was an award in her future. She should thank him for thinking her work was at least the best in the business. It wasn't, however, the life Naomi saw for herself.

"I suppose you've found this *fire* you speak of."

He turned then, not waiting for her to answer. The chair rolled through the door with a soft whir. Naomi stayed where she was. She didn't see the car outside or the people who always traveled with Burt, but she knew they were there. Burt surrounded himself with people to do whatever he wanted. The fact that she didn't fall into line with his plans must have cut him deeply. She felt sorry for him. The accident had changed him a lot, but their relationship had nothing to do with it and she was thankful he hadn't tried to use that as an argument.

Burt would get over her, she knew. It wouldn't take him long. His pride was hurt, but he'd recover that before he reached the airport. Naomi felt a small sting that she'd aligned her life with him, knowing he wasn't the right man. What would she have done if Adrian hadn't mixed up the dates and sent her and Stephen here at the same time? Would she have married Burt and lived that perfectly orchestrated life he had laid out for her. Would she never have known someone like Stephen?

Where was Stephen, anyway?

SEVEN

Stephen's feet pounded the sand so hard that it kicked divets into the air. Jogging wasn't his usual sport. He much preferred golf to running aimlessly along, but today he needed to run. He knew of Burt Mitchum, but he hadn't known about the accident that confined him to a wheelchair or that it was a permanent situation.

Naomi hadn't told him. Burt's unexpected appearance would have been enough of a surprise, but the chair forced Stephen to remember his own mother and her attention to a man she didn't love because of his handicap. Naomi had told him she wasn't going to marry Burt, but what would happen when she faced him and he sat in that wretched chair? Would she be strong enough? Would she choose love over duty? Or would she choose as his mother had done?

Love, Stephen thought. She'd never said she was in love with him. Only her actions had led him to believe she could be. After she confessed that she wouldn't marry Burt and the last week they had spent together, how could she leave him? How could she not know how he felt about her?

Stephen turned back toward the estate. He'd been gone long enough. When he left Naomi, she was still asleep. He remembered her against him, warm and loving. By now she would be up and would have discovered Burt in the kitchen if he didn't find a way to get to the second floor and join her in the bedroom. Stephen's gut clenched at the thought of her with him.

He came through the gate to find the estate exactly as he'd left it. It wasn't the estate that had changed, but himself. He came in last night with Naomi on his arm humming one of his songs. He'd awakened early this morning with a song in his heart and love overflowing. He'd gone straight to the piano and, like his previous bouts of inspiration, the song came to him as if it were waiting for him to write it down.

Then everything changed when he answered the doorbell and found Burt Mitchum sitting there in his battery-powered wheelchair.

Stephen braced himself before stepping into the kitchen. He didn't want to come upon Burt and Naomi by surprise. The room was empty when he came inside. Only one cup of forgotten coffee sat on the table. The pot was full and hot. The place seemed unusually quiet. Naomi was scheduled to leave today. Had she gone without saying goodbye?

Picking up the coffeepot, he took a clean cup from the cupboard, then returned it, deciding he didn't want any. He wanted Naomi. He'd had the chance. He could have told her he loved her. He'd had enough chances, but in all of them he froze, never said the words that would let her know he wanted her, not just to stay for the week, but to stay with him for the rest of their lives.

He left the kitchen and went toward his own rooms. He didn't feel much like staying here without her. It had been perfect for them. Their own little corner of paradise. Without her, he didn't think paradise looked so good. He might as well pack up and leave, too.

The music reached Stephen as he stepped into the huge living room. His feet faltered and his heart stopped before hammering in his chest. It couldn't be, he told himself. The sound was soft, tentative, amateurish, as if the player had learned to play years ago and hadn't touched an instrument since. Yet it was the most beautiful sound he'd ever heard. He started walking. In seconds his feet were flying across the carpet toward the music.

Toward Naomi.

They had spent so much time together in the music room, Naomi was naturally drawn there. The windows were open, the curtain anchored to the side, allowing the breeze to enter and bright light to fill the space. At another time Naomi would find the room happy, even soothing, but now she wanted to know where Stephen had gone. What had Burt said to him? It didn't take this long to go to Federal Express and return. Had he stopped for breakfast someplace? She wanted to go looking for him, but the island seemed huge when trying to find someone who might not wish to be found.

She went to the piano and sat down. Lightly she ran her hands across the black and white keys. Stephen's energy seemed to have left the room with the wind from the windows. Where the keyboards and floor were usually covered with discarded paper, today they were as neat as if the maid had just cleaned. The only papers were a few sheets of music which he'd printed from the computer keyboard attachment.

Naomi picked up the pages. There were three of them propped against the stand. The music was far beyond her comprehension, although she'd participated in several recitals as a child. She started to read the words. The title on the top stated, "One Candle." She didn't remember this one. Stephen had played the score for her. This song had not been part of it. She wondered if the song was something he'd decided on later.

Looking down, Naomi began to read.

Out there,
On another mountain
The light of
A thousand candles
Burns to the heavens.

From my mountain
I watch them flicker

Across the landscape,
Turning snow to blankets
Of dazzling diamonds.
Across the space of separate worlds
Our hearts found each other, touched,
Our souls met and spoke understanding.
Piercing the darkness
Separately and together
We raised our lights.

Time travelers,
Moving through thunderous storms
And loving reunions.
Our minds crossed miles
To bring us together.
We didn't know our enemy—Time—
Had come to walk between us.
As we paused
To change directions
My steps were quicker.
When I looked, you'd gone.

Out there,
Lost in the dark,
The light of one solitary candle
Faded, flickered, died.
And the light glowing from the
Thousand other candles knew
That one was missing.

Naomi put her hand to her mouth. Tears gathered in her eyes and spilled down her cheeks. Using one hand, she wiped at them. The song was about them, their meeting and the knowledge of a bittersweet end. She thought he loved her. But his was the light that had gone out and she could see it clearly. Even during sunlight she would know that one missing light.

Stephen burst through the door, hanging on to it for balance. She was there. Naomi sat on the piano bench, playing the song he'd spent the night writing. Once before he'd come upon her this way, sad, crying, without a friend.

She swung around on the seat when she heard him.

"I thought you'd gone." His voice was without breath.

"I couldn't leave." She looked down, using the back of her hand to dry her face.

"Why?"

She hesitated, turned away, and replaced the music on the stand. He approached her. Burt Mitchum had gone. She was alone in the room and out front there had been no car.

"Why, Naomi? Why didn't you leave with him?"

Her fingers pressed a discordant note. She was nervous. He watched her pull her hands back and close the dustcover. Stephen sat down next to her. She moved aside to give him room, but he kept his body touching hers.

"I need to know," he whispered.

"I—I haven't told you I'm in love with you."

Stephen knew he hadn't heard her correctly. He'd seen Burt, knew she would feel a duty to him. He wanted it to be different, but he knew she couldn't mean it. Why had she said she was in love with him?

"Where's your fiancé?"

"He isn't my fiancé any longer."

Stephen's head was spinning. This was too good to be true and he knew whenever that was the case, it was certainly the case. Could Naomi really be in love with him?

Naomi stood up but didn't move any farther than a foot away from the piano stool. "Am I wrong in thinking you're in love with me, too?"

Stephen stood and turned toward her. He took her arms in his hands. "God, no," he whispered. He studied her face, every feature of it, putting them together as he'd done before when he first discovered she stirred something in him more than friendship, stronger than he wanted to admit, even to himself. "Say it again."

"I love you."

"I love you," he replied. "I've always loved you." He pulled her close, wrapped her in his arms, and kissed her softly, still afraid she might tell him she was leaving. "I can't believe you didn't go with him. He's . . . ill," he finished, not wanting to say he was handicapped.

She laid her head on his shoulder. "He's not ill."

"But the—"

She pulled back a little to look into his face. "The wheelchair. If you love someone, Stephen, it doesn't matter if he is in a wheelchair or not. I'm not in love with Burt. I'm in love with you."

"How did he take it?"

"His pride was hurt more than anything else. Burt isn't in love with me. We both know that."

Stephen forgot about Burt at that moment. He would never think of him again. He only thought of the woman in his arms—the woman who'd defied him the moment she saw him, and the woman he couldn't stop wanting, wouldn't stop wanting until death separated them. He lowered his mouth to hers and kissed her passionately. Their bodies melded as their lives had done. He wanted her forever and he would take nothing less.

"Now that you aren't engaged to Mitchum any longer . . ."

"And you've finished your score . . ." she said when he stopped.

The smile in his eyes left, along with the one on his mouth. His face was deadly serious. "Would you be engaged to me?"

"What about this?" she gestured toward the sheet music.

"I wrote that with such fear in my heart. I knew it was our last night. That today you would return to your world and I would be left alone."

"My mountain?" she attempted a smile.

He nodded. "So will you marry me?"

"A long engagement?" She raise her eyebrows.

"A very long one," he said.

"Define *long.*"

"Have you ever been to a Hawaiian wedding?" he asked between pecks that covered her face.

"No," she said in that breathless, love-starved voice he loved so much.

"Anyone you care to invite who can get in within three days? Because I refuse to wait any longer than that."

"Adrian," she said. Their inefficient travel agent came to mind. "If it weren't for her, we wouldn't have met."

Stephen agreed and pulled her back in his arms, never again to let her go.

Dear Reader,
Hawaii is a beautiful place and I've visited several of the islands and talked to many of the original people more than once. The islands are rich with tradition, mystery, and wonderment, not to mention a virtual paradise of foliage. I regret I couldn't put it all in the story. I hope I captured some of the flavor of the island and that Stephen and Naomi were adequate tour guides.

I own a time-share condominium on Oahu and much of the setting in *An Estate of Marriage* was taken from the area where I vacationed. The idea for the novella came from a vacation I had several years ago. A travel agent booked the trip and when I arrived and checked into the hotel, there was a man in my room. The hotel had rebooked an occupied room. Although he was a very good-looking stranger, we settled the problem and I received another room. The characters in *An Estate of Marriage* solve their dilemma in quite a different manner. I hope you liked their solution.

I receive many letters from the women and men who read my books. Keep them coming. I appreciate your comments. If you'd like to hear more about *An Estate of Marriage,* other books I've written, and upcoming releases, send a business-size, self-addressed, stamped envelope to me at the following address:

Shirley Hailstock
P.O. Box 513
Plainsboro, NJ 08536

Visit my web site:
http://www.geocities.com/Paris/Bistro/6812

Shirley Hailstock

THEN CAME YOU

MARCIA KING-GAMBLE

ONE

Atlantis? Could it possibly be? Had the lost island really surfaced in the Grenadines?

Raven Adams tuned out the tour operator's voice and drank in the natural beauty around her. She remained rooted to the dock, staring at the abundance of tropical greenery and towering mountains, while the rest of her tour group plodded ahead, following the leader's bright red flag.

The operator's voice filtered in and out. "Bequia, pronounced phonetically *Beck-way,* is one of several Grenadine islands. St. Vincent, considered the mainland, is approximately nine miles away and can be reached by ferry."

When she could no longer hear him, Raven kept an eye on the bobbing flag. She slipped off her sandal and dipped a ruby-red toenail into the azure sea. It felt like bathwater, tepid to the touch. Raven longed to close her eyes and submerge her body in the warm Atlantic ocean. It had been a brutal past week and she was emotionally drained, but who wouldn't be after what she'd been through?

"Mrs. Adams, we're waiting," the tour conductor called, reminding her that she continued to lag behind the others. "You're holding up lunch at the Bougain Villa."

Startled by the *Mrs.*, Raven blinked her eyes. Where had that come from? That's right, she'd booked the cruise as a honeymoon couple and never bothered to change the record. Had she not been dumped, that rat bastard would be her husband. Be that as it may, she'd decided to take the trip alone. Frank had paid for it, so why waste good money?

What she'd discovered was cruising alone was a big mistake. The luxury schooner was chockablock full of adoring couples gazing lovingly at each other. It was too much to handle, and she'd spent almost every waking moment in her cabin. Today was the exception.

Raven caught up with the group as they climbed into a brightly painted jitney. She squeezed into a seat beside a huffing, puffing couple from the Midwest, both of ample girth.

"Hey, Rae," the husband greeted. "Ain't this about the prettiest place you've ever seen?"

Raven forced a smile. "Yes, it is, though I suppose we should reserve judgment. This is our first port of call."

"It's paradise, as far as we're concerned," his wife chimed in.

It was paradise for her, too, certainly a far cry from the slums where she'd grown up. For the remainder of the short ride, Raven gazed out of the vehicle, admiring the pastel villas and lush natural vegetation. With one ear she listened to the couple beside her drone on. Soon the jitney bounced down a narrow lane and entered a cobblestone courtyard. Raven was the last person to get out. She followed their leader's flag, inhaling the briny smell of ocean.

"Welcome. Welcome to Bougain Villa." A plump dark-skinned woman dressed in a colorful headdress and matching skirt stood on the steps of a patio, waving them in. Balancing a tray of exotic drinks in one hand, she motioned to Raven to take one.

"It's rum punch, a local drink," she supplied, answering Raven's silent question.

Raven removed the red hibiscus from the straw and tucked it behind her ear. She took a long draught of the potent liquid before finding a seat at the rear of the patio. After a few minutes of expectant silence, a middle-aged local introduced herself as the hotel's manager. She gave a short description of the island's history and how the site came to be built. Soothed by the punch and the woman's melodious voice, Raven relaxed.

After lunch, the group toured the premises, stopping to

admire the luxurious cottages perched on the bluff. These pastel villas were part of the resort, and a huge sign indicated vacancies. Immediately Raven made up her mind. She would return to the Starburst, pack her things, and remain on this island paradise. Later she'd call her travel agent, Candace, tell her she'd jumped ship, and arrange to have her airline ticket changed. For the next eight days she'd simply drop out of life.

That decision made, Raven wandered down a narrow dirt road and stopped when the trail dead-ended in a spectacular ocean view. A charming little villa, painted a delightful robin's-egg blue, had been erected only a stone's throw from the water. A tree laden with plums dominated the front yard. Raven had never seen plums that large before. The fruit tempted. Reaching up, she plucked a few.

"You're on private property," a gruff voice yelled.

Raven snapped to attention at the sound of the deep male voice. The man had an accent she couldn't place, part Caribbean, part Oxford.

"I'm sorry."

"I suggest you move on. You're trespassing."

"I didn't mean to." She felt flustered and just a tiny bit put out as his golden gaze raked her body. How direct could one be? This machete-wielding laborer, an employee, no less, dressed in torn denim shorts and a soiled T-shirt, acting as if he owned the place.

Raven recovered. "Are you always this rude to paying guests?" In less than an hour she would be a guest, so that was no lie. She made a mental note to let the front desk know how inhospitable he was.

"Didn't you read the sign?" the laborer persisted.

Raven bristled. "What sign?"

"The one that said, 'No Trespassing. Private Property.' "

Not feeling particularly friendly to the male species on the whole, she stood her ground. This one was downright impertinent. "There was no sign." At least she didn't remember seeing one. All the pent-up anger and hurt of the last week came to a head as she glared at the man in front of her and he glared back.

He was model good-looking, if you liked the type: his skin the deep rich color of a Reese's Peanut Butter Cup, his slightly pouted lips rich and full, the nostrils arrogantly flared. Much as she hated to admit it, she was drawn to his magnificent golden eyes and a body that seemed hewn out of volcanic island rock. For a moment, Raven had some difficulty reminding herself she was off men. A beautiful body and handsome face did not a good person make. She'd been suckered in before, and look how it had ended.

Without a backward glance at the rude employee, Raven retraced her steps.

Logan vaulted over the counter, then placed a hand on the shoulder of the man drying glasses. "Let me take over. You go on a break. You've already put in a twelve-hour day."

"Thanks, man." Phillip, the bartender, quickly slapped the towel into Logan McFee's hands, then took off.

Logan rolled up his sleeves and stepped up to the bamboo counter. The Tikki Hut was a central gathering spot for the yachters and tourists. He slipped an apron over his head and went about the business of washing and drying glasses.

"I'd like a yellow bird."

"Coming up."

Logan could pick Torey's voice out of any crowd. He poured liquor, added orange juice, and topped the drink off with a hibiscus. The flower reminded him of something . . . or someone. The tourist he'd encountered earlier. The one with the golden brown complexion and huge almond-shaped eyes. She was something. She'd complained about him to the hotel staff.

He handed the drink over, listening with one ear to Torey's chitchat. She flirted outrageously. He'd grown used to it, but basically she was harmless. Within the next half an hour the place filled up with the usual assortment of patrons. A diverse group rubbed shoulders with Bougain Villa guests: the affluent yacht crowd sporting suntans and colorful outfits, tourists from the surrounding hotels, a handful of locals, mostly men on the prowl, and the occasional Rasta there to play chess.

Logan made drinks, served them, and acted as general kitchen help. The two waitresses could barely keep up with orders. Outside on the sand, a calypso band pounded out a medley of tunes and a handful of people made a valiant attempt to dance. The chatter and exchange of tall stories continued nonstop.

In so many ways he'd missed this stress-free existence. On Bequia the passing of time meant nothing, and what a man did for a living was irrelevant. Not that he'd ever regretted moving to the States. He'd had to do so to pursue his dreams. To be successful in his own right.

"Hey, Logan. Make the lady a piña colada, will ya?"

A large, hulking blond man slapped some bills on the bar. Logan threw Buddy Swensen a ready smile. The old salt was a regular at the Tikki Hut. Rumored to be immensely wealthy, he made his home on a ninety-foot yacht.

Logan's smile froze as he recognized the woman sliding onto the now-vacant barstool. The Swede had ousted the previous occupant.

"Light on the rum," she said.

"And on good manners," he muttered with ill-concealed sarcasm. Her perfume, a flowery scent, wafted his way.

"What was that?"

Logan turned his back on her and began to fix the drink. If you could overlook the woman's personality, she wasn't too bad on the eyes. Outfitted in a tasteful red sarong, her makeup minimal, single braid hanging over one shoulder, she'd appraised him with wary brown eyes and found him lacking. He knew the type. No respect for natives and their right to privacy. No respect for anything that wasn't American. This time around he would use common sense. It would be a local girl or nothing.

Logan heard Buddy introduce himself, and the woman's slightly nasal American accent. "Raven Adams. My friends call me Rae."

"Then Rae it will be," Buddy said, chuckling.

The randy old goat. But *Rae* was a heck of a lot more down to earth than *Raven. Raven* sounded pretentious, like something from a soap opera. Logan added fresh pineapple, punched the button on the blender, and mouthed the name again. Grimacing, he poured the frothy liquid into a scooped-out coconut husk, added a touch of cinnamon, and stuck a fragrant frangipani in the straw.

The conversation continued. "So, Rae, is there a Mr. Adams lurking about?"

Logan kept his ears tuned. He turned, slapped a napkin on the counter, set down her drink, and as unobtrusively as possible eyed her fingers cupping the coconut husk. A diamond almost as large as any star twinkled from her left finger. Logan ran a damp cloth across the bar and grunted an answer to one of Torey's comments.

"Not exactly lurking," he heard the Adams woman say.

Noncommittal. Sly. Was there a Mr. Adams or not? She was a tough one, all right.

Not at all disconcerted by her evasiveness, Buddy continued. "So, Ms. Rae, what exactly is it you do, when you're not sitting under a Caribbean moon?"

Raven's laughter reminded Logan of crystal clinking. She had a friendly laugh, made you want to laugh with her. She tucked the frangipani into her tightly plaited braid and sipped her drink. "I'm a designer."

"Ah, an artist. Creative. Spontaneous. Beautiful."

Puh-leese! Logan rolled his eyes. Surely Buddy could come up with a better line. Still, he found himself interested, wanting to hear more. He'd had her figured as one of those high-powered executives. Someone used to throwing her weight around. Getting her way.

"No, a hardworking dress designer; one of Calvin's minions."

Logan continued to mix drinks, waiting expectantly for her to go on. She'd risen amazingly in his estimation.

Buddy surprised him by leaning across the bar, drawing him into the conversation. "You and Logan here should talk. Sounds like you two might have something in common."

The Adams woman's eyes flickered briefly, dismissing him. "I doubt that."

"Really, you do. Logan here's a—"

"Another beer, Buddy?" Logan slid a Carib across the bar.

"Don't mind if I do." The Swede deftly caught the bottle and brought it to his lips. He hunkered down, whispering something in Raven Adams's ear. She thought for a moment, then slid off the barstool and followed Buddy to the dance floor.

Logan fulfilled several drink requests, keeping one eye on the swaying couple. After a while he turned his back and bantered with flirtatious Torey.

Raven looked down from her tiny balcony onto the ocean. Overhead, a half-moon cast golden beams on crystal sand, and strains of music drifted over from the Tikki Hut. The festivities continued without her. It wasn't that early, nor was it that late. To escape Buddy, Raven had pleaded a headache. Why encourage a man old enough to be her father? Why encourage any man at all? And most definitely not that laborer-cum-bartender or whatever he was.

With a dismissive toss of her braid, Raven put the bartender firmly out of mind. Now what to do? She was much too wound up to fall asleep immediately. If she succumbed, she could guarantee waking every hour on the hour. It had been a while since she'd jogged, or wanted to; now endless stretches of beach called to her. Crime on this island was minimal, or so she'd been told. She could run on the moonlit beach till her aching body said no more.

Inside the cottage, Raven slipped into T-shirt and shorts and laced up her Reeboks. She considered locking the front door but decided against it. The desk clerk had told her that most guests never did. Windows in the cottages were left open to enjoy the cool ocean breeze. Break-ins seldom happened.

"Unheard-of in New York," Raven muttered, beginning her warm-ups the moment she hit the beach.

Half an hour of jogging did her in. Her aching sides and burning lungs forced her to stop. She limped slowly up the beach, groaning softly, vowing never to push herself again, at least not until she was in better shape.

An overturned rowboat caught her attention. On top of the hull a man reclined, his legs hanging off the side. Raven's spine grew ramrod straight. Crime-free or not, she didn't feel secure meeting a stranger on a desolate moonlit beach. A nearby cluster of almond trees served as a landmark. The Bougain Villa was a good half-mile sprint at best, but in her present condition, she'd never make it.

"Good evening."

The man's clipped yet lilting tone commanded attention. As he sat up, a moonbeam illuminated his face. She'd run into the bartender again. On his turf and all alone, it would be prudent to return his greeting. Earlier they'd started off on the wrong foot. She'd felt compelled to report him to the middle-aged woman in the back office—the one who'd given the welcoming speech. While he might simply have been having a bad day, what if she'd made him lose his job?

"Good evening," Raven replied, forcing a smile into her voice.

"You sound almost human."

She refused to be baited, but simply placed one foot in

front of the other and continued walking up the beach.

The man followed, catching up shortly. His closeness made her uncomfortable. He smelled like citrus and sucked up all the fresh ocean air. Curiosity prompted her to ask, "What exactly is it you do at the hotel?"

"A little of this and a little of that."

Evasive. "That means?"

A beat went by, then two. "I'm jack-of-all-trades. I help out wherever I'm needed."

Well, that certainly explained why she'd mistaken him for a laborer earlier. Later she'd been surprised to see him tending bar. Privately she'd wondered why a man who sounded educated had ended up doing odd jobs. She was determined to keep him talking, at least until the hotel was in sight and she was within screaming distance of other folks.

"What brought you to Bequia?"

"It's pronounced *Beq-way,*" he corrected. "I'm a native."

"You couldn't be," Raven blurted.

"Surprised?" One eyebrow arched.

"It's just that you don't speak like the majority of the people. The only one sounding remotely like you is the woman in the front office."

The bartender changed the subject abruptly. "Where are you from?"

"The States."

"That's obvious." Sarcasm laced his words.

What a moody creature. Temperamental, too. And she was alone on the beach with him.

Raven softened her tone. No point in antagonizing him. "I've been told the accent's a sure giveaway. I grew up in San Francisco but live in New York now."

"Your design job had something to do with you moving?"

He'd been listening to her conversation with the Swede. That made her even more uncomfortable. She tried answering him honestly. "No. Actually I won a scholarship to FIT. Fashion—"

"—Institute of Technology," he finished.

Raven continued, "Graduated, and never returned home."

Interesting that a native would know what FIT stood for. "Who are you?" Raven attempted to joke, at the same time quickening her pace. "We've talked for a while, yet we haven't been introduced."

"Logan McFee."

Was he for real? The name had to be fabricated. It sounded as if he were laird of a castle, not some hard-working island man.

"Rae Adams."

"Short for Raven," Logan brazenly finished.

"That it is."

He'd been listening to every word of her conversation with Buddy, that much was obvious. Now, why had she shared her nickname with him?

Spotting lights ahead and the silhouette of a building, Raven sighed with relief. The Bougain Villa at last.

"Where is Mr. Adams?" Logan McFee probed.

This time caution and the imp inside prompted her to answer, "He got held up by business and should be flying in any day." She practically flung her left hand in his face, hoping the moonlight would illuminate the sparkler on her finger.

She'd made the impetuous decision to dig the engagement ring out of the bottom of her purse and wear it. Warned by the cruise staff that men made it their business to hang around hotels and cozy up to single women, she'd hoped the ring would keep them away. She'd return it to Frank when she got back to New York. The two-carat diamond only served as a painful reminder of her gullibility, her lapse in judgment.

"And is there a Mrs. McFee?" Raven asked.

"There is, but she's not my wife." He chuckled.

A sense of humor, who would have thought? They'd reached the main building. Raven held her hand out. He clasped it.

"Nice meeting you, Mr. McFee."

"Logan."

"Nice meeting you, Logan."

"Where do you think you're going?" Logan McFee asked, still holding on to her hand. "I'm walking you to your front door. Can't risk you running into a mongoose or some other predator."

Raven feared she already had.

TWO

As promised, Logan walked Raven to her door, then bade her good night. He knew if he hung around, the temptation to keep the conversation going would be too much. Raven Adams fascinated him, as all artists did. He related well to left-brained thinking. But work called and he had a deadline to meet.

She'd seemed shocked when he'd simply shaken her hand and left her. She'd widened those enormous brown eyes and skittered off like a nervous calf. Logan had since revised his opinion of her. She wasn't a bitch, just terribly uptight. A little sun and salt water should take care of that. It always did.

Whistling softly, Logan took the long way home. Though every muscle ached, his brain continued working overtime. He'd come up with an idea, a subtle way to poke fun at New York City politicians. The artist in him couldn't wait to get to work.

How different his night would be if he hadn't come home. His mother's SOS had been, in a sense, a godsend, giving him an excuse to close up his spacious home on the north shore of Long Island and leave the cold behind. Since then, the manual labor he'd immersed himself in had helped dull some painful memories. No use in thinking about Beverly now. It was over.

A dim light flickered from behind white cotton curtains. Good, his mother was up. He knew she'd be gazing at tea leaves, dreaming her dreams, creating for herself a fanciful future. Logan smiled indulgently. Constance McFee had survived two husbands while managing to build a thriving business. She'd seen to it her two children had the best education there was. And when she'd needed him, he'd come running.

"Hello, Mother," Logan greeted, entering without knocking.

Constance abandoned the cup and stood, offering her cheek for his kiss.

Logan hugged her tightly and sniffed the air. "You've got curry on the stove."

"Ummm-hmmm. Hungry?"

"Starving." He suddenly realized he was. He'd risen at five, managed to get some sketching done, grabbed a fast breakfast, then spent the better part of the morning supervising the landscaping, in actuality doing most of the heavy work himself. When one of the snorkeling instructors called in sick, he'd taken her place. And so it had gone. Always went. There wasn't a job in the hotel he hadn't done.

Constance set a steaming dish before him. Logan dug in, making fast work of the rice, peas, and plantains accompanying his chicken while his mother hovered.

"Our new guest, Raven Adams, is quite stunning," Connie McFee said, pouring him a glass of sorrel beer.

Logan grunted. "Pretty is as pretty does," he said between mouthfuls.

Constance laughed. "Nothing like being quoted back."

"I should have remembered that advice the last time around."

"Psssh. Beverly was an evil one. Good riddance to bad rubbish." Constance refreshed her tea. "Were you that rude to warrant a complaint from Mrs. Adams? I didn't have the heart to tell her you were my son."

"Good. Let's keep it that way."

She sat across from Logan, regarding him. "Any particular reason why?"

He shrugged. "Raven Adams thinks I'm hired help, not worth her time. Why correct that impression?"

"Raven Adams is married; doesn't much matter what she thinks."

Logan felt a sudden need to rise from the table, scrape his dish, and place it in the dishwasher.

"Have to run, Mother. I've got work to do."

Constance's soft laughter followed him. "Sure you do. But you can't very well change your future. The tea leaves say . . ."

Logan cut his eyes at her.

". . . this is your year to fall in love."

The moment Raven entered the cottage, she sensed someone had been there. Even though a cursory glance around confirmed all was in order, a subtle jasmine fragrance permeated the air. Not her scent. Must be the maid's. She tried to shake the uncomfortable feeling she'd been the object of scrutiny, and got ready for bed.

In the bathroom, Raven splashed water on her face and grabbed a fluffy towel. Out of the corner of her eye she spotted a splash of color against the white tile floor. Reaching down, she retrieved a lime-green hair ornament. It wasn't hers, that was for sure. She hated green.

"Hmmm," she said, setting the object on the bathroom counter. "Probably belongs to the maid."

Yawning, she climbed under the mosquito netting draping her bed and promptly fell asleep.

She rose to the sound of a rooster crowing. Pushing aside the mesh cloth, she slowly made her way to the window, shoving back pastel sheers to get a better view. Outside, a picture-perfect day awaited: blue skies, fluffy cumulus clouds, and an ocean that didn't have a ripple. Raven sniffed, inhaling the salty air. Paradise, all right. The Midwest couple had been right.

Funny, but she hadn't thought of Frank once. Well, maybe once, and briefly, in direct correlation to the wedding gifts still to be returned. Raven's stomach rumbled. She pushed thoughts of her ex-fiancé aside. She'd eaten only a salad last evening and needed to remedy the situation.

Within half an hour she sat on the wraparound deck of the main building, sipping a cup of tea. When the manager walked by, she was enthusiastically attacking her plate of mango and papaya.

"Morning. You're up early," the middle-aged woman said brightly.

"Morning." Raven smiled, acknowledging the friendly greeting. Those golden eyes reminded her of someone's. She concentrated on her fruit, savoring every delicious bite.

Five or so tables down, a man sat bent over a book, totally absorbed in what he was doing. Raven sipped her tea and stared at the back of his head. They seemed to be the only patrons up at that hour.

The manager's steps slowed in front of her other guest. The two exchanged words. Raven couldn't hear the details of the conversation but guessed by the body language they were more than casual acquaintances. Sensing she was staring at them, they turned in her direction.

The bartender again. The man sure turned up in the oddest places. He smiled and waved at her. Raven waved back. Hotel management had a pretty liberal policy when it came to the staff, she decided. Here was Logan McFee, dressed like any tourist, sitting, enjoying the early morning sun.

He rose, handed the woman his book, and headed Raven's way. Was that a sketch pad he'd turned over? Raven gaped at the corded muscles in his arms, at his bulging biceps where the T-shirt's sleeves ended. His cutoffs fit as if they'd been sculptured on, emphasizing legs the envy of any soccer player. A cool ocean breeze ruffled her hair, but even so she felt flushed. Logan McFee's presence was beginning to have the strangest effect on her. Raven gulped the last of her tea.

Why was she reacting to a man she'd hated on sight? This laborer, bartender, or whatever he was, was clearly not her type. And the way he looked at her was disconcerting, as if he saw through the facade and labeled her a fraud.

As Logan drew nearer, Raven twisted the engagement ring around and around. The solitaire, set in a wide gold band, glittered in the morning sunlight. Had he seen it? A week ago she'd been certain Frank Dunn, a man more gorgeous than Mario Van Peebles, and equally as smooth, was the one. She'd been up to her ears planning a wedding that had never come off.

Frank had been a man's man, practical and decisive. A ladies' man, too, she'd later found out. Two days before the wedding, his secretary had shown up at Calvin's, visibly pregnant and willing to talk. Poof! Just like that, it was over.

His betrayal knocked her for a loop and flipped her heart inside out. But she'd survived and now love was no longer part of the equation.

"Do you have plans for today?" Logan McFee asked, bending over and placing chocolate-colored hands palms down on her table. He had long, slender fingers, the hands of an artist.

"Plans?" Already she'd lost sense of time. For eight glorious days there would be no schedules. No deadlines to meet.

"The water sports office opens in half an hour," Logan said, drinking up her fresh air. He flashed a boyish smile, and for the first time Raven noticed his chipped front tooth. "I'm giving snorkel lessons at ten. Join me."

She couldn't think of an excuse not to. Nothing would come. She stared at him.

"Logan," a high-pitched voice called.

He turned to acknowledge the new arrival. His face lit up when a honey-colored beauty wearing ridiculously short shorts waved and started toward him. The woman at the Tikki Hut. The one he'd flirted with outrageously. From the confident bounce to her walk, she must be his girlfriend. Raven disliked her on sight.

"Think about it," Logan said, covering Raven's hand with his before moving off.

Presumptuous of him to touch her. She stared at his long, muscular legs as he strode away.

"How many of you can swim?" Logan waited for the group to raise their hands before taking a silent count. At least six of the eight in his class, thank God. Raven wasn't among his snorklers and he felt let down and strangely out of sorts.

Since all age groups were represented and the strength of his swimmers was still to be determined, he kept them in the shallow water, showing them how to breathe and explaining the mechanics of the tubes. They seemed to get the hang of it, some picking it up more quickly than others.

"Am I too late?"

Raven Adams's voice produced a prickling sensation at the back of his neck. She stood on the sand, oversize sunglasses perched on the end of her nose, a hotel towel riding her hips.

"No, not too late," Logan managed. Momentarily forgetting his charges, he held his hand out and waded toward her.

Raven, engrossed in ditching the towel, ignored his offer of assistance. Her siren-red one-piece welded like a second skin, hugging her slender figure. Her legs ran for miles. Shapely. Endless. He barely had time to pick up his tongue from the sandy floor and stick it back into his mouth. She fixed those huge brown eyes on him.

"Do you swim?" he remembered to ask.

"Passably."

Could mean anything. He wasn't taking chances. Not until he saw how she performed in the shallows. He handed her goggles and a tube; the flippers, she'd already put on. The rest of his group waited.

Logan managed to get through the lesson somehow. It

had been his lucky day to have a snorkel instructor call in sick. As Raven glided through the water like a sleek angelfish, he turned his attention to the class. She was much more than a passable swimmer. The hour went by quickly.

Logan was putting the snorkel gear away when she came up behind him. Suddenly he was all thumbs. Never in his thirty-four years had he felt this clumsy.

"I still can't figure out what it is you do," she said.

Logan clicked the padlock in place and turned away from the locker. "Work for the Bougain Villa."

"I know that." She sounded exasperated. "But what do you do?"

He shrugged. "Anything that needs doing."

Raven toweled her dripping hair while eyeing him. In just that short time her skin had bronzed. "Okay, smart guy. That much is obvious. Are you a handyman? That's nothing to be ashamed of."

Glad she'd filled in the blanks herself, Logan decided to go along with the story. "Yes. Yes. A handyman."

"But you're educated?" Her eyebrows were two commas. Her tone registered puzzlement. "And I saw a sketch pad."

He arched an eyebrow, challenging her. "So?"

"You must be an artist, working here to make ends meet."

An artist she could deal with; a handyman, no?

"I do odd jobs and draw a little," he admitted, making it sound like he didn't have much talent.

"Me, too. I'm a dress designer."

"Then you're really good." He made his eyes go round. "Perhaps . . . well, maybe . . . you'd help me."

"With?" She tossed the still-damp braid over one shoulder, regarding him with those sherry-colored eyes of hers.

"My sketches. Give me some tips." He was hamming it up now. Having a good time at her expense. Lord, if she only knew.

"Sure. Let me know when you have free time." Fingering her braid, she walked away.

Raven showered, changed for lunch, and thought about Logan McFee. He was a strange man, but intriguing. Faced with all that sinew and muscle, she'd barely been able to concentrate on the snorkeling lesson. No one knew better than she that good looks, brains, and a dynamite body spelled trouble. Even though he'd made a conscious effort to downplay his diction, she could tell he was intelligent. It showed in the depths of his eyes.

Deciding she felt daring, Raven slipped on a pair of shorts and a skimpy halter top. The subtle scent of jasmine perfumed her things as she dug through her tote bag looking for two wooden bangle bracelets. Why did she have the distinct feeling her stuff had been gone through? Her underwear had been packed at the bottom of her bag, her accessory case on the side. The two were now reversed. A nosy maid?

Raven did a mental inventory of her belongings. A quick search revealed only a pair of thong panties missing. Victoria's Secret. Perhaps the maid had stolen them. It was a bold move on the woman's part, one that left Raven feeling violated and angry. Just thinking of someone fingering her personal items and taking them out of her suitcase disturbed her.

Maybe she was making too much of the incident, she thought while heading off to lunch. If it happened again, she'd be forced to report it. Too bad if the woman lost her job.

THREE

The Friday lunch hour was notoriously busy. To top that off, one of the waiters called in sick. It couldn't have happened at a worse time. The yacht crowd, anxious to start their weekend, were all ashore, clamoring to be fed. Locals, paychecks cashed, looked forward to long, sumptuous lunches. And Bougain Villa guests, rather than opting for tours of the mainland, had chosen beach and sun. Seeing the mob, Logan had simply grabbed a tray and pitched in.

He'd just delivered an order of fried conch and crab cakes when he spotted her. She was seated across from Buddy Swensen. He frowned. The section wasn't Logan's to serve, but a quick word with his waiter remedied that.

"What can I get you?" he asked, positioning himself directly in front of her.

Buddy's faded blue eyes regarded him warily. "Hey, Logan, you certainly get around. Ladies first. Rae, have you decided?"

Logan's teeth clenched. *Rae* implied they had solidified their relationship.

She lowered her head, perusing the menu. Her braid swung forward, brushing the top of the table. When she smiled at him, his spirits soared. "How's the codfish and dumplings?"

"Excellent. I made them myself."

He was lost in those wide brown eyes. Lost in that infrequent smile that reminded him of a ray of sunshine. Corny, but true.

She was still smiling. Smiling at him. "Then it's decided. Codfish and dumplings it is."

"Buddy?"

Logan barely heard what the Swede ordered. He recorded their drinks and moved on.

Later, the majority of patrons served, Logan perched on a barstool, wolfing down his lunch. Even from that distance, he remained conscious of the woman seated across the room, hanging attentively on Buddy's every word. Upon occasion, her laughter drifted his way. The yachter obviously had the hots for her. It was no secret Buddy liked his ladies tall, dark, and beautiful. Mr. Adams better get here soon.

"Hi, handsome, mind if I join you?"

"Not at all." Tossing Torey a welcoming smile, Logan patted the stool next to him. They'd dated once. It hadn't worked out. That didn't stop Torey from still trying.

"So Logan, how come I never see you except at work?"

She'd never been one to mince words. "You see me almost every night."

"Yes, and like I said, you're always working."

"And you're not?" He raised an eyebrow, looking directly at the briefcase she toted.

"Yeah, but talking up time-shares is second nature to me."

"Business is booming, I hear."

"Can't complain." She held a hand up before he could say another word. "And I swear, I'm not taking guests away from the Bougain Villa. The Frangipani's clientele is a whole lot different."

"Guests are guests, as far as I'm concerned."

"Seriously, Logan . . ." She crossed one honey-colored thigh over the other. There was a time when a jiggle of those thighs made him tremble. "Can't you talk to your mom about letting me buy her out? Would she at least entertain a partnership? Now that your stepfather's dead, she might have a change of heart, and it could resolve the issue of you going back and forth. These lengthy absences from the States are bound to hurt your career. Course, you could consider marrying me."

Logan chuckled. She was at it again. Had been for years. Lovable as she was, business came first. Torey's life centered around the almighty buck; she viewed the world through dollar-green glasses, eastern Caribbean currency taking second place. Logan signaled to a waitress, miming that Torey was to be served breadfruit and codfish, the same dish he ate. No need to consult her; he knew her as well as the back of his hand.

The conversation resumed. "Thanks for the proposal, but I don't think it would work. As to my career, it's doing just fine. Thanks to computers and express mail, the world really has shrunk."

"What about exposure? Keeping your name out front?"

"I'm not worried." Logan explained patiently, "In some states I'm a household name. And I'm not above doing the occasional interview."

He cast a furtive glance to see if Raven and Buddy were still in the restaurant. They were. The Swede had his head dangerously close to Raven's.

"Who's she?" Torey said, drawing circles on his forearm while following the path his eyes took.

"One of our guests." He was careful to keep his face expressionless.

"Buddy seems to like her."

Logan sucked his teeth. "Buddy likes women, period."

"Hmmm."

Torey's food arrived, and although she sat silently picking at it, Logan could tell by her scrunched-up face, the wheels turned. He braced himself for the next slew of questions.

"Hi, Logan."

Logan turned to see a petite, nut-brown beauty bearing down on them. Spotting the woman, Torey raised a napkin to her lips, muffling a colorful expletive. "I'm out of here," she said, sliding off the stool and picking up her briefcase. "See ya."

Logan was left to face Dawn on his own. It wasn't a

prospect he looked forward to. During the time he and Torey had dated, Dawn had made her life a living hell. Their dislike for each other continued even today.

Laughing distractedly, Raven listened to Buddy's tales with half an ear. On her way to the restaurant, she'd run into him and had been railroaded into having lunch.

"What are you doing tonight?" The Swede asked, downing his second Carib, his eyes never leaving her face.

Raven sipped on lemonade. That woman was buzzing around Logan again, claiming her turf.

"I haven't given it much thought. What's going on?" She said, practically throwing her left hand in Buddy's face. It didn't seem to matter. He purposely ignored the ring.

"Usually the hotel gives a beach party."

"Sounds like fun."

Surreptitiously, Raven glanced Logan's way. His girlfriend was no longer seated next to him; another woman had taken her place. She could tell by the body language he and the new arrival were more than casual acquaintances. *Logan McFee gets around,* she thought. Both women were exceptional-looking. Not bad for a guy with no prospects.

Buddy's voice penetrated. "Will you be there?"

"Where?"

"The beach party," he said, brushing a handful of longish blond hair, threaded with silver, off his face.

He was coming on strong. Too strong. Raven darted another glance in Logan's direction. He stared at her. The sizzling connection between them caused an implosion; electrical tingles started in her toes and quickly worked their way up. Logan must have felt the effects. Abruptly he left the diminutive beauty and headed her way.

"Can I get you anything?" he asked, turning those gorgeous golden eyes on her.

"We're fine," Buddy was quick to say.

But she wasn't fine. Raven felt as if someone had just set her body on fire. That someone was Logan McFee. And at that very moment she made up her mind to let things take their natural course. A fling with a handsome native might be just what the doctor prescribed to get over Frank. She'd been cautious her entire thirty years, and where had that gotten her?

Setting out to seduce this handyman was a crazy idea. She'd never been one for idle flirtation or casual sex. But even the women at work came back from vacations boasting of endless conquests and passionate nights spent with island men. And if Stella could do it and get her groove back, why couldn't she? Raven grinned, thinking of the movie she'd seen recently. Would Logan McFee allow her to seduce him?

Raven smiled her supermodel smile, turning on the charm. "Buddy tells me there's a beach party tonight." She tossed her braid and batted her lashes.

"That's right." Logan's golden eyes never left her face. His gaze radiated intensity. Heat.

"Will you be there?" Still smiling at him, she moistened her lips.

Logan's answering grin revealed the chipped front tooth. "As long as I'm here, I never miss it."

As long as I'm here? What did that mean? She wanted to ask him but was conscious of the yachter's quiet assessment. She and Logan had communicated their interest without saying the words.

Buddy rose and threw some bills on the table. "Will I see you at the party later tonight, Rae?"

"Count on it." Though her mouth smiled and her hand waved, her attention was no longer with the Swede. It was centered on the man hovering attentively. He'd cast a lustful spell on her.

Logan McFee had neither title nor position, yet she'd made up her mind to seduce him. Most probably because she knew there would be no earthly possibility of it backfiring. They had a snowball's chance in hell of falling in love. And though she sensed he was not a man to be trifled with, trifle she would. She'd made up her mind.

Logan watched the staff place colorful cloths on the tiny tables dotting the beach. Off to the side, an array of fruits, vegetables, and salads was artfully arranged on long buffet tables. A pit, partially hidden from sight, held a roasted pig. The smells wafting his way were simply mouthwatering.

Officially he had the night off. Not one of his mother's employees had missed the bus or called in sick. Still, he felt a certain responsibility to supervise the setup and make sure nothing was lacking.

Tiny white lights twinkled in the surrounding almond trees, competing with the full moon above. In less than an hour, the beach would be jam-packed with people, every table taken. Out to sea, yachters had already lowered their dinghies, readying themselves for the trip in.

Logan's mother placed an ample arm around his waist. Her soft voice whispered, "The place isn't going to fall apart if you lie down for half an hour."

He kissed her mahogany cheek, nuzzling the downy softness with his nose, inhaling the peach scent he knew so well. "I'm okay. How are you holding up?"

"As long as I keep busy, I don't have time to miss Jimmy."

Logan missed him, too. Jimmy McFee was the only father Logan had ever known. His biological father had been killed in a boating accident when he was barely two years old. Jimmy had adopted him, raised him, given him his name.

"Torey asked me to talk to you," Logan said, switching the topic before they both grew maudlin.

"What does that conniving little shark want?" His mother's smile took the edge off her words.

"To buy you out." He pressed a finger against his

mother's lips before she could protest. "Would you consider a partnership?"

"Not in this life. We'd kill each other. That woman's far too aggressive for me. Why would I be interested in turning the Bougain Villa into time-share heaven?"

Logan clicked his tongue. "Oh, Mother. There's something to be said about time-shares if marketed properly, and Torey's got the knack down pat. At least you'd be assured regular clientele."

"I already have regular clientele. Seventy percent of our guests are repeaters. Cruise dropouts like Raven Adams are a certainty each season."

"Raven got off a cruise?"

"According to half the island, she did."

Two workers bustled by, carrying heavy cases of soda. They nodded at mother and son. Logan acknowledged them with a two-finger salute, then phrased the question carefully. "Wasn't Mr. Adams suppose to join her?"

"Not that I know of."

But she'd said . . .

Constance squinted her eyes, appraising him carefully. "Forget Raven Adams. There are plenty of single women around willing to keep you happy. That Torey crawls all over you. And Dawn, well, that's an entirely different story."

The women she mentioned didn't fascinate him. Neither Dawn nor Torey had the cool self-assurance of a Raven Adams, nor did they have the mind of an artist. All wasn't right between Raven and the husband she'd left behind. He meant to find out what.

As the first guests started trickling down the beach, Constance McFee hurried to greet them. Spotting an obscure table where he could observe the action, Logan thrust his hands in the pockets of his chinos and headed off to secure it.

He'd just sat down when a man's voice said, "Mind if I join you?"

Logan looked up to see Buddy Swensen standing before him. Buddy had pulled out all the stops, discarding his usual uniform of tank top and shorts for linen drawstring pants and a striped T-shirt. The tangy citrus of his cologne was somewhat overwhelming. All this for Raven.

"Of course not." Logan patted the vacant chair beside him.

Buddy sat, long legs sprawled out before him. "How's your mother holding up?"

"As well as can be expected. She's burying her sorrows in work."

Buddy, used to getting attention, snapped his fingers at a passing waitress. "Two Caribs over here." When the woman left to do his bidding, he resumed the conversation. "Now that Jimmy's dead, do you think your mother would consider selling this place?"

Logan cocked his head, eyeing Buddy thoughtfully. "Why? Are you interested?"

"I might be. I'm always looking for good investments."

"I'll let my mother know, but I wouldn't hold my breath waiting for her to sell. The Bougain Villa is what keeps her going."

The waitress returned with their beers, set them down, and took off.

Buddy clinked his bottle against Logan's before taking a healthy slug. "So you're thinking about staying to help out?"

"I'm considering it."

Logan scanned the horizon, hoping for a glance of Raven. Lines were already beginning to form at the buffet tables, where loaded platters of chicken and souse had been set out. No sign of her yet. He turned his attention back to Buddy.

"What have you been up to?"

"I took a trip over to Canouan and Palm Island. Hobnobbed with the usual assortment of celebrities attempting to lie low. Ran into Mick, Sinbad, and some hot reggae group the locals are wild about. How are you keeping up with work from this distance?"

Logan was about to tell him when he spotted her. A vision in white, Raven was breathtaking. She wore a hooded gauze caftan. Two daring splits on either side revealed long shapely legs. She scanned the crowd, looking for someone, probably Buddy. Openmouthed, Logan watched her move easily among the patrons. He sucked in an audible breath.

"Lovely, isn't she?" Buddy's eyes followed the path Logan's had taken.

"That she is."

The Swede's blue eyes never left Logan's as he tossed back his beer. "I'd have no objection if you went after her. May the best man win." Once again he clinked his bottle against Logan's.

"Raven Adams is married."

"And so am I." Buddy shrugged. "Merely a formality. A piece of paper."

Raven headed their way. Buddy stood, waving to get her attention. As she picked her way toward them, the hood of the caftan slipped, and her shiny black hair was revealed. Tonight she'd let it hang down.

Cleopatra, Logan thought. This was what she must have looked like. All luminous almond-shaped eyes, skin the color of warm cinnamon toast, and hair so jet-black it was almost blue. Raven. No wonder she'd been called that.

If he were a poet he'd be inspired to write prose; a songwriter, he'd happily pen lyrics. The artist inside just wanted to draw her, commit her memory to paper. Logan picked up the pencil the waitress must have left behind, grabbed a napkin, and began to sketch.

He was almost done with his caricature when he sensed her presence, smelled her flowery fragrance, and felt the heat she radiated. His trembling hands were barely able to fold the napkin quickly and cover it with his palm.

"Hi, gentlemen, may I join you?" she asked.

Buddy held out a chair. "But of course."

Raven sat while Logan remained silent, his tongue refusing to cooperate.

"May I see that?" she pointed to the napkin.

How to handle her request? To say no would seem rude, but if he showed her his primitive sketch, she might be insulted. She hadn't a clue what he did for a living.

"It's nothing you would be interested in," he said, finally meeting her eyes. God, she was even lovelier up close.

"Logan's being modest," Buddy interjected. "Show her."

Reluctantly he handed the napkin over.

For a long time she scrutinized his sketch. While she did, Buddy waved a hand, gaining the attention of a nearby server.

"It's very good," Raven said at last, whiskey-colored eyes roaming his face. "Have you ever considered art classes? There are schools abroad that specialize in figure drawing."

"Uhhhh . . ."

Buddy's raucous laughter broke out. "Rae, Logan's a pro—"

"Drink," Logan said, plucking a rum punch off the returning waiter's tray and setting it in front of Raven. "Sorry, folks, have to run. Duty calls."

He was several feet away when Buddy called after him, "I thought you took the night off."

Logan felt compelled to acknowledge his words. "I did, but plans changed. My moth—manager needs me."

FOUR

"Who's the woman talking to Logan?" Raven's hands circled her third drink. She leaned in toward Buddy. The rum punch mellowed her and made everything seem fuzzy and out of focus.

The yachter's faded blue eyes scanned the bar Logan tended. "You must be speaking of Torey Barnard. She's a biracial Brit. Came here on vacation, fell in love with Logan, and decided to stay. Eventually she bought a rundown hotel, refurbished it, and now makes a fortune selling time-shares."

"I take it the two of them are tight?"

"Like hand and glove."

Raven narrowed her eyes as the woman flirted outrageously with Logan. She watched her lean across the bar and kiss him smack on his lips. For some fathomless reason, Raven wanted to scratch the woman's eyes out.

Picking up the empty glass, she slipped out of her seat, saying to Buddy, "I'm going to refresh my drink. See you around."

"I'll be happy to get you . . ."

His last words were lost as she headed off, weaving her way through inebriated patrons. Raven had sensed a certain interest on Logan's part most definitely worth exploring. Now or never, before the barracuda moved in.

Raven sidled up to the bar and plunked her glass down. Logan immediately ceased his flirtation and came over. "Refill on your rum punch?"

She batted her lashes, playing with him. "No. How about something different?"

"Rum and coconut water?"

"Sounds good."

Not entirely clear on what she'd agreed to, she accepted

he coconut husk Logan thrust at her. The drink sounded xotic. Tropical. She was on vacation; why not?

Raven tucked the ixora bloom accompanying the drink ehind her ear. She took a long draught of liquid. She'd asted coconut before, but this concoction was different. Heady. Potent. As she relished every sip, her eyes clashed vith Torey's furious ones. The time-share queen's message ame over loud and clear. Hands off her turf.

May the best woman win, Raven thought, widening her yes for Logan's benefit and raising her husk to toast him.

Someone had erected a limbo stick on the beach and everal adventurous souls were attempting to beat the odds s the rod moved lower and lower. Raven drummed her ingers against the edge of the bar, pounding out a rhythm vhile the calypso band played an enthusiastic rendition of Harry Belafonte tune. Tourist music. More guests lined p, taking their turns under the limbo stick.

"Mmmmm." Raven sipped her drink and set the coonut husk down.

"You like it?" Logan's rag moved from side to side, wiping at imaginary spots.

"Love it. That's not all I like." She winked at him.

Where had that come from? All her life she'd never been his brazen. What if Logan McFee bit?

Torey's eyes flashed dangerously when Logan planted oth palms on the bar. Ignoring her, he smiled his crooked mile and looked directly into Raven's eyes. "I don't think Mr. Adams would approve."

Raven snapped her fingers. "Presto. He's gone." She lucked the diamond ring from her finger and tossed it in er purse.

"Just like that?" Logan threw his towel at the man drying glasses alongside him. "Here, Phillip. You take over."

"You can't just abandon your job," Raven sputtered as e grasped her elbow and began leading her away from he crowd. On the way, they passed the Bougain Villa's nanager. She shot them a puzzled look. "You'll get fired."

Next, the petite brown-skinned beauty seen talking to Logan earlier tried to stop him, saying something Raven couldn't make out. "Not now, Dawn," he said, smiling vaguely and continuing on his way. Where was he taking her?

Cold sober, the crowd and music a mere buzz in the background, Raven faced Logan. His eyes never left her face. He folded his arms, staring her down. "What was that about?"

"Excuse me?"

"Ah, you're a tease? A minute ago you were coming on strong, sending smoke signals only a fool would miss. Is this what you were looking for?" He bent his head, brushing his lips against hers.

The word *no* stuck in her throat. Humiliation wasn't what she had in mind when she'd set out to seduce him.

Logan deepened the kiss. His tongue thrust in and out, sweeping the insides of her mouth, with each stroke sending her to the moon. A funny thing happened. She should have felt elated, over the top. She just felt used.

Raven's hands pushed against his chest. "Stop."

"Why?"

"Because I want you to."

His kisses ceased immediately. Tentative fingers touched her swollen lips. "Did I hurt you?"

"No."

She'd led him on. There was a name for women like her: CT. Still, she'd be a liar if she didn't admit that, much as he'd tried to humiliate her, she'd enjoyed his kisses and enjoyed being held by him.

"Come here," he said, surprising her by opening his arms.

She took a tentative step toward him. He met her halfway. They stood for a long time holding each other, swaying, waiting for their breathing to settle. When they finally separated, he said, "The truth, Raven—do you have a man or not?"

She felt the tears pricking her lids. Now was not the time to break down. Not on the beach, on this lovely Grenadine island with a full moon overhead and a perfectly beautiful man at her side. Some people never had this. Still, how could she explain to him she'd been cast aside, dumped? Thrown over for a twenty-something secretary, and that now she'd purposely set out to use him?

Raven answered honestly. "At one point I did."

He took her hand and they began walking up the beach. "And now?"

She shrugged.

"What is it you want from me?" Logan asked softly.

What exactly did she want from him? The directness of his question threw her off-kilter. She'd been bent on having a fling: a sizzling island romance, a hot affair. A rendezvous so alien to her nature it was bound to help her get over the hurt.

"You fascinate me," Raven admitted, looking up at his perfect face illuminated in the moonlight. She could have kicked herself the moment the words flew out. They continued walking, and an uneasy feeling soon surfaced. They were being watched. Followed. She sensed it.

Logan came to a full stop at a lit jetty where two dinghies were tied. Using the palms of his hands, he dusted off a spot and motioned to her to sit. Soon he joïned her, long legs swinging off the edge of the pier.

"What about me fascinates you?" he asked, sounding as if he didn't quite buy what she'd said.

How to find words that would not offend him? He was everything she'd promised never to become involved with. Handsome. Sexy. Brash. And underemployed. It wasn't that she wanted a man to take care of her, but she did expect an equal. A professional. Someone successful in his own right. Someone who didn't remind her that she'd once been poor.

"Is the difference between us the appealing factor?" he probed, not quite hitting the nail on the head.

"Maybe. Even I don't understand it."

Growing up, there'd been no father figure to speak of. Men simply came and went. At an early age, having grown tired of the procession of uncles, Raven had made certain promises to herself. First she'd get a good job and claw her way out of the ghetto, then stability and success would be hers. She'd accomplished both. Had she gone ahead and married Frank, wealth would have been a certainty. Logan McFee was too painful a reminder of the old life.

Logan bounded upright, brushing sand off his slacks. "It's getting late. Time to head back."

What had she said to produce this sudden change in him?

They retraced their steps, and although she tried, not even her efforts at small talk could break down the barrier that had resurfaced between them.

An hour later, Raven entered her cottage and immediately knew someone had been there. Call it woman's intuition. Instinct. Hadn't she left the curtains open? Now they were closed. She sniffed the air, picking up the slight scent of jasmine.

"My maid seems to have style and a heavy hand," she murmured, heading off to the bathroom.

Peering into the mirror, she examined her face, tentative fingers tracing tender lips. Lips Logan McFee had kissed. If he hadn't been so obvious in his desire to humiliate her, she might be lying beside him in bed right now, allowing those artistic hands free reign of her body. Ridiculous as it was, there was something about the man that attracted her.

"Buddy, despite his age, would be a far better prospect," she muttered. "At least he owns his yacht and has money to burn."

The Swede had told her he spent six months of each year cruising the Grenadine Islands, the remaining six in his homeland, managing his financial affairs. But Buddy was a married fifty-something, old enough to be her father, and certainly didn't turn her on.

Raven slipped the caftan over her head. She unsnapped her bra and critically examined her body in the mirror. At thirty she looked wonderful, at her peak, toned, firm, and in shape. "Not good enough for Frank, apparently."

Dismissing her errant ex-fiancé, she washed her face and slipped on an oversize T-shirt. Stifling a yawn, she headed for bed. Raven stepped under the mosquito netting and threw back the covers. By some freaky chance she looked down. A shrill scream ripped from her throat, swirling upward, spiraling in a sharp crescendo. Still screaming, she raced from the cottage.

The beach party was slowly winding down. It was the opportune time for Logan to take off. But he wasn't even tired. After minutes of wandering the property aimlessly, unable to shake the feeling of confusion that had settled on him like a heavy cloak at Mardi Gras, he lowered himself onto a rock. He had Raven Adams to thank for this feeling of befuddlement. Damn the woman!

Whatever had possessed him to kiss her? The woman was married. While Raven might have flippantly dismissed the existence of Mr. Adams, that didn't mean she was free. She might be one of those tourists out to have a fling with a native, add an exotic notch to that belt of hers. Just the thought had made him want to humiliate her. She'd been so damn certain that with a bat of those huge brown eyes she could have him. All of a sudden, Ms. Uptown Girl had turned into a vixen with a heavy come-on.

Well, he wasn't any woman's plaything. He'd been there, done that. American women were quite practiced at going after what they wanted. Take Beverly. She'd moved in on him quicker than he could say "Jack Sprat," and before he knew it, he was in a relationship. Then she'd taken what she could get, and moved off just as quickly, trampling all over his heart.

He'd sworn off Yankee women after that. They functioned like men did in the Caribbean; love 'em and leave 'em, and to heck with the consequences. This time around he'd stick with an island girl. At least they were honest about what they wanted, and despite what their men did, were loyal to a fault.

Logan heard a bloodcurdling scream to the right of him. He raced off in the direction of the sound and ran into his mother halfway.

In response to the concern etched all over her face, he called, "I'll take care of it," and raced off in the direction of cottage number five, Raven's cottage, where the noise came from.

He found her standing in front of the building, arms wrapped around her quivering shoulders. Logan acted instinctively, giving no thought to appearances, or that she wore a tiny T-shirt barely covering the essentials. Embracing her, he pulled her trembling body against his.

"What happened?" he asked, cheek pressed against her hair, the scent of her shampoo heavy in his nostrils.

Raven took several moments to gather her wits. Her voice trembled. "I found . . . this . . . thing . . . animal in my bed."

"Animal?"

"A beast. Huge. Furry. Feral."

Drawn by her piercing screams, a small crowd gathered, mostly hotel employees and people on their way home to bed, Torey among them, his mother bringing up the rear. Conscious of Raven's skimpy attire and the speculative glances thrown their way, Logan turned the silently sobbing woman over to his mother.

"Please take Mrs. Adams back to the main house," he said. For the onlookers' benefit, he made sure to stress the *Mrs.* "I'm going to check out the cottage."

Connie McFee placed an arm around Raven's shoulders, leading her off. "I'm Connie, honey. You and I'll have a nice soothing cup of tea together." She left the curious crowd gaping as Logan took the cottage's steps two at a time.

An initial assessment of Raven's accommodations led him to believe she'd overreacted. The room was clean. Neat. Everything in order. He approached the queen-size bed draped in mosquito netting, the scent of jasmine filling his nostrils. He stuck his head under the netting and reached down to caress the area where Raven slept. A chocolate mint graced the pillow, a sure sign turn-down service had been completed. A handwritten note read, *Sweet Dreams.*

Nice touch. He'd have to remember to compliment his mother. Simultaneously, he spotted a tiny gray mouse, the field variety, dead as the proverbial doornail, and equally as inert.

"Furry and feral, eh?" Logan chuckled out loud, his mirth soon disappearing with the realization the creature had been left in Raven's bed intentionally. Who would do such a thing?

Backtracking to the bathroom, he grabbed a handful of tissues and a plastic laundry bag, and returned to dispose of the rodent. Prior to leaving the cabin, he made a quick call to housekeeping. Wishful thinking on his end that at this late hour anyone would pick up. He'd have to change the bed linens himself.

"Have you ever had your tea leaves read?" the Bougain Villa's manager asked Raven.

Raven sat facing the woman, palms circling a piping hot cup of Red Rose. It occurred to her that even though she wore the manager's robe, they'd never been formally introduced.

"Actually, I haven't, Mrs. . . ."

"Connie. Would you like to have them read?"

Conscious of amber eyes roaming her face, Raven hesitated before nodding her agreement. What harm could it do?

"You're sure, now?"

"Yes."

Those eyes. That face. Both reminded her of someone.

"Set your cup down and let the leaves settle."

Raven complied and waited for Connie to sink into the chair next to her. She felt comfortable in the main house, letting this solid-as-a-rock woman take charge, and allowing the warm tea to soothe her belly. Finding that beast in bed had shaken her up badly; now the prospect of returning to the cottage, *that* bed, wasn't even to be contemplated.

For what seemed an eternity, Connie stared into Raven's cup, her brows tightly knitted. After a while a half smile curved her lips, and she murmured, "Just as I thought."

"What. What do you see?"

"Dear"—Connie's hand reached over to cover hers—"you've had a great deal of pain in your life. You grew up poor and always wanting things. At times there wasn't enough to eat. Am I right?"

A lump filled Raven's throat. She managed a nod.

Connie gave her hand a reassuring squeeze. "Those times are long over with. You've gained some modicum of success and have your finances in order. You're ready to take the next step. You've met your soul mate. Don't let him walk away."

Raven sucked in a loud breath. The manager was dead wrong. There was no mate. Soul or otherwise. Frank had been a mistake. She'd been attracted to him, but had chosen him more for the security he represented than actual love. She'd used him to thumb her nose at the world and as a sign she'd arrived. Scrawny little Raven Adams, the nappy-headed child with the bleak future, had been capable of snagging an attorney—albeit a philandering one.

Raven smiled wryly. Previously, she'd never given much credence to the mumbo-jumbo of fortune-tellers, even turning up her nose when co-workers suggested she visit a tarot card reader. But this woman wasn't the flamboyant, crystal-ball-toting type; she was levelheaded and down to earth. Her words had been uttered with such sincerity and warmth, she almost had Raven convinced.

"Go on," Raven urged.

Connie turned up her warm smile. "That's it. I can't see any more." She stood, stretched, and yawned.

Picking up on the hint, Raven rose. "Can I return your bathrobe tomorrow?"

"Certainly. But where do you think you're going, missy?"

"To bed." She'd imposed on the woman long enough.

As she headed for the door, Connie planted herself firmly in Raven's path. "Uh-uh. Not until my . . . Logan returns."

FIVE

Logan tucked in the edges of the top sheets and smoothed out the creases with one hand. He set another mint on Raven's pillow, made sure the mosquito netting was draped just so, then stood back to admire his handiwork.

It had been a long time since he'd substituted for the maid, and he hoped his hospital corners passed inspection. Not that Raven would know the difference. Logan stared at the newly made bed, conjuring up images of a naked Raven, her body trim and sleek, long shapely legs wrapped around him.

The image still firmly implanted in his head, he left the cottage and set off to see how Raven fared. When he entered the main house, he could hear the two women laughing. It had been a long time since his mother had sounded that lighthearted and carefree. The two were good for each other, he decided.

"There's Logan," Connie said as he entered.

"Is that thing gone?" Raven faced him, looking so vulnerable he wanted to wrap his arms around her and assure her that her furry, feral beast had been aptly disposed of.

"You will never see or hear from it again."

His mother eyed him, choosing her words carefully. "What was the problem?"

"Someone played a sick joke." More quietly, he added, "Dead mouse left in the bed. You'll need to question the maid in the morning."

"It is the morning," Connie reminded, lips pursed. "Take this child straight to bed." She practically pushed Raven into his arms. "I'll deal with this nonsense right now."

Visions of a naked Raven still dancing in his head, Logan snaked an arm out to steady her as she stumbled against him. It seemed the most natural thing in the world to place a hand on the small of her back. Big mistake. He longed to squeeze her shapely body until it molded against his, kiss those cinnamon-colored lips till they parted and she agreed to anything he asked.

He left the house, ushering her slightly ahead of him. On the way back to her cottage he came up with an idea. "If you're not tired, let's walk along the beach a bit."

"I'd like that."

Raven actually made it sound like she wanted to be with him and was relieved that he'd asked. His euphoria didn't last long, though. What if being with him wasn't what delighted her? What if it was simply the prospect of not being alone?

"Are we heading someplace in particular?" Raven asked, after they'd walked for a while in silence.

"To a beach that's off the beaten path."

They reached an unpaved road and Logan could tell by her rigid posture she recognized the area.

"This is where we first met," she confirmed, darting an uncomfortable glance his way. "As I remember it, you implied I was trespassing."

"You've got some memory. Incidentally, you were."

"And you were rude," Raven murmured, just loud enough for him to hear.

"Ouch. Was I that bad?"

"The worst."

He placed a hand on her shoulder, squeezing gently. "See the blue cottage? That's where I live. How would you feel if some tourist appeared out of nowhere, invading your privacy and stealing your plums?"

"I see your point," Raven said quietly.

The moon's beams played across her features, softening all the angles and making her appear younger than he thought she was, and equally as vulnerable. The smell of frangipani lay heavy in the air, mingling with her perfume and teasing his senses.

Logan felt a strong urge to kiss away the lines that had appeared between her brows, to slowly work his way downward until he captured her mouth, tasted her lips, and saturated himself in her kisses. Kisses that tasted sweeter than mango jelly to a man starving for a woman's touch.

He shook his head, trying to make sense of things. Trying to put perspective on his feelings. He knew he needed physical contact. It had been far too long since Beverly. Too long to remain celibate. But the truth was, his feelings for Raven Adams weren't purely physical. She appealed to him on a cerebral level.

But so, for that matter, had Beverly. She'd been his ideal woman. A graphic artist he'd met at an opening in Soho. The attraction had been instantaneous; a meeting of minds, or so he'd thought. He'd slept with her that first night and every night thereafter, mistaking lust for love, mistaking a cunning mind for a creative one.

Beverly had never really been interested in him as a person. She'd been more interested in his position in the art world: his contacts, and what he could do for her. And she'd left him the moment someone more famous came along. Ironic, now that she'd been dumped by her new lover, she wanted Logan back. That would never happen. Her deception still rankled and he'd never allow himself to be conned again.

They stopped in front of his tiny blue house with the gingerbread trim, and in unspoken agreement mounted the three little steps leading to the porch. Logan brushed off the topmost step and motioned to Raven to sit, then joined her.

Raven stared at the moon, shifting uncomfortably. The cotton fabric of his mother's robe made a crinkling sound, competing with the creaks and croaks of crickets and frogs. Refusing to think of how little she wore under the light robe, Logan blanketed his mind. Raven finally broke the silence that descended between them.

"Why would someone put a rat in my bed?"

"Mouse," he quickly corrected.

"Mouse, rat, whatever it was, it was intentional."

Their shoulders bumped and it took Logan a supreme effort not to put his arm around her. "I prefer to think it wasn't," he said quietly.

"Then how does a dead rat end up in bed? Did it climb under the covers and conveniently go into cardiac arrest?"

"Mouse," Logan automatically responded, smothering a chuckle at the vision her wry comment conjured up. The thought of a rodent purposely climbing into Raven's bed and dying, gruesome as it might sound, was hilarious. He was pleased she seemed more like her old self. Most women would still be in shock.

Raven flung long curly locks over one shoulder and began twisting her hair into a plait. Logan's hands itched to finish the job. The idea of weaving his fingers through that lustrous mass and massaging her warm scalp was far too tempting. Mesmerized, he watched her complete the braid.

"God, Logan, this view is beautiful," she said, staring out at the ocean.

"No place like it. Then again, I'm hardly impartial."

Raven's hair brushed his arm as she leaned forward, palms cupping her cheeks. The perfume of her shampoo floated on the breeze, mingling with the salty ocean smell.

"When I got off the cruise and spotted this place, I thought . . . well, I thought . . . I'd never seen any place quite so lovely. And when our tour operator told us that story about the mountainous peaks being the lost island of Atlantis, I was totally enchanted."

"I've heard the same story since I was a child. There's no proof, but it does add an aura of mystery."

"What's St. Vincent like?" Raven asked, casting him a sideways look.

Those lips. Those eyes. That body built for seduction. Was she married or not? It took every ounce of self-restraint not to pull her into his arms.

Logan's voice wobbled. "Lush. Mountainous. Beautiful. It's home to the oldest botanical gardens in the Western Hemisphere."

"Is that right? Sounds exotic."

"That it is, and busy. Would you like to see the sights?"

She graced him with a smile that made his heart flip-flop.

"Love to."

"What if I take you tomorrow?"

Her smile was quickly replaced by a frown. "It's already tomorrow. Don't you have work?"

"I'll take the day off."

"I'd love it if you could."

He stood and stretched. "Tired? I'll walk you back to the cottage."

"No. No. I'm fine. I like sitting here talking to you." Her tone was shrill, almost pleading. She'd put up a brave front but wasn't ready to go home yet.

"Come inside, I'll show you the house," Logan said, taking her hand. We'll share some Horlicks and you can fill me in on your life."

"Hor-licks?" Raven appeared taken back by his invitation, undergoing some mental debate.

"A barley-based drink. It's soothing and will help you sleep."

Releasing her hand, he shooed her into the house.

The inside was nothing like she'd expected. The three small rooms Raven could see were sparsely but tastefully furnished. Hemp throw rugs were artfully arranged on highly polished wood floors. In the living room, satin pillows sat piled on an old-fashioned mahogany divan. A stereo lay next to it on the floor and a wrought-iron goose-necked lamp, with a hand-painted shade, provided muted lighting. Positioned in front of the divan, a kidney-shaped coffee table held neatly stacked magazines. Besides that, the only other item was an antique rocker.

"Come into the kitchen," Logan said, motioning for her to follow him.

Raven entered a good-size room, large enough to hold a table with four chairs. The one and only window was open wide, letting in the cool morning breeze and the tangy smell of ocean. She sat on the chair Logan held out.

"Horlicks coming up," he said, extracting two mugs and a jar from teak cabinets overhead. He set them on the table, turned his back to her, and fumbled with a knob on the stove, then placed a copper kettle on the open flame.

Raven stared at Logan's broad back as he went about his business, at the way his head tilted to the side, at the strong column of his neck. He was beautiful from any angle and reminded her of the Carib chiefs she'd read about. How did such an articulate, gorgeous member of the male species end up tending bar and doing odd jobs? How could a handyman afford antiques? A cottage on the ocean? The place must have come furnished, she decided. Maybe the manager gave him a break or let him use it free of charge.

Logan straddled the chair beside her and angled it outward. She felt his gaze on her face.

"I'm waiting for the water to boil," he confirmed.

There was something so intimate about sitting in this man's kitchen at such an odd hour, with him only inches away, that made her uneasy. "Were you educated on Bequia?" Raven blurted.

"For the most part."

Logan's long fingers circled the base of the mug, drumming lightly. Raven's eyes were drawn to the tiny hairs on his knuckles. To his bronze arms. The same silky dark hair covered every muscular surface.

She took a deep breath, gulping in the cleansing morning breeze. "And you've lived here always?"

"Not always."

"You've traveled abroad, then?"

"Why do I have the feeling I'm getting the third degree?" He flashed her that devastating smile.

"I didn't mean to pry." But she had.

"Talk to me," Logan said, reaching out to stroke her cheek with his callused palm.

I wish you'd keep your hands to yourself so I can think straight. "About?"

"About you. Begin by answering one question."

"What would that be?"

He scooted his chair closer to hers and leaned forward. She could feel his warm breath on her face. He took her left hand and stared at her ringless fingers. She clutched the robe where it gaped, willing her knees to stop knocking, and hoping the table didn't vibrate.

"Are you married?"

Her body heated up under his scrutiny. The whistling kettle cut short her response. "N-n-o." She wasn't sure if he'd heard her.

Logan rose to turn off the stove. He put a spoon in the jar, scooped out a beige farinha-like substance, placed it in each cup, and poured water. Apparently forgetting something, he headed for the refrigerator.

Raven noted the way his chinos molded to his rump. He had an athlete's butt. High and slightly rounded. Just the way she liked them.

He returned with milk, poured it into the mugs, and set both containers down. "Then why were you wearing a ring earlier?" he asked, sipping on his drink.

To ward off men would sound vain. "I was engaged until recently," she said quietly.

"You changed your mind, but kept the diamond?" She could swear he smirked.

"That's not quite the way it happened." To avoid looking at him, she took a sip of the steaming liquid, then set the mug down. The drink tasted malty but delicious.

"He left you? Somehow I find that hard to believe."

"Believe it. Frank felt he was marrying down anyway. The twenty-three-year-old he had stashed on the side came from an old Atlanta family."

Logan's fingers circled her wrists. "I would never have guessed you had such poor self-esteem. Regardless of how humble your roots, you should believe in yourself. See yourself as the best. You are the best."

Raven could feel the moisture on her lashes. Where had he been when she was growing up? When she needed this pep talk? She took another sip of Horlicks. "Is that what keeps you going? Your belief in yourself?"

His fingers tightened around her wrist. Intensity flashed in his eyes. "Let me tell you something, Raven. . . ."

"Rae."

"My father died when I was barely three, leaving my mother with very little. Times were tough for a single parent, especially a poor island girl. We had no welfare system to turn to. I credit my mother for instilling in me a sense of pride and self-worth. She made me want to excel and encouraged me . . . well, encouraged me to be the best person I could."

He rose and crouched down next to her, the cooling cup of Horlicks forgotten. "Look at me, Rae."

How could she not? She was at ease with him, soothed by the Oxford in his voice, the slight Caribbean lilt to it. She was lost in those mesmerizing golden eyes. Dangerously attracted to a man she had no business with.

"You're more together than I am," she said, gulping the liquid. "To think I . . ."

"You felt sorry for me? Pitied me? Maybe looked down on me a bit?" He straightened, and taking her hand, pulled her up from the chair. "Bring your drink with you."

They relocated to the living room, where Raven sat on the divan, careful to keep a firm hand on the robe's belt. Logan squatted down to turn on the stereo, playing with the knobs until he found a Marley tune.

"Get up," he said, returning to stand over her.

She rose awkwardly. Was he proposing they dance?

He lowered himself onto the settee, long legs taking up the length of the furniture. He held his arms out, encouraging her to join him. She eased herself into the tiny space he'd left and perched uncomfortably on the edge. Logan's arms wrapped around her waist, pulling her down to rest against him, fitting her buttocks between the V of his legs.

" 'Lively up yourself,' " he sang in an off-key rendition of Bob.

She felt safe in his arms, cocooned in his warmth, mellowed by the smell of ocean, body, and man.

She stifled a yawn as he kissed the side of her neck, nibbled the lobe of her ear, and continued to sing in that slightly off-key voice of his.

Bob Marley's soothing lyrics were the last thing she heard before drifting off to sleep.

SIX

The rooster crowed for the third time that morning. Logan maneuvered his arm until he could see the face of his watch. He'd barely slept, but most definitely it was time to get up. Careful not to wake the woman cradled next to him, he positioned her off to the side, then set his feet on the floor.

All morning he'd drifted in and out of sleep, painfully conscious of Raven's perfumed body and tantalizing curves driving him wild. It had been sheer agony, lying there, holding but not really stroking her. He'd been forced to have a mental talk with himself and issue his hormones a stern warning. She'd trusted him enough to fall asleep in his arms. He couldn't violate that trust.

Logan stood and fastened the top button of the chinos he'd loosened for comfort. To ease the ache in his loins, he adjusted the crotch of his pants. He hadn't had an erection this large since . . . well . . . since college. He looked down on Raven, curled into a ball now, knees drawn to her chest, hands clasped under her cheek, an angelic expression on her face. This time he couldn't stop himself from reaching out and smoothing her hair.

She stirred and shifted onto her back, muttering something he couldn't make out. The robe gaped open. The T-shirt underneath bunched up around her middle, revealing a flat stomach and an outie belly button. Her legs seemed to go on for miles. His eyes were now riveted on her slightly protruding hipbones and moved downward to focus on the tiny scrap of silk covering her mound. Cut high on the thigh, the thong panties didn't hide much. The tug in his groin became a definite ache. Moistening his lips, he forced himself to move away. Sketching something, anything, would keep him busy. Keep him sane.

In the bathroom, he splashed water on his face, counted backward from a hundred, and changed into shorts. He didn't trust himself to remain inside any longer than it would take to make coffee. That task completed, he ducked into his bedroom, snatched his sketch pad from the floor, and tore a page from it. He wrote Raven a quick note. After setting the note on the table beside her, he grabbed his pad and raced from the house.

Outside, Logan stopped briefly to feed Skettel. He'd found the injured bird eons ago while hiking La Soufrière, St. Vincent's dormant volcano. The querulous parrot was a rare species and had to be close to Logan's age, if not older. He'd spent several months working with her, teaching her how to speak. When he left for the States, he'd turned the task over to the hotel staff. If anything, Sket's temperament had worsened with age.

"Hi, Sket," Logan said, removing a bag of seed from the storage shed and gingerly opening the bird's cage.

"Sket want a cracker, not that sh—crap," the parrot sang.

Logan chuckled. He'd tried to get the old girl to clean up her language, yet the expletive still slipped out. Especially when she thought he wasn't paying attention.

"You'll get what I give you," he said, filling her dish.

"Psssssh!"

This time he laughed aloud at the bird's efforts to suck her nonexistent teeth. She'd picked up the habit from the hotel help and he'd done nothing to discourage her.

"I'm off now, girl." Logan shut the parrot's cage firmly behind him. The macaw hung by one claw off her perch, eyeing him from her upside down position. Then began a high-pitched series of catcalls.

Logan waggled a finger at her. "Now, you be good, girl. Can't have you waking my guest."

But even as he headed for the beach, the catcalls continued.

"Pretty girl. Pretty girl."

Raven woke to the heavenly aroma of coffee, loud conversation, and raucous cackling. She struggled to a sitting position, managing at the same time to wipe the grit from her eyes. Sunlight poured through mullioned glass windows and danced off highly polished wooden floors. Slowly, the room came into focus. The rocking chair wasn't familiar, nor was the kidney-shaped table in front of her. Finally remembering where she was, she jolted awake.

Had Logan taken advantage of her? Her first inclination was to look down and make sure she was fully clothed. The bathrobe she'd borrowed gaped open, and the T-shirt underneath was practically up to her chin. She'd had too much to drink last evening. Too much booze and too little sleep. Heaven only knew what he must think of her. Raven adjusted her clothing, then, cushioning her aching head between both hands, sat up.

"Logan," she called softly, setting her feet down on a sheet of paper that littered the floor. She frowned when he didn't answer. He wouldn't have left without at least saying good-bye, would he? They'd made plans to tour St. Vincent—at least that's what she recollected. Raven reached down to pick up the paper she'd stepped on. Red lettering screamed her name. Her lips moved as she read his note in a whispery voice:

Raven:
I made coffee, help yourself. I've gone for a walk on the beach. Be back shortly.
Logan

He hadn't deserted her after all. She'd search for a spare toothbrush, clean up a bit, then go find coffee. Those goals in mind, she headed off purposefully.

With that business accomplished, Raven was faced with

the dilemma of what to wear. The sun was high in the sky and both staff and guests were sure to be up and about. She couldn't go traipsing about dressed only in Connie's bathrobe. Speculation would run rampant and she could kiss what was left of her reputation good-bye.

A pair of Logan's boxers and a T-shirt hung off a peg at the back of the door. She had no choice but to pull them on. His clothing still held his scent: a delightful combination of ocean and man. She stroked the silky material of his T-shirt and closed her eyes. This way she could easily pretend he was holding her. Scary, but she was on the precipice, close to falling over the edge. So dangerously close to liking a man who had no prospects and therefore was totally unsuitable.

Determined not to let her wandering thoughts entertain even the most remote romantic possibility, she sniffed the air, following the scent of freshly brewed coffee to the kitchen.

The high-pitched conversation that had awakened her earlier was louder in here. Raucous cackling and a vulgar screech floated through the open window. Raven poured coffee and stepped outside. She would find Logan, thank him for his kindness, then head back. And to avoid announcing to the entire world she'd spent the night at his home, she'd use the back door.

Outside, the warm sun caressed her bare legs and an invigorating sea breeze ruffled the leaves of nearby shrubs. Raven stopped to touch unfamiliar plants, marveling at the beauty of Logan's backyard. There was a charming little pond with goldfish and pastel-colored water lilies in it. A tiny scrap of lawn held a glider, a small patio table, and two chairs. Yellowish red shrubbery she'd heard someone call croton edged the yard. She bent to sniff a fragrant blossom of an unfamiliar bush and heard the high-pitched voice call, "Pretty girl. Pretty girl," followed by a series of sharp wolf whistles.

Looking in the direction of the sound, Raven spotted a

mammoth-size cage suspended off the limb of a mango tree. A macaw clung by one talon to its perch, beady eyes focused her way.

"Pretty, pretty girl, feed Sket a cracker," the bird ordered.

A parrot. How delightful. Intrigued by the talking macaw, Raven drew closer.

"Hey, there," she said, reaching a finger through an opening in the cage. Swifter than she could ever imagine, the parrot swooped down on her outstretched finger.

"Skettel! Don't you dare."

The bird came to a screeching halt centimeters from his target. Raven quickly withdrew her hand and, turning toward Logan, placed that same hand against her heart. "You startled me."

"I didn't mean to," he said, his eyes caressing her. "Nice outfit."

"It's not exactly a Calvin original, but it will do," she joked, pirouetting so that he could get the full effect of her borrowed garb.

The macaw, irritated that he was no longer the center of attention, flapped his wings and made a production of preening. Logan set down what looked like a sketch pad and admonished the bird with a waved fist. "How many times have I told you not to bite, Skettel?"

"Sket's a good bird. *Good* bird," the parrot chirped, opening his wings full span.

"Is that his name: Sket-le?" Raven asked, captivated by the warm interplay between pet and owner.

"Actually, it's Sket-tel," Logan said, ruffling the macaw's feathers and letting his warm smile wash over her. With the back of his free hand he reached over to caress her cheek. She smiled back at him, wondering what it would be like to have his hand on her body. In his white short-sleeved polo shirt and skimpy jogging shorts, he looked so handsome. Such a broad chest. Such muscular legs. *Focus, Raven, don't get carried away.*

"That's an unusual name," she managed to get out. "Does it have special meaning?"

He chuckled. "Actually, it's a local expression used to describe a bad, cheap, or wayward woman."

Was there a hidden message meant for her? Had he gotten the wrong impression because she'd come on to him, then spent the night?

"So I take it Sket was both wayward and bad?" Raven said, deciding she might be reading too much into his comments.

"That she was. Hence the reason she's caged." Two fingers tapped the metal bars of the macaw's prison. "Still interested in seeing St. Vincent?"

"Oh, yes. Most definitely."

"In that case, how about I walk you back to your cottage? You can change, and we'll meet at the main house in an hour. Plan on catching the ten o'clock ferry."

Raven stepped into a hot pink sleeveless jumpsuit and secured the toggles at the front. The jasmine odor lay heavy in the air, signifying another's presence. Scooping up a brush from the bathroom vanity, she struggled to work the snarls from her hair, then, finally giving up, she wove the heavy mass into a braid.

A touch of blush and a dab of mascara would be all that was needed to complete her makeup. She searched for the bag of toiletries she'd left out on the counter last evening. Funny, but she could almost visualize where she'd left the beige cosmetic roll—right over there. Maybe the maid had tucked it away in one of the drawers. Cool tile soothed her bare feet as she took small steps toward the vanity.

"Ouch."

Raven picked up one foot, hopping toward the mirror to examine the place where it hurt. Somehow she'd picked up a splinter. With one hand she squeezed the spot on her sole that had turned slightly pink, managing to open the drawer with the other hand.

As she'd thought, the cosmetic roll had been put away. Inside would be a pair of tweezers. Gingerly setting her foot down, she unfolded the bag, pausing when her fingertips encountered moisture. She spread the flaps wide to the pungent odor of a dozen assorted scents and a mishmash of browns, reds, yellows, and coppers. Liquids spilled over the edges, dripping onto the floor. Mixed in were shards of glass.

She stifled the sharp expletive before it came out. The maid must have dropped her cosmetics and ground the containers underfoot. Accidentally or on purpose? Was this the same maid who'd left her the rat last evening? What in the world had she done to the woman?

Among the mess, she somehow found tweezers. Giving them a quick rinse, she plucked the splinter from her sole, then methodically sorted the items that could be saved and dumped the remainder, including the bag, into nearby trash. No time to mull over this disaster. Logan would be waiting.

Quickly slipping on a pair of flats, she grabbed her purse and camera, planted a wide-brimmed hat on her head, and set off. While she didn't want to be responsible for anyone losing their job, enough was enough: This harassment couldn't go on. She'd stop by the manager's office on her way out.

Logan waited at the check-in counter of the main house. He looked even better than she remembered. He'd shaved and changed into khaki walking shorts, hiking boots, and a black T-shirt. Around his neck he wore a slim gold chain, and tied to one handle of his backpack was a bright red bandanna. He smelled heavenly, like sandalwood and man. He kissed her cheek and held her hand seconds longer than necessary.

"You look wonderful. Good enough to eat," he said.

Her heart actually pounded. Could he hear it? "Thanks. So do you."

"Ready?" Palm pressed against the small of her back, he prepared to steer her from the house.

"In a minute. Right after I speak to Constance." Her insides quivered and her knees knocked.

"Problem?" Logan arched a well-sculpted eyebrow, seeming to pick up on her inner distress.

It felt good to tell someone about the destroyed toiletries. Her fear that the maid was to blame.

"I'll handle it," Logan said, disappearing into the back room and returning several minutes later. "All taken care of," he announced, reclaiming her hand.

"What did you do? Please don't tell me you got the maid fired. Granted, she's the person with unlimited access to my room, but I can't prove she's the one. If she's innocent, I'd hate to see her out of a job."

The two desk clerks, young ladies in their mid-twenties, openly ogled Logan but seemed to glare at her.

"Not to worry," he said, "I arranged for security to increase patrol of your area. But meanwhile I've come up with some options."

"And what might those be?"

Raven enjoyed the feel of his fingers looped through hers. She dismissed the cautious voice at the back of her mind telling her to be careful. She was this close to falling for a handyman. Albeit a devastatingly handsome, intelligent one. But a handyman no less.

Logan continued, "We could move you to another cottage, less isolated and closer to this building, or . . ."

"Or?"

"You could move in with me."

She knew her face must reflect her surprise. She gaped at him openmouthed. "I'm sorry. I don't think I heard you correctly."

"Ah, but I believe you did," he said, hurrying her off. "Now, which is it to be?"

She didn't trust herself to answer.

SEVEN

On the ferry to St. Vincent, Raven and Logan sat hemmed in by a gregarious crowd. Logan studiously avoided making eye contact with a woman he once dated. For the most part he ignored the curious glances thrown their way. He'd grown up with these people. Knew how they thought, and knew that the moment he and Raven got on that boat together, they would be the topic of every Bequia gossipmonger.

His heart swelled in his chest as he acknowledged the men's envious looks. He knew they would willingly change places with him anytime. When the boat tooted its arrival into Kingstown Harbor, he took Raven's hand, guiding her through the debarking crowd and onto the dock.

"So this is St. Vincent," she said, looking around her.

"Not the most attractive part," Logan responded, pointing to the rusty barges and ramshackle buildings surrounding them. "We'll see the real St. Vincent in a minute."

Somewhere along the way his reservations about this woman he'd labeled an "Uptown Girl" had been cast aside. She might have snobbish tendencies, but she was intriguing as hell, and definitely passionate. He could tell by the way she'd kissed him back. Common sense told him he was getting in way over his head, even possibly setting himself up for a letdown. Still, he'd decided to go with the flow. Enjoy the few days they had left.

"Taxi," Logan called, making his way through the milling crowd and flagging down a blue sedan.

"Taxi? I thought for sure we'd walk."

"It's a fairly long trek. I didn't think your feet would hold up. Even I have a difficult time adjusting to ninety-degree weather." Logan waited for Raven to settle into the backseat before climbing in next to her.

Raven's chocolate gaze raked his face. "Adjusting? You started telling me you'd lived someplace other than Bequia, but you never did say where."

"London and the States."

Bug-eyed, she mouthed something that sounded like, "That explains Oxford," and in a louder voice eventually managed, "And you're back tending bar and doing odd jobs?" Disapproval dripped from each word.

"Sometimes a guy's got to do what a guy's got to do." He tapped the driver on the shoulder. "Can you turn up the air-conditioning?"

"Yeah, mon. Where yo go?"

"Botanical Gardens, please," Logan said.

During the ten-minute ride through narrow, pitted streets, Logan provided running commentary of the sights. He showed Raven the market square and, when they turned onto Back Street, the old courthouse. Off on a side road, he pointed out an ancient Catholic church that was Gothic in appearance. Leaving the busy town behind, they entered even narrower roads, eventually coming full stop in front of the gardens. A sign proclaimed it THE OLDEST IN THE WESTERN HEMISPHERE.

"Is that true?" Raven asked, pointing out the sign.

"So I'm told." Logan asked the driver to wait and guided her under the arched entrance and into parklike surroundings.

"God, it's magnificent." Raven's expression revealed she was totally captivated by the lush vegetation and natural beauty. He was certain she'd never seen anything quite as splendid in the States. Even he had difficulty not touching the leaves and budding flowers, throwing himself on the grass, rolling down the sloping hills, and pretending he was a child again.

A kaleidoscope of colors peeked from every nook and cranny. A dozen scents titillated his nostrils as they walked for what seemed miles without meeting anyone. All the while he told funny little anecdotes, ending with the tale of Captain Bligh, the party responsible for bringing the breadfruit plant to the island.

Logan slowed down in front of a shady flamboyant tree. Unzippering his backpack, he removed an oversize towel, flask, and two paper cups. After spreading the towel beneath colorful blooms, he crooked a finger. "Relax for a few minutes, Rae, and enjoy the serenity." He flopped down, and when she made no move to join him, patted the spot next to him. "Come sit."

It seemed like an eternity before she sat. Even then, she perched on the edge of the towel, afraid to bump shoulders; afraid to touch him. She did manage to remove her adorable hat and set it at her feet. He drank in the scent of her fragrant perfume—a delightful honeysuckle concoction—felt the heat coming off her skin, the flames sizzling between them. He wanted more than anything to scoop her up in his arms and kiss her senseless. Instead, he poured liquid from his flask and passed her a cup.

"What is it?" Raven asked, taking a tentative sip.

"Mauby."

Reacting to the acrid taste, she wrinkled her nose.

"It takes some getting used to. It's made from the bark of a tree."

The tip of a delicate tongue flicked out to take another sip. "I think I like it. Grows on you."

He longed to capture that tongue in his mouth, suck on it, and savor her sweetness. He gulped the remainder of his drink and set down his cup. "Are you still in love with what's his name?"

"Who? Frank?"

"Yes, Frank. The bastard. That excuse for a man."

She fingered the edges of the towel, refusing to meet his eyes. "Depends on your definition of *love*."

Plucking a nearby cattail off a bush, he tickled her earlobe. "If you can't give me a definitive answer, then it's no."

She squirmed. "Stop it." A chuckle broke free. "Why are you so interested?"

"A guy needs to be assured there aren't any obstacles in his way." His fingers pried the cup from her grasp, setting it down on the grass. "Rae?"

"Yes?"

"Is there?"

Her eyes told him more than words could ever say. He held her face between his palms, turning her head slightly, planting a kiss on her forehead, the tip of her nose, and on both slanted cheeks.

The smell of honeysuckle threatened to overpower him, going directly to his head, befuddling his senses. Other outdoorsy smells crept in: freshly mown grass, blooming roses, the cloying scent of gardenias. Through the tree branches the sun warmed his shoulders. There was no turning back. Raven's lips parted, inviting him in. Hoping to find his equilibrium, he pressed his forehead against hers. *Breathe, Logan, Breathe.* He was drowning. Drowning in her scent, her taste, the very feel of her.

"God, Rae," he said, before taking the plunge. Capturing her tongue between his teeth, he sucked on it. She clung to him, arms wound tightly around his neck, bringing him closer. Matching him move for move, her tongue circling his, giving as good as she got. He wanted to tear off her clothes, make mad passionate love to her on the emerald lawn. Instead, he fingered the top toggle of her jumpsuit, wondering if he dared take the next step.

Footsteps close by solved his dilemma. Elementary school girls, paired in twos, strolled only feet away, dressed in navy uniforms and crisp white shirts.

"The taxi's meter's still running. We'd better go," Logan said, leaping to his feet, then helping her up.

Hand in hand, they began a slow stroll toward the exit.

Later that evening, a red light blinked on the telephone when Raven entered her cottage. Looking around, she decided everything seemed in place. It would be so inconvenient to relocate; perhaps she could just have her locks changed. Of course, that wouldn't necessarily solve the problem if the maid was to blame. But moving in with Logan was out of the question. Not because she was concerned with appearances. She didn't trust herself to be in such close proximity to him.

Earlier his kisses had set her on fire, leaving her weak-kneed, addle-brained, and unable to think. She'd come to the conclusion she wasn't cut out for a fling. Not with him, anyway.

Raven picked up the receiver and dialed the operator.

"Do you have a message for cottage number five?"

"Yes, madam, Mr. Swensen said he'd be by at eight to get you."

Raven thanked the operator and hung up. She hadn't made plans with Buddy. At any other time she'd resent his high-handedness, but now she was glad to put space between her and Logan. She needed time to think.

Eight didn't give her much time to dress. She splashed water on her face and refreshed her makeup. Hurriedly she pulled on a tight little black dress, complementing it with silver jewelry. Making sure to close the windows and lock the door, she headed off to the Tikki Hut to wait for Buddy.

As luck would have it, she spotted Logan the moment she entered. He was tending bar while talking to the café au lait beauty she'd seen hanging around. He waved to her. She waved back, refusing to acknowledge the surge of jealousy she felt when the woman leaned across the bar and wrapped her arms around his neck.

"Hey, Rae, come save me," Logan called, rolling his eyes playfully.

She had no choice but to approach the bar. Every eye in the already crowded place was on her. She noticed Logan hadn't changed clothes and felt a momentary twinge of guilt. She had taken him away from his job. His living. Now he'd been forced to make the time up. He'd spent a fortune on the taxi, the lunch he'd insisted on buying, and their quick excursion to Mesopotamia: land of lush mountains and valleys.

Though her arms still lingered around Logan's neck, the woman loosened her grip. She turned to watch Raven approach.

"Hello, there—and you are . . . ?" she inquired in a voice straight from Liverpool.

Raven tried her best to smile, managing a stretch of the lips and a slight tilt of her head. She couldn't summon a word.

The woman broke the awkward silence. "Bloody hell, Logan, aren't you going to introduce us?"

Shrugging his strong neck, Logan managed to free himself from her hold. "Torey Barnard, meet Rae Adams."

"Raven," Rae corrected, holding out her hand.

There was a slight hesitation before Torey took it.

Logan's lips twitched. He didn't miss a beat. "You look nice," he said, his eyes feasting on the places where the lycra dress clung. He flung the towel he'd been wiping the bar with over his shoulder. "I'll get you something to drink, then we'll leave."

"Thanks, but no need to. Rae's with me." Buddy Swensen appeared from somewhere, placing a proprietary arm around Raven's waist. "Hope you're hungry," he said to her.

"I had a late lunch."

Raven could feel Logan's heated gaze on her face. Sense his confusion. She didn't dare look at him for fear of what she would see reflected in his eyes. Just hours ago she'd enjoyed his passionate kisses and had come dangerously close to making love with him. Yet here she was, dressed in her evening finery, ready to leave for God knew where, with a man old enough to be her father, and reputed to be rich.

"Good. Then we can have a late dinner on my yacht," Buddy said sotto voce.

"Private party?" Torey interjected. Her arm again circled Logan's neck.

Bitch, Raven thought, resisting the urge to belt this Torey person who thought she owned Logan. One backhanded slap would wipe the smug expression off the witch's face. Tuning out Buddy's response, she ventured a look Logan's way. Stone-faced, he'd escaped Torey's clutches, busying himself with the blender, steadfastly refusing to look at her.

"Just how many people did you invite for dinner?" Raven asked after Buddy had squired her from the Tikki Hut.

"Only a handful. Mostly people from neighboring boats."

She squelched her unease as they boarded the motorized dinghy that would take them to his ninety-foot cruiser.

When they stepped aboard, it was deadly quiet. The only person in sight was a worker swabbing the decks. He nodded politely at them.

"Where's everyone?" Raven asked.

Buddy shrugged, his arm circling her waist. "It's just you and me, babe. You might not have come if I told you otherwise. This way, please." He nudged her toward some steps leading down.

"I'd like to go back to the Bougain Villa," Raven said, refusing to take another step.

Buddy's fingers caressed her sides. He blew a long, slightly alcohol-smelling breath into her ear. "Don't be like that. This is our opportunity to get to know each other."

"Like hell it is. I want to go back."

Cupping her buttocks in his hands, he brought her even closer, grinding his groin against hers. "And how are you planning to do that. Swim?"

"If I have to."

In a swift motion, Raven brought her knee up, ramming it into a tender body part. Ignoring Buddy's anguished cry, she stumbled blindly across the deck and toward the worker, who'd set his mop down.

"You've got some bug up your bum," Torey said, stirring her rum swizzle with one finger.

"What?" Logan wiped the glass he was holding, slamming it down with a thud. He slapped his towel on the bar and glowered at Torey.

"Don't take your vexation out on me. Since that woman showed up, you haven't heard a word I said."

"And what exactly were you saying?"

Torey threw him a dazzling smile. "I wondered if you'd had a chance to speak with your mother."

"About what? Joining forces?"

"Right on the money, my lad. You aren't planning on hanging around forever." She arched her brows and pursed her lips. "Unless, of course, you're considering my proposal?"

Despite being annoyed with Raven, he managed a smile. "One small problem. I'm not in love with you. And I don't believe in business arrangements."

Torey sucked down her drink. "Pity. We could be good together." Her gaze left his momentarily. He heard her sharp intake of breath. "Oh-oh! Here comes trouble. You do a better job of handling that witch than I do. I'd as soon slap her face as look at her." She slid off the barstool and, still facing him, said, "Since you're not big on public spectacles, I'll leave you two alone. See ya." Taking off, she undulated her way through the crowd.

Dawn, whom he'd known since childhood, slid onto the stool Torey vacated.

"Hi, Dawn," Logan said. "What's it to be?"

"Ju-C for me. You know I don't drink."

Logan popped the cap, then slid the bottle across the

bar. He set down a napkin and placed a glass with ice in front of her. "Something on your mind?"

Dawn's liquid chocolate gaze caressed his face. "What happened to your girlfriend?"

Logan propped his elbows on the bar. "Who? Torey? We haven't dated in a while."

"Not that slut. The other one."

"Those are mighty strong words," he said as she took dainty sips of soda.

"Accurate, though. Foreign women are all cut from the same cloth. No morals." She slugged her drink now. "There isn't a man on this island Torey Barnard hasn't been with. And the other one's just the same. I saw her taking the dinghy over to Buddy's yacht. Guess she plans on spending the night."

"What's new with you?" Logan said, refusing to acknowledge the pain in his gut. Despite seeing Raven leave with Buddy, he didn't want to believe that of her. The hatred between Dawn and Torey he understood. He'd dated Dawn a long time ago, until Torey put in an appearance. But Dawn didn't know a thing about Raven—or did she?

"Same old, same old."

"How's the job?"

Dawn shrugged slim shoulders. "Dead end. Boring."

"Why don't you go back to school?" Logan asked, already knowing the answer.

"Who has time? Logan, I don't see why you can't take me back to the States with you."

He decided to play along. "And what would you do there?"

"Take care of you."

He chuckled and hoisted himself atop the bar, peering down at the diminutive beauty who stared at him adoringly. "Dawn, do I look like I need taking care of?"

"You always did."

"That was a long time ago," he said gently, remembering the vulnerable boy he used to be. Different by far from the macho males the island bred. Back then, his artistic soul had needed lots of stroking. And Dawn had risen admirably to the task.

"Big shot or not, you're still an island boy at heart," she reminded him.

"In many ways I am," Logan said evenly, privately thinking, *But you're no longer what I want. I want a woman with drive and ambition. One who loves me madly and one who takes loyalty seriously.*

"So you'll give us a chance."

He had to stop her before things got out of hand, before the tears came, as they had a tendency to. He hopped off the bar and waited for her to finish the Ju-C.

"Dawn, there is no *us*," he said quietly, walking away.

EIGHT

Raven surfaced in time to hear the drone of the dinghy's motor behind her. Inhaling deeply, she kicked out, slicing through the water with powerful strokes. Only a few more yards to shore. She could make it. She knew she could. She just had to concentrate on the twinkling lights.

"Raven," Buddy called over the noise of the dinghy's motor.

He'd be forced to dock the thing at some point. Could she outrun him?

"Raven, I'm sorry. I got carried away. You can't condemn a guy for trying."

She dove under the water, surfacing a few feet from the dinghy, treading water and gulping air. Had he seen her?

Her arms ached and her chest felt constricted. Face it, she was out of shape. Only another few feet to the shallows, or so she hoped.

"Raven, don't be mad. I didn't hurt you. Get in the boat and I'll take you back to shore."

She bit back an angry retort. It was a crazy thing she'd done, jumping overboard, but a necessary one. Buddy's employee hadn't wanted to jeopardize his job and she sure as hell had no intention of staying on his yacht. Minutes later, Buddy had leaped in the dinghy and come in hot pursuit. Now she'd be damned if she'd allow him to catch her.

"Damn you, Raven Adams!"

Logan threw his sketch pad and number two pencil on the floor. Instead of drawing the usual assortment of crooked politicians, tart one-liners emerging from their lips, his strip had taken a maudlin turn. A woman with a single plait dominated each cell; an assortment of broken hearts floated in the space surrounding her.

He hadn't meant for this to happen. Didn't want it to. Yet in a few short days he'd allowed this foreign woman to turn his world upside down and endanger his heart in the process. Suddenly needing air, he headed out. A walk might help put things in perspective.

Logan jogged by cottage number five. It was still blanketed in darkness. He raced by the Tikki Hut, registering the music's increased tempo. The tourists now echoed the lyrics of a lively calypso with more gusto than talent:

"Oh, me bucket have a hole in the center. If you think I telling lie, put your finger . . ."

The song was probably as old as he was. Hands in his pocket, he took the long way into town, strolling along Port Elizabeth's waterfront, past the bookstore, the Gingerbread House, and the Frangipani. Eventually tiring, he took a seat on the overturned hull of a fisherman's boat, crossed his arms, and gulped in the crisp night air.

What had he allowed Raven Adams to do to him? He didn't know what her motives were, but she'd skillfully played him. Toward what end, though? As far as she knew, he had nothing: No ambition. No drive. No money. He should have learned his lesson with Beverly.

The noise of a motorboat pulled him back to reality. He heard the slap-slap of water banging against the dock and watched a dark form emerge from the sea.

"Raven," Buddy Swensen's slightly accented voice called. "Quit being a bitch—answer me."

Logan eavesdropped shamelessly. Was this a lovers' quarrel or had the two gone skinny-dipping together?

"Dammit, Raven. You're trying a man's patience."

A larger silhouette he assumed to be Buddy hopped onto the dimly lit dock and quickly secured his dinghy. A figure waded to shore, blindly trudged in Logan's direction. Something wasn't right. Why had Buddy been in the dinghy and Raven in the sea? Was this some nocturnal frolic or something more serious? He didn't like what he was thinking.

Calling Raven's name, Buddy jogged toward the beach. The figure that Logan assumed was Raven felt her way in the dark, still heading his way, making more noise than she knew. She stopped a foot or two from him and instinctively his arm whipped out, pulling her against him. She screamed.

"Raven, baby. Are you all right?" Buddy yelled.

Logan clamped a hand over her mouth. "Shut up. Unless you want him to find you."

"Thank God it's you," she whispered, hurling herself at him, almost knocking him over. Winding her arms around his neck, she placed him in a choke hold.

"Come with me. I'll get you out of here;" he ordered. "I know a back way."

Half carrying, half dragging Raven, Logan navigated his way under a shady almond tree and led them to the brush.

Several minutes later, they came full stop in front of cottage number five

"I'll see you in," Logan said, placing an arm around the waist of a still-shaking Raven. "You can fill me in on what happened."

She leaned into him as if relishing his strength. "Thanks for caring."

Stepping inside the cottage he flipped on the light. "You must like this perfume," he said, wrinkling his nose, hoping to tease her out of the funk she'd fallen into.

She sniffed the air but remained at the door. "It's not mine."

Logan crossed to open a window. "Then whose is it?"

She didn't seem to hear him. She darted quick, nervous glances around the room.

"Something wrong?" he asked.

She clapped a hand across her mouth. "Someone's been in here."

"Are you sure?"

She pointed to the bed. "I didn't leave my suitcase out. Now it's packed."

Sure enough, her suitcase was perched on one of the chairs, assorted items of clothing pouring from it.

"Don't move," Logan ordered. "I'll check out the rest of the place."

He entered the bathroom, where the fragrance of jasmine seemed to grow stronger, and snapped on the lights. Scanning the room for signs of disorder, he read the lipstick-red message scrawled across the mirror: YANKEE BITCH GO HOME.

Logan returned to the outer room. "Get your things. I'm taking you home with me."

"I need to get out of these wet clothes."

"You can do that at my cottage."

"I'm not your responsibility, Logan."

"I just made you my responsibility," he snapped. He grabbed her elbow and moved her toward the overflowing suitcase. Focusing his anger on the case, he banged it shut. When Raven made a U-turn toward the bathroom, he blocked her path. "What is it you need?"

"Toothpaste. Toiletries."

"I'll get them."

She didn't protest or follow him. Taking the suitcase with him, he gathered the items on her vanity and tossed them in, returning to claim her arm. "Ready?"

"R-r-r-ready." Her teeth chattered so loudly he barely made out her words. He would kill Buddy. Kill whoever was doing this to her. An audible sigh escaped her when he placed his free arm around her waist. "Tell me that bastard didn't hurt you. . . ."

"I handled Buddy."

"You better not be lying to me," he growled, practically pulling her from the room.

"This has got to be someone's idea of a sick joke," Raven heard Logan say. He was in the kitchen, pouring red wine, the cordless phone glued to his ear. "Even so," he told the mystery person on the other end, "security needs to investigate, and quite possibly the police."

The police? Was he serious? She'd never liked the cops. They'd been regulars at the projects where she grew up. Even today, she could still see the look of contempt on their faces as they inquisitioned some poor black man who'd acted out. Sure, she was scared to return to her cottage, but who wouldn't be if they'd found a dead rat in bed? But she hadn't really been in danger. A nosy maid might have gone through her things, broken cosmetics, and helped herself to underwear. As a practical joke, someone had packed her things. Hardly a felony. Calling the cops was overkill.

Tightening the belt on Connie's robe, which had yet to be returned, Raven followed Logan into the kitchen.

"No police," she said, louder than she'd intended.

Ignoring her comment, he handed her a glass of wine. "Yes, that's Raven," he said to the person on the other end. "And no, I'm not letting her out of my sight." Chuckling, he added, "Now you're getting carried away. Better go back to your tea-leaf reading."

"Connie?" Raven asked.

"Yes. She's concerned."

The two were cozy. Odd, given Logan's lowly position. Boss and employee relations must be different on the islands, Raven decided. Picking up his glass of wine, Logan linked his arm through hers, escorting her into the living room. He popped a CD in the player and flopped onto the divan, tugging her down to sit beside him. After smoothing her curls, he outlined the furrows between her brows with his fingers.

In the background, Toni Braxton's sultry, liquid voice wove a spell, creating the illusion of safety. Logan's arms circling her body felt like home.

"Are you going to tell me what happened with Buddy?" Logan asked when the conversation lagged.

"Not much to tell."

"You were running from him. Your clothes were wet."

"He came on to me. I handled it."

"I'll kill him."

Raven heard the venom in his voice. She ran a palm across his clenched jaw, stroking the smooth, taut flesh beneath. "No, you won't. You're not a violent man."

Logan sighed: his warm breath caressed her face. "Why did you leave with Buddy to begin with? The man's a pig."

She tried for mirth but only a high-pitched squeak came out. "Now you tell me."

He drew her closer, nestling her head under his chin. "Do I scare you, Rae?"

"A little," she admitted. "Those were rather torrid kisses we shared earlier."

"Could this be love?"

He felt her startled reaction and tightened his arms so there would be no escape.

"Jeez, you're direct."

"I don't believe in playing games or wasting time."

Her teeth remained on edge as she contemplated his question. In love with him? In love with a handyman? Never in her wildest dreams had she ever entertained the most remote possibility. The thought of falling in love with a poor guy scared her. But what if she had? That was no crime.

Logan McFee was warm, understanding, and caring. Whereas Frank, with both money and position, had been . . . cold, impatient, and at times insensitive to her needs. Given the choice, she'd trade ice for fire. Logan, with his winning ways, had helped restore her faith in the male species. Forced her to feel again. Was that love?

"I'm in love with you," he said, breaking into her thoughts.

His declaration threw her. "You can't be. You barely know me."

"We've known each other a lifetime," Logan said, kissing the top of her head.

He sounded certain. Sure. All she knew was that her limbs turned to mush whenever he was close. Her entire body tingled at his touch. So what if their intellects complemented each other? Their finances didn't.

"I like you a lot," she reluctantly admitted.

"Not good enough for me," he said, drawing circular patterns with his fingertips where the robe opened in a V.

"Oh, Logan," she said, closing her eyes and melting against him.

"Time for bed," he said abruptly. "You've had a long day."

Pushing off the couch, he extended a hand to help her up.

NINE

Raven woke to the sound of loud conversation.

"Pretty girl. Pretty girl."

Sunlight streamed through an open window, warming her face. She stretched and watched the room slowly come into focus. An abandoned easel stood in one corner. Off to the side, an old seaman's trunk held neatly stacked magazines. Her open suitcase lay on the floor, spewing forth clothing.

Memory returned at long last. She'd spent the night at Logan's place. He'd given her his room and she'd sunk onto his comfortable mattress, passing out instantly. She set her feet on polished hardwood floors and crossed to the open window.

"So what am I to do, Sket?" she heard Logan say. He ruffled the macaw's colorful feathers.

"Sket want a cracker. Cracker," the parrot cawed, eyeing the feed in Logan's hand gleefully.

Logan's joyful laughter brought a smile to Raven's face. "You're useless, old girl." He was bare-chested, and the muscles in his back rippled when he hefted the bucket containing the macaw's food. With a swift motion, he opened the bird's cage and poured the seed into a container. Something deep inside Raven stirred; an uncensored reaction to all that male beauty.

Turning away, she almost stepped on a sketch pad littering the floor. Curious to see its contents, she flipped through page after page of artwork. Mostly the comic-book variety, but not at all bad for an amateur. Terrific, actually, and humorous, to boot. In one strip Logan had managed to capture her image perfectly, down to her braid. She didn't even want to consider the significance of those crazy hearts floating around her.

Dismissing the most ridiculous thought, she snapped the sketchbook shut. Logan McFee, an island boy with no formal training, was just extraordinarily talented. He couldn't be—The back door creaked.

"Raven, are you up? I've made coffee," Logan called.

"I'll join you in a minute," she said. "Right after I use the bathroom."

"So what would you like to do today?" Logan asked when Raven was seated at the table across from him, her fingers circling her almost empty coffee cup.

"Don't you have work?" Raven's brown-eyed gaze registered confusion.

Taking a sip of coffee, he shrugged. "Your vacation's almost over. I'll stop by the main office and work something out."

"I'd rather not take you away from your job," she insisted.

"You aren't."

Suddenly feeling the need to touch her, he rose and came around to place his hands on her shoulders. Bending over, he kissed the nape of her neck, nuzzling her braid out of the way. She turned, gazing at him with those huge brandy-colored eyes. He squatted down beside her, capturing her lips, drinking deeply of the honey that he'd tasted yesterday. Pulling her to her feet, he parted her robe, seeking the warmth of her flesh against his palm.

"Logan!"

"Yes, babe?" He kissed the lobe of one delectable ear. She smelled like honey and almonds.

"Make love to me."

He tilted her chin back until he could see her face clearly. "Now, that's an offer I can hardly refuse."

He'd ached with want for her all night, but reminded himself only a total clod would take advantage of her vulnerable state. Now, in the clear light of day, he'd be a fool to say no. Besides, it might be his only chance to show her that she was loved and to see if his feelings were returned. Foreigner or not, what they'd found was special.

Logan led Raven to the bedroom, where he slipped her robe off, letting it pool at her heels. He kissed one honey-brown shoulder. She tugged on the T-shirt he'd put on. "Take that thing off."

He practically ripped the shirt in his haste to get to her. A tiny scrap of lace was the only thing she wore. His palms settled around her copper-color breasts. He pressed his groin against hers and blew into her ear. Her rapid heartbeat told its own story and her soft sigh of acquiescence was a welcome thing. Logan settled against her, ready to put his heart on the line again.

Skettel's voice filtered in: "Pretty girl."

Logan echoed the Macaw's words: "Pretty girl."

Making mewling sounds, Raven nipped at the sides of his neck. Her manicured nails raked his back. At this rate they would never make it to bed. She tugged at the waist of his shorts, fingers slipping under the band to circle his shaft. With a swift kick, he managed to dispense of the garment. He pressed her up against the wall, his mouth replacing his hands, his tongue leaving a damp trail on her skin. Kneeling, he kissed her toes and laved the hollows at her ankles. Her hands entwined in his hair urged him to hurry. He worked his way back up, found her center, and plunged into her, letting her hot, pulsating sweetness fill his mouth.

"God, Logan," he heard her say.

"God, Rae. I can't take much more."

Dispensing of her panties with a yank of his hand, he pressed his flesh against hers, getting off on the sound of their synchronized breathing. He cupped her smooth buttocks, angled her hips, and lifted her off the floor. "Wrap your legs around me."

Eyes never leaving her face, he entered her. He felt her shudder, heard her sigh, and managed, "Stay with me, baby."

Eventually they found their rhythm. He was at an all-time high. Lost in her softness. Lost in her. His strokes were short and calculating, sliding in and out, and in again. He was almost there, at the brink of no return, as close to toppling over the edge as he'd ever been. Raven matched him move for move, so in tune that when the first spasms racked her body, he was ready.

"O-o-h Logan," she screamed.

Rational thought evaded him. He closed his eyes and let go.

Later, after a day of sun, swimming, and water-skiing, Logan tied his boat up at Port Elizabeth's Harbor. To Raven's surprise, he'd told her the small Sea Ray was his. Arm linked around her waist, he guided her through the tiny town, stopping to acknowledge several friendly greetings. While watching the yachts dock, they drank tea and ate buns at the Gingerbread house. There was still no sign of Buddy, thankfully.

It had been a long time since Raven had been this at peace with herself and totally comfortable with a man. She was so relaxed with Logan she let her defenses down, actually giggling. Logan McFee had taught her one thing: You didn't need money to be happy or feel free. While she hadn't yet told him she loved him, she'd planned on doing so before leaving Bequia. Somehow, some way, she'd make what they had work.

"Let's go home," Logan said, pulling her from the chair, his arms lingering around her waist. "I miss you already." He kissed the tip of her ear.

Two days left in paradise. She hated to be reminded her holiday was almost over. "Promise you'll show me how much," she said, pasting on a smile and kissing his cheek.

They stopped at the entrance of the Bougain Villa's main house.

"Shall we see what security's uncovered?" Logan asked, preceding her into the building.

Connie stood in the middle of the lobby conversing with the tiny dark-skinned woman Raven had seen speaking to Logan. A security officer, dressed head to toe in navy, flanked them. The woman's fisted hand punctuated her words, and although Raven couldn't decipher the thick island accent, she sensed the conversation was heated.

"What's going on?" Logan demanded, parking himself in the midst of the fracas.

"Dawn was found entering Raven's cottage," Connie said in a loud voice.

"I didn't break and enter, Mrs. McFee. Buddy asked me to give her this." Dawn opened her fist and released a flimsy black garment Raven recognized as her missing Victoria's Secret panties. Dawn's gloating gaze settled on Logan. Hostility flashed from her eyes when she looked Raven's way.

"Skettel Woman!" Dawn spat. "Bad as the day is born. No cartoonist can compete with Buddy's money. Logan here wasn't good enough."

Could Logan possibly be *the McFee,* the syndicated cartoonist? Was Mrs. McFee his mother? What an idiot she'd been not to have made the association. The eyes alone were a giveaway. She'd read about the National Cartoonist Society awarding McFee the prestigious Reuben award, but hadn't realized he was black.

The underwear settled on the white floor at about the same time Raven's heart did. Mortified, she stared at the woman hurling accusations at her, calling her every cheap name in the book. What must Logan, his manager, and the entire lobby think? Adrenaline finally kicked in when the desk clerk behind her snickered.

It was pointless defending herself. The condemnation in Logan's eyes told her all she needed to know. That and the manager's shocked expression. She'd been tried and found guilty. She'd botched things up badly. Humiliated, she bolted.

Logan debated following, but grabbed Dawn's arms instead. "Be quiet, you stupid cow. Look what you've done." He caught a glimpse of Raven's retreating back. As the security officer moved in, he said, "I've got it under control."

Connie's fingers dug into Logan's shoulders. "Release her. She's not worth getting into trouble for."

"All I wanted was for you to love me," Dawn wailed.

Logan looked at his mother's placid features. "You knew she was the one, didn't you?"

"The tea leaves told me so. That's why I had security follow her."

Dawn sobbed openly now. "Why couldn't you love me instead of that slut?"

His temples pounded. If Raven had slept with Buddy, why had she run away from him the other night?

"She stole that underwear," Connie said, giving the younger woman a stern-eyed look. "Her explanation doesn't make sense. Buddy's quite capable of delivering his own message. He would have used that underwear as an excuse to see Raven."

Logan's ex-girlfriend sniffled, wiping her nose on the back of her hand. "Buddy had other things to do. That's why he sent me instead."

"You came all this way to deliver a pair of panties?" His mother raised a skeptical eyebrow.

Both desk clerks tittered.

"Tell the truth, Dawn. Wasn't this your way of getting back at a woman you considered competition?"

Dawn hung her head but remained silent.

"The game's up." Connie's voice held censure. "I questioned the maid. She's already confessed to lending you the room key on several occasions."

"I didn't know what else to do," Dawn shrieked, pummeling Logan's chest. "I hate this island. I hate my stupid job. You were my only way out. And there you were, paying attention to a tourist and ignoring me."

Logan knew he should feel pity for a woman so desperate to change her life she would do anything. Instead he felt revulsion. What else would Dawn have done had they not stopped her?

"You're on the same level as the vermin you placed in Raven's bed," he said, walking away. "No." He shook his head. "You're worse."

TEN

"I'd like to place a call to the States," Raven sniffled, balling up a T-shirt and stuffing it into her already full suitcase.

"If you'll give me the number, I'll put you through," the cable and wireless operator said in a singsong voice.

Raven leafed through a leather-bound book, finally locating the phone number. What seemed hours later, her travel agent and good friend, Candace, came on the line.

"Hey, Ms. Thang, Frank called looking for you. 'Course I kept my mouth shut."

Raven skipped the preliminaries. "I need my ticket changed."

"Honey, you've got two more days in Eden. Why the sudden change of plans?"

"Something's come up."

Candace's fingers tip-tapped across her keyboard. "Can't do. Looks like you're stuck. LIAT's on strike and every coach seat on Eagle's gone."

Raven's colorful expletive would have made even Sket cringe. She couldn't afford a first-class ticket but couldn't stay at the Bougain Villa one minute longer. No way could she face Logan and the rest of the staff.

"Put me on standby," she said, coming to a decision.

"You got it, girl."

Fingers pinching his nostrils, Logan paced back and forth. "The desk clerk says she checked out, Mother. Packed her stuff. Settled her bill. And left without leaving me a message."

Connie, seemingly unperturbed, stared into her tea leaves. "I take it you went by cottage number five?"

"It's empty."

"And you've checked other hotels on the island?"

"No."

"Then what are you waiting for?" Connie broke away from her musing to reach for the remote phone. "Here," she said, holding the instrument out.

Five phone calls later, Logan hung up in a far worse mood than he'd been in to start. Raven wasn't to be found in any of the better hotels. After a few seconds, he again dialed.

"What can I do for you, luv?" Torey asked, before he could identify himself.

"I'm looking for a guest. Have you seen—"

"The Yank you've been hot for? As I was getting off the ferry this afternoon, she was getting on with all her gear. You two must have had quite a tiff."

Logan didn't bother answering. He simply disconnected the phone.

Tea leaves forgotten, Connie rose to place a comforting hand on his back. "It'll be all right. You'll see."

With Raven gone, nothing felt like it would ever be right again. Logan's palms cupped the sides of his head. Why had he gotten on his damn boat, hunted Buddy down, and forced the truth out of him? And even after that conversation had been had, why had he not turned the boat around and come home? No! He had to take the trip to Mustique, spend the evening at a local bar, drinking himself silly. Even now his head still pounded.

He'd been in no shape to bring the boat back to Bequia last evening. But after he'd sobered up, he'd had time to think. Raven Adams had slept with him without knowing his true identity. She wasn't the opportunist Dawn had made her out to be.

"When was Raven scheduled to check out?" Connie asked, rubbing his back like she used to when he was a little boy.

"Tomorrow."

"Bet you anything she's still on St. Vincent."

In spite of the rock weighing down his heart, Logan forced a smile. "Are those the leaves talking?"

She didn't confirm or deny. "Guests have been complaining nonstop that they're stuck. LIAT's on strike and coach seats on Eagle don't exist."

The rock around his heart shrunk to the size of a stone. "Ma, you're brilliant. There's hope." He hadn't called his mother that since he was, what? Eight. He kissed the top of her head. "Raven could be holed up at a hotel somewhere awaiting her flight." He glanced at his watch. "I've missed the last ferry, dammit!"

"There's always tomorrow. Now, speaking as your boss, you're officially fired." Her heart in her eyes, she smiled at him. "Go pack your things. I hired an assistant manager today, so you're free to head back to the States and that fun job of yours."

"Oh, Ma," Logan managed to utter. When Connie opened her arms, he practically fell into them.

"Standby passenger Adams, please approach the podium," a voice announced over the intercom.

Raven accepted the boarding pass the agent offered and returned to her seat. She tapped her foot impatiently. She wished they'd begin boarding. The longer the delay, the greater the opportunity for the passenger whose seat she'd taken to show up. Yesterday she'd spent the most horrible day sequestered in that hotel room. Now all she wanted was to get on that plane and put this whole business of Logan McFee behind her. When it came to relationships, obviously she didn't have what it took.

Never mind that she'd been wrongfully accused of having a fling with Buddy, she'd been humiliated and mortified in front of Logan. Renowned cartoonist McFee, that is. The man she'd initially treated as if . . . as if he were a lesser being. His bio in the newspaper article announcing his award had mentioned his degree in fine arts from a university in England. It had also stated he'd gone on to attend Cooper Union in New York. That same article had lauded him for two previous awards: the Banshee and the Elvi Seeger, two of the most prestigious citations bestowed on any cartoonist.

Raven thudded a palm against the side of her head. Yikes! What an idiot she'd been. Even if she'd stayed around to patch things up, he probably wouldn't let her forget how poorly she'd treated him. She'd even promised to give him tips to improve his sketches, when he could so easily have taught her.

"Flight 595 is now ready for boarding," the airline employee at the podium finally announced.

"Good-bye, St. Vincent. I'll miss you, Bequia . . . Logan," she mouthed, clamping on her straw hat, and picked up her Gucci tote. Giving a last, wistful glance around the small terminal, she proceeded toward the gate.

After being jostled by several passengers, she eventually found her seat and pressed her aching head into the cushion. The next thing she remembered was being jolted awake by a tap on her shoulder.

Raven opened her eyes to a smiling flight attendant. "Beverage?" the uniform-clad beauty asked.

"Yes, please. Orange juice."

"I've also been asked to give you this." The flight attendant thrust an envelope at her. "It's from one of our first-class passengers."

"Oh?"

Raven waited until the woman moved on before tearing the envelope open. Not knowing what to expect, she unfolded the stationery inside with uncertain fingers. No message. Just a sketch of some sort. A cartoon. Her heart stopped midbeat. It couldn't be.

The setting was a Caribbean one. In the first cell, a woman with a braid faced a machete-wielding man. In the next, the two seemed to resolve whatever issue they had. The third showed the man laying his machete at the woman's feet. *You've got my heart,* were the only words she registered.

Teary-eyed, Raven looked up just as the first-class curtain parted. Logan's golden gaze scanned the compartment, searching her out. She stood, waving, calling his name. They'd captured the attention of all of coach, but who cared? Dressed in a crisp blue shirt, a discreet designer monogram on the pocket, chinos hugging his trim hips, he bounded down the aisle toward her.

"Rae . . ." he said, skidding to a stop, flashing her that chip-toothed grin.

"Logan." Unable to believe he was standing there facing her, she reached out, laying her palm against his cheek.

When he covered her hand with his, she felt as if she would lose it in front of those fifty or so pairs of eyes looking at them.

"Come," he said softly, helping her gather her things. "When I found out you were on this flight, I reserved an extra seat up front next to me."

"But how, why?"

"My mother no longer needs me. I'm heading home to New York . . . to be with you."

"But Logan . . ."

"But Logan, what? I'm in love with you, Rae Adams. Head over heels in love."

"I love you, too."

Dropping her Gucci tote, Logan scooped her into his arms, passionately kissing her in front of the gaping passengers.

Around them, the crowd hooted and cheered, urging him on. A wild outbreak of applause accompanied their sensual kiss. Then, taking her hand, Logan led her toward the first-class compartment and into his life.

FAR FROM HOME

ROCHELLE ALERS

A good wife is her husband's pride and joy; but a wife who brings shame on her husband is like a cancer in his bones.

Proverbs 12:4

ONE

Only your children can hurt you to your heart.

Erika Williams sat at the kitchen table, staring at the cordless phone in her hand, her mother's words coming back to haunt her. And she had to admit that Rosa Lee Hampton was right. Her children had hurt her to her heart.

Her son and daughter waited until two weeks before Christmas to call and tell her that they would not be coming home for their school holiday recess. They had discussed it with each other, then decided they would remain in California with their father, his trophy wife, and their two-year-old half-brother. Chassie admitted, before ending the conversation, that her father planned to host a party where many of the more popular West Coast hip-hop artists were expected to attend.

Erika had muttered, "That's wonderful, princess," before she pressed the button terminating the call. But it was not wonderful. As a banquet manager for a major hotel chain, she had handed in her vacation request as soon as the memo was circulated earlier in the year. However, the hotel manager only reluctantly approved her request for the two weeks off during the most hectic party season of the year. Now, after her efforts to get the opportunity to spend the time with her children, she ended up losing them to the passion of rap and hip-hop performers.

She did not blame her eighteen-year-old daughter or twenty-year-old son as much as she blamed her ex-husband, because she knew Ronald's marriage to a woman half his age was floundering and he was grasping for a modicum of stability by embracing his children from his first marriage.

After twenty years of marriage, Ronald Williams had

waded out into the dangerous waters of infidelity and found himself ensnared in a paternity scandal with a much younger, woman. He moved out of his opulent Upper Saddle River, New Jersey, home after Erika filed for divorce, he flew to Los Angeles to witness the birth of his second son. Then, at the age of fifty, Ronald became a father for the third time. A barely five-foot-one-inch, 102-pound Taneequa Moore became Mrs. Ronald Williams a week after her twenty-first birthday.

Erika had to admit that their little boy was a beautiful child, but she never would have named her son Dackqwan DeAundray Williams. What saved the poor tyke was that everyone referred to him as D.W.

Thinking about Ronald and his subterfuge was not going to alleviate her predicament. She had two weeks to herself and she had no alternative plan. What had been a stinging disappointment was now a slow seething anger. The last time she saw her son and daughter was late August when they boarded their flight to return to Stanford University, and she knew she would not see them again until late May.

"Damn you, Ronald," she whispered between clenched teeth. They had discussed having their children spend Christmas with her, yet he had gone behind her back, bribing them with a showy gathering of popular recording artists so that they would remain in California.

How could she have ever loved him? How had she given him twenty years of her life and really not known the man? She had married up-and-coming record producer Ronald Williams at twenty-five, and a week past her forty-fifth birthday she had officially divorced a man who had fathered her two children, and who had also dishonored their union by sleeping with a young girl whom he claimed tricked him.

Taneequa Moore may have tricked Ronald Williams, but Ronald in turn had tricked Erika Hampton-Williams. But then, he had tricked her for the last time. She would not call her son and daughter to plead with them to change their plans. She had never groveled, and now at forty-seven that wasn't even a thought.

First she would brew a pot of coffee to fortify herself, then formulate an alternate plan how she would spend her hard-won ten-day vacation.

It took two cups of coffee and an advertisement in the newspaper for Erika to solve her dilemma. Her gaze lingered on the seductive headline: WHAT WOULD YOU PREFER UNDER YOUR FEET—SAND OR SNOW?

Picking up the telephone, she pushed a button, listening for the break in the connection. "Good morning, Your Vacation Travel. This is Velma."

"Velma, Erika."

"Hey, girl, what's up?"

She smiled at her college soro's familiar greeting, then sobered quickly. "There's been a change in my holiday plans."

There was moment of silence before Velma's voice came through the wire again. "Why?"

Erika took a deep breath. Her voice was steady, lacking emotion, as she related her telephone call from earlier that morning.

"No, she didn't!" Velma sputtered. "That little strumpet Ronald married should be—"

"Now, Velma, you know I refuse to discuss *her,*" Erika interrupted.

"Sorry, girlfriend. I forgot."

Erika did not openly discuss her children's stepmother. Not with anyone. What she had not done was dwell on her past life with Ronald Williams when all she wanted to do was look ahead and plan for her own future.

"You can spend the holidays with me," Velma offered.

"Thanks, but no thanks. I'm calling you because I want you to book a vacation for me."

"You really want to go away?"

"Yes, I do."

"Where do you want to go, and when do you want to leave?"

Erika's gaze swept over the listing of vacation locations, lingering on one of the U.S. Virgin Islands. "St. Thomas. I'd like to leave on the nineteenth and return on the twenty-sixth."

"Good choice," Velma murmured softly. "That's a Sunday through a Sunday."

Erika circled the dates on the calendar in front of her. "That will give me a week on the island and another week to prepare for the new year."

"What do you have planned for the new year?"

She shrugged, staring at the circled dates. "I don't know yet." What she did not plan to do was sit home alone and watch the festivities on television like she had for the past two years. Even Chassie and Derrick had found several parties to attend while she toasted Dick Clark with a glass of premium champagne before she crawled into bed *alone* several minutes after the new year.

As she shook her head, her gaze narrowed and she mumbled a silent, fervent promise. This coming new year would be different from any other in her life.

"Should I ask if you're traveling alone?" Velma queried.

"The accommodations will be for *one*." The single word was emphatic.

"There's one place I know would be perfect for you," Velma replied, the sound of turning pages crackling through the wire. "It's small, private, and everything is inclusive. I've had customers tell me that it's a hundred times better than Club Med. You'll have your own private bungalow only several hundred feet from the ocean, with all the amenities of a home away from home. It's going to be a little pricey, girlfriend, considering the season and the short notice."

"I don't care what it costs, Velma. Just book it."

"I hear you," Velma replied, laughing softly. "Give me

about an hour and I'll call you back with all of the particulars."

Erika smiled easily for the first time since she'd heard her daughter's voice earlier that morning. "Thanks, Miss V."

"Later, girlfriend."

She ended the telephone call and concentrated on listing what she needed to do and buy before she embarked on her impromptu vacation to the Caribbean.

It was now Wednesday, and she was scheduled to work Thursday, Friday, and Saturday evenings, which meant she only had three days to prepare for her trip. She had to go to the post office and place a stop on her mail, try to squeeze in an appointment at her regular beauty spa for a makeover, and shop for clothes for the tropical climate.

A sense of powerful relief filled her because she knew she had made the right decision not to remain in the States and spend two weeks alone, perhaps wallowing in a morass of self-pity and depression. She had spent the past two decades seeing to everyone else's needs before taking care of her own, but unknowingly the one telephone call had changed her—forever.

"Thank you, my children," she whispered, walking out of the ultramodern kitchen and up a curving staircase to the upper level.

After her divorce was final, she sold the enormous house in Upper Saddle River and purchased a three-bedroom, two-and-a-half bath town house in an upscale New Brunswick, New Jersey, community. She loved her new home, but not enough to spend the next two weeks sleeping late, watching television talk shows, or catching up on viewing the movie videos stacked on a table in her family room.

Calling Velma and booking a vacation to the Caribbean was the best decision she had made since she decided to dissolve her marriage to Ronald Williams.

Erika peered through the window of the aircraft, smiling at the inviting sight coming into view as the jet lost altitude in preparation for a landing at the St. Thomas airport. The slight smile playing at the corners of her lush mouth widened, allowing the passenger sitting beside her a glimpse of her straight white teeth for the first time. The overly friendly chatty man had sought to engage her in conversation from the moment he sat down beside her, but she had smoothly sidestepped his advances when she feigned sleep throughout most of the flight. She'd arrived at Newark Airport two hours before her scheduled departure time, checked in, and lingered over breakfast in one of the terminal's restaurants with the express intent of forgoing the ubiquitous airline cuisine.

Her fellow passenger's sharp gaze had noticed her ringless fingers before he flashed his too-bright porcelain smile, then ensued with a monologue that he was flying to St. Thomas for a month of fun in the sun. Her only comment had been, "That's nice," before she closed her eyes and concentrated on listening to the sound of her own breathing as it slowed until she was relaxed enough to sleep for over an hour.

The aquamarine-blue waters of the Caribbean, encircling the verdant mountainous terrain of the island, beckoned quietly for her to come and swim in its clear, seductive depths. Her smile widened. *I'm coming,* she mused. And she was ready for everything St. Thomas had to offer its native residents and many tourists.

The jet touched down on the runway, and within seconds of the seat belt light going off there was a flurry of rustling excitement as the flight crew and passengers prepared to disembark.

Erika gathered her oversize handbag, following the throng over the tarmac to the baggage claim area. She noticed a short dark-skinned man holding up a placard with her name printed on it in bold black letters.

"I'm Erika Williams," she informed him, offering a friendly smile.

He returned her smile with a bright one of his own. "Welcome to St. Thomas, madam." He extended his right hand. "I am Aldrich Hyatt, and I will be your driver during your stay on our beautiful island. Compliments of your travel agent," he added, inclining his head.

She shook the proffered hand. "Thank you, Mr. Hyatt."

Erika would also have to thank Velma for her thoughtfulness and concern. She knew Velma was apprehensive about her traveling without a companion and had secured the services of a driver to safeguard her well-being while on the island.

"I will get your luggage, madam."

She winced at the word *madam*. It made her sound old and staid. She was forty-seven, middle-aged, but she did not look or feel old. When she discovered that she had lost her husband to a woman half her age, she had taken a close look at herself, questioning what hadn't she done to keep Ronald from straying. But after a dozen sessions in a therapist's office she realized she had not been derelict in her role as wife and mother. What she had been was mother to her children *and* husband, and after twenty years of taking care of Ronald's every need he had finally grown up, deciding it was time for him to take care of someone. And that someone was thirty years his junior.

As she waited patiently for the driver to retrieve her luggage, Erika's confidence level escalated each time an admiring male glance lingered on her. She was pleased with her new hairstyle. It was parted off center and cut so that it framed her perfectly rounded face. Her regular stylist had highlighted her dark brown hair with streaks of gold and auburn, artfully disguising the liberal strands of gray which had come in at a steady rate the year she turned forty. She had to admit the overall effect of her new hairstyle was feminine and quite flattering.

Aldrich Hyatt reclaimed her luggage, led her out of the airport, and helped her into his taxi. Sitting on the backseat in the rear of the spacious old sedan, Erika stared out the window as the driver drove slowly, carefully out of the airport toward Charlotte Amalie. She was charmed by the city's narrow streets and quaint Danish architecture. She lost count of the number of yachts and cruise ships anchored in the large natural bay surrounding the city. She also had not missed the numerous duty-free shops offering everything from fine jewelry, liquors, and cameras to perfumes, silks, and lace.

They arrived at the small private resort near Sapphire Beach and a wide smile curved her lips. Velma had selected the perfect vacation retreat. Mr. Hyatt unloaded her luggage from the trunk of his car while she checked in at the front office. She listened intently as the friendly desk clerk outlined the amenities the resort offered before she handed her a map. The map denoted the location of several restaurants, recreational facilities, and the resort's many gift shops.

Within twenty minutes she was seated in a jitney, along with her bags, and a slender dark-skinned man drove her to her bungalow. The bungalow assigned to her was charming. It was constructed in stucco, painted a pastel pink, and boasted a red-tiled roof; its interiors claimed natural rattan furniture with pink, green, and white floral accessories. The front door opened to a panoramic vista of palm trees and verdant green hills, while the rear offered a view of the beach and the Caribbean from a charming marble-tiled patio.

It was as if she had come to paradise—a place where she could finally heal and discover who Rosa Lee Hampton's firstborn actually was. It would be the first time in her life wherein she would think of herself and only herself. That was a heady feeling.

She checked the telephone, electricity, and running water, finding everything in working order. The one-bedroom structure contained a living/dining area, a small utility kitchen with all of the modern appliances, a full bathroom, and a bedroom with French doors opening out to a copse of palm trees and the beach.

Drawing the pale pink vertical blinds, she kicked off her shoes, then removed the serviceable corduroy slacks and pullover sweater she had selected out of necessity for the twenty-degree New Jersey weather. Hanging up the slacks in a wall-to-wall walk-in closet, she mentally catalogued what she planned to do.

Picking up the telephone on the bedside table, she dialed the extension for one of the restaurants at the resort and made a dinner reservation for one for seven that evening. An hour later, after emptying her luggage, she took a cool shower, set her travel clock alarm for six, then lay across the bed to take a nap.

TWO

Erika sat in the waiting area of the restaurant, taking furtive glances at a tall silver-haired man who looked vaguely familiar. They had been sitting opposite each other for more than half an hour, staring, while waiting to be shown to a table.

Glancing away, she tried placing where she had seen him before. And, given his elegant bearing, she was certain that if she had been introduced to the man, she definitely would not have forgotten his name or his face.

The maître d' returned, a slight frown deepening the grooves in his lined forehead. "I'm sorry, Senator Phillips, but there has been an unfortunate faux pas. The clerk neglected to reserve your table."

Jordan Phillips's mouth tightened noticeably as he stood up. "Are there *any* available?" His light brown, gold-flecked gaze shifted from the formally attired maître d' to the attractive woman who had been waiting for a table longer than he had.

The maître d' nodded. "I have one that seats four."

"Is the lady waiting for someone, Mr. Nelson?" he questioned softly.

Patrick Nelson glanced over at Erika, his dark gaze lingering on her smooth bare shoulders under a gold silk slip dress. "I don't believe she is."

Jordan leaned closer. "Then perhaps we can share the table."

Inclining his head slightly, Patrick smiled. "I will ask her." Turning on his heel, he made his way over to Erika, who rose gracefully to her feet with his approach. "Madam, I would like to propose an offer to you."

A professionally waxed eyebrow shifted delicately. "An offer?"

"There has been a slight mix-up with reservations." He paused, watching Erika's large eyes narrow. "You are dining alone and so is Senator Phillips. But there will not be a table available for either of you for more than an hour."

"But I've been waiting for half an hour," she countered, unable to keep a thread of annoyance out of her voice. She hadn't eaten anything since early that morning and doubted whether she could sustain her energy level after going without food for more than twelve hours.

"I do have one available now, but only if you are willing to accept Senator Phillips's invitation that you share it with him."

Now she knew who he was. He was the U.S. senator from Connecticut. And as one of only three African-American senators, he was a highly visible member of Congress.

A slight smile touched her lush mouth. She had shared a table with heads of movie studios, record company executives, popular athletes, and locally elected officials, but never a member of Congress. Her smile faded. She was hungry—no, starving—and she was willing to share a table with anyone to assuage her appetite.

"Tell Mr. Phillips that Ms. Williams will accept his offer."

Nodding, Patrick let out his breath in an audible sigh. "Thank you, madam."

Jordan watched the interchange between Patrick and the woman who he hoped would agree to share the table, his gaze cataloguing everything about her. She was average height, perhaps five-five or- six, and claimed a body that was firm and slender. Her medium brown skin was clear and flawless, as evidenced by the expanse of bare flesh displayed by the revealing dress.

He liked her hair. It flowed around her face, the blunt-cut ends feathering softly under her delicate jaw and chin. Her eyes were large and round, giving her the look of a startled child. But he knew she had not been a child in a long time. He had estimated she was either in her late thirties or early forties, because when he had stared openly at her she returned his stare with a direct one of her own. He noticed that not only was she secure but also quite comfortable with her femininity.

And she was very feminine. Her well-groomed hands and feet, and the choice of dress which flattered her body, piqued his interest in a woman for the first time in more than five years. It was as if, when he'd buried Lynette, his wife of twenty-three years, all of his interest in women had died with her.

Patrick's smile gave him his answer. "Ms. Williams has agreed to share your table."

"Thank you, Patrick."

Jordan took a half dozen steps, bringing him to Erika's side. He extended a large hand. "Jordan Phillips."

Smiling up at him, Erika took the proffered hand. "Erika Williams."

Still holding her smaller, slender hand, Jordan placed it in the curve of his elbow. "I'd like to thank you for sharing my table this evening."

Feeling the solid muscle of his forearm under the sleeve of his cream-colored jacket and inhaling the sensual fragrance of his masculine cologne, she nodded. "I'd like to thank you for asking."

Jordan shifted a pair of still-dark eyebrows, then flashed a slow smile. "Please, Miss Williams. The pleasure is all mine."

"Erika," she chided him softly.

"If it's Erika, then you must call me Jordan."

Patrick bowed slightly from the waist. "Please follow me." He quietly directed a passing busboy to remove two chairs from the table in the corner near a large potted palm plant.

Jordan waited for Erika to precede him into the restaurant, then followed her as Patrick led the way to their table. His gaze was fixed on the velvety skin on her back and the haunting vanilla-based fragrance clinging to her bare flesh. Everything about Erika Williams was stunningly mesmerizing—from her stylishly coiffed hair to her lightly made-up face, flattering dress, and beautifully modulated voice. She was perfect, and he wondered why she was in St. Thomas dining alone.

Patrick moved to pull out a chair for Erika, but was usurped when Jordan stepped in front of him. He seated her, lingering over her head. A rush of desire shot through his body, bringing with it an unexpected heaviness in his groin when he stared down at the soft swell of breasts rising above the gold silk.

Gasping audibly, he bit down hard on his lower lip, hoping Erika was not aware of her effect on him. He wasn't impotent, but at fifty-three his sex drive had decreased appreciably. There were extended periods of time when he realized he could survive emotionally and physically without sleeping with a woman. And there had only been two women since he had become a widower. Both times the women were available and quite willing to share his bed.

Don't lose it, Phillips, he warned himself. What was wrong with him? He had picked up a woman in a restaurant and within minutes his body had betrayed him when he thought about her not only sharing his table, but also his bed.

Rounding the table, Jordan sat down, his golden gaze fixed on Erika's bowed head as she studied the menu. The strands of her straightened hair fell over one eye, and he laced his fingers together to stop them from reaching out and tucking them behind her ear. He smiled when she did reach up and tuck the streaked strands behind her left ear. The flickering light from the small oil candle caught the brilliance of a large diamond stud in her pierced lobe. He had attended enough parties in Washington, D.C., to assess the quality and worth of jewelry with a single glance. And the diamonds in Erika Williams's lobes rivaled any he had seen gracing the ears of women whose wealthy husbands headed large corporations or were visiting foreign dignitaries.

"Do you drink champagne?" he asked, his sonorous voice breaking the comfortable silence.

Her head came up slowly, her gaze fixed on his firm mouth. Erika preferred studying the menu rather than the man sitting across from her in this restaurant that resembled an indoor rain forest with a profusion of potted palms and blooming orchids.

But she found Jordan Phillips attractive, too attractive for her to ignore. He was tall, at least an inch or two above the six-foot mark. She wasn't aware of the breadth of his shoulders until he sat down. But it was his golden brown face that fascinated her. It was angular, almost raw-boned, with high, arrogant cheekbones. Laugh lines fanned out at the corners of a pair of slanting eyes that were a clear light brown with brilliant flecks of gold. He had elected to cut his silver hair close to the scalp to camouflage the thinning spot at the top of his head.

Everything that was Senator Jordan Phillips screamed intelligence, elegance, and breeding. And she kept up with enough current events to know that his wife had died shortly after he was elected to his second term in Congress.

"Yes, I do," she replied, her voice low and very controlled.

Jordan smiled, his slanting eyes crinkling attractively. "Good. Then I'll order a bottle and a platter of hors d'oeuvres."

"What are *you* celebrating?"

He sobered quickly, his expression becoming impassive. He wanted to say their meeting each other, his interest in her, and the revival of a desire he thought he had buried with Lynette.

"A beautiful night in St. Thomas," he said smoothly.

"That it is," Erika agreed.

"Where are you from and when did you arrive?"

"I arrived this morning from New Jersey."

"You don't sound like New Jersey."

"What do I sound like?"

Jordan visually traced the shape of her full, lush mouth outlined in a vermilion red. Leaning back on his chair, he closed his eyes and crossed his arms over his chest. "Say something else."

Erika laughed lightly. "What do you want me to say?"

"Tell me a little about yourself," he urged, still not opening his eyes.

She decided to play along with him. "There's not much to tell. I was born, raised, and educated in New Jersey. I'm also divorced."

Jordan opened his eyes. "Any children?"

"Two."

"You left them with their father?"

A slight frown appeared between her eyes. "They decided to spend Christmas with their father and his wife."

It was Jordan's turn to frown. "*They* decided? I thought you would've worked out a holiday visitation agreement prior to your divorce."

"That wasn't necessary. My son is twenty and my daughter is eighteen."

"Your children are *that* old?"

Erika bristled at his tone. "They're not old," she replied defensively.

"How old were you when you had them?"

She went suddenly still, realizing he thought she was younger than she actually was. "I was not a teenage mother." She was twenty-seven and twenty-nine, respectively, when she gave birth to her son and daughter. "I'm forty-seven."

Jordan's golden gaze lingered on her face, then moved slowly down to her chest before reversing itself. "I don't believe it. You're gorgeous!"

Lowering her gaze in a demure gesture, Erika could not

stop the heat suffusing her face and chest. "Thank you, Jordan."

Leaning forward, he placed his hands over hers. "Say it again."

Her head came up and she gave him a direct stare. "Isn't one thank-you enough?"

He shook his head. "Say my name."

Her delicate jaw dropped slightly. "Jordan?"

His fingers tightened slightly over hers before he pulled away. "Yes. I've never had anyone say my name the way you do. You make it sound very French."

She repeated his name to herself several times, realizing that she did put more emphasis on the second syllable. "You have the perfect name for a politician."

"I don't think that's what my parents had in mind when they named me. My father wanted me to follow in his footsteps and become a doctor."

Now it was Erika's turn for her interest to be piqued. "Your father is a doctor?"

"Was. Both my parents are deceased."

"I'm sorry, Jordan."

He shook his head. "Don't be. Both my parents lived until they were well into their eighties. And I must admit they shared a wonderful life together. My father was the only black doctor who had a private practice in a suburb of Hartford for many years. My mother was his nurse."

Resting her elbow on the table, she supported her chin in the heel of her hand. "What made you decide to go into politics?"

"The civil rights movement. I came of age during the sit-ins, boycotts, and marches. I graduated law school and secured a position with a Connecticut law firm that specialized in cases involving civil rights violations."

"What made you decide to run for public office?"

He wanted to tell her that it was Lynette's father who urged him to enter the political arena, but decided not to. He did not want to spend his time discussing his late wife with Erika. He had had a lot of time to prepare for Lynette's death. They'd been married for thirteen years when she was first diagnosed with the terminal illness which finally claimed her life at forty-five. His life with Lynette Collins-Phillips had been filled with love and an interminable suffering which ended with him holding her in his arms when she drew her last breath.

"I was approached by a group of men who decided I would make an ideal candidate. I had managed to exist without the taint of scandals or infidelity hovering in my background, and the fact that I am African-American was a plus."

"Didn't you win by a landslide victory?"

He nodded. "It was substantial."

"Don't be so humble, Jordan," she chided with a wide grin. "You put a serious hurtin' on that man."

"I suppose you're right. It was the press that reported that took him more than a week to concede."

"Was the report of him being on a suicide watch credible?"

Jordan motioned for the waiter standing several feet away. "Now, Erika, do you want me to repeat gossip?"

"No. Just the truth."

He gave her a long, penetrating look at the same time vertical lines appeared between his eyes. "It's true."

Picking up her menu, she laughed softly as tears filled her eyes. She heard Jordan order a bottle of champagne along with a platter of appetizers. She put down the menu and opened her purse to withdraw several tissues to blot her moist cheeks.

"You're a cruel, heartless woman, Erika Williams," Jordan remarked, shaking his head. "The poor man was depressed."

"The poor *old* man was not depressed, but humiliated that a brilliant, younger, virtually unknown opponent had hastened his retirement. How old was he when you defeated him?"

"Eighty-two."

"Much too old to waste taxpayer dollars by napping during proceedings or missing roll call."

"You're right about that. Have you thought of a career in politics?"

"Never. The closest I come to politics is voting regularly."

"At least you do that."

The arrival of their waiter preempted further conversation as he opened a bottle of chilled Taittinger Comtes De Champagne, filling two flutes with the pale, sparkling wine. Another waiter followed with a platter of appetizers.

"Are you ready to order, Senator Phillips?"

Jordan looked at Erika and she nodded. She scanned the numerous selections on the menu. Tilting her chin, she smiled across the table at Jordan. "Why don't you order for both of us?"

"Is there anything you're allergic to?"

"No."

He ordered without glancing at the printed menu. His choices included several seafood entrées, with a variety of vegetables indigenous to the region.

Erika noticed all the restaurant personnel were familiar with Jordan, and he with them. "How often do you come here?"

His long fingers played with the stem of his flute, his gaze fixed on the bubbling liquid. "I've come here for the past five years. I fly down after Thanksgiving and go back to Connecticut for the new year." His gaze moved up, meeting her questioning one. "And you?"

"This is my first trip."

I hope it won't be your last, he mused. Raising his glass, he waited for her to raise hers. "Thank you for allowing me the honor of sharing your lovely presence."

She hesitated, wanting to make her own toast, but decided against it. "You're quite welcome," she said instead, then took a sip of the premium wine.

Jordan and Erika spent the next ninety minutes dining, talking, and drinking champagne. She could not remember the last time she enjoyed talking to a man. He hadn't mentioned his wife except to say that he was a widower. He related stories about growing up with his three brothers, admitting that the levels of testosterone reached explosive proportions because they were so competitive. His oldest brother had retired from the Army as a two-star general, while another brother taught constitutional law at Yale Law School. His youngest brother had gone into partnership with another restaurateur and together opened one of the more popular dining establishments in the D.C. area.

The mention of restaurants ignited a spark of excitement within her. "I want to gain another five years as a restaurant banquet manager before I go into business for myself."

Jordan dabbed the corner of his mouth with a linen napkin. "What kind of business are you interested in?"

"I want to open a small bed and breakfast."

He gave her a wide smile. "Where?"

"It doesn't matter."

"You would relocate from New Jersey?"

"Sure."

"What about your children?"

Erika went still. "What about them?"

"You would leave them?"

Leaning forward, she stared Jordan down. "I did not leave them. They left me. They've elected to go to college three thousand miles away, and even though I did not want them to leave the East, the final decision was theirs. I've been a good mother and I love my children with all of my heart. But what I've had to realize is that I can't hold on to them because I don't want to be left alone."

"Does it bother you to be alone?"

Easing back against the cushioned seat of the chair, she stared over his broad shoulder. "At one time it did."

"And now?"

A small smile played at the corners of her mouth. "Now it doesn't bother me."

Biting down on his lower lip, Jordan nodded slowly. "Good for you." He placed his napkin beside his plate and let out his breath. "I don't know about you, but I'm either going to have to walk or dance off this food before I turn in for the night. What would be your choice?"

Erika gave him a dazzling smile. She had enjoyed his company so much that she did not want the night to end—not yet. "I'd say that dancing would be more fun."

Rising to his feet, he pushed back his chair and extended a hand. "I hope you're not a princess like Cinderella who will disappear on me when the clock strikes midnight," he teased.

Taking his hand, she allowed him to pull her gently to her feet. "I don't know. Perhaps we should tempt fate and find out."

Jordan had spent nearly two hours in Erika Williams's presence and concluded he liked her. Liked her a lot. She was open and direct as well as intelligent and beautiful. And he was willing to tempt fate and see her again.

Jordan danced with Erika under a star-littered St. Thomas sky, reveling in the warm ocean breeze washing over them. They had gone to one of the three nightclubs in the resort catering to a couples-only program. One club was set up for an adolescent crowd, another for seniors who favored big-band music and ballads made popular during the Second World War, and the third for those who favored disco music.

Erika hadn't realized how much she missed having a man's arms around her as they moved in unison to the music of a love ballad. She missed feeling the unyielding power in a broad chest against her breasts. And she missed the natural scent of a male body mingling with the fragrance of a sensual masculine cologne.

Curving her arms around Jordan's waist inside his

jacket, she pressed her cheek to his shoulder. Her marriage to Ronald hadn't ended when he confessed to getting another woman pregnant, but years before that. It had ended when his business trips became more frequent, and when they stopped taking vacations together. It ended once their lovemaking tapered off to one or two times each month. And it all ended once the all-consuming desire she had had for her husband died completely. There had been a time before and during her marriage to Ronald Williams that she could not keep her hands off him. Her libido had been so strong that early in their relationship they spent entire weekends in bed together.

She had rationalized that she was older and premenopausal, and therefore the decrease in estrogen had affected her sex drive. She had blamed herself for everything, but after finding herself in Jordan Phillips's arms she knew she had been wrong.

The moment Jordan pulled her to his body, her breasts reacted swiftly. And she was certain he felt the hardening of her nipples against the fabric of his crisp shirt because his breathing had quickened and his hold on her waist tightened. Their bodies were fused from chest to thighs, an invisible bond drawing them together.

I don't believe it, the voice in her head screamed silently. *I want him!*

Jordan's hot breath swept over her ear. "I've just discovered something."

"What's that?" she mumbled against his hard chest.

"It's after midnight and you're still in my arms."

Pulling back, Erika smiled up at him. "That should prove that I'm not a princess."

Jordan returned her smile, his gaze lingering on the shape of her sexy mouth. "Yes, it does, Erika Williams. It proves you're a queen." He stopped dancing, ignoring the other couples moving around them. Closing her eyes and shaking her head, Erika whispered his name.

"Yes!" he hissed, countering her hushed entreaty. The

single word, though spoken softly, sliced through the music coming from massive speakers set up around the space. He released her body to cradle her face between his large hands. "I don't know what it is about you, but I find myself wanting to do things with you that I have not thought about in years. I fell in love with Lynette from the first time I saw her. I was eight and she was six. We grew up together and married. And once I married her, I was never unfaithful to her. I wanted children, but she couldn't have any. Then she got sick and I remained faithful to her until the very end."

Erika's breasts rose and fell heavily as her uneasiness spiraled. "What is it you want me to say, Jordan? Should I be flattered that you want me?"

"No. It has nothing to do with flattery."

Erika pulled away from him and walked off the dance floor. He caught up with her, his arm going around her waist. "Then you are quite an exceptional man, because I gave Ronald the children he wanted, while never denying him my body, and still he was unfaithful."

"Then he was a fool."

Erika wanted to tell Jordan that even though she was forty-seven she was a novice when it came to having affairs. She had given Ronald Williams her virginity, and he had been the only man she had ever slept with.

Her shoulders slumped in resignation. "What is it you want from me, Jordan?"

"I want to get to know you."

"Know me how?"

"In every way possible," he replied.

"That's not possible."

"Why, Erika?"

"Because I'll only be here for a week. I'm scheduled to leave the day after Christmas."

He smiled, pulling her closer to his side. "A week is more than enough time."

Shifting slightly, she stared up at him in surprise. "You're kidding me, aren't you?"

He shook his head slowly. "No, I'm not. We're not kids. We'll know within days whether what we're beginning to feel for each other is the real thing."

He'd said *we*. He knew she wanted him. "And if it's not?"

"If it's not, then it should be easy for us to turn and walk away."

She let out her breath slowly. He was making it easy for her—for them. Could she afford to take the risk and give in to her emotions? Could she have a week-long affair with a prominent politician, then go back to the States and pick up the pieces of her life as if she had never met or known Jordan Phillips?

She realized they were two lonely people whose first loves were lost to them—forever. Could she afford to take a chance to find love again?

Why not?

What did she have to lose?

After all, she was far from home.

Nodding, she said, "You're right, Jordan. We're not kids."

Hand in hand, he walked her back to her bungalow and waited for her to open the door. "Have you made plans for tomorrow?"

"No." She hadn't made any definite plans.

"What if I pick you up around ten? We'll share brunch, then go for a tour of the island."

Flashing a tired smile, she conceded. "I'd like that very much."

Lowering his head, Jordan brushed a gentle kiss across her cheek. "Sleep well," he crooned.

"You, too."

She watched him as he walked in the opposite direction, his hands thrust in the pockets of his suit trousers. The glow of the overhead streetlights positioned along the path created a halo around his silver hair as he stopped suddenly and stared back at her.

Heat suffused her face as she raised her hand and waved. She wasn't disappointed when he returned her wave. Her teeth flashed whitely against her brown face when she smiled. Stepping back into the bungalow, Erika closed the door.

Kicking off her sandals, she flicked the wall switch, flooding the living room with light from a table lamp. She hummed to herself as she made her way to the bedroom and flopped back on the firm bed.

"I like him," she whispered softly. Then, in a louder voice, she said firmly, "I like you, Jordan Phillips."

THREE

Erika awoke at dawn to the sound of rain pelting the glass of the French doors. The comforting sound lulled her back to sleep, but it was the chiming of the telephone that woke her hours later.

Groping for the receiver, she picked it up. "Hello."

"Good morning."

She sat up quickly at the sound Jordan's voice, staring at her travel clock. It was nine forty-five. There was no way she could ready herself in fifteen minutes.

"Jordan," she moaned softly. "I'm still in bed."

His deep laugh came through the wire. "You're not the only one who overslept this morning."

"Is it still raining?"

"It stopped a little while ago. Is our date still on?"

"Of course." She ran a hand through her mussed hair, pushing it off her forehead. "Pick me up in half an hour." She hung up, slipped out of the bed, and headed for the bathroom.

Erika opened her door and found a Jordan Phillips who looked nothing like the man she had shared dinner with the night before. Instead of a tailored suit, silk tie, and imported loafers, he had selected a pair of laundered khakis, a white T-shirt, and a pair of running shoes. His silver hair was concealed under a tan baseball cap, and his golden eyes by a pair of sunglasses. She did not know which Jordan she preferred—the sophisticated politician or the laid-back vacationer.

Jordan's gaze devoured Erika behind the dark lenses. Seeing her in the full sunlight was a visual feast. The flawlessness of her face overwhelmed him. It was clear, smooth, and gave no indication of aging. And he noticed, for the first time, that her eyes were not as dark as he originally thought. They were a warm cinnamon-brown, ringed by thick black lashes.

His smile widened. "You look very nice."

"Thank you." She did not know why, but she felt like a young girl on her first date. She had not been single in so long that she had almost forgotten courtship protocol, unlike many divorced or separated women who jumped back into the dating game with the express intention of securing another husband.

But she had to admit that she had taken extra care with her appearance in preparing for her outing with Jordan. She had selected a tangerine-orange A-line dress with a squared neckline and capped sleeves. The softly flowing lightweight fabric skimmed the curves of her body, ending several inches above her ankles. The stylish natural straw cloche covering her hair was an exact match for her leather sandals. She had decided to forgo makeup and had applied a light cover of moisturizer to her bare face along with a coat of shimmering lip gloss. Closing the door, she slipped the magnetic key into her woven purse.

Jordan took her hand, holding it protectively as they strolled leisurely in the direction of the restaurants. He glanced down at her enchanting profile under the hat. "How hungry are you?"

"Not very. But I could use a cup of coffee."

"We'll have just enough time to stop for coffee," he stated mysteriously.

Erika stopped suddenly, forcing him to stop. "Where are we going?"

"I thought we'd take a hop over to San Juan."

Her mouth opened, closed, then opened again before she managed to say, "San Juan? I thought you wanted to take a tour of St. Thomas."

"We'll have plenty of time to tour St. Thomas. Don't you want to see San Juan, St. Croix, and St. John?"

"No. I mean, yes. What I mean is that I hadn't planned to go island hopping."

He studied her intently for a moment. "What had you planned?"

"I'd planned to shop, snorkel, and lie on the beach."

Jordan did not want to pressure her, but he wanted her to share his enthusiasm when they toured historic Old San Juan, the ruins and restored plantations and sugar mills on St. Croix, and the U.S. National Park on St. John.

"I just thought I'd offer."

Erika sensed his disquiet and registered the disappointment in his statement. "How do you intend to do all of this island hopping in only seven days? I'll go with you, but don't forget I'm leaving in less than a week."

A slow smile softened his features. "Thank you, Erika," he whispered reverently. He pulled her against his body, his head came down, and he moved his mouth over hers in soft, gentle joining that left her trembling with desire. Both were breathing heavily when she pushed gently against his chest.

She managed a tremulous smile. "You're quite welcome."

Jordan glanced down at his watch. "Let's go if you want coffee. We don't want to miss our driver, who will take us to the airport."

"Do you drink coffee?"

He shook his head. "Never touch the stuff. I prefer tea. Especially afternoon tea."

"What is it you like about it?"

"I think it's the ritual."

"When you're back in the States and passing through New Brunswick, why don't you stop by and we'll share afternoon tea?"

He gave her a sidelong glance. "Is that a invitation, Ms. Williams?"

"It's an open invitation, Senator Phillips."

"Don't be surprised if I show up on your doorstep one of these days."

"I'm going to hold you to that promise, Jordan."

"And I won't disappoint you."

Erika found the thirty-minute flight on a commuter plane a harrowing experience, while Jordan did not seem to mind the dip and sway of the small aircraft. She had sat beside him, gripping his hand so tightly that the imprints of her fingernails were clearly visible on the palm of his hand.

"We'll make the return trip by boat," Jordan promised, curving an arm around her waist and leading her across the tarmac.

Leaning heavily against his side, she nodded. She did not trust herself to open her mouth to speak because she feared embarrassing herself as she swallowed back a wave of nausea. She shuddered to think what would have happened if she had actually eaten breakfast.

They stopped to eat a late breakfast of scrambled eggs with onions and peppers, broiled chorizo, and hot buttered slices of cocoa bread with several cups of steaming hot tea, then headed for Viejo San Juan.

Erika felt as if she had stepped back into the sixteenth century when she strolled along the narrow cobblestone streets of the National Historic Zone. Withdrawing a small compact camera from her purse, she snapped frame after frame of thick-walled colonial-style municipal buildings and other structures housing shops offering pieces of art, local crafts, exquisite jewelry, and hand-rolled cigars.

She lingered outside one shop that featured a showcase window filled with a display of religious jewelry. "Do you see something you want?" Jordan questioned close to her ear.

"Yes. It would be perfect for my brother."

"Brother? I don't know why, but for an odd reason I thought you were an only child."

Looping her arm through his, she pulled him into the shop. "Don't let Father Dennis hear you say that." He stared at her, baffled. "Even though we were raised Methodist, my brother is a Roman Catholic priest," she explained, offering him a saucy smile.

Jordan waited patiently while Erika selected a pair of rosary beads made of sterling silver with a yellow gold crucifix. Watching her made him realize there was no way he could get to know her in a week; even if he lived with her for the next twenty-five years, she would remain a mystery. She was so different from Lynette, who had been as easy to read as an open book. He knew he had surprised Erika when he suggested going island hopping and counted himself lucky that she had accepted, while Lynette usually agreed to anything he suggested.

It had taken hours after he had gone to bed to fall asleep because he had not been able to erase the image of Erika's hauntingly beautiful face and sultry voice from his mind, questioning how a man could be unfaithful to her. Her ex-husband had to be a certified fool to permit any woman to come between them.

Erika paid for her purchase, tucking the small package into the bottom of her purse. Jordan opened the door for her and grasped her hand once they were out on the sidewalk.

"Why did your brother decided on the priesthood?"

An expression of sadness settled into her features. "It was either the priesthood or the morgue."

He went completely still, staring at the pain in her eyes; pain she could not conceal. "You don't have to talk about it if you don't want to."

Taking a deep breath, she shook her head. "It's all right. I've learned to deal with it. My father was a cop, and my brother saw him murdered in a robbery gone bad," she began slowly. "Whenever my dad had weekends off in the summer, he made it a practice to drive across the George Washington Bridge and take Dennis to a baseball game at Yankee Stadium. On the way back from the Bronx after a Saturday night game, they stopped in Paterson to pick up milk and eggs for Sunday breakfast. They walked into a little grocery store where a couple of teenage boys were waving guns at the owner, ordering him to empty the cash register. The man must have hesitated and bullets started flying. My father drew his service revolver, not knowing there was a third robber standing lookout. He shot Daddy in the head and he died instantly.

"Dennis had just turned thirteen, and he couldn't handle his anger and pain. Over the next three years he got into every kind of trouble imaginable. He cut classes, defaced property with graffiti, and once broke the windshields of every car on our block. It went on and on."

"Didn't the police arrest him?"

She shook her head. "No. He was the son of a hero cop who had been killed upholding the law. My mother was assistant principal at the high school, so even there he was protected. It used to rip my heart out to see her face whenever one of the officers from the local precinct escorted Dennis home after he'd been picked up for some infraction of the law.

"Two days before I was scheduled to leave to go to college, I confronted him. I had mixed feelings about living on campus and leaving him alone with my mother. I tried telling Dennis how much he was hurting not only himself, but Mama. He looked at me, then spewed out the foulest language I had ever heard. I went temporarily insane, and I picked up everything I could get my hands on and threw it at him. The next thing I knew, my mother was pulling me off my brother. He had just sat there and let me hit him. Blood gushed from his nose where I had broken it.

"He left home that afternoon, snuck into the Catholic church, and spent the night on one of the pews. The pastor found him the next morning. I don't know what Father Gallagher said to him, but Dennis came home and apologized. He went back to school, graduated with high honors, and entered the seminary. He's now the priest at the same parish where he once sought sanctuary."

Her voice faded away and seconds later she found herself in Jordan's arms, her face pressed to his shoulder, as he pulled her close and permitted her to feed on his strength. "I'm not proud of what I did," she mumbled against his chest. "If my mother hadn't come into the room when she did, I'm certain I would've killed my brother."

"But you didn't. You did what you had to do, and thankfully it worked."

"I wanted to kill him." Her voice broke with emotion.

"That's understandable, given the circumstances. But he was spared so that he could become a saver of souls."

Pulling back, Erika stared up at Jordan as a look of incredulity filled her gaze. "That's what he says."

"He sounds like a very wise man."

"He is a wonderful man," she confirmed.

Tilting his head, Jordan stared down at the glint of moisture filling her large round eyes. "How did you feel about your father's death?"

"I hated him for a long time for risking his life for a few dollars. I just could not understand his heroic Rambo tactics until I had to face the realization that Daddy was a cop; he was always on the job, and there was no way he was going to stand by and let those kids shoot that frightened old man without taking some action. It took a while, but I forgave him for abandoning us."

Lowering his head, Jordan brushed his mouth over hers. Erika savored the kiss, the feel of his lips warm and sweet on hers. She did not know what it was about Jordan Phillips that prompted her to tell him about her brother. When Ronald met Dennis for the first time, he did not question his brother-in-law's vocation.

And it was only now that she realized Ronald had never been interested in anyone else but himself. He coveted his wife and children as possessions the same way he prided himself on the assessed value of his home, luxury cars, and designer clothes. They had become extensions of his personal and professional success.

She had not known Jordan for twenty-four hours, yet interacting with him helped her to see what she had not been able to acknowledge for twenty years.

"Thanks for your ear and your shoulder," she whispered against his parted lips.

His lids lowered over his golden eyes, concealing his innermost feelings from her. "Why don't you thank me again?" he teased.

She noticed a man watching them intently, a smile curving his mouth, and she eased out of Jordan's embrace. "Not here." The rising heat in her cheeks had nothing to do with the rays of the hot Puerto Rican sun.

Laughing softly, he curved an arm around her hip. "What else do you want to see?"

"I want to see what some of the art galleries are offering." They had planned to visit the historic fort, El Morro, before returning to St. Thomas later that evening.

"Thinking of picking up a few pieces?"

"Maybe, Senator Phillips."

Jordan sat opposite Erika on the fast-moving tender, watching the wind whip her hair around her face. She had removed the straw hat and turned her face into the spray of rising waters as the boat sliced a path through the clear blue of the Caribbean.

They had spent more than six hours touring Puerto Rico's capital district, and when they finally boarded the boat for their return trip to St. Thomas, both were exhausted. But he had to admit to himself that it was a comforting tiredness. He had managed to spend most of the day with a woman who unknowingly had offered him peace—a peace he had never experienced before. With Erika he was able to relax completely; he did not think about returning to Washington, D.C., and the upcoming session of Congress. And it was in Washington that he felt most lonely.

It was a social city. Not a week went by when he did not receive an invitation to a dinner party, concert, or a fund-raising event. And then there were the invitations from the White House to attend a reception dinner for a foreign dignitary. These were the soirees when he was expected to attend with a date and he usually asked one of two women to accompany him; both were aware of his reluctance to establish a more permanent association, and had come to the realization that an invitation would never read, *Senator and Mrs. Jordan Wayne Phillips.*

He did not know what it was about Erika Williams that was different; what was it that made him want to spend every second, minute, and hour with her? There was no doubt that she was a beautiful woman, but it went beyond physical attractiveness. Closing his eyes, he tried sorting out the emotions she elicited in him.

He had felt her pain when she told of her ex-husband's infidelity and her childrens' decision to attend college on the West Coast, and he also felt her vulnerability when she told of her father's brutal, untimely death and her brother's behavior, which had caused a rift in her family.

She had endured a lot pain in forty-seven years. Pain most people did not encounter during their entire lifetime. Opening his eyes, Jordan continue to stare at the woman who had unknowingly crept under the barrier he had erected to keep the opposite sex from penetrating. He had married a woman he had loved all of his life and he did not want another woman to supplant the memory. He had married for life—in sickness and in health. But Lynette died, leaving him alone to grieve for the loss of her companionship. He stiffened, his pulse accelerating. Now he knew what it was that drew him to Erika Williams.

Companionship!

He wanted and needed her to share not his bed, but his life. He wanted her to accompany him when he attended the glittering D.C. parties; he wanted her to share vacations with him; he wanted to lie beside her at night and talk before they closed their eyes to fall asleep. He wanted and needed to spend whatever time he had left on the planet with her as his partner, and in turn he would love her and protect her until his last breath.

He had less than a week to court her and win her trust. An implacable look of determination fired his sunlit eyes at the same time a smile parted his firm lips. Erika returned his smile and he moved over to sit beside her. He was not disappointed when she slipped her hand in his, her fingers squeezing gently.

FOUR

Erika stood in the middle of her living room, staring up at Jordan staring back at her. She had known him for only twenty-four hours, yet she knew she was not the same woman she had been before he'd offered to share a table with her.

She liked him—that she could not deny. But then, what was it about him not to like? Physically he was perfect: tall, dark, handsome, and elegant. He revealed he played tennis two or three times a week at a D.C. sports club to control his weight. And she was surprised when he disclosed that he tipped the scales at one hundred eighty-five pounds. Despite being six-one, he appeared to weigh much less.

She'd found him gentle, his manners impeccable, and for a fleeting moment she wondered how her life would have been if she had married Jordan Phillips instead of Ronald Williams. She dismissed the thought as soon as it entered her head because of her son and daughter. She would have married Ronald ten times if only to have Derrick and Chassie. She loved them with all her heart, and they had become a great source of joy in her life, in spite of their recent defection.

She knew Jordan was interested in her—that he had openly admitted. And she was aware that he wanted more than a partner to share meals or outings when he went island hopping. He wanted a physical liaison, and so did she. Each time he touched her, she thought she would dissolve in a spasm of uncontrollable ecstasy where she would beg him to take her to bed and reignite the passion that died before her marriage ended.

She did not want to seduce Jordan, but she was willing to let go of her iron-willed self-control that had kept every man who had expressed an interest in her at a distance since she had rejoined the ranks of women who were deemed single.

"I would like to have dinner here," she said softly.

Jordan arched a sculpted black eyebrow. "Here?"

She smiled. "We can order room service and have a picnic on the patio under the stars. I've had my fill of crowds for one day."

And she had. By early afternoon the streets of Old San Juan were teeming with tourists jostling for space along the narrow streets and in the many shops and galleries. Even the restaurants were filled to capacity once they decided to stop for a late lunch. After a lengthy wait at one of the popular upscale eating establishments, they had left without being seated.

Jordan gave her a long, lingering look, prompting her to suspect that he was opposed to her suggestion. Then, without warning, his expression softened, his eyes crinkling as he offered her a sensual smile.

"That's a wonderful idea." Why hadn't he thought of it? After spending nearly six hours with Erika, he suddenly realized that he did not want to share her attention with other people. When, he had to ask himself, had he become so selfish?

"I'll order the food," she suggested.

"And I'll bring the incidentals," he offered mysteriously.

She gave him a sidelong look. "What incidentals?"

He ran his forefinger down the length of her nose. "That will be my surprise."

She felt a quiver of excitement, but successfully concealed it as she glanced at her watch. "What time do you want to eat?"

Jordan peered at his own watch. He wanted to return to his bungalow to shower, shave, and change his clothes.

"Eight."

She nodded. An hour was enough time to order food,

then ready herself for dinner. "I'll see you back here at eight."

Erika stared at her reflection in the full-length mirror on the bathroom door, a slow smile tilting the corners of her mouth. A silk cranberry-red shaped ribbed knit tank top hugged her upper body like a second skin, emphasizing the fullness of her breasts and toned waist. Working out at a local health club had slowed the pull of gravity waging a devious and calculating war with her middle-aged body. A pair of black cotton knit slacks rode low on her hips, elongating her torso to make her appear taller and slimmer.

She swept her hair off her face with a headband that matched her ribbed top, and a shimmer of moisturizer, a sweep of mascara over her lashes, and wine-colored lipstick adorned her simply made-up face.

Clasping her hands together, she mumbled a silent prayer that the night would go well, not realizing it was the same prayer she had whispered at seventeen when she went out on her first date with a boy. It appeared as if she hadn't come that far in thirty years.

I'm ready, she told herself. And she was ready for Jordan Phillips.

The doorbell chimed melodiously ten minutes before the hour and she opened the door, staring through the screen door at two young men dressed in the colorful floral shirts worn by the employees of the resort. Both carried large covered trays.

"Please take them around the back and put them on the table on the patio."

"Yes, madam," they chimed in unison.

They had transported the food from the restaurant to her bungalow in the jitneys used to transport employees and vacationers around the resort's boundaries. She left the door open for Jordan, then made her way through the living/dining area to the patio.

The weather was perfect for outdoor dining. A half-moon, surrounded by millions of stars in a navy-blue sky, silvered the water and the pale sand on the beach. The daytime temperature had dropped to a balmy seventy-five and a calm ocean breeze provided a sensual backdrop for their nighttime picnic.

She watched the two men set the table with a lace tablecloth, china, crystal, and silver, then light several wicks floating in a large bowl filled with a sapphire-blue oil. She had not planned to seduce Jordan, even though the setting was perfect.

The waiters had just completed setting up the table when Jordan rang the doorbell. "Enjoy your evening, madam," the taller of the two stated, offering her a wide grin.

She returned his smile. "Thank you."

Taking a deep breath, she made her way to the living room. The sight of Jordan standing on the other side of the screen door rendered her motionless. He was dressed entirely in black, and the color emphasized the contrast of his burnished-gold eyes in a deeply tanned face. Her gaze was fused with his until it inched lower to the two colorful shopping bags he held in either hand.

Pushing open the door, she smiled. "Please come in. Everything is ready."

Leaning over, he kissed her forehead. "Not everything," he replied cryptically.

She led the way to the rear of the bungalow, Jordan following. She did not know how, but she felt the heat of his gaze on her back. "What did you bring?" she questioned the moment they stepped out onto the patio.

Jordan set the bags down, then reached into one and handed her an exquisite crystal vase and a bouquet of pure white orchids wrapped in pale pink cellophane. "A little something for a beautiful lady." She stared numbly at the vase. "Take it, Erika," he urged.

"Lismore," she whispered, not moving. "How did you know I collect that Waterford pattern?"

"I didn't," he admitted. "Perhaps it's because I also like it. Are you going to stand there and let the flowers wilt, or do you want me to put them in water?"

"I'm sorry." She took the vase and flowers, retreating to the kitchen, where she filled the elegant crystal vase with water, then arranged the rare blooms to display their delicate beauty. When she returned to the patio, Jordan had set up a portable stereo player and the distinctive voices of Marvin Gaye and Tammi Terrell singing "If I Could Build My Whole World Around You" floated clearly through the speakers.

He took the vase from her, positioned it in the center of the table with the candles, then pulled her into his arms. "May I have this dance, Ms. Williams?"

She smiled up at him. "But of course, Senator Phillips." Now she knew what he meant by incidentals: music and flowers. Without his admitting to it, she knew Jordan Phillips was a romantic at heart.

Burying his face in Erika's sweet-smelling hair, Jordan sang Marvin's part while she sang Tammi's. The song ended, seguing into another duet when the duo sang "Aint Nothing Like the Real Thing."

The taped selections continued with Motown classics, which elicited good and some not-so-good memories for Jordan when he reluctantly led Erika to the table, seating her before he took the opposite chair. The soft lighting from a fixture over the French doors and the flickering glow from the four wicks floating in a sea of blue oil cast flattering shadows on his bewitchingly beautiful dining partner's round face. The light also caught the brilliance of the large gems in her ears.

She gave him an demure smile. "I hope you'll like what I ordered."

"I'm sure I will."

Erika felt a shiver of uneasiness when his smile did not quite reach his eyes. There was something different in Jordan's mien that hadn't been there before. He seemed more serious, almost brooding, and she wondered if he was remembering the times when he had dined and danced with his late wife. Was there something about her that reminded him of Lynette Phillips?

"I didn't know whether you wanted wine, but I ordered a bottle," she continued, her voice sounding too strident for her own ears. Why, she asked herself, was she babbling like an anxious adolescent girl trying to impress a boy she had liked from afar, who now had taken a few minutes of his time to notice her?

Jordan smiled again, this time warmth lighting his golden eyes. "I'll have a glass later."

She extended a delicate hand to the covered dishes. "Will you do the honor of serving?"

He uncovered the dishes, nodding his approval of her choice of different seafood entrées. They began with a shrimp cocktail, served with a tart, piquant sauce, then followed with an exotic green salad made with snow peas, pink grapefruit, cooked shrimps, scallops, and tomato with a honey-yogurt dressing.

They sampled portions of baked Mediterranean sea bass with oven-roasted potatoes and several slices of fish steak with a creamy leek sauce.

Erika drank one glass of a chilled white wine, then switched to a bubbling mineral water to counter the taste of the spices triggering an unnatural thirst. "How much time do you spend in D.C.?" she questioned Jordan after one of the taped songs faded.

"Too much," he admitted. "I have a house in Georgetown, but I return to Hartford whenever there's a recess."

"You don't like Washington?"

He smiled at her over the rim of his water goblet. "Let's say I prefer Connecticut."

"Connecticut and St. Thomas," she replied, returning his smile.

"Especially St. Thomas. I've thought about buying vacation property down here."

"Beachfront property?"

He shook his head. "No. Farther up in the mountains. If I decide to buy, would you come to visit me?"

Erika's expression sobered. He was asking her questions she knew she would be unable to answer. "I don't know."

"Why not?"

"Because I haven't planned that far ahead. My life is not as predictable as it used to be."

"That happens when you get older," Jordan stated solemnly. "Life throws you a curve, and if you're not grounded, you don't recover too quickly or easily."

Giving him an intense stare, she tried analyzing his statement. "Is that what happened to you, Jordan?" Her voice was soft, cloaking. "Is that why you haven't remarried?"

He stared at the burning floating wicks rather than at Erika. "I thought I was prepared to lose Lynette, but what I was not prepared for was the loneliness." His head came up, impaling her with the brilliance of his glittering light brown eyes. "I miss the company of a woman."

"But you should not have a problem getting a woman in D.C., or for that matter anywhere," she argued softly. "Not with the way you look." She did not want to say that women would gravitate to him based solely on the fact that he was a member of Congress.

Jordan inclined his head. "Thank you for the compliment, but it's not quite that simple."

"Why?"

"Take yourself, Erika. You've been divorced for how long?"

"A little over two years."

"Have you dated since your divorce?"

"A few times," she admitted honestly.

"Why is it you've come to St. Thomas alone? Why didn't you come with a man?"

She had questioned him, and without giving her an answer he had become the inquisitor. He had deftly turned the tables on her.

"There was no one I felt comfortable enough with to want to see him every day for a week.

"Why?" The single word sounded like the crack of a whip.

Flinching slightly from the tone of his voice, she said angrily, "Because he'd bore the hell out of me."

A slow, sensual smile softened the grim lines around Jordan's mobile mouth. "You've answered my question for me."

"Which means what, Jordan?"

"You are the first woman I've met who hasn't bored the hell out of me. You make me laugh, Erika. And it's been a long time since I've done that."

Reaching across the space of the table, she covered his hands with hers, squeezing gently. "If that's the case, then I'll try to make you laugh many more times before I leave."

"Do you have to leave next Sunday? Can't you stay a little longer?"

She wanted to tell him that she wanted to stay—forever, if that were possible. But it wasn't possible. She had a life back in New Jersey, and when she left St. Thomas she would leave with wonderful memories of the island and the man who helped her realize that there was life after Ronald Williams.

"No, I can't, Jordan."

"You can't, or you won't?"

A quick shadow of annoyance swept across her face. "I cannot and I *will not.*"

Leaning back against the tufted rattan chair, Jordan saw an expression of unspeakable determination on Erika's face and realized he had made a gross mistake. Erika Williams was not Lynette Collins. He could not coerce her or bend her to his will.

Rather than speak, he nodded in acquiescence, then filled his wineglass before topping off Erika's. He raised his glass to her and was not disappointed when she touched her glass to his in a toast.

"It's been a wonderful evening," he whispered.

"That it has," she agreed, smiling.

"Here's to a beautiful dining partner who has excellent taste in food."

Heat flared in her face as her smile grew wider. "Don't forget I have excellent taste when selecting the perfect dining partner."

Jordan took a sip of wine, then put down the glass. In one smooth motion, he pushed back his chair, stood up, then rounded the table. Within a span of seconds Erika was in his arms, his mouth covering hers in a kiss that was nothing like the others they'd shared.

His tongue traced the soft fullness of her lips until they parted, then inched into her mouth with an agonizing slowness that made her clutch the fabric on the back of his shirt in a punishing grip. His kiss was slow, drugging, while leaving her mouth burning with a fire that swept down to her breasts, belly, and still lower to the moist, pulsing area between her thighs.

A silent voice screamed to Jordan to end the kiss, turn, and walk away, but he couldn't. He was caught in the spell of a woman who had no idea what she was doing to him. Whenever she looked at him he felt as if she could see into his very soul to the real Jordan Phillips. Could see under the tailored clothing he favored, into the mind crowded with an infinitesimal amount of legal data he had learned over the past three decades; and beneath the professional deportment he had affected since becoming an elected official, to a man who had denied his own sexuality rather than choose a woman to share his bed. Could see a man who, when he fell in love, loved hard and loved deep.

And he hadn't changed much in forty-five years. At eight, he had taken one look at Lynette and fallen in love with her. And now at fifty-three he had taken one look at Erika Williams and had also fallen in love with her.

His hands moved from her back, down to her waist, and lower to cradle her hips. His breathing quickened with the heaviness settling into his groin, his desire spiraling out of control.

Erika knew the moment they had passed the point of no return as her passion rose to meet Jordan's. His grip on her body tightened when she felt her knees weaken with his deliberate sensual assault on her senses.

Everything that was Jordan Phillips seeped into her: his strength, masculinity, and repressed passion that silently called out to her own.

Emotions she had not felt in years rushed back, buffeting her with heat, chills, and a soft throbbing in the secret place between her thighs.

The banked fires flared to life, engulfing her as they seared her flesh and her brain. She wanted Jordan. She wanted and needed him to make love to her.

And it did not matter that she had met him the day before. All that mattered was that he wanted her as much as she wanted him. They weren't kids who, after making love, would wallow in guilt and shame. They were adults who shared a common emotional denominator: loneliness.

Pulling back to catch her breath, she breathed heavily against his chest. "Jordan?" Her voice was soft, whispery.

"Hmmm-mmm." He moaned as if in pain. What he feared was spilling his passions and embarrassing himself. It had been a long time since he had been with a woman. Too long.

Erika swallowed several times, trying to relieve the dryness in her throat. "Please. Let's go inside."

Bending slightly, he swept her up in his arms and carried her over to the French doors leading to her bedroom. He managed to support her body and open the doors at the same time. The space was dark; the only available light coming through the partially closed blinds was from the patio.

The sound of their labored breathing was magnified as he lowered her gently to the bed. Undressing her and undressing himself would give him the time he needed to bring his volatile passion under control.

"Jordan?" There was no mistaking the apprehension in Erika's voice.

He lay down on the bed beside her, pulling her close to his body. "Yes, sweetheart?"

"I'm not on—I'm not taking anything. You'll have to . . ."

"Don't worry about anything," he interrupted. "I'll protect you."

Those were the last three words Erika remembered as she gave herself up to the passion Jordan Phillips wrung from her.

FIVE

Erika felt as if she had stepped outside of herself, observing what was about to take place in slow motion. A shaft of light rippled over the foot of the bed, outlining Jordan's tall body as he slipped out of her embrace to undress. She lay motionless, watching his shadowed figure when he slowly, methodically unbuttoned his shirt, then placed it on a chair beside the bed. His shoes, socks, and slacks followed. A glint of white glowed in the muted light, and she knew it was his underwear. All he had to do was remove his briefs and he would be totally nude. There was no going back—not now, not for either of them.

Jordan returned to the bed and again lay down beside Erika. All of his senses were heightened. He noticed her slight trembling along with the increase in her respiration.

He did not want to frighten her, but bring her pleasure—a pleasure he was certain she would also offer him. Lacing his fingers through hers, he smiled in the semidarkness.

"Are you all right?"

She nodded, then realized he could not see her in the darkness. "Yes," she sighed.

Why, she wondered, hadn't she realized how deep his voice was before? There were so many things she hadn't realized about the man who was to become the second lover in her life, because all she knew was that she had known him for twenty-four hours and within that span of time he had lit a fire within her she had not felt in years. Being with Jordan made her feel protected. And the first and last man to make her feel totally protected had been her father.

Jordan squeezed her hand. "I want you to tell me what you like."

Turning to him, Erika laid her free hand along the side of his face, her heart filling with tenderness for the man sharing her bed. "I like you, Jordan Phillips," she whispered, her warm, moist breath searing his throat.

He smiled. "Not as much as I like you, Erika Williams."

"I think that's debatable."

His smile broadened. "Would you care to place a wager?"

Her trembling subsided with their easy banter, replaced by a slow, mounting desire and growing respect. "What would I wager?"

Jordan chuckled softly. "I could suggest a game of strip poker, but you already have me at a distinct disadvantage."

"What if you undress me? Then we would be even," she said suggestively, her voice lowering to a seductive whisper.

"You're a shameless woman, Ms. Williams."

"Only with you, Mr. Phillips."

Needing no further urging, he moved over her prone figure and looped his fingers in the waistband of her slacks. The scent of her perfume mingling with her natural feminine scent intensified with each article of clothing he removed. Reaching around her back, he unclasped her bra and eased the straps off her shoulders, the lacy fabric falling to the floor. He heard her slight intake of breath at the same time he placed both hands over her breasts, his thumbs making light sweeping motions over her nipples.

It was his turn to gasp when she swallowed back a soft moan. His fingers lingered on her high, firm, full breasts before caressing the slender column of her neck, the velvety softness of her shoulders. They retraced their path to the curve of her waist, hips, and still lower.

Her panties was the last barrier concealing her nakedness; the heat coming from her hidden sex scorched Jordan's palm as he covered the mound. His fingers traced the elastic waistband, then curved around her back, his hand sliding between her heated flesh and the lace to cradle her hip.

"May I love you, sweetheart?" he asked close to her ear.

Erika felt her eyes fill. Ronald had never asked permission to share her body. "Yes, Jordan. Yes, you may."

Jordan moved down her body, removing her underpants. He touched her body like a sculptor, molding every dip and curve. He alternated each caress with a brush of his lips, lingering over bared flesh in his quest to find her source of pleasure and eventually his own.

His mouth was rapacious, his tongue was relentless, and Erika's body dissolved in a trembling mass of throbbing lust. Writhing, she was eager to touch Jordan's body, but he lingered between her thighs.

She moaned his name over and over until it became a pleading litany. Her head thrashed back and forth, tears leaking from under her eyelids and the moisture streaming into her hairline and onto the pillowcase.

He answered her plea, moving over her body, parting her legs with his knee. She inhaled sharply at the contact of flesh meeting flesh, arching off the mattress when he entered her celibate body with a smooth, sure forward motion.

Pleasure she had forgotten, pleasure she did not know existed stunned her with its intensity, and she moaned aloud with each strong relentless thrust of Jordan's hips. Her body vibrated liquid fire as the heated passion radiated from her throbbing core.

Everything ceased to exist for Jordan—everything except the woman whose heart pounded in rhythm with his. Threading their hands together, he clasped them to their sides, increasing his cadence until he did not know where he began or she ended. Then without warning he exploded, taking Erika with him as fulfillment shattered them into erotic fragments of ecstasy. Breathing heavily, he released her hands and supported his greater weight on his elbows.

Reversing their positions, he cradled Erika to his chest, placing tender kisses over her moist forehead. He felt her shaking, followed by a soft chuckling. His deep laugh joined hers, and by the time they lay side by side, they were laughing uncontrollably.

"It was wonderful," she admitted.

Jordan gathered her to his moist body, holding her tightly. "That's because you're wonderful. I don't think I'll be able to offer you a repeat performance for a while," he teased as his breathing slowed to a normal rate.

Erika pressed her lips to his hard shoulder. "There's no need for an instant replay when you get it right the first time."

His heart swelled with her compliment. "Thank you, sweetheart."

"No—thank you, my darling," Erika countered.

They lay together, reveling in the aftermath of complete physical fulfillment until they finally succumbed to the sated sleep reserved for lovers.

SIX

Erika rolled over, encountering a solid bulk and coming awake immediately. Her eyes crinkled in a smile. Jordan lay with his head cradled on a muscular arm, smiling down at her.

"Good morning," she whispered shyly.

Throwing an arm over her waist, he pulled her closer. "And a very good morning to you, too."

Jordan stared at the woman whose bed he was sharing, trying to sort out his emotions. He wasn't eight or even forty-eight. He was a fifty-three-year-old man who had fallen in love with a woman on sight and had slept with her within twenty-four hours of their meeting. He hadn't planned it, but he realized when the opportunity presented itself, he'd picked her up at the restaurant; she'd caught his attention while they waited for a table, and she had to have known he was more than interested in her each time her curious gaze encountered his.

He'd found himself in love for the second time in his life, and what he could not understand was, why Erika Williams? What was there about her that drew him to her like a bee to a flower, a moth to light, and sunflowers to face the sun?

Even his making love to her was a startling experience. During his marriage he had always been a conventional lover, yet he had offered Erika a raw sensuality he had never shared with any other woman.

She placed a smooth, slender leg over his hair-roughened one, grimacing and swallowing back a soft moan. "Did I hurt you?" he questioned perceptively.

Pressing her face to his chest, she shook her head. "No. It's just a little tightness in my upper thigh."

Jordan released her, pushed back the sheet, and went

to his knees. "Lie on your back and I'll give you a massage."

Erika reached for the sheet, clutching it to her breasts and hoping to conceal her nakedness. "No!"

He reached for the twisted linen, easing it from her clenched fists. "Let it go, sweetheart."

She did let it go, at the same time she closed her eyes. It was one thing to make love in the dark and another to reveal all of herself in the morning light. And she did not know Jordan well enough or feel comfortable enough with him to parade around in the nude. She did not see the vertical lines appearing between his eyes when he stared at her clenched fists, compressed lips, and tightly closed eyes.

"Look at me," he urged in a quiet voice. She shook her head, not complying. Straddling her motionless body, he sat back on his folded knees. "What's the matter, Erika? Are you embarrassed because you slept with me?"

Her eyes opened and she gave him a direct stare. "No."

"Then what is it?"

Biting down on her lower lip, she ran a hand through her mussed hair, pushing it off her forehead. "My body," she replied softly.

His golden gaze swept over her full breasts. "What about your body?"

"It's not . . ." Her words faded.

"It's not what?"

"It's changing. It's not as firm as it used to be," she explained quickly. "My breasts are sagging and so is my behind. I work out to slow down the pull of gravity, but—"

Jordan stopped her words when he placed a finger over her mouth. "Your body is perfect. You're perfect. You're in better shape than a lot of women half your age." This wrung a smile from her. "I'm not exempt from the aging syndrome. There's snow on the roof and places south of the border," he teased. "Gravity has taken its toll on me also. Take a look, sweetheart."

Erika's gaze shifted slowly downward, her eyes widening when it lingered on the source of Jordan's maleness, then quickly reversed itself. Seeing the appendage that had offered her so much pleasure revived her desire for him all over again.

"You're a very smooth liar, Senator Jordan Phillips," she said in a crooning tone. "You are perfect."

"And you are very good for my ego," he countered, his hands inching up her inner thighs. "Relax and let me work out the knots in your muscles."

Erika closed her eyes and gave herself up to the healing touch of Jordan's strong fingers as he kneaded the muscles in her thighs, legs, and feet. Forty minutes later they shared a shower, cleaned up the remains of their dinner, then prepared for a morning of snorkeling in the clear turquoise waters in a cove several miles from their resort near Sapphire Beach.

Erika strolled the streets of Charlotte Amalie on Jordan's arm, peering through the windows of the many duty-free shops. She stopped in front of a gift shop; she still had to purchase Christmas and Kwanzaa gifts for her mother, children, and Velma. She had given her co-workers at the hotel their gifts before she began her vacation.

"I'm going to go in, Jordan."

He smiled at her. "I'm going to the jewelry store across the street. I'll meet you back here." Angling his head, he brushed a light kiss across her soft, moist mouth.

She watched him cross the cobblestone street, her gaze lingering on his tall, lean frame. She felt a slight fluttering in her stomach when she recalled the sensual passion she had shared with Jordan. Sleeping with him, while sharing her body, had changed her, and she knew what she felt and was beginning to feel for him went beyond a simple liking. However, she was mature and levelheaded enough to know that love was not an emotion she would acknowledge or could even consider.

She had fallen in love once, and once was enough for her. Not now. Not when she was older, more vulnerable. No. She would enjoy Jordan Phillips's company, and when it came time for her to return to the States, she would leave him on St. Thomas with the memories of a passion she had experienced far from home.

Jordan carried a small shopping bag containing his Christmas gift for Erika. He had completed all of his holiday shopping before leaving the States. There were not many names on his list for gift-giving: his brothers, their wives, and gift certificates to his four great-nieces and five nephews. He usually feted the people who worked in his office with a dinner at his brother's restaurant, handing out gift certificates to stores they favored. The task of uncovering which stores they preferred was an assignment his personal secretary relished with a childlike glee. It usually took her six months to unearth everyone's preferences. When she had come to him with requests for selections from Victoria's Secret for five of the six females, he had inquired whether the shopping mall would issue a generic certificate wherein the women could make a purchase from any of the shops. Charges of sexual improprieties and sexual harassment were rampant in the workplace, and he was careful not to test the limits of what could be construed as inappropriate behavior.

Thinking of sex elicited a smile when he remembered what he had shared with Erika Williams. It was as if he had been created male to complement her femaleness. Never had he had a woman reach so deep within him to invoke a reckless passion in which he wanted to spend hours just feasting on her body. And she had offered up everything he sought from her—and more.

"Well, well, well. Senator Jordan Phillips. Happy holidays."

Jordan turned, staring down at the smiling face of a woman he managed to catch a glimpse of each time he attended a social function in the Capitol district.

His gaze narrowed behind the lenses of his sunglasses. "Happy holidays, Allison." The greeting was flat, lacking any hint of warmth. "What are you doing so far from home?"

Allison DeWitt's bright red hair and sparkling green eyes were shielded from the brilliant Caribbean sun by a wide, stylish straw hat and oversize sunglasses. The chatty, brilliant reporter for the *Washington Post* had managed to get the ear of many of the most powerful men in the nation's capital. Her coverage of national politics was a combination of witty political satire and sordid gossip. Her column had become a favorite and was syndicated in more than two hundred other newspapers throughout the country.

Allison gave him a dazzling white-tooth smile. "Taking a much-needed vacation away from a very cold and snowy Washington, D.C. Off the record. I must commend you for a wonderful session. As an important member of the Banking, Housing, and Urban Affairs Committee, you waged an outstanding battle for additional funding to build new housing for the residents in Appalachia and the Mississippi Delta."

He arched a dark, sweeping eyebrow. "I simply did what I pledged I would do during my reelection campaign."

The reporter wrinkled her pert freckled nose. "You're too noble to be a politician, Jordan."

"Should I take that as a compliment?"

Allison threw back her head and laughed. "Coming from me—yes." She peered at the gaily wrapped slender box in the shopping bag. "Shopping for a lady, Senator?"

He followed her gaze. "Why would you say that?" There were several times when Allison hinted in her column that he had had affairs with other women while Lynette lay dying. She'd tried using people close to him to substantiate her suspicions, but failed with every attempt to tarnish his reputation.

"I don't know whether I'd call it instinct or intuition, but it looks as if that cute little box contains either a bracelet or a necklace."

Jordan's stoic expression did not change. "I didn't know you added X-ray vision to your other superpowers," he said facetiously.

She pursed her lips in an attractive moue. "Bingo, Jordan. I must tell you that you're quite an anomaly in Washington. And I must admit that you're quite a refreshing one. You've become a very eligible bachelor, yet you've not been linked with any particular woman. Have you been holding out on us?"

Jordan found himself tiring of Allison's inane banter. He knew where her topic of conversation was headed, and he had no intention of giving her anything about his private life that she could use in her column.

"Us or *you,* Allison?"

"Come on, Senator Phillips," she crooned when he did not respond to her query. "Relax. I'm here as a tourist, not a reporter."

"There's nothing to tell," he stated grimly. "There will never be *anything* to tell."

The reporter was astute enough to know she wasn't going to get any information from Jordan that would prove titillating enough for her column.

"Are you vacationing by yourself? Because if you are, I'd like to invite you to . . ." Allison's words trailed off when she saw an attractive African-American woman walk up behind Jordan and curve an arm around his waist.

She focused her sharp gaze on the couple, missing nothing. The familiarity with which the woman touched Jordan and his natural response to her was charming. His expression had softened considerably as he smiled down at her.

Extending her hand, Allison smiled at Erika. "Allison DeWitt."

Erika stared at the red-haired woman, taking the proffered hand. "Erika."

"Allison is a reporter for the *Washington Post,*" Jordan explained in a quiet, sonorous tone.

"It's nice meeting you, Allison," Erika said, flashing a friendly smile.

Allison shifted a pale eyebrow. "The pleasure is all mine." She turned her attention back to Jordan. "As I was saying, if you're not busy, why don't you and Erika join me and Hugh for dinner?"

"Maybe another time," Jordan replied quickly. What he did not want to do was give Allison more grist for her renowned rumor mill. As much as he tried avoiding the inevitable, he knew his name would eventually appear in her column. He was an elected official, used to the gossip and innuendos, but what he did not want was for Erika's privacy to be invaded because of her direct association with him.

"Maybe I'll see you around again." Allison's statement came out like a question.

"Maybe," Jordan replied noncommittally. "Enjoy your vacation."

"You, too," she returned. "Nice meeting you, Erika."

Shifting a bag filled with gaily wrapped packages, Erika wound her free arm through Jordan's, smiling at Allison. "It's been a pleasure." She waited until the red-haired woman walked down a street and disappeared around a corner before she looked up at Jordan's impassive expression. "She seems very friendly."

"She's prides herself on being nice and friendly. She's known as D.C.'s Rona Barrett."

Erika's jaw dropped slightly. "She's a gossip columnist?"

"Her actual title is political analyst."

A look of concern filled her gaze. "Has she written anything negative or sordid about you?"

He shook his head. "That's only because I've never given her cause, even though there was a time when she expressed an uncommon interest in my personal life."

Biting her lip, Erika shook her head. "If I had known that, I never would've acted so friendly in front of her."

His eyes burned amber fire behind the dark lenses. "If I'm not concerned about my reputation, then you shouldn't be."

She stiffened as if he had struck her. "It's not only your reputation that's at stake, Senator Phillips."

"I would never do anything to compromise you," he countered.

"And the same goes for me."

Closing her eyes, Erika realized she and Jordan were standing in the busiest shopping area on the island of St. Thomas arguing about each other's reputation when there was no certainty that Allison DeWitt would even deem their relationship worthy enough to write about in her column.

"I'm ready to go back if you are," she stated in a bored tone.

"I'm more than ready." His voice, though quiet, had an ominous quality.

They were silent during the ride back to the resort, each preferring to stare out the window at the passing landscape. The driver arrived at her bungalow and she turned to look at Jordan for the first time since she'd entered the taxi.

"I'll see you later."

Reaching up, he removed his sunglasses. "What time?"

"I'll call you."

Not waiting for him to assist her from the car, she pushed open the door and stepped out, feeling the heat of his fiery gaze long after she'd closed the door to the bungalow behind her.

She left her shopping bag on a small round table, then made her way across the living room to the sofa. She sat down, staring out into nothingness.

We had a lover's spat, she mused, her eyes filling with tears. She wasn't in love with Jordan, yet they were verbally sparring as if they were. Slipping off her shoes, she pulled her legs up to her chest and lowered her forehead to her knees.

Jordan did not care whether his name appeared in newspaper gossip columns, but she did—especially when the world had known her husband was sleeping with a woman more than half his age before she discovered their affair.

Allison DeWitt could write anything she wanted about Senator Jordan Phillips, but not about Erika Hampton-Williams. What she refused to do was make the same mistake—twice.

SEVEN

The sun had set and a half-moon silvered the beach while Jordan sat in the darkened living room, waiting for the telephone to ring. He had had hours to analyze the dynamics of his verbal exchange with Erika after their encounter with Allison. He sensed she was upset by the fact that Allison was a reporter, but she had not revealed anything about herself which would make her a subject for a torrid exposé.

It's not only your reputation that's at stake, Senator Phillips. He replayed her words over and over in his head. *Who are you, Erika Williams?* he asked for the first time. What was it in her background that prompted her to avoid media coverage? He hadn't missed the fact that when she introduced herself to Allison she had offered only her first name, which would make it a bit more difficult for Allison to uncover her true identity.

Williams, he mused. Was it her maiden or married name? Who had she been married to? Had the man garnered his share of public spotlight? Had she willingly shared the spotlight, or avoided it?

Closing his eyes, he tried recalling her ex-husband's name. He knew it began with an R.

Roland? Ralph? *Ronald!* Ronald Williams. Why was the name so familiar?

It took another hour before his sharp mind went through a mental listing of subjects and connected with the music industry. A slow smile spread across his face when he recalled Erika's statement about her ex-husband's infidelity. He had to be the same Ronald Williams who owned REWind Records.

Jordan remembered seeing the man at his brother's restaurant in D.C., but the woman dining with the recording music mogul was not Erika. The scantily attired woman who had sat more on Ronald Williams's lap than off appeared young enough to be his daughter. But then he knew she could not have been his daughter, because daughters usually did not touch their fathers' bodies as provocatively as this young woman had done.

All of the facts fell into place. Erika lived in New Jersey and so had Ronald Williams. The brilliant stones she wore in her ears cost more than some people earned in a year. And the man who had given her a life most women dreamed about had dishonored her by becoming involved in a paternity suit with a very young woman—a woman young enough to be his own daughter.

Curses, silent and coarse, exploded in Jordan's head. How could he? How could the man not recognize and realize what he had? Burying his face in his hands, he waited until his respiration slowed and his temper cooled. Then he made his way to his bedroom to plan what he had to do to win Erika Williams's heart.

It was the telephone and doorbell ringing simultaneously that awoke Erika the following morning. Scrambling from the bed, she picked up the telephone receiver. "Hello. Please hold on," she said breathlessly.

Reaching for the bathrobe hanging on the back of the chair near the bed, she slipped her arms into it and rushed to the door. Totally disoriented, she opened it to find Jordan smiling at her.

"Good morning," he announced cheerfully. He hoisted a large wicker hamper against his chest. "I have a breakfast delivery for Ms. Erika Williams." *Also lunch and dinner,* he added silently.

Tying the belt to her robe around her waist, she nodded. "Please come in. I have to take a call."

He walked in, pushed the door closed with a broad shoulder, then made his way over to the dining area while Erika retreated to her bedroom.

Gray skies and a softly falling rain precluded any outdoor activity, canceling his idea of chartering a boat which would take them to St. Croix for a day of sailing and sightseeing.

He emptied the oversize picnic hamper, removing containers of dishes he had specially ordered from the resort's head chef, then set the table and waited for Erika to join him.

"Calm down, Chassie," Erika ordered her hysterical daughter. "I can't understand a word you're saying."

"I—I called you, but Grandma answered the phone."

"That's because I forwarded my calls to her house."

"She gave me this number," came a sniffling childlike voice through the wire. "Where are you, Mama?"

Closing her eyes, Erika shook her head. "I'm on vacation. Where are you?"

"I'm at my apartment."

"I thought you were at your father's."

"I left last night. I told Derrick to drive me back."

Erika felt her pulse racing. "Why? You told me you were going to stay with him until classes resume."

"I hate her, Mama. I hate what she's doing to Daddy. She's nothing but a hoochie mama bitch!"

"What your language, young lady. I'm not one of your friends." Even though Erika knew Chassie was referring to Ronald's young wife, she refused to condone her daughter using language she felt belonged in the street.

"I'm sorry, Mama. But she's disgusting. She's fooling around on Daddy and—"

"Stay out of it, Chassie. I told you before that your father willingly married Taneequa knowing who she is."

"But she's sleeping with—"

"Stay out of it!" Erika repeated, raising her voice. "After all, she is his wife."

"That's what Derrick says."

"And your brother is right."

"But I feel so sorry for Daddy," Chassie continued.

"Where's Derrick?" she questioned, changing the subject. The last person Erika wanted to discuss was Ronald and Taneequa Williams.

"He went back to Daddy's house after he dropped me off."

"Are you going back for Christmas?"

"No. I'm thinking about coming back to New Jersey to spend Christmas with you."

"I won't be there, princess. I'm not coming back until Sunday."

"How can you do this to me?" Chassie wailed.

Erika closed her eyes, struggling not to lose her temper. "Do *what* to you? You never considered my plans when you decided you were going to stay in California because your father decided to have a *party* where you'd have the opportunity to mingle with your music superstars up close and personal. It did not matter that I put in for a vacation at this time of the year because I wanted to spend the Christmas holidays with my children. And not once did I say to you or Derrick how can you do this to me.

"When did you become so selfish, Chassie Williams, that you think only of yourself? Your father decided he wanted another wife and he got one. Maybe not the one you'd want for him, but she's still his wife. What about me? What if I decide I want to fall in love again? Why shouldn't I be happy?"

There was a swollen silence before Chassie's voice came through the wire again. "Are you in love with someone, Mama? Have you found someone you want to marry?"

"I don't know, princess." Her voice was a hoarse whisper.

"Is he nice, Mama?"

Opening her eyes, Erika smiled. "He's very, very nice."

"Good for you. I can't wait to tell Derrick and Daddy."

"Don't do that, Chassie," she warned. "Please don't say anything. Not yet."

There was another pause. "Okay, Mama, I won't. Can you tell me who he is?"

"No, baby, I can't. At least not now."

The conversation ended a minute later, and when Erika hung up she felt better than she had in a long time. She hadn't lied to her daughter, because she wasn't certain whether she was in love with Jordan. She hadn't known him a week, yet he had become a part of her existence since her arrival on St. Thomas.

She had promised to call him after they'd returned from their shopping excursion, but did not keep her promise once she realized how close she had come again to having her life dissected by the press.

Sighing heavily, she rose to her feet and retraced her steps to the living room and found Jordan standing with his back to the French doors, hands thrust into the pockets of his slacks. Her gaze went from his closed expression to the table set with china, silver, and glassware.

Jordan's gaze moved slowly over the silken garment clinging to her curvy body, unable to believe that she looked so delightfully seductive with her tousled hair and unmade up face. She had complained about her changing body, but he found her body perfect. In fact, he found everything about Erika Williams perfect.

She was shockingly feminine, intelligent, and claimed a teasing sensuality he could not resist. Whenever she smiled at him or touched him, she ignited a desire he had not felt since adolescence. Erika was a woman who did not bore him, and he knew instinctively that he would never tire of her companionship.

A slight smile tugged at a corner of his firm mouth. "Are you ready for breakfast?"

Crossing her arms under her breasts, Erika successfully concealed her own emerging smile. It had only been hours, but she hadn't realized how much she had missed him. And as it was, they had so little time left for them to be together.

"Do I have time to complete my morning ablution?"

He inclined his head. "Yes, madam."

Lowering her arms, she picked up her floor-length robe and matching nightgown and curtsied deeply, giving Jordan a generous view of the tops of her breasts rising above the pale lace trim of a navy-blue silk ensemble.

"I shall return." Turning gracefully, she swept out of the room, Jordan's deep laughter following her departing figure.

EIGHT

The next two days passed quickly, days and nights blurring into one. With each sunset and sunrise Erika and Jordan held on to and treasured their precious moments together.

She felt comfortable enough with Jordan to reveal how she had learned of her ex-husband's infidelity from reading a newspaper article in which the reporter hinted of a scandal wherein a twenty-year-old singer had accused the president of REWind Records of getting her pregnant.

Reliving the incident brought her to tears—angry tears—while Jordan gathered her protectively in his embrace, holding her until she was once again in control of her emotions.

They spent most days touring St. Thomas and sailing to St. John and St. Croix, reliving a history which included the importation of Africans to the New World to support the ongoing institution of the slave trade, and most nights they ordered room service and they dined alone.

Erika sat on the beach with Jordan, watching the sun rise over the ocean. It was Christmas Day, and once the sun set hours later, it would signal her last night on St. Thomas. Streaks of lavender, mauve, then a bright blue brightened the sky filled with puffy white clouds.

"It's so beautiful here," she whispered reverently.

"Yes, it is," he agreed. "It's been magical." Closing his eyes, he mumbled a silent prayer that she would change her mind and stay. But he knew it was a futile prayer.

Moving closer to him, Erika settled herself on his lap, her arms curving around his neck. "Merry Christmas." Her moist breath swept over his ear, causing him to shudder while he inhaled the delicate fragrance clinging to her bared flesh.

Turning his head and opening his eyes, he stared at her staring back at him. "Merry Christmas, sweetheart."

Closing her eyes, she snuggled closer, feeding on his strength. "Jordan?"

"Yes."

"We're going to have to get some sleep. We've been up for almost twenty-four hours."

"Twenty-two," he countered, slurring the two words.

"Okay," she conceded. "Twenty-two."

"I want to give you my Christmas present before we turn in."

She sat up, becoming suddenly alert. "You didn't have to buy me anything."

"I know I didn't, but I wanted to."

Reaching up, she cradled his lean cheeks in her hands. Her dark eyes lingered on the shape of his slanting eyes, high cheekbones, and his strong, stubborn chin. She committed everything about him to memory, because she would need the memories when she boarded her flight to return to the States.

"I have a little something for you, too."

He frowned at her. "No, Erika."

"Yes, Jordan."

"You're not making this easy."

"Good-byes are never easy. But remember you promised to come for afternoon tea."

He managed a sad smile. "You're right. I did promise."

She moved off his lap and stood up. Moments later he also rose to his feet. They made their way back to the bungalow, each lost in private, tortured thoughts as they realized their time together was drawing to a close.

Erika sat on the middle of the bed, unwrapping the long, slender box Jordan had given her after she'd showered, secured her hair in an elastic band, and pulled a nightgown over her scented body. He had flashed a mysterious smile, then excused himself before he walked into her bathroom to shave and shower. She was exhausted, but found herself too wound up to relax.

Jordan had chartered a boat to take them to San Juan, where they checked into a Condado Beach hotel. They'd spent hours dancing, dining, and gambling in the hotel's casino. It was as if he had wanted to relive their seven days together in twenty-four hours. Neither wanting the day to end, but knew they had to face the inevitable. This would be their last day together on the magical island of St. Thomas.

Her fingers were steady as they peeled away the paper to reveal a highly polished teakwood box. She unlatched the lock and opened the box to reveal a single strand of magnificent Mikimoto pearls with a pair of matching earrings. Her fingers were trembling when she removed the necklace and examined the exquisite gold clasp set with a smaller pearl that was surrounded by a circle of sparkling diamonds. Closing her eyes, she willed the tears not to fall. She fastened the perfectly matched pearls around her neck and replaced the diamonds in her ear with the pearl studs.

Jordan walked into the bedroom, a towel draped around his slim hips, and found her propped up against a mound of pillows wearing the pearls and nothing else. The light coming through the partially closed blinds revealed the contrast of the pale baubles against her full brown breasts. She extended her arms and he dropped the towel, sat down on the bed, and pulled her into his embrace.

"Thank you, Jordan," she whispered against his smooth cheek. "They're beautiful."

"They'll never match your beauty, Erika."

"I'll treasure them always."

He buried his face against her scented neck. "I hope they'll come to mean as much to you as your diamond earrings." He did not know why, but each time he noticed the diamonds he felt a rush of envy—envy that she continued to hold on to something Ronald Williams had given her.

"They are more special than my diamond studs. Each time I wear the pearls they will remind me of the magical week I shared with a man I never want to forget."

"Have you forgotten Ronald Williams? Do you remember him every time you look in a mirror and see the diamonds?"

She laughed, her voice low and seductive. "Yes, I do." Pulling back, she smiled up at Jordan's impassive expression. "I can still remember the night I met him for dinner at what had been our favorite restaurant in Upper Saddle River. My lawyer had filed the documents needed to make the divorce final when Ronald called me, saying he wanted to talk to me.

"We were very civil during dinner, but before dessert was served he handed me a beautifully wrapped box. It was covered with silver foil with a black velvet ribbon. He urged me to open it, and I did. Ronald had purchased a diamond necklace totaling at least seven or eight carats. He claimed it was for my birthday, but I knew it was more of a token for a reconciliation. I thanked him for the gift, then calmly ate my dessert.

"A week later he called again, begging me to take him back. Of course I refused, hung up the telephone, then went to my jeweler and traded the necklace for the earrings. I think of the earrings as an *'I finally got rid of the philanderer and now I'm free'* gift to myself."

Jordan stared at her smiling face, completely surprised by her disclosure. He knew Ronald Williams would always be a part of her life because they shared children, but he could not rid himself of the nagging fear that she still loved him.

"Good for you," he whispered quietly as his head came down and he covered her mouth with his. He kissed her lips, throat, shoulders, nipples, belly, and still lower to the furred triangle at the apex of her thighs. He kissed every inch of her flesh, leaving his invisible brand as she lay panting, her chest heaving.

He was a selfless lover, offering all of himself, then found himself on the receiving end of Erika's unbridled passion when she straddled his thighs and tasted his flesh.

The world outside ceased to exist for the lovers as they celebrated Christmas in their own special way. Their bodies and their passions were gifts they shared unselfishly. And when the fulfillment they had held at bay until the last possible moment exploded, they gave in to the explosive ecstasy taking them beyond themselves.

It was only after they lay together, their breathing back to normal, that Erika realized she had welcomed Jordan Phillips into her body and into her life. And what she had denied from the first time she shared her bed and her body with him was that she had also fallen in love.

Erika walked back into her house, feeling numbed. She had refused to allow Jordan to come to the airport to see her off, and he had refused to open her Christmas gift to him. It was as if they had retreated behind facades where they were polite strangers instead of passionate lovers.

It had taken a week—only seven days—for her to meet and fall in love with the perfect stranger. And she had another seven days to reflect on how her life had changed and what she had become before returning to the routine of getting up and going into the hotel where she would resume her duties as a banquet manager.

Walking up the staircase to her bedroom, she stripped off her clothes, made her way to an adjoining bathroom, then stood under the spray of a shower with the water beating down on her head and body until she sat on the tiled floor, weeping uncontrollably.

She cried for having discovered love for the second time in her life, and for losing love for the second time. And she waited until the water cooled before she rose to her feet and turned off the shower.

She blotted the water from her body with a thick, thirsty towel, then used a smaller one to towel-dry her hair. Returning to the bedroom, she called her mother, then Velma, then lay across the bed and fell asleep.

Velma Parker's dark eyes sparkled in appreciation when she opened the package Erika handed her. Her best friend and sorority sister had brought her back a large bottle of her favorite perfume.

"Thanks, girlfriend. You didn't have to give me anything."

"It was the least I could do for you, Miss V."

Velma examined Erika's deeply tanned face. "You must have had a good time, because you look wonderful. I can't remember the last time I saw you glow."

Erika stared at Velma's exotic face with her flawless sable-brown skin, large clear brown eyes, full mouth, and high cheekbones. The flickering candle on the small table in their favorite restaurant cast a flattering glow on her delicate features. She and Velma had married within six months of each other, but Velma and her husband had maintained a solid marriage for more than twenty years. Their decision not to have children solidified their relationship; they lavished each other with gifts and undivided attention.

"That's because I'm in love."

Velma's eyes widened. "You're what?"

Running her tongue over her lower lip, Erika stared down at the sparkling liquid in a water goblet. "I met a man on St. Thomas, fell in love, and slept with him. But not necessarily in that order."

Velma reached across the table and held Erika's hand in a punishing grip. "You did what? Girl, are you crazy? Don't you know how dangerous that is? It's not like it was years ago when we were—"

"Do you actually think I would sleep with a man without protecting myself?" she interrupted hotly.

Velma winced. "I'm sorry, girlfriend. I know you haven't had a lot of experience with men," she apologized.

"More than you have, Velma Parker. I've slept with two men to your one."

"You're right, girlfriend." Both women had married the first men they had slept with. Velma and Robert Parker had remained faithful to each other, while Ronald Williams slept with his wife and any other woman who offered herself to him.

"How was he?" Velma asked quietly.

"Wonderful."

Erika truthfully related her week-long affair with Jordan Phillips, leaving nothing out. She felt as if a weight had been lifted when she finally revealed Jordan's name.

"No!" Velma squeaked. "No, you didn't! You mean to say you had an affair with *the* Senator Jordan Phillips?"

Leaning against the cushioned chair back, Erika nodded slowly. "The one and only. Everything was perfect: the island, the man, and his lovemaking. Cinderella had nothing on me because instead of having a few hours with the prince, I was allowed seven wonderful days and nights."

"Are you going to see him again?"

She shook her head. "I don't know. We didn't exchange addresses or phone numbers. When the time came for me to come back, I just left."

"Didn't he ask you to stay?"

"Yes, he did."

"Why didn't you, girlfriend?"

"For what, Velma? To prolong the inevitable? It was better we ended it when we did. Perhaps I'll book another trip to St. Thomas next year, and maybe I'll run into him again."

"You'd wait a year?"

"Sure. Why not? It would be worth it."

Velma gave her a skeptical look, shaking her head. She loved Erika like a sister, but always found her to be a little too controlled. "You know you're invited to celebrate the new year with us. Robert decided he wanted to have a few friends over New Year's Eve, and I want you to come."

Erika gave Velma a squinting glare. "I'll come, but only if you and Robert promise not to try to set me up with one of his buddies."

"I promise."

"Then I'll come."

NINE

Erika examined several ensembles hanging from a rack in the closet in her bedroom, trying to decide what she would wear to the Parkers' New Year's Eve celebration later that evening. She had considered several dresses, then decided against them because she thought they would be too dressy. One, in particular, was better suited for a formal wedding or a black-tie affair. After eliminating the dresses, she selected a black silk jacket with a mandarin collar and a pair of matching slacks. Opening another closet, she searched the many racks for a pair of black silk pumps. She counted a half dozen pairs with varying heel heights, reaching for one with a two-inch heel at the same time the doorbell chimed melodiously from the lower level.

A slight frown appeared between her eyes. It was ten-thirty in the morning, and she wasn't expecting any visitors. Her step was light as she walked out of her bedroom and down the staircase to the door. Peering through the security eye, she went completely still. The magnified face of Ronald Williams stared back at her.

What was he doing in New Jersey, and why had he come to her home? She opened the door and glared at the man whom she never expected to see again, except at their children's graduations or weddings.

Ronald Williams felt as if someone had kicked him in the gut when he saw the woman who had been the love of his youth. He hadn't seen her in two years and he noticed the changes in her immediately. She had lost weight—not much, but enough where her body appeared slimmer, firmer. Her thick hair was cut and streaked and was styled in a mass of tiny curls that floated around her face like airy bubbles.

"I'm sorry to come without calling, but I need to talk to you."

Erika's gaze took in everything about the man whom she had once pledged her life and future to, seeing the obvious changes others never would have noticed. He was impeccably attired, but a visible stubble of gray dotted his jaw. The glasses he usually wore only after many hours of reading were now perched on the bridge of his nose as he squinted at her.

Nodding, she opened the door wider. Ronald bent down to retrieve a monogrammed leather carry-on bag, then made his way through the entryway and stepped out into the spacious living room. A slight smile curved his mouth under his neat mustache. Cool colors of beige and pale green enveloped him as he admired the elegant furnishings Erika had selected to decorate her home.

"Please sit down, Ronald."

He slipped off his topcoat, placing it over the back of an off-white silk-covered love seat. He waited until Erika sat on a matching armchair, then sat down.

Ronald stared at a grouping of silver-framed photographs of his children on a side table rather than at the woman who had given birth to the little boy and girl whose smiling images evoked memories of another time. A time he wanted to recapture.

"Why are you here?" Erika asked, her voice completely devoid of emotion.

His head came around and he stared at her. "I want a reconciliation," he stated without a preamble. "I'm sorry I hurt you—"

"I've heard this before," she countered, interrupting him.

His eyes narrowed slightly behind the tinted lenses of his glasses. "Please let me finish."

She nodded, closing her eyes, crossing her legs, and folding her arms over her chest. "Go on."

"I've had to do a lot of things I'm not particularly

proud of, but cheating on you is something I'll regret to my grave. I had it all and then I lost it all. I thought ultimate success was purchasing a million-dollar home, having a custom-tailored wardrobe, and riding around in luxury cars. But my true success was marrying you and providing for Derrick and Chassie.

"I don't know what possessed me to marry that child," he continued. "She doesn't know the first thing about being a mother and even less how to conduct herself as a wife."

Erika opened her eyes, wanting to tell Ronald that she did not want to hear his sob story; she did not want to listen to him bad-mouth his wife. After all, shotgun marriages were no longer in vogue.

"I can't understand why she would want a two-year-old boy to wear his hair with little plaits sticking out all over his head," he whined unattractively, "because every time someone says that he's a cute little girl she catches an instant attitude." Leaning forward, he rested his elbows on his knees, wagging his head from side to side. "Dackqwan DeAundray," he mumbled under his breath. "What the hell kind of name is Dackqwan? I always thought a *q* was followed by a *u*." His head came up and he met Erika's amused gaze. "You think it's funny, don't you?"

She stood up. "I think you should be with your family, Ronald. I'm certain your wife and children are waiting for you to help them celebrate the new year. Shall I call a taxi for you?"

He shook his head, rising to his feet. It was over. He had pleaded his case, but she had ceremonially dismissed him.

"No, thanks. I have a driver waiting for me."

Erika watched Ronald pick up his topcoat, throw it over the sleeve of his suit jacket, then pick up his carry-on bag. Her expression was unreadable as she led the way to the front door. He had a driver, yet he had not left his coat or bag in the car. Had he actually expected her to invite him to stay? Had he expected her to allow him back into her life and into her bed?

She was proud of herself; proud that she could remain so calm in Ronald's presence; proud that she hadn't been swayed by his impassioned plea for forgiveness or for a reconciliation.

Placing her hand on the doorjamb, she glanced over her shoulder at her ex-husband. "Have a safe flight and good health in the new year."

He nodded slowly and managed a tired smile. "Thank you, Erika."

She opened the door, her jaw dropping and eyes widening in shock when she saw Jordan Phillips poised to ring her doorbell.

"Jordan." His name came out in a breathless whisper.

Tilting his head, he winked at her. "Am I too early for afternoon tea?"

She saw the heartrending tenderness of his gaze before his expression changed, hardening, when he saw Ronald standing behind her. Slipping her hand in his, she squeezed his fingers. "Ronald was just leaving. Jordan, I'd like you to meet Ronald Williams. Ronald, Jordan Phillips."

Ronald was momentarily speechless when he recognized the Connecticut senator. Knowing Erika was lost to him was compounded by the presence of a man who looked at her with naked, unabashed love.

He extended his hand. "Senator Phillips."

Jordan took the proffered hand. "Mr. Williams."

Ronald managed a half smile. "I'd better be going if I'm going to make my flight." He gave Erika one last, lingering look. "Good-bye."

"Good-bye, Ronald."

He walked out of the house and Jordan walked in. Erika waited a full minute before she closed the door to her past, then prepared herself to face her future.

Her penetrating gaze took in everything about Jordan

Phillips in one sweeping motion. He was casually dressed in a pair of tan cords, a matching wool pullover sweater, a pair of low-heeled brown boots, and a supple waist-length brown leather jacket.

Jordan was equally entranced with Erika. Her hair was styled with soft curls that framed her beautiful face. He surveyed her trim hips in a pair of fitted jeans under an oversize T-shirt. She hadn't worn shoes, but a pair of thick white socks.

"How did you find me?" Her eyes were shimmering with a love she was unable to hide or disguise.

Jordan crossed his arms over his chest, shaking his head. "How many Erika Williamses do you think live in New Brunswick, New Jersey?"

She affected a similar stance, hoping to appear indifferent to his presence while her heart pumped uncontrollably. "I'm not listed in the telephone directory."

"I have my methods, Ms. Williams."

Her gaze widened. "Legal methods?"

He took three steps, bringing him only inches from her. All that he remembered about Erika Williams came rushing back with the velocity of a roaring twister sweeping up everything in its wake. He inhaled the familiar perfume clinging to her skin and hair, the velvety flawlessness of her round face, the firmness of her body, and the quiet sensuality she wore as proudly as a prized medal.

He had thought he could have gone on, pretended that the week he had shared with her was a fluke, a capricious escapade, but he was wrong. He had fallen in love with her, and he wanted her in his life—forever.

"I have my methods," he repeated. Reaching out, he pulled her gently to his chest. "I've come to your home because you invited me for afternoon tea. And I've also come because I want to invite you to accompany me to a New Year's Eve party. I know it's very short notice, and I apologize for that. But what I won't apologize for is falling in love with you, Erika Williams."

Tears of joy shimmered in her large eyes as her gaze met and fused with his. Their single, magical week together had resulted in a love so strong and tender that time or reason would never be able to explain the whys.

Her arms curved around his neck, pulling his head down. "And I will never apologize for loving you back, Jordan Phillips." Standing on tiptoe, she touched her lips to his, sealing her promise.

Jordan deepened the kiss, his hand slipping lower to cradle her hips. There was no mistaking his surging desire when his hardness searched through heavy fabric, searing her with heat.

"Will you come with me?" he questioned between soft, nibbling kisses.

"Yes," she moaned. Pushing gently against his chest, she reluctantly ended the kiss. "I have to make a phone call and cancel my former plans for tonight." Lacing her fingers through his, she pulled him in the direction of the kitchen. "Make yourself at home, while I call my friends. You can start the tea if you want to. And I have the perfect little cakes to—"

"Erika. Sweetheart," Jordan interrupted, placing a finger over her parted lips. "It's too early for afternoon tea. By the time we get to Connecticut it will be the perfect time to share tea."

"Oh." The single word said it all.

"Yes, oh. I suggest you pack a bag for an overnight stay, because I doubt whether we will be coming back to New Jersey after the party."

"Are there any other surprises you're keeping from me?"

"The party is at the governor's mansion."

She arched her eyebrows at this disclosure. "Oh, I see. Which means it's probably a formal affair."

He nodded. "It will also give me an opportunity to wear your Christmas gift."

It was her turn to nod. She had given Jordan a set of

mother-of-pearl cuff links and studs set in gold. When she saw them she thought they would be a perfect complement for a formal dress shirt.

"When do you want to leave?"

He glanced at his watch. "Whenever you're ready."

"Give me half an hour."

"Take all the time you need, my love."

She flashed a tender smile. "Thank you."

She left him in the kitchen and made her way to the staircase, her pulse racing with a renewed happiness. He had come to her. He loved her. She loved him.

She made it to the top of the stairs, then clenched her fists while closing her eyes. Then she did what she hadn't done in years. She executed a jig, her arms and legs pumping like a piston, then she walked into her bedroom, her eyes shining with a joy she would not control or conceal.

The telephone call to Velma took less than a minute, and when she hung up she went to the closet and pulled out a platinum-hued silk chiffon camisole dress. It was perfect for a New Year's Eve celebration at the governor's manison. And for the second time that morning she went through the ritual of selecting shoes and underwear.

The blood sang through her veins when she retrieved an overnight bag and filled it with more casual garments. The smile that softened her mouth was still in place when she descended the staircase forty minutes later and handed the bag to Jordan. He waited patiently while she secured her home, then took her hand and led her to the car, where a driver waited to begin their journey to Jordan's home in Hartford.

They sat in the back of the spacious sedan, sharing a smile. A smile recognized by lovers all over the world.

Erika found herself in Jordan's arms as the minutes on the clock inched closer to twelve to signal a new year. The lights from a dozen glittering chandeliers ringed his silver hair in a white glow as he stared down into her eyes.

"I love you, Erika," he whispered close to her ear, "and I want what we shared on St. Thomas to never end."

Her head came up, and the mass of curls she had swept up off the nape of her neck moved as if they had taken on a life of their own. "What are you saying, Jordan?"

"I'm asking whether you'd consider marrying me. I know it will probably mean you relocating, but you did say you would operate a bed and breakfast anywhere."

"What are your future political plans?" She had heard whispered remarks that the governor was grooming Jordan for his seat when he retired at the end of his term. And that was in another three years.

"I've been asked to run for governor."

"Do you think I'll make an adequate first lady of the state of Connecticut?"

Jordan's smile was dazzling. "You'll be perfect." His brilliant gaze lingered on her sexy mouth, the pearls in her ears, and the matching single strand resting on the soft swell of breasts rising above the revealing neckline of her exquisite pale gray dress.

"Then it's yes, Jordan. Yes, I will marry you."

They did not hear the assembled count down the seconds to the new year as they moved closer, sealing their love and their promise to hold on to the island magic they had found on St. Thomas.